When **Kali Anthony** read h... at fourteen she realised two ... never be too many happy en... ... ... one day she would write them herself. After marrying her own tall, dark and handsome hero, in a perfect friends-to-lovers romance, Kali took the plunge and penned her first story. Writing has been a love affair ever since. If she isn't battling her cat for access to the keyboard, you can find Kali playing dress-up in vintage clothes, gardening, or bushwalking with her husband and three children in the rainforests of South-East Queensland.

Bella Mason has been a bookworm from an early age. She has been regaling people with stories from the time she discovered she could hold the dinner table hostage with her reimagined fairy tales. After earning a degree in journalism, she rekindled her love of writing and she now writes full time. When she isn't imagining dashing heroes and strong heroines she can be found exploring Melbourne, with her nose in a book, or lusting after fast cars.

AWOKEN BY REVENGE

KALI ANTHONY

HIS CHOSEN QUEEN

BELLA MASON

MILLS & BOON

First published in Great Britain 2024
by Mills & Boon, an imprint of HarperCollins*Publishers* Ltd,
1 London Bridge Street, London, SE1 9GF

www.harpercollins.co.uk

HarperCollins*Publishers*, Macken House, 39/40 Mayor Street Upper,
Dublin 1, D01 C9W8, Ireland

This book contains FSC™ certified paper
and other controlled sources to ensure responsible forest management.

For more information visit www.harpercollins.co.uk/green.

Printed and Bound in the UK using 100% Renewable Electricity
at CPI Group (UK) Ltd, Croydon, CR0 4YY

AWOKEN BY REVENGE

KALI ANTHONY

MILLS & BOON

As a wise woman once said to me...

Even the smallest flicker of light
can overcome the darkness.

CHAPTER ONE

AN AMPHIBIAN WAS giving her trouble. Louisa pushed her glasses up her nose, staring down at the recalcitrant creature she'd sketched. Her illustration brief had been clear. He was meant to be a cute frog with a golden crown. The perfect frog prince for a sweet children's story. Instead, he sat there on the page, crown jauntily askew. His froggy little mouth turned up into a kind of smirk. Arms crossed, as if in some way judging her...

Louisa could never accept that. No judgement was allowed anywhere in her life, any more.

Though it was a familiar smirk on that mouth of his. Sly, knowing. Recognition niggled in the recesses of her memory, yet she still couldn't place it. Louisa blew out a slow breath. Sometimes your characters worked against you and today was that day. She tried sketching him again, this time with a billowing cape. A rakish wink.

Although surely frogs in children's stories shouldn't be rakish, should they?

'Play nicely,' she said to the frog on the page. She could have torn the paper out, tossed him away and shown him who was the real boss, yet something about his familiar smile forced her to keep him for now. Louisa turned to a fresh sheet of crisp white paper. She would get him right. She *would*. She had a deadline for her illustrations, and she never missed a deadline. Timing was everything. She lived by it.

Instead of challenging herself with misbehaving frog princes, she immersed herself in the world of the story. A verdant, magical forest, with fairies and animals come to life on the page. A mythical world where she didn't have to think about a gleaming coffin lowered into sodden ground in a snowdrop-carpeted cemetery. A grave in the English countryside her great-aunt Mae had loved and would lie in for ever.

Louisa rubbed at the yawning ache in her chest. No. She didn't have to think of grief. Right now, she could think about another world entirely. A world of make-believe. Her favourite place.

She inked a watercolour wash of green, the detail of leaves. It was as if she were in that picture, strolling through the forest like a lost princess with the breeze whispering through her hair. Possibility abounding as her brush slicked across the page and her heart tripped along at the mystery of *discovery*. Half in reality, half out of it. Picking up some blue because in this world she created the sun always shone and the sky remained a perfect hue...

A clanging gong sounded in the distance. She tried ignoring it, even though the doorbell could challenge Big Ben for loudness. A ringing doorbell couldn't be right. It was Wednesday, and no one was due today. The house empty, staff on one of their days off. Just her and her work, in what should be blissful silence. Of course, tourists would occasionally drop by on days the home wasn't open to the public, but a polite sign on the door usually saw them on their way. Anyhow, since Mae's passing Easton Hall had been closed, which was made clear on the house's website. No. Everyone in the area knew the home's schedule, and none would be impolite enough to disturb it. She could ignore the demanding sound with impunity...

Yet the knowledge that there must be a stranger outside gnawed at her consciousness like a worm in an apple. Louisa stilled. Her brush held above the page, a splat of blue dripping onto it as she was rudely wrenched from the world of her illustration into cold, hard reality.

She looked down at the livid blue blot now bleeding over the page, marring her picture. At least it was only a working drawing, and not the final copy. The error wouldn't put her behind her schedule. Louisa loathed the idea of missing her deadline almost as much as she loathed unscheduled strangers at the door. In recent times those kinds of strangers hadn't meant anything good.

That infernal doorbell gave another chime. Whoever it was wasn't going away. Since Mae had been laid in the ground, a number of people had visited the property. Buyers' agents, mostly. Looking to see if Easton Hall was for sale, given the owner's passing. All vultures, as if the estate were some kind of carcass to pick away at, rather than a loving home.

She could try to ignore them, yet they were known for their doggedness and the housekeeper, Mrs Fancutt, and her two Pomeranians weren't here to help her evict them. Right now, she was alone.

It was her job to see the intruders off the property.

'There's more to the world than you've experienced, Louisa. Be brave.'

The last words Mae had spoken to her. Tears pricked Louisa's eyes, but she blinked away the burn. Her great-aunt had lived a long and eccentric life and had loved Louisa fiercely. Swooping in when one medical professional had *finally* refused to believe her mother's lies. Giving her a home when her mother had died just prior to a trial that would have laid ugly secrets bare.

That Louisa wasn't sick all those years as her mother had claimed.

Mae had ensured she'd gone to school again, trying to give her a normal life. Getting her the help she'd needed when her mental scars had threatened to overwhelm her. If Mae's last message to her was to be brave, that was what she'd be. In her twenty-four years, she'd fought bigger demons than strangers on her doorstep.

Louisa washed her brush. Pulled her long hair back into a rough ponytail and stomped to the front door. Realising as she peered through the spyhole to an amorphous blur that she'd forgotten to take off her reading glasses again. But what did it matter? She'd be working again in no time and sometimes the world was better when everything was a little soft focus. She took a deep breath, turned the giant iron key, and yanked the ancient oak door open.

A man in dark clothes stood on the gravel drive with his back to her, seeming to survey the land before him as if he owned it. Whilst he was at an inconvenient distance for her glasses, his silhouette could only be described as *sharp*. His hair like a blot of ink on his head. Something about him made the heat creep up her chest and prickle her cheeks.

Everything about his demeanour screamed authority. She wanted to say something, but she feared her voice was trapped and all that would come out was a croak. Then he turned. Began to move towards her as if he were made of liquid, his movements so rolling and fluid. The only thing making her realise he had solidity and weight was the heavy crunch, crunch, crunch of his shoes on the gravel drive. And she had to say something because he'd get to the stairs soon and she had a wild premonition that if he made it to the top, he'd never leave…

She held up her hand. 'Stop right there.'

He did. Closer now, a little less soft focus. The corner of his mouth quirking in a way that seemed all too familiar. That sensation of recognition overcame her. Give him a billowing cape, a jaunty crown and a rakish wink and this man was her frog prince made human.

It was as if she'd drawn him to life.

Her heart thumped an uncomfortable rhythm. She should take off her glasses, but she didn't want him to think that she wanted to get a better look at him, even though she did.

Desperately.

'You haven't answered any of my lawyer's correspondence.'

That voice of his. Smooth, rich and decadent. Like treacle tart with clotted cream. *So good*, yet *so bad* if you indulged too much. Louisa was sure this man could make reading chess moves sound like some kind of midnight intimacy… But correspondence? That sounded official and *not* like an estate agent. All things official she left in the hands of her solicitor. Any mail redirected there. Although the man had talked of retiring and sometimes did seem increasingly overwhelmed in his small, overstuffed office in the village.

Though…this man spoke almost as if he knew her. How could that be? In recent years whilst caring for Mae she'd not ventured much further than the local village and if he'd lived there, she would have remembered him. He wasn't the sort of person you'd ever forget. Sure, everyone in the local area knew her. In the early days of her arrival, she'd been *'Poor Louisa Cameron…' 'Lost her parents…' 'Too young to be living with an old lady...'* She'd heard it all. Once, those whispers had chattered in her head. Especially when she'd believed that someone would come to take her away from the only home she'd felt safe in for years.

'Everything goes to my solicitor. He must be busy.'

Even though the man was soft focus at the bottom of the stairs, she saw his brows rise on his high forehead. 'What you call busy, I'd call incompetent. You weren't at the reading of the will.'

Mae had told Louisa she'd be looked after. *'You will always have a home.'* Her solicitor had confirmed that Easton Hall was her place to live, for ever. Why would she need to go to the reading of a will with all her relatives? If she never saw another Bainbridge again, it would be a happy day. They didn't deal with life when it became real and messy. Elegantly brushing said messiness under vast antique Axminster carpets so it wouldn't tarnish the family's pristine name.

All they cared about was their money, their reputation and keeping up appearances. The ones who had come to visit Mae nearer the end had tried to ingratiate themselves. Get her to leave here for a care facility, *'for her own good'.* But it was never about what was good for Mae. Only themselves. Each of them wanted a piece of the Bainbridge estate, Mae being holder of the most coveted prize, Easton Hall and its surrounds. She'd cackle when they left. *'Watch the silver as they walk out the door!'* How sad that she hadn't been far wrong. Mrs Fancutt had reported finding one of them poking about the teaspoons in the good cutlery service after one visit...

'There was no need for me to go. I know everything I need to.'

'Do you?'

In those final days of Mae's life, she'd promised Louisa she didn't have to worry. So Louisa believed her because Mae had always kept her promises. Of course, if this man had been at the reading of the will, that meant he might be a lawyer too. In his dark suit, he had an official kind of demeanour. Except...there was something more. Standing near the bottom of the stairs with his hands thrust into his trouser pockets in a casual yet authoritative way, it was as if he were *entitled*.

Bainbridges were the most entitled of the lot with their wealth, and good name paid for through cynical attempts at philanthropy to gain kudos, not putting their money where it mattered most. Yet he didn't look like anyone from that family with his dark hair and warm brown skin. Bainbridges tended to an almost vampiric type of pale. She supposed she was of Bainbridge stock too, though she didn't look much like the rest of them with her colouring, taking after her father. Something she'd come to be thankful for, even though her luminescent mother had bemoaned her red hair, green eyes, and freckles if she spent too much time in the sun.

'We need to talk, Louisa.'

That decadent voice of his drew her out of her introspection. Which was a good thing because introspection was a bad place for her to be even on her best days. He'd begun moving again, slowly this time. One step. Pause. Two steps. Pause. Though she couldn't describe any of the moves as hesitant. Each pause more like a silent demand for permission to move further, from a man she doubted sought permission from anybody, to do anything.

'What are you doing?'

'I thought it was self-evident. Coming closer, since I'd rather have a discussion where I don't have to raise my voice or, even better, need to communicate with two paper cups and string.'

Paper cups and string… What an odd thing to say. Yet a memory came drifting back of a magical summer as a six-year-old, staying with Mae here as she often had when her dad was sick. A common occurrence as the motor neurone disease began to take its awful toll. She remembered exploring Easton Hall. Running wild through the rambling gardens chasing butterflies.

There was a boy who'd come to stay too. He'd seemed so much older and wiser, at twelve. A cousin, Mae had told her when they'd first met. Though her mother had later said he wasn't a *real* Bainbridge because he'd been adopted, as if that were some kind of disqualification. And they'd played, trying to make a string telephone, which had worked in the end, to their surprise.

'I've had so many adventures,' Mae had told them. *'Make your own and make them stupendous.'*

It had been the last moment of happiness before a whole mountain of misery for Louisa. But she'd created special memories during that time. More importantly, stories of those stupendous adventures had been what she'd recounted to Mae in her last months. Those adventures had made Mae laugh. Maybe Louisa had taken some creative licence, but so much of her past was a blur of sadness and sickness and pain, what did it matter that she exaggerated? Trying to hold on to those few snatches of brightness as tightly as she could.

It seemed as though the sun had always shone in that summer of innocence and joy. There wasn't a day that hadn't been perfect.

The man was halfway up the stairs now, and somehow the squirming sensation in her belly didn't feel like the be-

ginnings of dread, but something far more...anticipatory.
Almost like excitement. Though it was remiss he hadn't
told her who he was, when he clearly knew her name. As
he climbed with his long, powerful legs he became clearer
and sharper. As if she were inking in the details of an illustration she'd been commissioned to complete. His suit
in a dark charcoal grey, pristine white shirt gleaming in
the sunshine like the snowdrops in that old churchyard.
As he came closer the niggle of recognition didn't pass.
It grew and grew.

Then he arrived at the top of the stairs and that recognition hit her with a wallop. Because that tanned-skinned,
dark-haired little boy who she'd thought completely unlike
his insipid Bainbridge namesakes, with all his vibrancy
and life, was standing right in front of her. All grown up,
filled out and angular with broad shoulders, narrow hips
and cut cheekbones. His brown eyes she'd once thought of
as warm and hinting at constant mischief as a child, now
remote and cool. Like the flat stones they'd gathered in
the stream running through the estate to skip in quieter
waters. He'd taught her how to do that and she'd squealed
when her stone had skipped twice.

He'd been less impressed. His had skipped six times.
Sometimes more.

He *regarded* her then, seeming to glower in the same
ominous way as the slate-coloured sky behind him. A
storm threatening. Louisa's breath hitched. She smoothed
her hands down the front of her crushed dress. Feeling
too soft and unkempt for him as he stood there sharp as a
blade. Not a dark hair on his head out of place. The neat
stubble on his strong jaw clearly by design, rather than a
neglect to shave.

She'd bet he neglected nothing.

'Matty.'

Not his given name of Matteo. He'd been Matty to her. The adopted Bainbridge who'd apparently conquered the world and made his fortune independent of his family. Almost to spite a name that tended to open every door. Yet what on earth was he doing here? He'd not visited Mae in that last year of her illness, or at all in the time Louisa had lived at Easton Hall. Though her great-aunt would mention him and his successes. She had tended to keep some things close, to be tossed out occasionally like little treats of sweets…

'Louisa.'

The way he said her name was soft and smooth, almost like a caress. Though he'd called her Lulu when they were children. Her father's nickname for her. One her mother had loathed because it apparently sounded undignified.

She'd never understood why a child's name needed to be dignified.

'H-how are your parents?'

Louisa wasn't sure why she sounded so breathless, as if she'd run a mile. It was a normal kind of question, wasn't it? Although she had no real practice at small talk, since her contact with strangers was restricted to telling tourists about the history of Easton Hall and its surrounds, which was a well-practised script.

His mouth thinned. Eyes narrowed. That look could slice you clean through, leaving you eviscerated. Then he shrugged, but it was somehow stiff. Almost an attempt to be dismissive when she suspected there was an enmity running seams deep.

'I've no idea. I haven't seen them in years.'

Mae had mentioned some family estrangement, so she didn't press. Especially not to ask about his sister, not right at this moment. She'd gathered even as a child that Felicity was a tender point for him. She'd been envious of the idea of a sibling back then, when she was a lonely only child. Matty had said, almost like a challenge, that he had a sister and she was sick. Louisa had known all about sick people, so she'd left well alone. Even then, she'd wanted the fantasy of a perfect summer rather than being haunted by the spectre of illness and death.

She suspected they both had.

Matty didn't ask about her family in return, but she didn't think that rude. The last time she'd glimpsed him was through streams of tears at her father's funeral, eighteen months after that summer at Mae's. He'd stood there, almost fourteen, sombre in a dark suit looking so grown up to her almost-eight-year-old self. She hadn't cared about anything that day because her world had ended.

'What are you doing here?'

It wasn't as if this were a social visit. All economy and business, he didn't even offer her condolences when she'd spent over half her life with Mae. She wasn't sure she liked it, missing the smiling sunshiny boy she'd glimpsed all those years ago. But then, she'd changed a great deal too. She wondered what he thought of her.

Whether he thought of her at all.

'Had your solicitor passed on any of my solicitor's letters, you would have known.'

His mouth was a thin, stern line. He looked as if he rarely smiled, no laugh lines round his eyes. The consummate businessman he'd reportedly become.

In response, she pasted on her brightest smile, because she'd come to believe life was too short and tenuous not to try and fill it with a little happiness.

'Well, now you're here you can tell me. Would you like to come in for a cup of tea?'

'I could just as well be inviting you inside, Louisa.'

How…odd. His voice was so cold. What had happened to him to strip him of any warmth? She was caught by the inappropriate desire to reach out, to touch. To see if he felt as cold as he looked. The prickle of something entirely unpleasant began to march down her spine. A warning.

'What do you mean?'

His mouth quirked into the pretence of a smile. His lips curling at the edges in a way that should seem happy, yet it didn't touch his eyes. They remained cold and hard as those river stones in the stream running through the estate.

'Since I'm now owner of Easton Hall.'

CHAPTER TWO

'WHAT? NO!'

Matteo didn't tell lies. His life was founded on truth since he knew the pain of lies by omission. No sugar coating. His word was his bond.

He was known for two things in both his personal life and in business. His ruthlessness and his honesty.

He looked at the woman now gripping the old oak door as if it were the only thing holding her up. Her fingers slender and pale, biting into the dark wood. She stood there in a long, soft white dress as if she'd stepped from another time. Like a woman from a pre-Raphaelite era painting, an artist's muse burst from the canvas. With red hair in a thick ponytail over her shoulder. Tendrils loose and curling round her heart-shaped face. Her pale skin dotted with faint freckles he remembered as darker from running in the sunshine over a long-ago summer.

But she wasn't a child any longer. On any objective assessment, she'd grown into an exquisite woman. The heat of admiration curled a seductive journey deep inside.

A woman he should not be suffering errant attraction to. One he was about to evict…

Not evict. Politely ask to leave, with handsome compensation for doing so. And once she was gone, this would represent his sweetest victory. The adopted and disdained

Bainbridge inheriting the jewel in the family crown. Its most coveted possession, Easton Hall. A dream he'd had since his nineteenth birthday when he'd finally cut the false cord that had tied him to this family that wasn't his by blood. The family that had all but abandoned their adopted child in favour of their natural-born one.

He knew those who considered themselves the 'true' Bainbridges wouldn't like it, and he was prepared for the fight. They were crooked to the core, if his quiet investigations into their charity interests were anything to go by, and had far more to lose than he did. In fact, they were unable to match him in any way. Still, there'd already been murmurings at the reading of the will. Unhappiness that he'd been appointed executor when he wasn't a real Bainbridge, and others claimed to be more qualified. Wanting a part of the vast property riches here when they weren't entitled to any of it. Threats of challenging the will.

They could all go to hell.

He'd vowed then that if there was any way he could take this place for his own, he'd ensure none of that cursed family ever graced its halls again. The house would be lost to them *for ever*.

His victory was almost complete, but for the woman standing in front of him, mouth gaping like a hooked fish.

'Are you going to let me in?' he asked.

They needed to discuss the predicament in which they found themselves. The estate was crumbling. Mae had talked of her worries about it and keeping up with the specialist work this home required to bring it back to its former glory. Especially being asset rich and cash poor, as were so many of those whose money and history were as old as the dirt upon which their homes stood. Mae had refused his help when alive. After her death he'd tried to send out a structural engineer to assess the state of the property, but the man hadn't even been able to set foot in the house. Reportedly being chased away by a terrifying woman and a threat, which seemed fanciful.

'Easton Hall is my *home*.'

She tore off her glasses and looked up at him with her beautiful green eyes. He'd been struck by them even as a twelve-year-old. Reminding him of the freshest new growth of spring. Of the moss at the edge of the stream that ran through the property.

So many of his memories of her had been frozen in that time, of someone small and pretty. A young if sometimes annoying little friend for a child starved of friendship and family, relegated to boarding school. Other boys' families occasionally took him in for school holidays, feeling sorry for him because he had a sick sister. What none of them realised, and what he'd concluded over those long years of her treatment, was that his family had wished he'd been the one to fall ill. The adopted one, instead of the beloved natural child...

The only glimmer of joy had been staying with Mae here, in this old ramshackle house. In that hazy summer where there were few rules, and two children were allowed to run wild in an imaginary world fighting dragons, catching frogs. It was as if the two of them had finally become the children they hadn't previously been allowed to be, when surrounded by grown-up problems like illness and death.

But there was no point to those reminiscences. He hadn't got to where he was, well past his first billion with an impressive property portfolio of boutique hotels and retreats for those who wanted intimacy, luxury and privacy, by having any form of sentiment. Business was the language he spoke, and he was unparalleled in his sphere.

That was his world.

'I'm sure this must come as a shock. I'm sorry for your loss.'

He tried to sound conciliatory, because he needed to work with her. And in some ways, he did feel some sympathy. She'd lived with Mae since before her teens. Being Mae's carer for the past twelve months meant she'd likely have expected to inherit the whole estate herself...

'*She needs to be looked after, Matteo. Promise me you will.*'

Mae's request during their last conversation. A promise he'd made with no thought, because it had sounded important to her and who was he to deny an old woman some sense of peace? Only now he realised the impact what he'd agreed to might have on his ultimate plan for this place.

Louisa narrowed her gaze. 'It's your loss too. Yet *you* weren't at the funeral.'

Matteo stared right back, ignoring her disapprobation. He wasn't a coward. Though his mobile phone weighed heavy in his trouser pocket. The unanswered messages from his sister, Felicity, saying she wanted to talk, taunted him. He ignored the sensation. He'd been occupied with a deal for a new property in Bali, that was all. She knew he was busy.

'I was in South East Asia on business. Once I found out, I couldn't make it back in time.'

Mae would have understood. She always did. Wrote him letters, which his assistant opened and scanned, sending them to him via email. A card each birthday... He and Mae would talk on the phone, about Easton Hall, about taking care of her interests. Talked a little about Louisa and her talents as a children's book illustrator too. How Louisa had come to be like the daughter Mae had never had. Then their last call, which he'd realised only after her death had been her goodbye to him. One full of warmth, where she'd told him how proud she was of him. And she'd made him make the promise he was now beginning to regret.

'*She needs to be looked after.*'

Still Mae had left its execution to his own judgement. He could do more to carry out her wishes, here, now, than he could ever have done when she was alive, given she was so stubborn and headstrong. As much as it had frustrated him, he'd admired her for that. Taking on Easton Hall after her husband had died, almost unheard of when the natural course would have been for Great-Uncle Gerald to have left the home to his nearest male Bainbridge relative, rather than his young wife...

Now, Matteo studied the young woman standing inside the home that he would soon add to his property portfolio. A woman who looked soft and innocent, and in need of the protection he'd promised. All he knew of the world was that it was cold, hard, and unforgiving. How would Louisa navigate that now Mae was gone?

'Felicity came,' Louisa said.

Those words tore him from his introspection. Felicity hadn't ever met Mae. Why had she even been at the funeral?

'I'm glad she could make it.' He tried to sound charitable. The words ground out of him, as if forced.

Louisa cocked her head, inspecting him in some way. For what, he wasn't sure, though it gave him a sort of prickling feeling at the back of his neck, almost as if she was judging him.

'She seems well.'

Everyone in the family knew of the tragedy of Flick, as they all called her. The child whose birth had been seen

as a kind of miracle, till she'd become cursed by a childhood leukaemia diagnosis. Then her remission and appar-
ent cure seemed like another miracle.

'I understand she is.'

'She's your sister. Don't you know?'

He could sense the judgement that infused every word.
Louisa didn't have siblings, so how could she possibly
understand? He and his sister didn't talk about it, when
they talked. Her past forgotten. She'd reached out to him
about five years earlier on his birthday and that was how
it had been between them since. Texting. Calling on the
celebrations. Birthdays, Easter, Christmas. That had always been enough.

'We both travel for work. There's not much time to talk.'
Louisa seemed to be good at picking at his old wounds.
Time to shut the conversation down. 'Unlike now. I have
all day to speak with you and keeping me out here isn't
going to help. There are things we need to discuss.'

Louisa hesitated for a moment, worrying on her pink
bottom lip with her teeth. 'I was told I'd have a home for
ever.'

He might have cared once, when he'd been capable of
it. But that child with the capacity to love and care was
gone. Ground out of him by constant disappointment. Love
didn't matter. Caring didn't matter. People shouldn't be
disposable, yet he'd learned that he was. Twice. His birth
mother, whoever she was, abandoning him on a hospital
doorstep. Then the family who'd adopted him, who hadn't
wanted him either. Not when they finally had a child of
their own blood...

Blood always won out, in this family at least.

They hadn't cared about him, until he'd become successful. *Finally* claiming him as a Bainbridge when he craved

to rub their noses in the certainty that he wanted nothing to do with them. Would have changed his name to eschew the family completely, had he known who he really was. But all his searches had been fruitless. Not even genealogy DNA testing, his last hope of finding his birth family, had turned up a relative. It had only given hints at his heritage. Italian. Which accounted for his colouring and his name. It gave him nothing more.

He was truly alone.

'You'll be looked after,' Matteo said. He'd promised Mae, and he delivered on his promises. Louisa would see reason. He'd ensure that she was well compensated, with a bank account so fat and full she could do whatever she dreamed. Travel the world, buy a home of her own, drape herself in jewels. He'd learned over the years that was what people wanted.

His riches.

She might look innocent and guileless, but she'd be no different.

No one he'd met ever was.

Louisa could barely catch her breath, as the heavy weight of dread crushed her chest. She hardly believed a word Matty said. He had to be wrong.

Yet why would he lie?

No, it would be okay. It *had* to be okay.

Still, a voice inside Louisa's head shouted a warning that if she let him in, she'd lose the only home she'd ever really had. The only place she felt safe. She was torn between being polite and listening to that voice.

The same voice that had whispered once that she wasn't really sick. That it was her mother making her ill, hurting her whilst claiming it was love. The voice that had told her she needed to get *someone* to listen because no doctor, no matter how clever they were with all their medicines and needles and procedures, could make her well.

That voice had saved her life.

But this was *Matty*.

She looked up at him, towering above her. Broad. Strong. Handsome…

No. Why was she thinking like this? He'd come to take away…everything. Then he raised an eyebrow, his lip quirked. And in a flash, he wasn't Matty at all. He was the man that boy had grown into. Matteo Bainbridge. Carrying an arrogance and assertion that seemed to hold her in some kind of thrall. An almost cool disdain for everything around him. Something about it made her tingle all over, though she didn't like to think too hard why that was.

Mae had always taught her to be polite. To be a good hostess, even though her great-aunt had stopped entertaining years ago. But one thing Louisa was certain of: had Matteo arrived on Mae's doorstep whilst she was alive, she would have welcomed him in with open arms.

Louisa felt obliged to do the same.

She forced herself to prise her fingers away from their death grip on the door. Stand back a little, although she wanted to slam the ancient wood firmly in his face because that door had protected the home from any number of invaders in the past.

Still, if he really did own the home, she needed to hear what he had to say.

'Okay, come in.'

None of that sounded like a good hostess, at all. Still, Matteo's lips curled into a smile that looked every bit the frog prince she'd just drawn, and kind of gloating as well.

'Thank you.'

She gestured him inside as he seemed to sweep in exactly as if he owned the place. Which, if she believed him, he did. He cast an appraising eye over the threadbare Axminster, looking around him as if searching for what was wrong, rather than focussing on what was right.

'Follow me to the kitchen.'

He didn't follow, of course he didn't. A man who looked as if he ruled the world wouldn't follow anyone. He moved into lockstep beside her, but it seemed almost uncomfortable. As though he had to adjust his pace, slow it to fit hers.

'Where's Mrs Fancutt?' he asked. 'I'd like to speak with her about chasing away my structural engineer.'

Louisa missed a step, falling behind Matteo's long, powerful stride. Hurried to catch up. She didn't want Mrs Fancutt getting into trouble. She was Easton Hall's long-term housekeeper. If Matteo was telling the truth and the home was really his, the woman deserved to be kept on in the role.

'She did no such thing.'

She rather had, with a little help from Louisa, but Matteo didn't need to know that.

'Comments about setting the dogs on him and talk of muskets sound familiar?'

Maybe it did but she'd never admit it. The heat rose to Louisa's cheeks. She hoped he wouldn't notice.

'Mrs Fancutt owns two Pomeranians who aren't in the least bit threatening...' At least that was the truth, though the man who'd arrived claiming to need to inspect the house didn't know that. 'And it was an invitation to see the armoury, where there might be a tiny bit of damp around a window frame. Your structural engineer seems to lack any kind of fortitude. Heaven help him if he came across a decent bit of dry rot. He'd be overcome.'

'You seem to know a great deal about the conversation.' Matteo's voice was smooth and cool as silk.

If he blamed her, then so be it. 'Why wouldn't I? I have a vested interest in avoiding trespassers on the property.'

'He wasn't a trespasser, he had my permission.'

'Well, he didn't have mine.'

'What are you going to do? Set the unthreatening Pomeranians onto me?'

'Sadly, Mrs Fancutt is on a day off. I'm sure she'll be sorry to have missed you. I'll say hello to her for you. Give Binky and Bess a pat.'

Yet after today, would she have a place here at all? She breathed through a wave of grief that overtook her. The yawning ache that simply opened inside. She'd lost her father, and it had been as if the world had broken apart. Staying in pieces for years. Now she'd lost Mae and, in many ways, it was the same, the corresponding loss of all that was safe and secure. Her world tilting on its axis yet again because those she loved always left her...

'Perhaps I should be making you the tea?' he asked.

That jolted her from her inertia. He was trying to take over already. Take the home that had been hers for twelve years. Louisa straightened her spine.

'I'm fine.' She'd just needed a moment. That was all. She kept walking but, out of the corner of her eye, thought she could see Matteo glancing her way. As if waiting for her to crumble. That wouldn't happen. She might bend, but she wouldn't break.

The kitchens sat quiet and empty given it was a day off for the staff here. She loved the space with its exposed brickwork, worn stone floor and huge stove. She'd thought the room magical when she'd first arrived in the home, food always available whenever she was hungry, because her mother had never fed her enough.

'There are things you're allergic to which make you ill.'

Louisa had come to learn, after those years of pain and deprivation, that she was allergic to nothing. It was yet another lie her mother had told in the pretence of love. Making sure to keep her thin and weak, so that she'd appear as sick as her mother claimed her to be.

Louisa didn't know why all these memories were assailing her now. She'd put her past behind her, begun making a future. She didn't want to think about her childhood and that hunger, deprivation and pain. Instead, she placed her glasses on the counter and put on the electric kettle to boil. Made the tea in her favourite yellow teapot, poured two cups. All the while a sensation prickled between her shoulder blades. She tried to ignore it but knew Matteo was watching.

'You said we needed to talk?' she asked, carrying the tea to the table before sitting down. He took a cup, black. No sugar. Looking at her as though she were a bug under glass, and he were conducting an inspection.

An uncomfortable sensation.

Matteo lifted the tea and took a sip, the sunny yellow cup dwarfed in his hands.

'I'm surprised you know so little about Mae's will.'

It sounded like the bite of criticism. Her mother had been an expert in its delivery. She ignored the sting. That didn't mean it didn't hurt.

'When I came to live with Mae, she promised I'd have a home for life. After she died, my solicitor confirmed that I never had to leave Easton Hall. It might be a surprise to you, but I trusted Mae and believed her.'

Matteo looked round the kitchen as if taking stock,

his golden-brown eyes cataloguing something he already owned. What did he see? The heart of the home as she did, or that everything was a little worn? The stove in need of restoration. A tap, drip-drip-dripping into the sink.

Then he fixed that assessing gaze on her.

'Apart from inheriting Easton Hall and its contents, I've been appointed executor of Mae's estate. After some money left to charity, you've inherited the remainder. Her personal effects. Jewellery.'

'What about a place to live?'

His perfect lips thinned a fraction. A tiny muscle in his stubble-covered jaw clenched. Matteo placed his hands on the table, clasped them together. The cuffs of his shirt a gleaming white against his golden skin.

'That's what we need to discuss. Mae's will grants you a right to reside in Easton Hall for as long as you want, until it stops being your principal place of residence...'

A bright spike of relief skewered her. She shut her eyes against the tears that once again threatened. She could stay here. She didn't have to leave. Louisa hadn't known how tightly she'd held herself. How little she'd breathed since she first saw Matty on the doorstep. Her shoulders dropped as she let out a slow exhale. It was as though she began to wilt as some of the tension bled from her.

'...or until you marry.'

Louisa snorted. Marry? Mae had always lived in hope for her and there were things that intrigued Louisa about a marriage. The physical side of a relationship, especially after she'd found those old leather-bound books in a re- mote part of the library here. An erotic collection of inked prints she'd once pored over. There'd been one of a woman clearly wearing a wedding dress in one of them...

A heat began to ignite in her chest, thread through her

veins as Matteo brought the teacup to his perfect lips once more. Took a swig, his Adam's apple bobbing as he swallowed.

'What's so funny about the idea of you marrying?' he asked.

Getting married meant finding a man when she barely went to the village any longer. Where would she even meet anyone? And falling in love? A shudder ran through her.

She'd had first-hand experience of what was done in the name of love. The pain it wrought. Why would she ever look for that?

'I'll leave marriage to other people. Like you, since you sound so keen on it.'

Now Matteo snorted, then checked himself. 'I travel too much to be tied down. Whereas you're young. It might not sound like an attractive prospect now, but it will be.'

As if he were so ancient. 'You're only six years older than me.'

'I left home in my teens and built my business from nothing to be one of the premier luxury hotel groups in the world, whereas you're...'

'What?'

He cocked his head, gaze drifting over her. Likely taking in the dress she wore, in fine white cotton with pretty pintucking and lace. One of her favourites from the number that she'd first found as a teenager in a trunk in the attic, which she'd been told were from one of the previous Bainbridge wives from the early nineteen hundreds. Her clothes were a particular hit when she took tours of the home talking about the history of the place. People thought she dressed up for the role. They didn't realise this was what she liked to wear. And she'd never really cared that it made her stand out, before today...

'You're a young woman who's devoted her life to caring for an elderly one.'

He said that as if it were a bad thing.

'Do you understand love, Matteo?'

He reared back, sitting straighter in the chair. Eyes a little wider. Looking uncomfortable.

'We're talking about property. What's love got to do with this?'

Most of what had happened to her had been kept hidden. The public had never found out about the charges against her mother, just the way the exalted Bainbridge family had wanted, because heaven forbid their perfect name be tarnished. Then her mother died of a heart attack before the press had got wind of what she'd subjected Louisa to. There was no point rehashing the truth when the lie that the last of her parents to pass away was beloved was so much more palatable.

'Mae took me in when I was an orphan.' Had given Louisa a home when all she'd had to look forward to was foster care, because no other Bainbridge had had any interest in her and her problems. Her father had been an only child with no relatives left to care for her. 'Everyone else in this family was only ever interested in the family name, or what Mae might have been able to gift them. Mae gave me far more than material things. She gave me a home, a safe place to land. And I loved her for it. Why wouldn't I care for Mae?'

The woman had sacrificed years of her later life, looking after Louisa, more a mother than her own ever had been. Had made sure she'd received the professional help she'd needed to overcome the death of her father and her mother's abuse. Louisa would have done *anything* to repay her.

'I'm sure there are many things you'd like to do now that your caring duties are over. I have a proposition for you.'

She'd had a lifetime as a child being told what was good for her, especially by men like the various doctors who'd 'treated' her, believing her beautiful, fragile-appearing mother when she'd said there was something terribly wrong with her only child.

For years, no one had believed Louisa. She'd become tired of her voice not being heard. It remained a struggle to speak up some days, because she was still unsure anyone listened.

'Of course you do.' Her voice came out too soft, too quiet. Louisa was simply pleased she could get the words out at all.

'I want Easton Hall outright, and I'm prepared to pay well for you to relinquish your right to reside here.'

She stilled. Her heart almost missed a beat. If she agreed to that...

'Where would I live, then?'

'Anywhere else you want.'

A tight band wound round her chest. Crushing the air from her. She could hardly breathe again. This home was the only place in the world she'd ever felt secure. All she had. Mae had promised she'd always be safe, and Louisa had believed her when there was no one else in the world *to* believe. There was nowhere else to go. She *couldn't* leave here.

'You haven't been listening. This is my *home*.'

'It's an old house, which is in dire need of restoration. Mae neglected it. Given that, I have an offer for you.'

He smiled, and *this* time it met his eyes. That smile was glorious. Some might call it a winning smile. Matteo reached into the inner pocket of his suit jacket. Pulled out a folded white piece of paper, placed it on the tabletop and slid it over to her. She opened it. It was an official-looking document that talked about giving up her rights under Mae's will for a sum of money. She stilled.

All those zeros at the end couldn't be right. She'd never seen so much in her life. The offer was designed to be an amount no one could refuse...if money was what you were interested in.

'Why do you want Easton Hall so badly? It looks like you're offering me an extraordinary deal. Surely that's bad business?'

Matteo's eyes narrowed. 'What does it matter to you if you're going to take it?'

And there was the part where she knew he could never understand, what this place meant to her.

'It matters to me. You're probably a man who has homes all over the world. Why this one?'

He shrugged. Sat back in his chair. Head cocked. Eyes cool and assessing as if weighing her up again.

'The home will be well utilised. My company, Arcadia, will turn it into a boutique retreat.'

So, not a home. She looked about the old kitchen that had fed generations of families. Thought of Mrs Fancutt, who'd been here most of her working life, managing the house, doing the cooking. Of all the people who worked to keep the house going. Generations of families had been employed here. If it became a 'boutique retreat'...

'Will the staff be "well utilised"?'

'Given that they're all older, they'll be comfortably re-tired, which I'm sure they'll enjoy.'

'Have you asked them?'

'I beg your pardon?'

'Have you asked whether they'd enjoy it? Do you know the answer to that question?'

All the times they'd sat here in the kitchen at this old

table in the evenings, Mae included, and played cribbage or other card games. Betting with toothpicks as if they were made of gold. He'd never understand this wasn't just a job to them. At the funeral, there'd been punishing grief. These people had been promised jobs, and homes for life too. On the day Mae had passed, each of them had said they wouldn't leave here, leave Louisa. It was more than her home; it was theirs as well.

She shook her head. 'No, this isn't happening.'

'What do you mean, *"This isn't happening"*?'

Louisa folded up the piece of paper, which held no temptation for her at all. Slid it back across the tabletop to him.

'Thank you for your kind offer, but I'm not leaving.'

The change in him was profound. His eyes narrowed, the colour of them turning. How warm brown could suddenly look ice cold she wasn't sure, but he achieved it. She'd kidded herself even thinking he was the boy she'd met so long ago. The memories of that time entertaining Mae in her last months—they were a mere fantasy. This man before her had no sentiment. He was all calculation.

'I'll add another hundred thousand.'

The way he said it. Who could toss money around like that with no care?

She shook her head. 'If Mae knew what you were planning, she'd turn over in her grave.'

Matteo stood, planted his hands flat on the tabletop.

'She knew *exactly* who I was. Ask yourself, why didn't she leave the home to you? A woman who spent what should be the best years of her life caring for an elderly lady. Surely you'd have expected repayment for that? It must come as a terrible shock that you weren't made executor too. That the house was left to me. But Mae assessed my experience and my resources, and she clearly made a judgement about yours. She knew that looking after this place was beyond you, which is why I'm here. I'm doing you a favour.'

Each word shot like another poisoned arrow deep into her heart. Tainting memories of a woman Louisa had thought she'd known. Yet he didn't understand. Matteo would take this place and tear the soul out of it. Tear apart everything she loved. She couldn't let him.

She smoothed her trembling hands over her dress. Stood. She'd made a terrible mistake allowing him to come in here. Underestimating him. She wouldn't again.

'Thank you for your considered offer, but I've heard enough. You can leave now.'

'That's where you're mistaken, Louisa.'

The way he said her name, as if he was in some way mocking her. She gritted her teeth. 'How am I in any way mistaken?'

'Thinking that I'm going to leave. I own the house, and I'm moving in.' He crossed his arms. Mouth a thin, cold line. The ominous grumble of thunder rolled in the distance. 'Today.'

CHAPTER THREE

MATTEO WOKE TO a ferocious wind howling outside, as rain lashed the rattling windows. Even though Easton Hall was made of stone, it was as if the whole house trembled against the storm's onslaught.

He'd taken the spare room he'd used here as a boy that single summer he'd stayed. Ignoring Louisa's mutinous glares as he'd brought his bags inside and removalists had come with a small truck to drop off computer equipment. If she refused to move out, then she'd have to get used to him moving in. Living here meant nothing. He had no house in the UK. On the odd occasion he was in the country, he stayed in one of his hotels. This was as good a base as any and the home needed to be assessed. He could use the time to do that, and to convince her to leave in the process.

He had all the time in the world to spare for *that* project.

Matteo tried closing his eyes, but his mind ticked over with work. Sleep had been an elusive state in his life. Owning an international business meant it was always daytime, somewhere. Right now, he had too many ideas crowding inside his head of how to turn this property into the newest jewel in his hotel chain's crown. Giving his clientele the type of authentic 'English country house' experience they'd pay handsomely for.

With those thoughts whirring through his head, he gave

up all pretence that he'd get to sleep any time soon, and turned on the bedside lamp, which lit the room with a dim glow, occasionally flickering as the flashes of lightning and cracks of thunder raged outside. Grabbing his mobile phone from the bedside table, he made a note to ask the engineer he'd rebooked to assess the building's lighting protection system, assuming it had one.

Matteo propped his arm behind his head, and scanned his emails, seeing a report from his chief operating officer about a prospective property in Spain. Through the window ahead of him, flickering blue lights reflected in the glass slicked with rain. He ignored it, but a piercing cry rent the darkness. He sat bolt upright. What was that? A vixen's cry? Though how could it be? It was the wrong time of the year and most definitely the wrong weather for that.

Matteo strained to listen for the noise again over the wind and rain. In the end, he left the comfort of his bed to investigate, dressed only in his boxer briefs. He raked his hands through his hair and peered outside at the persistent flashing lights close by. An emergency vehicle, he assumed as gusts of wind hurled at the home in a vicious assault. A tree down across the road? An accident? Who could tell? Anything was possible in this weather.

As he watched, a blazing white light burst outside with an instantaneous crack and boom. The lights in the room died. Matteo gripped the window ledge, heart thrashing in his chest. He enjoyed storms, the power of nature, but that had to be a direct strike on the house. Apart from the roar of the wind it was as if an ominous silence fell over Easton Hall, before he heard a creak and groan as if the home itself moaned in protest. All of him stilled. Waiting. For what he didn't know, a sixth sense filling him with dread.

He turned on his phone torch and went to the door of

his room, opened it. Above the noise of the storm there was a faint crackling sound. A taint to the air, like burning plastic. Smoke?

Fire.

Louisa.

He didn't think as he strode down the hall. The torch app from his phone cast its trembling light in the darkness. He coughed at the thickening acrid scent. Electrical? No flames. In the ceiling?

They had to get out.

'Louisa!'

Matteo knew from a multitude of fire-safety plans for his hotels that these old buildings were a tinderbox of ancient wood, ready to ignite. If on fire, in no time the whole place could explode over their heads.

'Louisa!'

The chill air bit his naked skin. Threadbare carpet felt rough under his feet. He tried to remember her door. Which one? Guess. He pounded on the dark oak outside one room. Would she be asleep? Somewhere else in the house?

Movement made him stop. A figure in ghostly white appeared as the door in front of him partially opened. Hand up against the light of the phone torch he'd pointed her way.

'Matty, what happened?'

She coughed. The air thicker, hazy.

'Lightning. We need to leave now.'

She froze. Gripping the door as if paralysed.

'C'mon. We have to go,' he snapped through gritted teeth as she stared at him with her huge green eyes, wide in what looked like terror. Yet she still didn't move.

'Take my hand, Louisa.' He held out his arm. Hand, palm up. As the wind still rattled the home round them, he willed his breathing to stay calm, measured, as she reached out, paused, drew back.

'I—I haven't… M-my things. My art. I can't.'

Then an alarm burst to life, another and another with their shrill and piercing sound. She clapped both of her hands over her ears.

Enough.

'We don't have a choice.'

This was taking too long. He stepped forward and simply swung her into his arms. She didn't fight. There was no struggle. Louisa went limp as he held her tight. His phone in one hand attempting to light the way as he tried to keep as low as possible, the air a flare of grey, thin smoke in front of him as they both coughed. Finding the stairs. A crash sounded. Falling masonry? Louisa flinched in his arms. He gripped her tighter, her body soft against his.

'We'll be okay.'

It was a promise. When he made those, he kept them, since so often in his life promises made to him hadn't been met. By some miracle he found the stairs, began walking down as fast as he could, reaching the bottom and heading through the house towards the front door as voices called out.

'We're okay,' he shouted. As he did, a beam of light cut across them.

'No one injured?'

He shook his head as firefighters and police milled about in the entry, escorting them towards the front door.

'Anyone missing?' a firefighter asked. Droplets of water on his uniform glittering in torchlight.

'Not us.' Matteo drew Louisa closer to him, 'There are some staff who live here. It's their day off. I don't know if they got out.'

'They all seem accounted for, sir. You might check, after we get you seen by the paramedic.'

Matteo nodded as they walked through the front door into a carnival of flashing lights of emergency services. The frigid gale hit him like a slap. He'd forgotten he was only partially dressed, the weight and heat of Louisa against him keeping him warm. Somehow tethering him, not letting the fear of what might have been get too much of a grip on his consciousness.

Around them, emergency services worked. Kept him moving forwards. The gravel of the drive was sharp and cutting on his bare feet. Someone wrapped a blanket round him. Led him to an ambulance. He told them their names. Relinquished Louisa even though he didn't want to lose the sensation of her in his arms. The perfect fit. Sat as the adrenaline that had been rocketing through his body bled away and the world simply spun round them.

Against the backdrop of night, flames licked the roof of the house. Then hoses. Water jets. Shouts and movement. The warm glow of fire guttering. Dying. Igniting again in a fight to remain alive.

Little by little he came back to himself. Turned round as Louisa was huddled on a gurney.

If he hadn't been awake. If the fire alarms hadn't worked. If emergency services hadn't been close...

If he hadn't been here at all and Louisa had been alone in the house.

No.

Louisa coughed. Eyes wide as the ambulance officers asked questions. Not answering them.

'We've inhaled some smoke.'

They came at him with an oxygen mask but he waved it away. 'I'm fine. Look after her. I think it may be shock.'

The ambulance officers nodded, placing a blanket round Louisa too, covering her soft, sheer nightgown. It struck him then how out of place she was in all of this. How breakable she appeared.

Something of himself seemed to break inside too. At how fragile life could be. How one day everything seemed fine and the next, everything changed. One moment he'd had a healthy little sister, then came the unexpected bruising. The listlessness. Till her awful diagnosis. The chemo. The infections. Constant terror that one day he might come home and she'd be gone, for ever.

He stood. No. He'd hardened himself to it all and the pain of that time had gone away. He didn't need to remember. Tonight, there were things he had to do. Plans to make. He'd wanted to get Louisa out of the house, and the universe had granted him the perfect opportunity.

'I have staff to check on,' he said to the ambulance officers. 'Can I go?'

Louisa seemed to wake up from her inertia. Sat bolt upright on the gurney.

'No!'

'They need to check you over,' Matteo said.

She shook her head violently, her hair swirling round her shoulders. 'I'm fine.' Tried to get up. Swayed. Her breaths short and shallow.

She looked just like Felicity had. Dark rings under her eyes, stark in the harsh light. Skin so pale she was almost translucent. Memories came flooding back of Flick being taken away in an ambulance all those years ago. The old fears. He shut them down.

'Let them look at you.' He made his voice stern. The voice of the businessman whose staff did exactly what he asked when he asked it. Louisa's eyes widened, mouth trembling. He wished then that his tone had been gentle. But he had no time for softness and gentleness. That had ended in his teens. And yet he couldn't move. Heart still pounding behind his ribs as if fighting for an escape.

'Don't let them do anything to me.' Her voice was the barest whisper.

What in hell's name would they do to put that fear on her face?

'It hurts, Matty.'

One of the last conversations he'd had with his sister as a child, when she'd been in hospital, undergoing the awful treatment that would save her life. It was as if a hand grabbed his throat and began throttling him.

Had something like that happened to Louisa? No, it couldn't have. She'd been a healthy child the last time he'd seen her at her father's funeral, and Mae had told him nothing. Though whatever the reason, he knew fear when he saw it.

'I'm right here. I won't go anywhere.'

Matteo wanted to do more. Overcome by the almost overwhelming desire to take her into his arms again. Smooth his hands over her. Tell her it would all be okay. Hold her. Yet that made no sense. Shock, that was it. Like her, it must be affecting him too. The desire to cling to the nearest life. Instead, he pinned the ambulance officers with a glare of warning.

'They won't *do* anything to you other than check you over. Isn't that correct?'

One of them nodded, turned to Louisa. 'We'd like to take your blood pressure. Listen to your heart and lungs. Is that okay?'

Louisa looked at him, almost pleading.

'I'll hold your hand if you're afraid,' he said.

'Okay,' Louisa said, never once looking at the man and woman attending to her as they began their work. Each gently narrating what they were doing. Taking care until they finished.

One ambulance officer made way for him, and he took Louisa's hand. Small, pale. Cold. He wrapped his fingers round hers. Gave a gentle squeeze. It brought him back to the hospital visits with Felicity. How small and scared she was. The ever-present dread that the time he saw her would be the last, till his parents sent him away and the only things he had were vague reports begged from the people who should have loved him as much as they loved their own true daughter.

His gut twisted into sickening knots. The memories that came flooding back, of the flashing lights, the medical care, the fear. Like a nightmare that had gone on for years till the news had finally come that Flick was in remission. She'd stayed in remission ever since, yet each year on that date he waited for the call that would tell him the cancer had come back, even though she was now in her twenties with no signs of relapse, and his sister was considered cured. Still...

'Everything all right?' he asked.

'Blood pressure's a little low, heart rate's a little high. Lungs are clear. Otherwise, no injuries. We'd like her to stay here a little while, have some oxygen. Take her observations again.'

'Are you okay with that, Louisa? I can ask them to call me over when they want to look at you again. For now, I'd like to go and check on Mrs Fancutt and talk to the others.'

The column of her slender throat moved in a swallow. 'That's fine.'

He stood and strode to a small group, huddled near a fire

engine under some hastily erected cover. The rain wasn't heavy any more but driven by the wind and stinging his bare legs as he held the blanket tight round him.

'Everyone okay here?' They all nodded, asked about him. Of Louisa especially.

'We're both fine.'

The housekeeper looked at him, her normally tidy grey hair a mess of being woken from sleep and the weather. 'Are you sure?'

'We have no injuries.'

'That's not what I meant. Miss Louisa hasn't been outside the house in months, other than to attend the funeral. She hasn't left the property other than to visit the village in far longer.'

Matteo stilled. He spent his time travelling, visiting his properties, working. He had 'homes' all over the world. His house in Italy when he'd sought to find his birth parents in earnest. The gleaming modern masterpiece of an apartment in New York, a chateau in the Loire Valley... He shook his head. Home was where he laid his head for the moment, not any one house or apartment.

'How long is "far longer"?'

Mrs Fancutt hesitated. 'Years.'

He stilled. What kind of life had she led? Louisa had talked about love but what held her here? He could hardly believe his great-aunt would compel her to stay. However, what did he know? This whole family was steeped in self-interest.

'She needs to be looked after...'

'Has she ever travelled? Been out of the country?'

'Never, though Mae, God rest her soul, did try. Even got her a passport. Used to tell Louisa of her adventures when she was a young woman. Encouraging her to go on her own. She never did.'

Matteo glanced over at the ambulance. No wonder Louisa was reluctant to leave Easton Hall. She didn't know what kind of world was out there waiting to be explored. With the money he was prepared to give her, she could do anything she wanted. An idea struck him. Louisa was trapped in an existence steeped in the past, yet she was a young woman with a big future in a wide world.

Whilst she might not believe him, he simply needed to show it to her.

Louisa sat in the back of a large black car. The luxury vehicle easing through the glaring, crowded streets of Milan. How could it have been only days since the storm and fire? That time had seemed to pass in a complete blur. All the while, Matteo had been there. Taking charge, taking control. Calmly talking to staff about what would happen until Easton Hall could be properly assessed. How their wages would be protected. Sourcing a replacement passport because hers was trapped in a house they couldn't now enter till it was deemed safe.

Then he'd simply told her she was coming with him, bundled her into a private jet and flown her to one of his luxury hotels in northern Italy.

She'd tried to marvel at the flight, her first. The sky, so vast. The clouds like spun sugar in the sky. Yet it was as if she were cut adrift, having lost everything safe and familiar. Sitting in the back of the ambulance had brought back memories, taking her to dark places she hadn't been in years. The nightmares she'd once suffered regularly, returning. Yet she didn't have her sketchbook with her to draw them when she woke, to take away their power.

She took a deep breath. The lack of her art things carried a greater worry, that she'd fall behind on her illustrations when she had a contract to fulfil. A deadline, and Louisa *never* missed those. She'd tried to explain that to Matteo as well, yet he'd simply waved away her concerns. Said that he'd look after her. Told her to have some time off and have fun, when Louisa was convinced they had different meanings for the word. Like today, when he'd arranged a personal stylist to come and take her to buy clothes, on his account. They'd sourced a few simple dresses in the UK before leaving, but, with everything else trapped in the house, even she could see that she needed more.

'Milan is the city of fashion,' he'd said, as if that meant anything to her. The woman sitting next to her in the soft white leather seats seemed to understand the assignment. Elegant to a fault with glossy, smooth chocolate hair. A sharp black suit. Vibrant, multicoloured silk blouse with a stylishly asymmetrical bow at the neck. Barely there make-up. Long, manicured nails.

A picture of perfection, who'd seen Louisa, pursed her lips, looked her up and down. Then nodded once and simply said, 'Come with me.'

No conversation about what she might like. Nothing. Now Louisa's belly churned as if it were full of snakes. Why did she feel so...judged? Her needs were simple. Maybe Matteo had said something when arranging the day? Perhaps that he'd found her in some way lacking? Though why that should even matter, she couldn't be sure.

He was the enemy. Trying to take away her home. She shouldn't care less about what he thought of her. Should she?

They pulled up outside a building fronted with smooth cream marble. Windows of glistening glass. Gleaming gold accents. No name on the shopfront. A man in a dark suit opened the car door and she followed the stylist out into the harsh summer sunshine. The humidity of the day draped over Louisa like a damp blanket. Likely making her hair frizz, the floral cotton of her pretty dress crinkle and hang limp.

It didn't seem to affect the woman she was with, who still looked crisp and cool as though she'd just stepped from a freezer. Cutting her way through the throng of tourists on the footpath who parted in her wake, whereas Louisa felt hemmed in, pressed on all sides.

She scurried to catch up, dodging a couple who'd stopped in front of her to take photographs, as the stylist strode through the door of the shop. Dagger-sharp heels, clicking staccato on the marble flooring as she entered. Leading Louisa through the back to a kind of showroom with plush couches, champagne on ice and racks of vibrant clothes. A couple more perfectly presented women entered. Assessing her. She spied herself in a wall of mirrors. Long red hair curling at the ends. No make-up. Floral cotton dress. Ballet flats.

'Please take a seat.'

She was guided to a couch, handed a glass of champagne. Some strawberries. She didn't want the champagne right now, although the berries looked delicious. She put the glass down as a conversation in Italian swirled round her. Talking *about* her, she was sure. She bit into a strawberry and a burst of juice exploded from the luscious fruit, dripping onto her dress. Leaving a blot of pink on the fabric as she was being…studied.

'Can I please have a napkin and some water to clean this before it stains?'

'You won't need it. A man like Signor Bainbridge has

certain…requirements for a woman and how she's dressed,' the woman said to her. Louisa wasn't sure of her name. They hadn't even really been introduced. She'd just swept in like a perfect, perfumed tidal wave and washed Louisa away with her.

'He does?' Louisa couldn't understand. Wasn't this trip about clothes for her? Why should Matteo care what she wore? Although he was paying, which didn't sit right, but that was another thing he simply waved off in his imperious kind of way.

'Of course. We will cater for all of them here. We have many ideas for you.'

What about her ideas for herself? She knew what she needed, what she wanted. What she liked. Though she supposed these people were professionals. She could sit back. At least it was cool here, out of the sunshine and the humidity.

They began taking clothes from the racks, holding them up for her. Suits as sharp as theirs. As sharp as Matteo's own. Black, a colour she swore she'd only wear to a funeral. Bejewelled dresses with plunging necklines. Crystal-covered stilettos when she'd never worn a pair in her life and would likely break a limb or her neck if she tried. Nothing looked like *her* or felt like her style, at all. She was happy to try something new, but this? She kept shaking her head as the assembled women's lips thinned, eyes narrowed, brows creased.

'What *do* you like to wear?' one of them asked.

She waved her hands up and down her body. 'Dresses a bit like this. I also wore vintage clothes at home. I felt… pretty in those.'

'And what if you were to go to a formal dinner? A

cocktail party? Accompany Signor Bainbridge on a business lunch?'

'I—I'm a children's book illustrator. Why would I go to anything like that?'

They all muttered amongst themselves. Seemed to change tack. Out came underwear. Filmy lace. Embroidery. Barely there. Beautiful. But how would it even look on her and *why*? Something uncomfortable prickled at the back of her neck. A heated sensation that was part unpleasant and part sliding temptation. Did they think…?

'I'm not Matteo's lover.'

The women stopped their bustling. Stared at her.

'What does it matter what you are?' the stylist asked, one perfectly plucked brow raised. 'We must do *something* with you. Perhaps your hair. It's so…long. Cut. Highlights. Then you'll feel like a new woman and want clothes.'

It was as if a hand grabbed Louisa's throat and cut off her breath. She loathed the thought of anyone cutting her hair after her mother regularly had when she was a child, even taking to it with thinning scissors to reduce its thickness. To try and make her daughter look ill. Louisa had vowed that she'd *never* be subjected to that again. She stood, but the women completely ignored her. All nodded at the fine idea of changing her into someone else, and went back to talking amongst themselves.

The thing was, Louisa had accepted herself long ago. Mae and counselling had shown her that she was enough. And so, her mother's barbed comments had dimmed over time. Why wasn't she blonde, unfreckled, thinner, taller? Now, these women were a reminder of how others saw her. Tears burned the back of her nose. She didn't need to be turned into someone else because some strangers wanted to squeeze her into a box that didn't fit.

'No,' she said.

'Come dici?' the stylist asked.

Even though Louisa couldn't speak Italian the phrase was said in a way that clearly meant, *What on earth are you talking about?*

Louisa shook her head. Right now, she had to go. Today wasn't fun. It was another kind of nightmare.

'This is all a mistake. I won't wear those clothes. I refuse to cut my hair. I want to go back to the hotel. We're done here.'

CHAPTER FOUR

MATTEO STRODE INTO his suite. It had been a successful morning in all respects. Arriving in Milan, finalis-
ing the negotiations for another property. He shrugged off
his jacket and tossed it onto a chair and loosened his tie.
Undid the top button of his shirt. Rolled up his sleeves. It
was only the afternoon—however, something had pulled
him back here. He was keen to see how Louisa's own day
had gone. The first step in showing her all she'd missed in
life, living with Mae. What woman didn't love shopping
for clothes? Milan was the perfect place to do that. Such a
magnificent city with its combination of history mingled
with modernity. Even though he'd anticipated her shopping
trip would take most of the morning, perhaps she might
have been able to do some sightseeing as well?

That thought piqued his interest—what she thought of
her first foreign city. He glanced at the door that joined
his suite to hers. Walked to it. Knocked. He was almost
surprised when it opened, so he walked through.

Louisa faced away from him, staring out of the hotel
windows onto Milan's rooftops. Hair tumbling down her
back in glorious waves of red. Still wearing a floral dress
from a small boutique in the village near Easton Hall they'd
managed to visit after the fire. Pretty, to be sure, but nothing like what she could find in this city. Though he was

surprised the suite wasn't full of packages. He'd been clear that money was no object in the stylist's efforts. There was to be no impediment to securing anything Louisa wanted.

'How was your day?' he asked.

She turned. He expected a beaming smile. Strangely craved it, since Louisa hadn't smiled once since they'd met only days ago. What woman didn't deserve a little happiness after what she'd been through?

Except there was no smile. Her face a mask of almost forced neutrality.

'I couldn't find anything to wear.'

Impossible. He'd been explicit, and the stylist was an expert. Perhaps Louisa didn't want to spend his money, although he'd tried to reassure her that she needed clothes. A couple of dresses and one hauntingly sheer nightgown were not enough. Even Louisa could see that...

Then he noticed. Her eyes, rimmed pink. Her nose, a little pink too.

Had she been crying?

He took a step forward, then another till he was close. She looked up at him, her lips trembling at the corners a fraction. Eyes bright with what he feared were tears. A heat boiled in his gut. He'd expected smiles, not sadness. He tamped the rising anger down. Trying to get to the bottom of what had happened. People did what he asked, or they paid.

It seemed someone would be owing him today.

'Didn't you see anything you liked?'

As he looked down on her, Louisa's pupils flared wide. The green of her eyes seemingly more vibrant in this moment. Captivating, like the verdant grass round Easton Hall.

'They showed me things I'd never wear. I tried telling them but they...'

She bit her lip as she hesitated. Took a jagged breath.

'Tell me,' he said, his jaw clenching. The way her eyes tightened, her soft pink lips turned down… Clearly today hadn't been a good day.

'The way those women looked at me. They didn't make me feel beautiful. They wanted to cut my hair.'

A shudder tremored through her as a blaze of fury tore through his veins. Not beautiful? How could they not see? And how could *anyone* suggest cutting off her hair, that glorious river of fire? He couldn't comprehend it.

Moisture pooled in the corners of her eyes. No. This was *not* what he'd asked for or envisaged. He craved to reach out, hold. Soothe. But why? Seduction of innocents wasn't the game here. Showing her what she'd been missing out on in life was, and he'd failed. Spectacularly.

Failure wasn't part of his repertoire. Time to fix what others had clearly broken.

'You are beautiful. That's a fact and not open for discussion. As for your hair?' What he wouldn't give to plunge his hands into the thickness of it. Find out whether it was as silky as it appeared. 'Anyone who'd consider cutting it would be contemplating a *crime.*'

Her mouth opened a fraction, with a breathy inhale. 'They thought I was your lover. Said you had…expectations.'

His brain snagged on one word. *Lover.* The heat that had flared in his gut rushed low. How she'd felt in his arms when he carried her from Easton Hall. The soft weight of her against his naked torso. What if they had been lovers? He'd carry her to this bed like that. Her head thrown back in ecstasy as her green eyes glazed in passion. Hair spilled like blood across his pillow. He could count every freckle on her body. Kiss each one…

No. He almost shook his head to rid his mind of the intoxicating fog of those imaginings. Innocents weren't for him. He'd been focussed on business for too long, that was all. What with investigating the Bainbridge family's charities' interests for fraud and then planning his quest for revenge, he hadn't been with a woman for some time. No wonder he was reacting like an eighteen-year-old with no control over his own body.

He took a step back. Turned round. Clenched his fists and willed his inconvenient arousal away.

'The *only* expectation I had was that you'd find clothes that you liked. My error was the choice of stylist, which I'll rectify immediately.'

She gave a shaky laugh. 'Not those women again, they didn't like me much.'

They weren't paid to like her. They were paid to do their job. To ensure she felt beautiful and cherished, and to make the whole process fun. The failure of his mission quelled his remaining desire like being doused in chilled water. He turned back round to face her. Noticing how... worn she seemed.

'She needs to be looked after...'

'Have you eaten?' he asked.

She shook her head. 'I kind of lost my appetite after being told something needed to be *done* with me.'

How *dared* they.

'If you had an appetite, what would you like?'

'A cheese toastie.'

He picked up his phone, ordered one for each of them. Whilst it wasn't something traditionally on the room service menu here, he had no doubt the hotel chef would make the best damned cheese toastie Louisa had ever eaten.

'Food first, shopping next.'

One of her hands gripped the fabric of her dress, twisting it in her fingers. 'I'm not keen to relive the experience.'

'You'll enjoy this, I promise you.'

Matteo was intent on recovering the day. A few phone calls later and he'd spoken to another woman. One he'd been assured could help him. She seemed more than amenable to dropping everything to search out suitable clothes and deliver them to his hotel. She asked about Louisa's style, and for a photograph of her, which he promised to send. 'Country look, cottage core,' she'd suggested. He didn't understand what that meant but it didn't matter. This time, he'd stay to supervise the process.

Failure was *not* an option.

Louisa didn't want to go back to more clothes shopping, but she was powerless to resist. How had she not recognised what a force of nature Matteo was? He'd simply stormed into the room and taken over. Whilst she couldn't understand the Italian he'd been speaking on the phone; his voice had been terse. Command and authority. All for her. Something about it had been...electrifying. To watch him work, take charge. She could imagine mere mortals simply rolling over and doing his bidding with no fight at all.

Was that what he'd expected of her, when he'd said he wanted her out of Easton Hall?

She couldn't think of that right now. As much as she'd stood up for herself earlier in the day, the cold words of three impeccably styled women had still taken their toll. She'd felt old-fashioned. Unattractive. Past insecurities calling to her in their nasty but seductive voices. Yet when she'd told Matteo...

He thought she was beautiful.

What did he say? That it was a fact *'not open for dis-*

cussion'. And she realised he was the first man other than her father to say that about her. With his words it was as if she basked in the warm, golden glow of spring sunshine. Though she shouldn't, Louisa found his approval hard to resist even though his aims and hers weren't aligned.

'How was your toastie?' he asked.

A perfect concoction of crisp buttery bread, melting cheese and the bite of mustard. 'I've never tasted better.'

The corner of Matteo's lips quirked. 'I'm sure the chef would like to hear that.'

'Do you always stay in your hotels, or do you have a home base anywhere?'

This place was a masterpiece of elegance with warm earth tones, jewelled accents, and sleek modern styling. The freestanding bath was almost like a swimming pool, with a chandelier above it that had made her feel like royalty as she'd wallowed in the tub. Everything a picture of sheer opulence. Yet she couldn't imagine this was where he spent all his time, though why she held that unshakable view she couldn't really say. It just seemed the hotel was somewhere he'd created for others, not himself.

'I have lots of places to live,' he said, arms out wide. 'Take your pick of country. Italy, France, the US.'

'Are they all your *homes*?'

He cocked his head to the side. A tiny frown creased his brow. 'I own them. I stay there. Isn't that enough?'

She shook her head.

'Not where you sleep. I'm talking about somewhere where you're happy to be. Every time you walk through the door, it's a relief. Your safe space, the one that holds your fondest memories. The place that you can be entirely yourself?'

That was what Easton Hall had been to her. A sanctuary. She'd spent so long feeling as though she'd had to hide, with people not listening to her. There, she could be who she was without any question. Today out in Milan had simply reaffirmed what she'd always thought: Easton Hall was her place. Where she fitted, like the final piece slotted into a puzzle.

Matteo's eyes widened, then he frowned. 'That's not what a home means. It's a place to stay.'

That was why he thought paying her off would convince her to leave Easton Hall. How could she ever convince someone who didn't understand the true meaning of home how important a real home was to her?

Before she could carry on the conversation his phone buzzed an alert.

'Ahh. I promised food then clothes. The clothes have arrived.'

The delicious toastie in her stomach seemed to have congealed to a solid rock in an instant. She took a deep breath, steeling herself for more judgement and humiliation.

A gentle knock sounded at the door and Matteo opened it. In walked a woman, once again with impeccable style. Though not sharp in black and bold colours but somehow more accessible in pale grey trousers, a soft cream blouse, and pastel-coloured scarf casually tossed round her throat. She shook Matteo's hand, her whole demeanour business-like. Louisa stood and the woman turned, a wide and warm smile on her face. Introduced herself as Sylvana. Directed a couple of men with clothing racks into the suite. Louisa scanned the racks and her shoulders dropped a fraction, relaxing. No black to be seen.

'I hope you like what I have to show you. Please take a seat and we'll go through what I've found.'

Louisa glanced at Matteo. Was he going to stay? She

guessed so, the way he'd sprawled on the lounge like a panther making itself comfortable in the sun. She sat in an armchair as Sylvana took dress after dress from the racks. All breathtakingly beautiful. Some she wouldn't wear, many she would. The woman reorganised the racks into the clothes Louisa might like and the clothes she didn't.

All the while Matteo watched, staring at the selections, then looking at her. What was he thinking? Imagining her in the clothes, wondering whether they'd suit her? The man was inscrutable, even though the awareness of his gaze brushed over her like the soft, expensive fabrics Sylvana invited her to touch to ensure she liked the feel of them against her skin.

'I hear that your house recently caught fire, which is why you have no clothes,' Sylvana said, with a look of real concern on her face as she began wheeling the clothes rack with Louisa's selections into the bedroom. 'I'm sorry. But let's start the fun by trying these clothes on.'

'I'm not sure this is my idea of fun,' Louisa said. 'I usually wear vintage day dresses that I found in the attic in my old home.'

Sylvana put her hand to her chest. 'Oh, *davvero*? I studied fashion history here in Milan. Those pieces would be irreplaceable. Were they lost in the fire?'

Louisa shrugged, rubbing at the tight ache in her chest even contemplating the loss. 'I don't know. Maybe. The fire was put out quickly, but no one can go into the house right now.'

'*È terribile!* Let's hope, then. This is at least a beginning. Not vintage masterpieces, but something I think you'll be comfortable in.'

She tried on the clothes. Not vintage, as Sylvana said, but dresses that still made her feel a little like a princess. With skirts that twirled as she spun round in them, big sleeves, glorious colours of greens, blues and pinks. Brighter, bolder than normal.

'You should show Signor Bainbridge,' Sylvana said.

Louisa's heart seemed to do a little twirl of its own in her chest at that suggestion. 'Really?'

'He's a man who stays, so he must want to see. Go,' the woman said, with a shooing motion of her hands.

Louisa peeked round the open bedroom door. Matteo still lounged on the couch, phone in hand. Shirtsleeves rolled up showing his strong, tanned forearms. He noticed her in mere seconds, lifted his head. She felt almost silly. What did she know about men's...wants? Surely he couldn't care less about the clothes she wore?

'You are beautiful. That's a fact and not open for discussion.'

'Sylvana said you might like to see one of the dresses?'

He put down his phone on the couch next to him, removed his tie. Her gaze fixed on the slice of brown skin at his throat, the hint of hair on his chest.

'Of course.'

She hesitated a moment before stepping out of the bedroom, brushing her hands down the skirt of fabric patterned with large royal-blue flowers. Did a little pirouette because she wasn't sure what else she was supposed to do, this was all so new for her. The full skirt swayed round her legs.

'Perfetto,' Matteo murmured, his voice deep. Rumbling right through her. Suddenly it was as if she'd run a mile. The way her heart thrummed. Her breath catching in her chest.

'Would you like to see another?'

His lips curled into a slow, appreciative smile. The type

of smile that could make a woman lose all sense. 'What do you think?'

Heat flared to her cheeks. 'Okay. Yes.'

She ran back to the bedroom, put on another dress. This one in autumn colours with a ruffle at the neckline and tiers in the skirt that went down to her ankles. Sylvana smiled, handed her a straw hat. 'Wear it with this.'

She placed the hat on her head, trying not to run back into the room to show Matteo. Instead, she took a deep breath, counted to five and then attempted to stroll. As she left the bedroom, she noticed that he wasn't on his phone again. It was as if he'd been waiting for her. His eyes, heavy lidded. His lips parted. She did another twirl. 'What do you think of this one?'

'Bellissima.'

Didn't that word mean beautiful? His voice was rough, a rasp. A shiver of pleasure at the sound shimmied up her spine. She was intoxicated by his approval, giddy with it. This was wrong. He wanted to take away her home. Yet why did it seem so right? No, it meant nothing. It was simply the moment, that was all. She'd had an awful morning, he'd been kind. And what woman wouldn't want to be told she was beautiful by a man who looked like a bronzed god? Yet…his gaze raked over her, golden brown eyes molten. Then he leaned forwards, hands clasped in front of him. As though he wanted to get closer to her somehow, except was holding himself back.

Awareness shimmered over her, the sparkle of goose-bumps. Time slowed syrupy and sweet. And whilst she'd listened to his words, with the heat in his gaze she began to believe them. She might have felt like a princess before, but the way he looked at her right now?

It made Louisa feel like a goddess.

* * *

Matteo sat back on the plush sofa as Louisa almost skipped back into the bedroom. Her dress of golden tones had matched her hair. With the straw hat on her head and freckles dusting her nose and upper chest, she looked like the embodiment of summer. He couldn't wait for the next change because this was a plan working. What he'd hoped for. Louisa was having fun.

She almost bounded out of the bedroom this time, in a dress of pinks and oranges. The hem ruffled. Shorter at the front, longer at the back. The neckline a little deeper than the others, nestling in her cleavage. Myriad tiny buttons down the front that any red-blooded man would crave to undo, slowly. To unwrap the prize of her gentle curves, to see if those freckles he'd observed earlier covered her whole body.

She stopped in front of him, not moving. Waiting. Feet bare. Matteo wasn't sure why the ability to see her toes struck him as so intensely intimate. Ridiculous. He lifted his hand, twisted his finger in a circle, and she twirled for him. Arms out, hair spilling wild round her as the hem of her dress swished about her calves. A smile broke free on her face, then she laughed. It burst through him bright and joyous as the first rays of sunrise over the horizon. There were no words to adequately describe how she looked in this moment, so he didn't try.

'I think you might enjoy shopping after all.'

It was as if a little light died. Cloud passing over the sun. Louisa worried her bottom lip in her teeth again, as if her insecurities had returned. 'I—I didn't enjoy the city or the stores, but this was fun. Yes.'

Something about the scene gave him pause. Milan had been an error. He'd brought her to a busy metropolis when she'd spent her formative years in the country. This hotel, a marvel of modernity in a bustling city, didn't fit Louisa. There were so many other areas of Italy he could see her enjoying more. Matteo didn't want her overwhelmed, he wanted her...overcome. With the beauty and wonder of new places, so she'd see that life at Easton Hall had been a trap, holding her back.

She'd asked him earlier whether he had a home base. That wasn't a concept he understood. He hadn't even felt as if he'd had a home as a child, being shunted to boarding school, not wanted by his adoptive parents. Everywhere only temporary. However, there *was* one place that was closer to Louisa's description than the rest. The first house he'd ever purchased, when he'd discovered his heritage was Italian. A place he'd taken no one before.

A place where he hoped Louisa would finally grow her wings and fly.

CHAPTER FIVE

LOUISA WATCHED AS the landscape slid by through the car's tinted window. Matteo had told her he had some surprises for her, then organised for their belongings to be packed, bundled her into another luxury vehicle and they'd exited his hotel, leaving the bustle of Milan behind them. Whilst she'd admired that he'd been a man of action in the days earlier, she was a little tired of being...bundled. Some hints might have been nice, minus the arrogance of Matteo's certainty that she'd like what he had in mind.

Though she did rather enjoy this. They'd left the city and headed north, so she'd been told. Now, their car travelled along a narrow road bordered on one side by houses, stone walls and greenery, and on the other, a vivid blue lake before a backdrop of mountains. It was vast. Take-your-breath-away beautiful. The sunshine sparkling on the water, little boats dotting the surface.

Lake Como, he'd told her as the water had first come into view. At least he'd finally told her *something*.

Though talk about take your breath away... She dragged her gaze from the view to glance at Matteo, sitting next to her. Looking effortlessly casual in navy-coloured chinos and a white polo shirt that only accentuated the warm brown of his skin. A large golden watch gleaming at his wrist. He was talking on his phone again. Giving instructions in Italian. She wondered where he'd learned the language so fluently, and why. Another question that she wondered whether he'd give her an answer to. Even though he never seemed to stop working, he looked well rested, as though he had no worries in the world.

As if it were his to rule. When she still wasn't sure some days why life was so chaotic and hard.

Oddly her life seemed a little less chaotic and hard now that Matteo was in it. Which was difficult to understand when he wanted to evict her from her home. She could refuse him. Say she was going to stay. Though she wasn't sure how that would work, since the place was currently unliveable...

'Where are we going to this time?' she asked as the unfamiliar countryside flew past.

'My villa.'

A tiny thrill ran through her. What would one of his houses be like? A modern masterpiece or something else? She'd noticed a subtle change in him as they'd travelled. He seemed more relaxed now, something about him less hard, more...fluid. Such a presence about him, he filled the cabin of the car with it. In this enclosed space the scent of him was like walking through some heady spice market. It scrambled her senses.

Then Matteo smiled and *that* smile reached his eyes, the corners crinkling as if he was truly happy. In that moment, she could barely breathe.

'You'll enjoy it,' he said. 'I promise.'

Promises were fraught things. They led to so much expectation yet often failed on delivery. Bitter experience with her mother had taught her not to believe in them.

'Isn't there a quote, promises were made to be broken?'

'I don't break mine.' It was said as a fact she should

simply accept. 'And I told you I have a few surprises for you when we get there.'

He didn't say anything more, yet the faint, self-satisfied smile on his face as they reached an ornate iron gate, which opened before them like magic, told her that he was pretty pleased with himself.

The car's tyres crunched on a gravel drive that followed the lake. Soon, they pulled up outside a magnificent two-storey villa, painted a warm ochre with blue-shuttered windows. The gardens surrounding were clipped and re-strained, unlike the wild tangle of Easton Hall. Yet whilst it was all so unfamiliar, something about the surrounds eased a tension inside her. It was as if her whole body could let out a sigh. The privacy of it all. Expansive lake on one side, tree-covered hills to the other.

He opened the door of the car, got out. She followed.

'Home sweet home,' she said.

'As I've said before, I don't have a home. Not as you de-fine it. This is a convenient base when I have to take care of business in Italy.'

'Then why have it at all?'

'It was good value.' He shrugged his broad, strong shoulders. 'I contemplated turning it into one of my hotels.'

He led her towards the front door of the villa. She took a moment to stop, look out over the gardens terraced down to the lake beyond. Sucked in a deep breath. The air here was warmer than home. Scented with jasmine and citrus blos-som. To the right of the door sat a plaque: Villa Arcadia.

Arcadia was the name of his hotel chains.

'Which came first?' she asked, nodding to the sign. 'The house or the hotels?'

Something triggered in the back of her brain. Arcadia

meant something. Louisa couldn't remember what. She'd have to look it up.

'The house. It's the first I ever purchased.'

He unlocked the door and led her inside to an entrance hall with a marble floor topped with a Persian carpet runner. Furniture, the warm honey of polished antiques.

'Why nowhere in the UK?' she asked. She would have thought his first property purchase would have been there.

'I have an affinity here. My heritage is Italian.'

That admission surprised her. 'How do you know?'

Back when she was young, her mother used to speak of the benevolence of Matteo's adoptive parents. How they'd taken in a foundling as their own, as if it was some great charity. Yet in her family's eyes, it hadn't made him a true Bainbridge.

'Family history DNA.' He shut the front door behind him and all of him seemed to shut down too, close off with the clear warning that this wasn't something he wanted to talk about, so she didn't press.

'I thought you'd want to see your surprises,' he said. 'Come with me.'

Matteo gave her an encouraging smile to accompany the deft change of subject, focussing on her once more. Another smile that didn't reach his eyes. He showed her through the house, in many ways like his hotels with its neutral colours. Bright with sunlight in every room. Yet this place was burnished with age. The eclectic combination of antiques with modern touches giving the villa an elegantly casual nudge into the present, which strangely felt like him.

'I-it's beautiful.'

Most rooms she saw opened onto a view of gardens or the lake, with expanses of glass. There was simply no place for any darkness here.

'Thank you. I hope you'll enjoy it.'

He led her up an internal staircase to the second floor, down another corridor, to a closed door.

'This is your room,' he said with almost a flourish as he pushed the door open and she walked inside.

Louisa took a few moments, scanning the space. The room had another glorious view of the lake but that wasn't what held her attention. The space disoriented her because, whilst there was a different view outside, the inside seemed achingly familiar. Her heart stuttered.

It was almost as if her room at Easton Hall had been lifted complete and placed here. Her bed. The rocking chair in the corner that used to be her father's. The rug on the floor. The paintings on the walls. *Everything*, down to the sketch pad and pens on the bedside table. Matteo stood at the door, head cocked to the side. Watching her. Not as if she were someone strange. But with a look on his face that was softer than she'd seen before.

Her heart filled with something warm and bright as the sunshine outside. A sensation gifting her that most cherished of feelings, *hope*, that in the mess of all of this, something could go right for once.

She didn't know what to do, what to say. It overwhelmed her. Instead, she ran to Matteo and simply hurled herself into him. He caught her with an 'oof' and then his strong arms wrapped round her. Keeping her together. Keeping her safe. Like the night he'd carried her out of Easton Hall when she'd been too paralysed to move.

Tears prickled her eyes.

'Thank you. It's everything I could have wanted,' she said, her voice cracking. Burying her face into his muscular chest. His heart thumping a steady, comforting beat. Other things came to her awareness. How solid he was.

The heat and muscle of him. His stance didn't change, but something about him relaxed into her. The way they began meld together. His hands loosely stroking up and down her spine. She breathed him in, the scent of freshly laundered clothes and the spicy scent she'd begun to associate with him in the car…

She craved to simply absorb him into her. Have him fill every empty space. Her nipples tightened in her bra. Heat built between her legs. Naked want became like a living thing. Grabbing her by the throat, leaving her breathless. He shifted his legs, spread them a little wider, his hand on her back drifting a little lower before stopping. He loosened his arms, and she looked up at him, tears pooling in her eyes. Not caring that he could see the emotion.

'You can't know what this means to me.'

'I wanted to make you feel at home.'

His eyelids were hooded, golden brown eyes almost drowned out by his fathomless pupils. His lashes, impossibly long. Stubble darkening his angular jaw. Matteo's lips parted as if trying to get more air, then his gaze flicked. To her eyes, lips, throat. His Adam's apple bobbed in a swallow.

She wished she could be the sort of woman who'd know what to do here, rather than a person who sketched her fantasies instead of acting them out for real. If she were the type of person who took chances, she might get up on her toes and press her lips to his. But chances meant risk and risk had ceased to have any part in her life, long ago.

She tried to give him a happy smile, which halted with the merest of frowns creasing his brow as she stepped back from his embrace. Trying to pretend that nothing had happened, when it was as if the world had tilted on its axis.

'How did you manage it? I thought we couldn't go into the house.'

'You'd be surprised what I'm able to do,' he said.

She wasn't, not now. Louisa thought he could achieve just about anything he put his mind to. Somewhere in the far reaches of her consciousness that realisation sounded a prickle of warning, but she was too overcome to pay it any attention.

'I heard you talking to the stylist about your clothes. I'm having them professionally cleaned. The soft furnishings were smoke damaged, but I requested as close a facsimile as I could get for your room here.'

'I-it's very kind of you.' What more could she say? She was completely overcome by the thought and his generosity.

He shrugged. 'It's okay.'

The unmoved expression on his face told her he thought it was nothing.

'You don't understand.' She shook her head. How to make him see that this meant something more? 'It shows that you thought of me. For so many years, people only thought of themselves. This is rare, because in my life not many people have been kind.'

Kind? He wasn't kind. Other words were routinely used to describe him. Business magazines called him driven. His opposition called him ruthless. Women he dated might have called him focussed during the early stages, then remote just before their fling inevitably ended. He was a man who got what he wanted, and one word *never* used to describe him was kind.

He'd brought her things to Italy for his own ends because he wanted her comfortable. *Comfortable* was the place where he would encourage her to relinquish her right to reside. She'd see a world not to fear, but to explore. Why would she ever want to go back to Easton Hall after that?

Matteo turned and walked to the window, placing his hands on the ledge, pretending to look at the magnificent view he never really had the time to stop and take in anymore. Willing himself not to turn round, take Louisa into his arms again. Kiss her. He almost laughed. A *kind* man wouldn't be thinking those thoughts.

It had been another moment with Louisa in his arms. The softness of her body. The curves. The warmth. With another woman, he might explore the situation. But he was no fool. There was no way she could be anything other than entirely innocent. Whilst he was all for something more casual, for a woman like her with sex would come love. They walked hand in hand, which was why in the past he'd only dated woman with the same sense of world-weariness as himself. Women who knew what they wanted, took it when offered, and walked away. This was a woman who'd want romance and gentle words, seduction and softness. Eliciting her sighs of pleasure. They'd be the sweetest of music...

Why was he even thinking of that? None of these things were for him. He didn't do romance. He certainly didn't do love. He didn't know what it was. His childhood had proven to him that it didn't exist.

Those thoughts were enough to crush any desire right out of him. He realised long ago that his sole purpose in life was to succeed *despite* his family, to exact his revenge of taking their most prized possession. His success was the only thing that made people want him. Buzzing about like bees to the wealthy honeypot. It was how it had always been, people wanting him, not for who he was, the orphaned boy, but what he could provide them. For his parents, being an heir until his sister was born and he was cast aside. As for others, it was all about his power, his position. At least people were transparent that way. No longer would anyone fool him into believing they wanted Matteo Bainbridge the *man*. It was easier to know they wanted him for material things. Life was predictable then. There were no cruel surprises.

Matteo took a deep breath. He couldn't stare out of the window indefinitely. There was more he needed to show her. He turned round and Louisa was looking about the room. For the first time since leaving Easton Hall she seemed calmer. All of her, smoothed out. A slight smile on her face as her gaze fell on all of her familiar things. He wanted her to look at him again as if he was a man who could solve all her problems. There was something gratifying about it, something that stroked an ego he didn't even realise was important to him. If it could get him what he wanted in the end? All the better.

'There's more to show you,' he said.

'More? Haven't you done enough with this?'

She swept her arms wide around the room. This was nothing. Paying an engineer to urgently assess the living spaces of Easton Hall to safely allow people to collect her things. Hiring a team of interior decorators to find what matched the items that were smoke-and-water-damaged, fit everything in. Sure, he might have told them what room he thought suited best in the villa. The one with the finest view because Lake Como was beautiful at this time of the year.

But it happened because of his money, for no other reason.

Sadly, she didn't seem to want the money to leave Easton Hall. That would change. It always did. He just had to find the right price.

'I want to make sure you have what you need here,' he said. 'It's downstairs this time.'

She laughed and it was a joyous sound, like birdsong in the early morning. 'Why didn't you show me that first?'

'I thought you'd want to know where you were sleeping. That seems important to you.'

The smile on her face dimmed a little, all of her becoming more contemplative. 'So few people understand.'

He didn't. Not at all. Still, he could pretend.

But the thought of that pretence made something in his chest tighten. He rubbed at it, a strange kind of ache. Because in this moment he *wanted* to understand what made someone desire a place, a sense of belonging. Wanted to understand the woman.

Something about Louisa fascinated him. With so much hidden he was almost compelled to unravel all her secrets. What made a young woman stay in a home caring for her older relative? Eschew everything that appeared to signify modern style? Over the past years, working most days and rarely taking a break, he seemed to have lost his curiosity. Every interaction was one of problem and solution. Week after week, always on the move, putting out spot fires. With Louisa, he had the overwhelming desire to simply stop and learn more.

In the past, that curiosity had been dangerous.

'Do you want to know why you don't look like your parents?'

His whole life Matteo had been surrounded by people with blonde hair, pale skin and glacial blue eyes. He'd never really thought about why his skin tanned in the sun or his eyes were brown until his older cousin had pointed it out.

Then, he'd wanted to know.

'You're a fake.'

Curiosity killed the cat...

He'd approached his parents and that day they'd told him

the truth. That he was adopted, but it didn't make any difference. Until Felicity came along and fell ill. Then their
lies were exposed.

Yet his adoption was old news. Not something he needed
to think about any more. Being curious about Louisa would
never be a bad thing. If he learned more, he could work
out how to get her to leave Easton Hall.

All he needed was the right trigger point.

He almost looked forward to seeing how the game would
play out between them. Whether he could coax anything
more than the occasional whisper of pink on her cheeks
from her. She seemed so…restrained. Then a vision flashed
into his head of his fingers running through her glorious
red hair, gripping it, drawing her head back to expose her
perfect pale neck…

No. He needed to remind his errant body that seduction
wasn't the game here. He was simply reacting to a beautiful woman unlike anyone he'd ever met before. It was
the novelty of her.

Novelties always wore off.

'Come with me,' he said, motioning out of the door of
her room.

They went back down the stairs, Louisa walking beside
him in one of the dresses she'd modelled for him a couple
of days earlier. It gave him a strange sense of satisfaction
to see her wearing what he'd provided for her. To know
that she liked it.

'I can see why you have an affinity for this place,' she
said. 'I think it would be easy to love.'

There was that word again. Love. He didn't understand it.

'The UK's never seemed like home to me.'

'Why?'

What admission could he make that didn't damn him?

The adopted child, unwanted by his birth mother. Unwanted by his adoptive family. What did that make him? Better to talk about what he could answer.

'When I found out I had Italian heritage, I visited here.'

To see if he could find any hint of the family he'd been sure was out there, somewhere, even though the DNA testing had turned up no relatives. It was as if his birth mother, father, had dissolved into the past as though they'd never existed. He was the only evidence that they'd lived at all. In the end he had himself, and that was what mattered.

Except he now had responsibility for Louisa too...

She looked over at him. 'And you felt something.'

'Yes.'

'If it were me, I'd say it felt like I'd come home.'

Was that right? It couldn't be. He hadn't wanted or needed a home in years, and it was freeing.

'No. Here was a place to start.'

Italy was the country of firsts. This property, his first boutique hotel. Milestones of his success. That was all.

'Have you ever looked for your birth family?'

'A little.'

A lie. He'd paid a small fortune to a well-regarded investigator, without success. Matteo needed to shut the conversation down. He didn't do this, the sharing. It was meaningless, reminding him of all that was wrong in his life rather than focussing on the important things, like moving forwards. Like the anticipation of showing Louisa the next room he had for her. Perhaps receiving another hug. Though how much better would a kiss be? Would... *more* be...?

'Did you find them?'

Louisa had stopped so he did too. He looked at her, face soft, full of what he feared was *empathy* when she shouldn't really care. No one else ever had. His throat tightened. Matteo shook his head.

'My birth parents? I've accepted I never will.'

She reached out, not with an exuberant full body hug, but with her hand. Touched his forearm, squeezed. Her grip surprisingly strong. He'd always thought of her as so small and fragile, yet he was beginning to think he might have underestimated her.

'I'm sorry, that must be difficult if you've wanted to meet them. Especially if you and your family...'

Her hand was hot on his forearm, burning like a brand. He pulled his arm away. Louisa rubbed her palm with her thumb. Her mouth slightly open. Those moss-green eyes of hers looking at him, as if deep into his soul. He didn't like that look, or what she might find there if she searched hard enough.

'I accept my life. It doesn't bother me. Anyhow, this isn't about me, it's about you.'

He smiled, but there was no pleasure in it. The type of smile he'd cultivated to use in business, one that did the job with no emotion underpinning it.

'O-okay.'

Louisa seemed hesitant as he led her to another room he'd chosen, one that had been an informal lounge. Large French doors leading out onto a paved terrace, decorated with pots of citrus trees, lavender and flowers. One of the best views of the lake from the bottom floor.

As Louisa walked in her gaze turned straight to the corner. Instead of flinging herself into his arms, she ran over to it. Her art desk, where she did her illustrations.

'Her work's really something.'

That was what one of his contractors had said, after they'd called him to report successfully moving her things.

The jealousy that had spiked through him at those words, when *he'd* never seen her pictures, was like a knife to his belly. He wanted her to offer. To show him. Yet she didn't say anything other than to check through the sketchbooks, as if cataloguing whether anything was missing. Louisa opened a drawer, peered inside the desk. Rummaged through everything with gentle, almost reverent hands.

'It's all here.'

'I should hope so. When I ask people to do a job, they do it.'

There was no excitement this time. Not like upstairs. He didn't know why that disappointed him, or what he'd really expected. She walked over to the doors leading to the patio. Tested one almost as if she wanted to escape, but it was locked. The light shone in from outside, and she was backlit, the skirt of her dress becoming sheer, her legs silhouetted like a soft pastel smudge through the fabric.

She said nothing, just looked out at the lake.

'I hope you're happy. I know how important the deadline is to you.'

Louisa reached up her hand to her face as if brushing something away. Then she turned. Her smile was a tremulous, fragile thing. Her eyes a little red, gleaming with tears. It was like a gut punch, striking all the air from him. He started forwards.

'Louisa.'

Like a few days before, he wasn't sure why the reaction to her tears was such a visceral thing. As he moved closer, he wanted to take her into his arms, wrap her tight and soothe those tears away. He could. It wouldn't take much. A few steps.

Instead, he stayed right where he was.

'Thank you, I...' She took a deep breath, her shoulders

rising and falling. 'Your thoughtfulness... In my life... nothing's ever really felt like it was about me.'

'That's not fair.'

'Life's not fair.'

The words carried so much weight. A heaviness falling across everything. Of course, both her parents had died, leaving her in the care of Mae, who, in the end, she'd had to care for too. 'No, it isn't.'

She nodded, then turned back to the scene in front of her. This was one of his favourite rooms in the house. He hoped she liked it too.

'It's perfect. I couldn't have asked for more in the circumstances.'

That was his reminder. He had a job to do, to convince her to leave Easton Hall. To fight off the family too, who were still making noises about challenging the will...

'The world's a beautiful place.' He had hotels and retreats in some of the most sought-after places on the planet. 'Venice, with its spectacular arched bridges and canals. Jaipur, the Pink City. Or the Whitsundays, with some of the most exquisite beaches in the world. I've been almost everywhere.'

'I've never been to the beach.'

She said it quietly, almost as if it was some terrible admission. He couldn't fathom it, not ever having seen the ocean. Not having travelled. Why hadn't Mae pushed her harder? He gritted his teeth. Instead, Louisa was hidden away when there was a whole world to explore. If she was afraid to go on her own, he could show it all to her. The bright lights of New York, in the city that never slept. The pyramids of Egypt, with all their history. The beauty of Paris, the romance...

Why was he thinking of romance? Never once had

thoughts of it entered his head before, not even when he'd bought his first hotel there. It was simply another place to stay in his nomadic life.

'I have a beach here. On the lake. There are a few public ones but mine's private. It might not be the ocean, but I can show you if you like? We could go there now.'

He wanted that look on her face again, of joy. Her laughter.

She smiled. It was a fragile, tremulous kind of thing. 'I'd like that. Maybe a bit later? I want to set up my workspace first. Make a start. I—I've never missed a deadline before, and I'd like to get back on track.'

His gut clenched, almost like disappointment. Though why he should have any sense of that was beyond him. He had work to do. Another brief report from the structural engineer to read about Easton Hall. Insurance claims to consider. After that, he'd take her to the lake. They could treat this like a holiday for her, a grand adventure. Then she'd see that returning to live in a mouldering old stately home in the country was a complete waste. That there was a world to see and he'd pay her very well to allow her the means of doing so. If she travelled, she could stay at any one of his retreats or hotels, then he'd know she was safe and looked after. He'd be fulfilling his promise to Mae.

It all made complete sense. Though he wasn't sure why the bile rose bitter in his throat, thinking of it all.

'How long do you need?'

'A couple of hours?'

She walked back to her desk. To the brushes and the sketchbooks. Her paints. There, he witnessed a look. It was difficult to define. Something like true happiness.

Had he ever found anything like it in his work? It was

more a means to an end. Something he was good at. Was it his passion?

Matteo wasn't sure. What he did drove him every day. He'd done better than he'd ever believed possible when he'd first started out. Was known around the world as providing the finest luxury retreats and hotels where privacy and comfort reigned. A home away from home only…better.

And what made him the best of the best were his drive and perfectionism. He rarely had a day away from it. Allowed himself no distractions. Yet Louisa seemed to be occupying more and more of his thinking time. Easton Hall he could understand, given that was part of his plan, yet that place and Louisa were inextricably bound. He needed to keep his eyes on the prize, finally wrestling the home away from the clutches of his family and into his business. The ultimate win.

He watched Louisa getting to work. Today, her hair was bound in a long plait down her back. How he longed to see it loose again, spilling long and red in its perfect copper waves.

Later.

'I'll be back in two hours, then,' he said, before walking to the door. Already, Louisa had begun immersing herself in her work. She'd slipped on reading glasses. The first time he'd seen her in them since the day he'd arrived at Easton Hall. They made her look…cute. Almost studious. Another side to her that he craved to explore.

He shook his head. No. She was a distraction he needed to ignore.

Yet why did leaving the room seem like one of the hardest things he'd ever done?

CHAPTER SIX

ON HER BEST days Louisa would fall into the rhythm of her illustrations. The scratch of the ink pen on the page. The flow of the watercolour washes, the coloured pencils. Today, though, something was different. It was as if the sunlight in Italy changed her drawings. The brightness of it all. Everything vibrant and glowing. Her colours more saturated. She pushed her glasses up her nose. On her page sat another frog prince roughly sketched out in ink. Never without his jaunty smirk, because that was his signature. Hopping about with his crown askew on his head. She smiled. Her characters often took on a life of their own. She added a few sprigs of lavender to the foreground. A lake in the midground. Castle and mountains in the distance.

Could she incorporate the evolution of her drawings into the story? Start the colours softer and, as the story went on, let them increase in vibrancy?

It was unlike her normal style, but it was an idea.

Something about the freshness of it all excited her. Whilst she loved her work it had been a while since the creativity had given her the kind of squirming thrill in her belly when things just *worked*. She added a few butterflies to her sketch. Bright little bursts of colour. Like the butterflies flitting about in her stomach right now, bouncing about like popping candy. Though that might have less to do with her drawing and more with something else.

Matteo was going to show her a *beach*.

She'd seen them in photographs, of course, as a teenager when scouring the vast library of Easton Hall. So many glorious books, most age appropriate and some, well, not so much. Great-Uncle Gerald had had a diverse collection and she'd found quite a stash of erotica when she'd gone searching. She looked over at the beige covered sketchbook in her pile containing the drawings she did, just for herself. Her nightmares so they lost their hold. Her fantasies. The pictures no one would ever see…

A sharp knock sounded at the door, and she jumped. Those butterflies in her belly flapping about as if caught in a strong gust of wind.

'Come in.'

Matteo sauntered inside and her breath hitched. He'd changed into something more casual. Shorts, showing his legs. The strong calves sprinkled with dark hair. Another polo shirt that gripped him in all the right places. The whole of her flushed hot. She was sure that she'd gone a bright shade of pink, and that realisation made her skin burn even hotter.

She'd never really noticed men before. There were men who worked on the estate, but most of them had been with Mae for years and were much older. There was a young man in the grocer's in the village who had a nice smile when she walked through the door. But he didn't make her blush. He didn't make her breathless. He wasn't this elemental force like Matteo. A whirlwind she wanted to be swept away by.

Where had that thought come from?

'Are you ready, or do you still need more time?'

As Matteo walked towards her she closed her sketch pad. Something about him seeing what she did made her feel vulnerable. She drew pictures for children's books whereas he ran a global company worth…she didn't know how much, but a man who had a private jet and houses all over the world must be doing very well for himself.

'No, I'm ready.'

From the clothes Matteo had organised for her there was nothing she'd selected that looked at all beachy so her dress would have to do. She took off her glasses and left them on the drawing board before they headed out of the house, down a paved pathway towards the lake. Passing pots overflowing with a riot of flowers. Petunias. Geraniums. Bougainvillea. The place so unlike her cool green home. Everything here somehow…supercharged.

Hyper-real.

'Do you stay at this house often?'

She had so many questions. Even though you could search for him online, it really didn't tell her much about the man. All she knew was from that brief summer as children and her conversations with Mae. How well he'd done. How he and his family didn't get along. But she was sure there was so much more to him. She just didn't know why she wanted to know it all.

Matteo shrugged. 'Not really. Not anymore.'

He'd walked ahead a little, his long powerful stride making her scurry to catch up, though she couldn't really complain. This way she could get a glimpse of his broad shoulders, how well his shorts fitted, moulding to his body. Was it objectifying? She wasn't sure. Did he do the same to her? Even the thought he might made her cheeks heat.

'What made you stop?'

He slowed his steps so she could catch up. 'Circumstance. Business. I don't stay anywhere for long.'

Not having any real place to call home, no matter how beautiful the surroundings, seemed surreal to her. 'I can't imagine travelling around all the time.'

'I can't imagine not. You can make the world as large or as small as you want. I prefer mine large.'

'Is that like saying, "You need to get out more, Louisa"?'

He chuckled and she loved the sound of it. Warm, rolling with a twist of wickedness. The way it made her tingle, want to curl up her toes in her shoes. He turned to her, smiled. That smile was like a mouthful of hot chocolate on a winter's day. Rich, decadent. Addictive.

'I am.'

People had tried before, even Mae. So many not understanding why she was happy to live in Easton Hall. No one could comprehend her past, how a stable home was everything she'd ever wanted. How much she owed to Mae. The woman had given up years of her life to look after a broken teenager. It was the least Louisa could do, to give up some years of her life looking after Mae in return.

What drove Matteo to remain constantly on the move? There had to be something behind it. Wasn't it normal to seek a home, to have a retreat, a singular place to stay? Though she supposed he made retreats all over the world. That was his business, what he did. Homes away from home for the rich and famous, when he didn't personally have one he called his own.

They rounded a corner following a manicured path through a small copse of trees, which then opened onto an expanse of grass with the magnificent lake beyond.

'Almost there,' Matteo said as he began to walk a little faster, almost as if he was excited. She picked up her pace to keep up with him. After a short distance the path led to a tiled terrace with a balustrade overlooking the lake. Stairs, down to the water.

'I'm sorry I couldn't give you sand. Pebbles will have to do.'

She followed him down the stairs and onto the pebbles of the private beach, uneven under her ballet flats. In a few spots along the bank there were artfully planted trees. Under one ancient tree sat an outdoor table, chairs.

The magnificent blue of Lake Como lay out in front of her. Mountains framing the scene. The late afternoon sun, warm on her body. A cool breeze caressing her skin. The magic of the scene seemed to unknot her. Her shoulders slowly dropping. Tension in her neck loosening. Matteo kicked off his shoes, walked to the water's edge and waded in to his calves, overlooking the view as if he ruled the whole lake. She followed to the water's edge and a shiver ran through her. How it seemed so dark and impenetrable.

'You coming in?' he asked.

She'd love to be like him, take off her shoes, throw away caution, but a little voice began whispering in her head.

'My mother would never have approved.'

Why did that woman still enter her consciousness, always holding her back whenever she wanted something for herself?

'Why not?' Matteo asked.

'Well, for one, germs. She'd say you never knew what lurked in unchlorinated water.'

He snorted. 'Every day is about risk. Your mother's not here now.'

No, she wasn't. Louisa walked to the water's edge. Took off her shoes, the creamy pebbles cool under her feet. Water lapping the edges just ahead. It all seemed so overwhelming, how fathomless all of this was. It was as if the world shifted under her feet and she was trying to find steady ground.

Then she looked over at Matteo. His patient smile. Somehow, everything seemed to solidify.

'Come on in,' he said. Could he see her struggle? Years of conditioning that was sometimes difficult to shake. Her dress brushed at her calves. It might get wet, though she supposed she could hold it up. There were so many decisions...

Matteo walked back towards her, the water sluicing around his legs till he was only ankle deep. 'I'm warning you, it's probably a bit cold given the lake's fed by the mountains. But you'll like it—'

'I don't know how to swim.'

The words simply blurted out of her. It seemed like such a huge failing. Another thing her mother had stopped her from doing.

'What if I'm not there when you're swimming, and you drown?'

Always so much fear. Louisa hadn't understood at the time, but now she believed it had less to do with love and more to do with control. Her mother had never stopped to think that the greatest risk to Louisa's health was not knowing how to save herself. Or maybe she hadn't really cared.

Matteo frowned. 'You don't know...'

His voice was incredulous, drifting off as if he couldn't even finish the sentence.

'How to swim.' Her voice, in contrast, sounded firm, because she wasn't broken. Not many people knew how much she'd endured, what it had taken to survive. She just needed to convince herself of that strength, some days.

Sunlight glittered on the water's surface. It looked so inviting, if she could forget the fears that plagued her when faced with something new.

'The water's shallow here. There's no drop off. Take my hand.'

She hesitated. Matteo held out his arm, palm up. That gentle, encouraging smile still warming his face.

'I won't let you fall.'

She looked down at her feet, toes so close to the water. Took a deep breath. Hitched her dress into her underwear as something about Matteo's gaze darkened, melted. Then she reached out, his warm fingers clasped about her own as he gently guided her to him. At the first touch of the icy water on her feet she sucked in a breath, her heart skipping in her chest as he drew her close.

Not into his arms as she had been earlier in the day when they'd first arrived. In that moment when his body had felt so hard and solid. Initially she was just trying to be thankful till it morphed into something else. Something she refused to give voice to but would keep her up late in the dark of her own bedroom. Fuel for the drawings only she would ever see in that secret sketchbook. Her fantasies, where they'd always remain. How could there be a reality with him? She could never forget he was the enemy.

Yet why did she feel as if he was turning into something else?

Matteo squeezed her fingers. 'Not so bad?'

She shook her head. There was no bad in this moment. It was all good. Really good. Something bubbled up inside her, an unusual sensation. Joy. A sense of freedom. Like when she'd been a child and sent to Mae's. Even though her father was ill she'd used to play in the stream on the grounds of Easton Hall. Especially the summer Matteo came to stay too. She'd had no fears then, not really. At the time she hadn't understood her father was going to die. She was a child who wanted to forget that her dad was sick, and her mum wasn't emotionally available.

Matteo had seemed so brave then, that little bit older, a bit wilder. And after a while they'd played in the stream together. Explored secret corridors behind the walls of the house. Eaten a glut of berries from the kitchen garden till their hands and lips were stained and their bellies ached.

She could be like that child again. Full of wonder, wanting to explore. Louisa realised somewhere during her journey over the past twelve years she'd lost it, become stuck. She let go of his hand, slipped hers away from his warmth. That summer had created some of her best memories, ever. Together she and Matteo had always been up to something. Getting into all sorts of mischief...

Louisa gasped at a memory long buried.

'You made me kiss a frog.'

Was it her imagination, or had flags of red just flashed across Matteo's bronzed cheeks?

He placed his hand on his heart. 'Never.'

'No. You *did*. You found one and told me if I kissed it, it'd turn into a prince, marry me and I'd be able to have a tiara and a pony.'

'You're a children's book illustrator. Do you think you might be getting caught up in your own stories?'

There was a niggle of doubt now, that maybe she had it wrong. That unpleasant splinter that told her she wasn't enough. Not to keep her dad alive, not for her mum... Yet she looked over at Matteo and the corner of his mouth quirked in a sly grin. Like that recalcitrant frog prince she'd been trying and failing to draw just the way she wanted him.

She pointed at him, waggling her finger. 'You. You're fibbing.'

He chuckled again, and the sound of it, that unrestrained mirth, made her toes curl into the pebbles beneath her feet in the cold waters of the lake.

'It wasn't one of my finest moments. But to be fair, I didn't think you'd fall for it.'

She planted her hands on her hips. 'You knew I'd do it.'

'How could I? It was clearly made up.'

'I was six.' She kicked her foot at him, and some water splashed over his calves. 'I hero-worshipped you.'

She looked down at his shorts, not wet exactly, but the fabric darkened where some fat droplets of water had hit the fabric.

'Hero-worshipped me?' Something about the tone of his voice deepened. Became rougher, a bit like the gravel on the drive into his villa.

'You know it, and you loved it. You pretended not to, but you liked the fact I listened to everything you said *and* believed it.'

She kicked her foot again, and another splash of water hit his legs.

His gaze narrowed, became more intense, but that wicked quirk of his lips remained. 'You're playing a dangerous game.'

Louisa cocked her head, 'And what game is that?'

'If you don't stop now, it's one where you're about to get very wet.'

'You wouldn't dare.'

He reached his hand into the water and flicked some at her. She kicked back at him, and this time water hit his shirt.

'Right.'

He began surging towards her so she grabbed her skirts higher and giggled, running up onto the stones of the beach as he followed. She tried to run faster but her dress was too long, and she wasn't really trying very hard anyhow. Her heart pounded as pebbles crunched behind her and she took off. Heart thump, thump thumping in her chest. Trying to make it to the stairs, laughing now because there was something about this that was such a thrill. Everything forgotten but the chase.

She suspected Matteo wasn't trying very hard either. It was more about the anticipation than the capture...

Till an arm snaked round her waist and she was pulled against a solid, muscular body.

She squealed and kicked her feet as he swung her into his arms and moved back to the water's edge, waded in, the sound of it rushing with each strong stride.

'Don't you dare!' she squealed.

'I told you.'

She squirmed some more but if he let her go now, she'd be in the water.

'I don't believe you will,' she huffed, looking up at him. His eyelashes so long. Gaze heated. Eyes sparkling with mischief and something far darker.

'Play with fire, get burned.'

'We're in water, that saying doesn't work.'

'You know what I mean. I told you I'd get you wet. I keep my promises.'

Something about this moment was loaded. His strong hold, her squirming against him. How she was so hot it was as if she'd go up in flames. How the thought of being dropped into ice-cold water right about now seemed almost welcoming.

He cocked his eyebrow. 'What'll it be? Are you going to behave?'

She'd always behaved, always done everything she'd been asked. If she did, she'd been told, she'd get better. All lies. Right now, she wanted to change her script. To do something unexpected for the first time in her life.

'Why do I want to misbehave, to be bad so...badly?'

It was freeing, this sensation. She threw her head back and laughed.

'We can be a little bad,' he murmured as he lowered his head, his lips skimming her throat. Her laughter stopped on a gasp, the sensation of it like an electric shock. His lips gentle, drifting over her skin. There was no laughter now, the only sound from her was half sigh, half moan. Her nipples prickling in her bra. Heat arrowing between her thighs. The need for him all-encompassing.

She wanted. As she'd never wanted anything or anyone before. It overwhelmed her, her whole body a mess of sensation.

Did he want her as much as she craved him?

His lips traced back towards her face, her jaw. Light brushes till she turned her head and their lips touched. Breaths intermingled. Slow, luxurious. Hypnotic. She became a captive of the sensation. Opening for him. His tongue slipped into her mouth, the barest of touches with her own.

Then the kiss slowed, stopped.

Matteo pulled back, looked deep into her eyes. Pupils blown wide, his own irises almost black.

'Before I drop you in the deep end, I need to teach you how to swim first. Slow, gentle steps.'

Could he see it on her face, the *need*? If self-combustion were a thing, she'd have gone up in his arms. Burned them both away to ash till they mingled and drifted out across the lake. He could be talking about swimming, she supposed, but she was sure this was something more.

What had just happened between them? How could she have let it?

Matteo walked out of the water, released her, letting her go slowly, and she slid down the full length of his body. So hard and uncompromising. She was almost disappointed that he hadn't carried out his threat, or promise, or whatever that all just was. The thoughts and sensations tangled through her in a mess of desire.

'I'd like that.' Her voice was breathless, as though she'd run a mile. Though his was probably a false promise. People had made those to her all the time, especially her mother.

'Take this medicine, it'll make you feel better.'

'This doctor will cure you.'

Any medicine only made her sicker, and no doctor could cure her because there'd never been anything wrong in the first place.

Those thoughts were like being plunged unceremoniously into the deep, dark waters of the lake. All the heat, all the want, simply…gone.

Matteo nodded and whatever had just happened between them passed.

'I—I should get back to work,' she said, her limbs limp like overcooked pasta. She wasn't sure her legs would carry her back to the house.

'I'll see you at dinner, then. It'll be around eight. I'll come and find you.'

'Thank you. Until then.'

She grabbed her shoes. Began walking back to the stairs, almost stumbling as she went, she was so unsteady. He didn't follow, just remained standing on the pebbled beach.

'I'd like to see what you do,' he called out from behind her, almost like an afterthought. 'Your drawings.'

Now it was her turn to nod.

Though she tended not to allow anyone to see her work until it was finished. As though if someone witnessed what she was doing, the magic would suddenly be gone. 'Once I have something to show you.'

'I'll look forward to it.'

She wasn't sure why she found that so hard to believe.

CHAPTER SEVEN

HE'D MADE A serious error of judgement. It had been days since those moments at the lake where some kind of enchantment had overtaken him and he'd brushed his lips across Louisa's perfect, tempting throat as she laughed. Lost any sense in the moment. Took her perfect mouth with his own.

Why do I want...to be bad...so badly?

That same phrase could apply to him as well. From the moment his lips had touched her skin, he'd been a condemned man. Doomed to crave more of her. Her gasp, the breathy moan. The way she'd opened for him. Tongue tentatively touching his own. It was all he could think about. Whereas Louisa?

He wasn't sure. Fearing he'd frightened her. He knew passion and desire, and believed she'd been as affected as him. The colour high on her cheeks as she'd slid down his body. The way her breath had hitched. Nipples obvious points against the soft fabric of her dress. Except, now, it was as if she'd disappeared. Locking herself away with her artwork. Barely coming out for meals as if she'd been avoiding him. All he knew was that Louisa was keeping to herself. So absorbed, it was as if he didn't exist.

He needed to apologise for it, fix it somehow, even though he wasn't sorry at all. His body craved more of her. His mind? Matteo shook his head, trying to get the persistent vision of her head thrown back in his arms, her laughter, from it. How he'd imagined her head thrown back, not in laughter, but in ecstasy...

He couldn't. Shouldn't.

Why?

That one word had run through his head like a broken record. They were both adults. Clearly attracted to each other.

Why, why, why?

He could add more words to that single one his brain locked onto, like some kind of chant. *Sheltered, innocent.* He'd lost his own innocence years ago. Life teaching him how cold and cruel it could be. Yet that afternoon on the lake when he'd shown Louisa her first beach, he'd simply *taken*. Thinking more clearly, as he was now, for someone who'd lived her life locked away it must have come as a shock. He should apologise. Her avoiding him, becoming fearful of the world, was not part of his plan.

Eyes on the prize, Matteo.

Louisa had her whole life, now in front of her. A world she needed to see. A right to reside she needed to relinquish. He wasn't going to get that by seduction, as tempting as she was.

Matteo made his way to the space he now called her workroom. Knocked gently. Opened the door when there was no answer because she might be avoiding him, but they *needed* to talk. Perhaps she was walking about the grounds. She seemed to love the gardens here. He'd catch flashes of her gleaming copper hair in fiery contrast to the trees and shrubbery, but when he went to find her, she'd be gone. Disappearing like a ghost.

It was beyond frustrating. As was the way she'd been

so non-committal about him seeing her artwork. It wasn't as if she'd said no.

It was that she hadn't really said anything at all.

He walked to her drawing table, art supplies neatly put away. The sketchbooks that she drew in, stacked beside it. He looked at a few scraps of paper tacked to the table, almost like a mood board. Sketches of ink pen, a little frog in a crown. A frog with personality judging by the way that crown sat slightly askew. An almost...smirk on its wide froggy mouth. Her attention to detail, the frog's princely little outfit. A red fitted jacket that looked like velvet though how she'd achieved that with pen, ink and what appeared to be coloured pencil was beyond him. Little yellow-and-blue-striped bloomers. His spotted skin. It was extraordinary.

He smiled. Wanting to find out more about the story she illustrated. To his shame he'd not paid much attention, and this was such an integral part of who Louisa *was*. Committed to her work, clearly taking pride in it, worried about deadlines.

He glanced at the carefully stacked sketch pads.

'Her work's really something.'

The words of that contractor who'd packed away her things. He'd almost berated the man for looking but why should this artwork be hidden? Yet another temptation in his path, yet this wouldn't hurt anyone if he gave into it. A quick scan of her illustrations and he'd leave. Continue looking for her. Which one to choose? He grabbed the sketch pad at the top, one with a beige cover. Placed it on the tabletop and opened.

These drawings were different from the sketches tacked to her desk. No whimsy about them at all. Pages filled with dark ink and nightmare creatures hiding in the shadows with twisted faces and evil grins. Hands reaching out of the darkness.

Nightmares.

That night of the storm. The cry that had him out of bed. Had that been Louisa? A heat rose inside him, like anger. He wanted to know what had caused the fear and horror he saw on these pages. To *fix* it, somehow. Matteo kept turning more pages, and the pictures changed. Drawings of people now, or disembodied parts of them at least. Hands, feet, eyes. All in exquisite detail.

They somehow felt intimate. However, he didn't think they were from life. Still, the bitter spike of something like jealousy overcame him, because they were all of a man. Although there was a familiarity about the sketches. Matteo couldn't put his finger on it… He kept going, and then he saw it. A full drawing of the statue of David on one page. On the other, Louisa had drawn him, not as the statue, but as if he were a real person. They must be from pictures. She'd never travelled before. The brilliance of them, sketching marble then making that marble come to life in pencil, pen and ink.

He should stop. This book was obviously private, unlike the sketches for her work. Yet he couldn't. He was like a man possessed. Here was the woman she hid. What other secrets would he find? He wanted to know more of what made Louisa tick. He flicked over pages of detailed drawings, until the drawings changed again.

A sketch of a couple. If he'd thought that the pictures of David were somehow intimate, this *was* about intimacy. She'd inked so few lines on the page yet there was no hiding what this drawing was about. The pair, naked. You couldn't see their faces but there was no doubt what they were doing. He turned the page, another scene. A couple lying on a bed. Rumpled sheets. The man's hand lazily resting on the woman's stomach. This was like looking through a window, except into Louisa's soul. Then the detail drawings. Hands clutching sheets, backs arched. Fingers pressing into flesh. Bodies connected.

Heat roared over him, rushing low. The weight of his desire overcoming sensible thought. He couldn't stop turning page after page. They were magnificent, erotic. Couple after couple making love, kissing. Touching. Questing mouths and hands. Such a contrast to the innocence Louisa always portrayed to the world. He lost himself in her pictures, not thinking whether he should or shouldn't.

Not thinking much, other than about a need to see *more*. He fixed on the last picture, a naked couple entwined, wrapped together and also wrapped in what looked like… wind. With scattered leaves whirling about them as if they'd both been picked up into the air. The woman, hair long and wild, curling round them both in the maelstrom. The man. Dark hair, mouth at her throat…

Were they her fantasies? In a general continuum of the acts of lovemaking they were tame enough. But that they'd come from her at all, given for the best part of her life she'd been isolated… Here he'd spent time berating himself for kissing her, yet these pictures weren't soft sketches filled with innocent love and romance. They scorched the pages with yearning and passion. A need he knew exactly how to fulfil…

'What are you doing?'

He hadn't heard the door open. Matteo snapped the sketchbook shut. A fresh heat burned through him but this wasn't desire, it was something like shame.

Louisa looked to the sketchbook under his fingers and stormed up to him, eyes narrowed, lips thin in anger. She reached out, hand trembling. Snatched the book from the desk's surface, holding it to her chest.

'You had no right. That's private.' Her voice was so quiet. As if he'd somehow forced his way into her life and exposed her deepest secrets. Her face flushed red. Her pale skin hiding nothing. He liked the way she blushed, but this time it wasn't something sweet and innocent. The way her mouth dropped, it was as if she were humiliated.

'I know.'

The taint of guilt slicked over him then. He'd embarrassed her by invading her space, her privacy. It had been the wrong thing to do and he was sorry, in some ways. In others, he wasn't sorry at all. Because he'd learned something about Louisa today.

That she desired.

'They're things you shouldn't have looked at. Things I never—'

'I'm sorry, Lu— Louisa.'

She whipped round, her hair swirling like the woman in the last picture, long, loose. Glorious. Like this, in her fury, it was as if she were on fire.

'Oh, really? Then why were you in here?'

He held his hands out, placating. 'I was looking for you. I didn't know where you were, and I haven't seen you much over the past few days. I thought you were avoiding me.'

'I was *working*. Something I thought you might understand.'

'I do.' Or at least, he did now. He'd not really thought much about her work before. When she'd first worried about missing her deadline and needing her things he'd dismissed her, told her she should take a break. To have fun. Now... 'You're exceptionally talented.'

Her skin flared an even brighter red. Louisa chewed on

her lower lip. Clutching the sketch pad to her chest. Her fingers blanched white around the edges.

'You know what I think?' he went on. 'I think you're feeling ashamed right now of what I've seen, and you shouldn't.'

'How do you know *anything* about what I'm feeling?'

'Because I'm human. Those pictures are all about humanity. Passion. It isn't something to be ashamed of, or to hide. It's normal, and I won't judge you for it.'

It was as if she almost folded in on herself. Shoulders drooping. Hair covering her face. 'You're lying.'

'Why would I lie?'

He wanted her to face him, to be proud of what he'd seen. Instead, she snorted, turned her back to him. Walked to the French doors overlooking the lake and stared outside.

'People lie all the time, Matteo. They say one thing, mean another. Think only about themselves, not caring who they hurt in the process.'

His gut clenched, hard and angry. He wanted to ask who had hurt her. Who'd put that haunted look on her face. Who'd made her draw, not those pictures of lovemaking and ecstasy, but the darker ones. The ones that looked like, not what she craved, but what she feared. Yet he was also angry at himself. How wounded she appeared, all because of his curiosity, when he should have known better.

People were entitled to their secrets. She could keep hers. All he'd been looking for was a way in, and he'd found it. Anything to show her that living in a huge old home in the country with only staff for company was a waste. That she was a woman of passion and desire. Someone who clearly wanted more, and the world was there for her taking.

He needed to repair what he'd done here. She wanted

truth, and he wanted trust. The only way he could achieve either was to give a tiny bit of himself. Not one that would crack him open *too* wide, but enough for Louisa to know that he was telling the truth.

Matteo shook his head, began to prise open the vault to the memories he preferred to keep hidden. Part of him rebelled at the disclosure, because truths could cause the most painful of wounds if twisted against you. But this was Louisa. *Lulu.* As harmless as a kitten.

'I know what it's like to be lied to,' he said, 'and I promised myself I'd never do that to another person. Even if the truth hurt.'

Louisa held on to her sketchbook as if it were a kind of life preserver. The only thing keeping her afloat. The one she'd especially wanted nobody to see. It contained her darkest nightmares, where the fear overcame her. Waking her in the night. Compelling her to draw because if she captured them on paper, they might stop tormenting her. Then those other dreams, her fantasies. The ones that taunted her in another way. She'd captured them to make them real, because she'd never wanted a relationship but, sometimes, she *wanted*. In the end she'd learned that dreams couldn't hurt you. Not like people.

People were all risk. Little reward.

Though the way she'd seen Matteo when she'd stood at the door, paralysed. The intensity on his face as he looked at her most private sketchbook. The unalloyed fascination as his hands touched the pages gently, almost reverently.

Before the shock and anger overtook her, she'd imagined those fingers touching her.

That last drawing, two people caught in a whirlwind. She'd felt like that down at the lake, in his arms. When his lips slipped over her skin. Their kiss, which rocked the very core of her. It was like discovering a part of herself that had been missing for so long. Here, in this glorious sunshine, far from everywhere familiar, the fears that plagued her nights had begun leaching away. Turning into something more heated, insistent like a ceaselessly beating drum.

Need.

He'd been right, she had been avoiding him. Her work being a convenient excuse. But she couldn't think about that right now, not with the man those recent desires had begun tangling round standing right in front of her. A man who claimed he knew how much untruths hurt. If they talked about him, he wouldn't talk about her and what he'd seen.

'Who lied to you?'

He turned away, walking to the glass doors overlooking the lake, hands in his pockets. As if he was trying to distance himself from some memory. Nothing about him was open right now. He'd closed himself off from her.

'When I was six, an older cousin told me I wasn't a real Bainbridge. That I was adopted and I'd never be one of them. I was a fake, a phony. Until then, I'd had no idea.'

Her stomach dropped. She couldn't imagine what that would have been like. How could anyone say that to a child? Though she understood this family. They were only after perfection, not failure. Blood and legacy were the only things important to any of them.

'Matteo, I'm—'

He cut off her words of sympathy with the slice of his hand through the air. Okay, so he didn't want to talk about it. That she understood all too well. The sympathetic looks from the police after her mother had finally been found out. The empathy from her psychologist. In the end she was sick of it all. Of being thought of as unwell for so many years, then being thought of as somehow broken. When all she'd wanted was for things to go back to how they were before her father died. When she was a normal child with her whole life ahead of her.

'It was a gift,' he said, yet his voice sounded choked. 'I finally realised why my parents didn't treat me the same as Felicity. Sent me away when she got sick. It made sense. I wasn't theirs.'

She shook her head. 'No, that can't be right.'

'It can. What other explanation is there?'

'Your parents had adopted you. They *wanted* you.'

He turned. Mouth a thin, brutal line.

'They wanted what every Bainbridge wants. An heir. Someone to carry on the family wealth, the family name if they're lucky enough to have a boy. Don't worry, I've reconciled myself to the realisation.'

Yet everything about him now seemed so hard and tense. As if one wrong move and he'd crack and break into a million pieces.

'Have you?'

'It is what it is. I can't change it. They got their true heir in the end.'

'Are you sure about that? What about Felicity?'

'What about her?'

Louisa had been surprised to see Felicity at Mae's funeral. It had been clear she was a Bainbridge, the pale skin and hair a giveaway, yet Louisa had never met her before. Then she'd introduced herself, whilst seeming to search the small crowd of mourners as if looking for something, or someone...

'I get the idea you don't see her much. Have you asked

her whether it's what she wanted? Whether she thinks of herself as the sole heir?'

He shook his head. 'Of course not. I don't see her because she's working as a nanny and travels a lot. Both of us are busy.'

He reached almost reflexively into his pocket, pulled out his phone. Seemed to think better of it, shoved it back as if it might burn him. Louisa knew all about avoidance of the things that hurt you the most. Sometimes the greatest kindness was to let someone hide.

Hadn't she been hiding long enough?

'Did you want to see some of my illustrations?'

Matteo's eyes widened at the sudden change of subject. 'I'd love to see what you want to show me.'

Words loaded, replete with meaning. Was there an answer?

Everything.

No. Where did that come from?

She didn't know. These thoughts, they intruded when she was around him. Insistent things that whispered she was entitled to whatever reward Matteo could provide to her. She'd waited long enough.

'I don't really show people my work before it's finished.' She grabbed a sketchbook and placed it on her table. Sure, she'd struggled with the pictures, and these were the sorts of drawing she'd generally file in a cabinet when done. Putting the characters who'd invaded her brain to bed. When she gave her drawings over for the last time, it was as if she set her characters free. And set herself free as well... till the next project held her captive.

'Why?'

How to explain something that made little sense, even to her? 'It's like when I share my illustrations, they stop being mine and become someone else's. Like the other person takes some of the magic away.'

He hesitated then, his hand halting over the page.

'I don't want to ruin the magic for you. I know how important your work is.'

Something inside her warmed. He understood part of what this meant to her. Her mother had always disparaged her 'doodling'. In spite of the woman, she'd built a career on it but still occasionally heard that critical voice, telling her what she was doing had no value.

'It's okay,' she said.

'I feel privileged.' Matteo's voice carried a weight, as though he meant it. 'What book are you illustrating?'

'A reimagining of *The Frog Prince.*'

'Always children's stories?'

She nodded. 'I like them, the innocence of it. And I love the idea that something I'm doing is giving children joy.'

The only thing that had given her much happiness as a child was reading. In those illustrated children's books she'd found an escape. Some days, after her father had died, when she was in and out of hospital, books and the fantasy world she could immerse herself in were all that had kept her going. It had been something her mother couldn't steal from her.

She wanted to give that escape to other children as well.

'Have you ever thought of writing your own?'

Louisa stilled. There were other sketchbooks. The stories she'd written and drawn for Mae. About two children and their stupendous summer adventures, which had made Mae laugh. But they were more personal, private things. Created because she'd wanted to make a woman she loved remember happier times. Some of the happiest times of Louisa's own life.

Still, she shook her head. 'It's not for me. Let the author take the accolades. I'm not really into the idea of book signings and publicity.'

Matteo frowned, skewered her with his hot brown gaze that saw too much, even though he didn't say anything in response.

She opened the first page of her sketchbook and slid it over to him.

'Here are some working drawings, the ones I did when I was a bit stuck.'

They stood side by side. The man somehow radiated heat. The warmth from his body slid through her. His presence was palpable as a touch, like a finger gently stroked down her spine. Goosebumps skittered across her skin.

How could the proximity of a person do this to her? This sparkling sensation that lit up every nerve of her body. Made her catch her breath whenever he was close.

Made her want him closer...

Matteo chuckled, dragging her away from those tempting thoughts. He'd turned to the page of the frog she'd sketched the day he'd first rung the doorbell at Easton Hall.

'He looks like a frog with attitude.'

'He was giving me trouble. He always has.'

'Have you wrestled him into submission now?'

She laughed. 'That's not really the way it works for me. They have a mind of their own. Sometimes they don't want to be drawn the way you want to draw them. Hence these sketches. Trying to convince him to do what I wanted.'

'That sounds—'

'Odd. I get it.'

No one truly understood. They nodded with a fixed smile on their face when she tried to tell them.

'No, it sounds fascinating. Like to get the perfect drawing you have to understand the characters, and for that, they become real. That takes some imagination, Lulu. I don't know how you do it.'

She stilled at his slip. The use of her nickname. Yet he didn't seem to have noticed. Perhaps she was reading too many things into it. Her imagination had always been the safest place to reside, after all. It was easy. Real life, that was the hard thing. She still struggled with it.

'I don't know how you run a multimillion-dollar business.'

'Billion-dollar.' The corner of his perfect lips quirked. 'Add a few more zeros.'

She laughed and smacked him in the arm. 'Sorry, Mr Businessman, for underestimating the number of zeros your business has.'

'My business is easy. It's about understanding what people want and giving it to them.'

Could he see what she wanted? Could he imagine it at all? A shiver ran through her. She repeatedly imagined seeing his body now, having felt it under his clothes. Obsessed about looking at every part of him. Even though some days she thought he could peer right inside her soul, he wasn't a mind reader. Except, he'd seen those intimate drawings. They were her imaginings too. It wouldn't take much to connect that those desires now involved him.

Which was another of the reasons she'd hid. Wanting him; when he was the man who sought to take everything away from her. Though he hadn't mentioned anything over recent days. Maybe he didn't need to add Easton Hall to his empire after all?

'I call what you do impossible,' she said.

'I call your illustrations impossible. But here we are, proving we're both making the impossible happen.'

He reverently turned a few more pages. The way he touched the paper again. Gently. With long, strong-looking fingers topped by perfect square nails. Drifting over the paper, almost as though he wanted to feel the drawings on the page.

'Extraordinary,' he murmured. The word was so quiet, it was almost like an exhale. There was something about his reverence that slid through her with pleasure. Winding its way on a seductive journey through her blood, heating her from the inside out.

'Thank you. The work seems to have become a bit easier here, since I've settled in. Something about the sunshine. It's making everything brighter.'

He looked up at her, slowly, almost assessing. As if he'd come to himself and remembered something long forgotten. 'I should let you get back to it, then. So you can finish. When you're done, I'd like to take you out to dinner.'

'Oh.'

Louisa didn't know what to say. She'd never been invited out to dinner by anyone before. A tiny kind of thrill skittered round her belly. She wasn't sure if it was based on excitement or on fear.

'There's a little *trattoria* close by,' he said. 'It's hidden away, used more by locals than by tourists, so it won't be too crowded. How long do you think you might be? I thought we could celebrate meeting your deadline.'

'Maybe a day or two?'

He smiled. 'It's a date.'

She nodded as he walked from the room. A date? That was simply an expression. It meant nothing. Though Louisa didn't know why she simultaneously wished it were true.

And hoped it wasn't.

CHAPTER EIGHT

MATTEO STOOD, WAITING. Glass of Scotch in hand. His phone buzzed an alert, which he checked. The car would be here soon to take them to his favourite little restaurant in town, tucked away in a cobbled alley. He'd asked the owner to set up a table for a celebration. Initially they'd thought it represented an engagement until he'd disabused them. He'd told them it was a special night nonetheless, and the owner seemed somehow pleased, promising a table in a quiet corner.

His plans seemed to be working. Louisa's talk of how the sunshine helped her pictures. He'd known getting her away from the UK would work, though the reasons seemed a little hazy right now. The raging desire for revenge not quite as sharp. He mused why that might be. Working seven days a week for months might be the cause. Likely he'd needed a break too. To simply stop and enjoy the sunshine himself...

Matteo downed the last, short sip in his glass, settling the strange sensation in his gut that had overcome him. Almost like anticipation, but that couldn't be right. He checked his watch. Almost time to go. This was a simple meal, nothing more. Another step in showing Louisa that there was more to life than living in the rainy old English countryside. She could chase the sunshine all round the world, if she wanted, he just needed to make her feel as if it were her idea.

'I'm ready now.'

Louisa. It was as though his imagination had conjured her. He turned, ready to let her know the car was about to arrive, except his voice was stolen. Simply dying in his throat.

She was unlike he'd ever seen her before. Dressed not like someone who'd stepped out of the past, but like a woman who slammed him straight into his future. A vision in green. The dress still long, soft and flowing, but cinched at the waist with a golden chain. The fabric vibrant and silky, lovingly caressing her curves. The front dipped into a tantalising vee between her breasts. Round her bare shoulders she wore a sheer wrap in the same colour as the dress, yet threaded through with gold like the chain, so it shimmered under the lights. Her hair tumbled round her shoulders and down her back in gleaming copper waves.

He froze, struck silent. As if this was a moment in time he wanted to stay captured in for ever. Like a scene from a movie, the type written about in books. A realisation that this woman was nothing like she seemed.

The blood in his veins rushed low as if he were some teenager, and he willed his body under control. Why was he so surprised? She was a stunning woman. He'd known that. Yet something about tonight seemed to have woven her in a kind of magic.

She gave a tremulous smile and tightened the wrap round herself. Was she still insecure about how she looked? In that moment, Matteo wanted to hurt whoever had ever made her doubt herself, her appearance. Her style.

'You look exquisite.'

His voice ground out all rough and dark, as if he'd just

found it after years of silence. Her eyes widened, cheeks flushed a glorious pink. If he had buttons to push, she was activating every single one with her soft, alluring innocence. Completely unaware of how she affected him.

'Thank you.'

Her own voice sounded breathless. As if she couldn't believe what he was saying now. What he'd told her before.

'You are beautiful. That's a fact and not open for discussion.'

'I—I wasn't sure about the dress, but it was a celebration so...'

'It's magnificent on you.' That earned another flush of pleasure. He wanted more. To capture every one all for himself.

'And I'm surprised. It's not like what you usually wear.'

'Sylvana suggested it. For fun, to try out something different. She said the green would look lovely with my hair...or something.'

Yet another thing she'd been prepared to try that was new. What he'd been hoping for. Soon, she'd want to explore the world without him. Yet why did that thought give him the sense of a deadline? One he never wanted to meet.

'You look *beyond* lovely. You always do. But tonight, you could be a siren, luring a man to his doom.'

'Oh, I'm not sure about that.'

'Trust me. I'm a man.'

She gave him a small smile that was imbued with a shy kind of pleasure. 'And I'm luring you to your doom?'

'Right now, I'm hungry. Dinner first, doom later.'

Louisa threw back her head and laughed, the sound lighting up the room like a firework. He could listen to that unrestrained sound of pure joy, every day. His phone buzzed another alert and he pulled it from his pocket.

'Car's here.'

'I'm a little bit excited about this. I've never been to a restaurant before,' she said, almost like a throwaway line as they headed for the front door and he locked up.

Never been to a restaurant? It seemed inconceivable and yet there was no doubt in his mind she told the truth. It underscored once more how sheltered she was. How little he understood of her, or her life.

A driver held the car door open for them and Matteo helped Louisa in. Her hand soft and warm in his. She lifted her dress and he glimpsed a hint of golden shoes as she slid into the seat. Her slender ankles.

What was happening to him? When did the hint of cleavage and the sight of shapely ankles ever attract him before?

He couldn't say. But it seemed that they did now. He wanted to wrap his hands around her ankles as he eased her legs apart. Kiss up and up till his mouth reached the heart of her. Make her scream his name. Recollections of those drawings of hers flooded back. A man's head buried between a woman's thighs. Hand gripping his hair, holding him tight. Holding him in place. That was the meal he craved right now…

Matteo took a deep, steadying breath. Fantasies were fine. It was the reality that could come back to bite you and that was a sobering thought. She looked up at him in anticipation, probably wondering why he was standing there. What would she do if she could delve inside his head, read his imaginings? Run to him, or away? He'd never know. Matteo hopped into the car next to her. After a blissfully short drive achingly aware of her presence next to him, they pulled up at a street at the bottom of a hill.

'Are we here already? We could have walked!'

'We can walk back after the meal, if you like.'

He could imagine that. The moonlight over the lake. Strolling back to the villa, hand in hand…

Where had that absurd thought come from? He'd never once held hands with a woman.

Matteo shrugged it off as he hopped out of the car and tipped the driver. Leading Louisa up a narrow street to a red door in a centuries-old wall. Just a small sign with the words Trattoria Galante announcing what lay behind. He pushed it open and they walked through a softly lit hall.

'Signor Bainbridge!' The ebullient owner welcomed him almost like a prodigal son returned. 'I have a special table for you both.'

They were led through premises bustling with locals, with its old stone walls and tables with checked cloths, towards the rear. Louisa seemed a little wide eyed, almost overwhelmed. He settled his hand on her back. Gently guiding her through. Trying not to forget how new this was for her. The bile rose to his throat. Anger at Mae, for taking in a child who she seemed to have kept hidden away rather than showing her the world. Not ever having been to the beach. Never having eaten in a restaurant.

Why?

Mae had done all of those things before her husband had died. She must have known what a young woman needed out of life, and yet she'd kept Louisa there like some hermit. It made no sense.

He flexed his fingers on the small of her spine. He'd started now, and he'd complete the job. She wouldn't want to go back to Easton Hall after he'd finished with her. He could take her to all his properties. His boutique hotel in Paris, his resort in the Maldives. His island in Australia.

There were any number of places and he'd show them all to her...

Except that wasn't his job. His job was to set her free and watch her fly. Yet the ideas took hold and wouldn't let go. How he'd love to see her bury her toes in pristine white sand for the first time. Step into the turquoise waters of a tropical beach. To watch her relish the food at each of the finest restaurants he knew. He could show her the world, yet somehow, he knew...

That was the most dangerous fantasy of them all.

They sat alone in a small courtyard. Above them strings of lights wound through a vine-covered pergola glimmered like fireflies. Candles flickered on the table, lending everything a soft glow. It looked as if she'd been dropped into some kind of wonderland. If she'd allowed herself to dream of the perfect date, then this would have come close.

Of course, dreams couldn't hurt you. Not like people.

People were all risk. Little reward.

Anyhow, she'd never have a date because relationships weren't in her repertoire. What was the point of a relationship if you didn't want love? That hadn't ever been something she'd searched for, not romantic love at least. Love didn't mean happiness to her. Her mother had said she'd loved her and done terrible things. Love meant loss, obsession. Something unhealthy.

There was nothing healthy about it.

That didn't mean she couldn't enjoy tonight, though she wouldn't let her imagination run away from her. Matteo was simply being kind again. He'd used the word 'date' as a figure of speech, that was all. Yet it was as though he'd stolen a little piece of her heart when he'd brought her here to this romantic setting. The tableware gleaming. A pristine, starched white tablecloth. A little vase of geraniums adding a vibrant splash of colour in all the green.

She pulled her reading glasses from her small clutch, put them on and looked down at the menu, but it was in Italian. Her stomach grumbled.

Matteo chuckled. 'Hungry?'

He was so devastatingly handsome. He'd taken off his jacket, now sitting across from her in a white shirt that accentuated the golden colour of his skin. His eyes flickering chocolate in the candlelight.

'I don't understand anything on the menu.'

'There's no risk. Everything here's good but I can order if you like. Surprise you.'

Matteo picked up the menu himself, held it in his long, strong fingers. How they'd touched her as he'd guided her through to their table, sending a shiver of pleasure up her spine. How she wanted him to touch her like that again…

He smiled and a flicker of heat ignited deep inside her, glowing like the candles on the tabletop.

'Since this is a celebration, how about something that sparkles? Have you ever had champagne?'

The heat rose to her face. Embarrassment. What must he think of her, especially given her admission she'd never been to a restaurant before? The man was so…urbane. He probably drank champagne all the time.

'I wasn't totally sheltered. Mae opened a bottle on my sixteenth birthday. Dom Perignon, I believe.'

He raised an eyebrow. 'How forward-thinking of her.'

'In many ways, she was.'

A deep, unrelenting ache stabbed in her chest. She rubbed at it. Louisa missed Mae terribly. The love she'd shown Louisa. The care and patience. Allowing her to be herself, to find her way in her own time. Even though in

later years Louisa seemed to have become somewhat…
stuck.

No, not stuck. Settled. And there was nothing wrong
with that.

'Did you enjoy it, the champagne?' Matteo asked.

'I remember it was fizzy and I thought it tasted sour, so
not really. I only had a few sips.'

Matteo chuckled and the sound rippled right through
her in waves of something like pleasure. 'Do you want to
try again?'

Louisa slipped off her now unnecessary glasses and
tucked them into her bag again, giving herself some time
to answer. She could say no, but wasn't tonight all about
trying something new? Different clothes, different food.
Living, when everyone else she'd loved was dead.

'Why not?'

One of the waitstaff approached as if summoned tele-
pathically. Matteo ordered in Italian, barely even looking
at the menu.

'So, what are we having for dinner?' she asked.

'It's a surprise.'

An uncomfortable sensation skittered through her belly.
Something almost like nerves. She always enjoyed certainty. Her life at Mae's had been ruled by it. Though
nothing over the past weeks had been certain, and she'd
managed to survive it, so far.

'Don't you enjoy surprises?'

Matteo seemed to be able to pick up her emotions. Sense
what she needed. She didn't know how he managed it, but
she didn't want to ruin tonight with her insecurities. Louisa shook her head.

'It's perfect. Thank you.'

'Finishing your illustrations is an achievement you should be proud of. It's worth celebrating.'

'Do you celebrate your achievements?'

A slight frown creased his brow. 'Not really.'

'I guess you have so many. If you celebrated each one, all that champagne. Would you ever be sober?'

His eyes widened for a moment, then he threw his head back and laughed. She loved the sound. Deep, throaty. The smile meeting his eyes, which crinkled at the corners in amusement.

'There have been failures along the way. Don't think I'm perfect.'

In so many ways, to her, he was. The hard, honed businessman melting away. For the briefest of flashes, he became Matty again. The young boy she'd remembered seeming to return, for rare moments at least. She'd take those where she could grasp them, no matter how fleeting.

The waiter arrived once more with a bottle, which he opened with a slow hiss and pop. Poured. Matteo took his glass. Raised it to her.

'I hope you enjoy this a little better than your last attempt,' he said. 'To you, Louisa. Congratulations on finishing your illustrations on time.'

'I always finish them on time.' But the toast shouldn't be to her. It should be to someone else. Someone she felt was in so many ways forgotten in this story. She raised her own glass.

'To me,' she said, with tears in her eyes, 'and to Mae.'

He murmured in acknowledgement and their glasses clinked together. She took a sip of hers. The drink burst across her tongue, somewhat tart and refreshing. She swallowed, trying to look a bit sophisticated, but the bubbles tickled her nose and she coughed.

'You okay?' he asked.

'It's quite lovely.' And dangerous. It fizzed inside her the same way as her insides did when she looked at him. The way he made her feel alive. 'I think it's a drink that might get people into trouble.'

'I'm all for trouble.' He raised his glass again. 'Here's to that as well.'

It was her turn to laugh, but memories of Mae brought back memories of Easton Hall. As much as Lake Como and Matteo's villa were beautiful, Easton Hall was *home*. A home she wanted to go back to.

'What did the engineer say about the house?' she asked. Matteo's face blanked smooth as a pond on a windless day. He took a long sip of his champagne.

'He's assessed the structure. Insurance is next.'

Which didn't answer the most important question. 'When can I go back?'

'Easton Hall requires repairs and rewiring after the storm damage.'

'That might be the case, but it's my home.'

His eyes narrowed. His focus merciless, like a glaring spotlight in the dark. 'Where you locked yourself away.'

'No, I didn't.' It was as if a solid weight pressed on her chest, making it difficult to breathe. The place wasn't her prison. She'd made a life there, taking tourists on tours through the house. There wasn't a day she hadn't felt safe, secure. 'You don't understand.'

He sat back, eyebrow raised. 'Enlighten me.'

How could she share the terrible things her mother had done? So few people knew. Mae. Some doctors. The police. It had all been well hidden in the end. For the best, everyone said when her mother died. She didn't know where to even start, so she took another sip of champagne. Breathing through the relentless pressure bearing down on her. Before she was forced to say anything more, a waiter arrived with some food. A plate filled with pillowy-looking balls in a creamy sauce. The memories of her past faded with the scent of cheesy deliciousness.

She didn't want to look up and face Matteo's relentless gaze, so she ate. The flavour burst across her tongue in its richness. She moaned.

'Oh. My. Goodness. What is this?'

Matteo's fork was partway to his mouth. His eyelids hooded.

'It's a local speciality. Gnocchi with Taleggio cheese. Have you never had gnocchi before?'

She took another forkful and it was as if a world of flavour had opened up to her.

'No.'

Mrs Fancutt was a traditional cook, but her food was beautiful. Not quite like this, but it hadn't mattered to a half-starved child what she ate, so long as no one tried to stop her.

'Didn't you ever wish—?'

'I was happy for a home. That might be difficult for you to fathom.'

Matteo placed down his fork. 'I'm trying to understand.'

'There's nothing much to understand. I'm a simple person. A creature of habit. I like things the way I like things.'

'They keep you feeling safe,' he said.

Louisa stilled. It was the first time someone had voiced how she'd felt.

'Yes.'

'And stable?'

She nodded. How did he know?

'Because you lost your father and your mother and the world ceased to be a safe and stable place.'

'Yes.'

It was such a simple and painful summation of her life, even if lacking some important context.

'I understand.'

'Do you. Do you *really*?' How could anyone? But Louisa wanted him to. She *craved* it.

'When my cousin told me I wasn't a true Bainbridge and I confronted my parents, they said nothing would change. Then Felicity was born, was diagnosed with leukaemia.'

Matteo drained his glass. The waiter came and refilled it. Topped up hers.

'I was a little boy who was afraid he'd lose his sister,' he said, not quite looking at her. 'My parents didn't care. They sent me to boarding school, where I stayed. Forgotten. Everything I'd come to believe, that I should have parents who cared about me, a stable family—that ended. And I swore when I got older that I'd never be in that position again. So, I understand, Louisa. I understand all too well.'

She reached out to place her hand over his. Stopped. Matteo's face had hardened, the anger palpable in the air. She knew what it was like to be surrounded by sympathy when you didn't want it. When you wanted to forget, to move on. The problem was, you followed yourself wherever you went.

'That's what drove you,' she said.

'I created a life. I created a business. All *despite* my family.'

He'd been so shut off from her, and yet it was as if he'd opened a door to himself, no matter what it must cost him. What would it be like to share the burden of what had happened to her? Sure, she'd spoken to a psychologist in those early days. A person who was professional and at arm's length. But the only other person close to her who had known what had happened was Mae, and she was gone.

In that moment, Louisa had never felt so alone in the world. With no one to speak to when dark thoughts and nightmares had threatened to crush her. No friends, no family. She was orphaned in all respects. Yet Matteo was here. He seemed to want to listen.

And perhaps if he knew what had happened to her, he'd understand why Easton Hall was her safe place, one she never wanted to leave.

Matteo knew he was almost glaring at Louisa, daring her to say anything about what had happened to him. Yet she sat there in empathetic silence. When she'd reached out her hand to touch him, he'd craved her softness even though he didn't need it. He'd spent his life not needing others, because people let you down. He had himself, and that was enough.

Yet the disappointment when she pulled her hand away. He took a slow breath. No. He wasn't looking for sympathy. He'd been trying to understand, because if he was going to get Louisa to leave Easton Hall then she needed to trust him. To feel a connection.

It had all been calculated until the words had simply... left him. Things he'd spoken to no one about. Not even his own sister. How could he gripe about those old wounds to her when Felicity had almost died? So he'd cursed his family to hell instead. Yet why had the words felt so good leaving him? Like ridding himself of some kind of poison. All he knew was that he'd told her more than he'd planned, things that he tended to keep to himself, because if she understood him, perhaps she'd let him understand her.

He was sure there were things that she desired. She was

just hesitant to reach out and take them. Well, he feared nothing.

'It seems we've both done things *despite* our families,' she said.

He nodded. 'My family cast me aside. Your parents passed away. It must have been hard, losing them so young.'

The waiter came and cleared their plates. Placed another exquisite dish on the table. A traditional fish speciality. He hoped Louisa enjoyed fish. Her first mouthful of the gnocchi seemed to have transported her in some kind of orgasmic bliss. He'd become instantly hard, realising that everything was new to her.

What he could introduce her to. All kinds of new experiences. How would she react? Those intimate sketches exposed her fantasies. He could show her reality. A heat began to stoke deep inside at the possibilities. Would she look at him with the same pleasure as she had eating a new food? How would she look being touched intimately for the first time...?

No. Once again he needed to remind his body that his job wasn't to seduce her. It was to convince her to leave Easton Hall. Yet wasn't that a seduction of sorts? He'd simply have to strike the right balance.

One that retained his sanity in the process.

'It was hard losing my father.' Louisa toyed with her fork, turning it as if staring at the candlelight reflected from the silver. Almost as if she was avoiding something. He guessed this would be a difficult conversation for her. At least she'd loved her parents. Had something to lose. His parents were still alive, and he'd lost them all the same.

Or perhaps, he'd never really had them at all.

He tried some of the fish, which was superb as always.

Letting the silence stretch. It wasn't a comfortable one, but he knew that when people tried to fill it, they often made important disclosures. Louisa wasn't just a closed book, it was as if she were one written in a foreign language that he needed an interpreter to decipher.

'My mother…'

Here it was. The key, he was sure.

'She was arrested before she died.'

Everything in him stilled. Mae had never said anything to him about this, only that Louisa's story was a tragic one and hers to tell. He'd assumed that the tragedy was the death of both parents.

Clearly not.

Now he saw the space she'd left in the conversation as one for him to fill. As if what she had to say was too big and terrible to say without prompting. She dragged her bottom lip through her teeth, the evening taking on a terrible weight.

'Why was your mother arrested?' he asked.

Her knife and fork hovered above the plate. 'My mother…she…'

Louisa looked up at him, her eyes tight. Her knuckles whitening as she held her cutlery in a tight grip. His heart rate kicked up as he waited. She was opening herself up to him, but he wasn't sure what he'd find when she did.

Louisa's chest rose and fell as if she was taking a steadying breath.

'My mother was arrested because she used to hurt me.'

CHAPTER NINE

THE WORDS HAD been trapped, but Matteo's question had seemed to be the key to her voice, and they'd come out all in a rush. Maybe he hadn't heard. He simply sat there, staring at her. Mouth opening slightly as if wanting to speak. Closing. Then he put down his cutlery, knife and fork crossed on his plate.

'When you say "hurt"...'

The psychologist had known when Louisa had walked into their office what had happened. She'd received a referral, Louisa's records. Mae had known too. The only person she had ever really had to tell fresh was the police officer who took her statement.

She had never told another soul who hadn't known or suspected something of what had gone on first. Now it was as if she couldn't stop.

'My mother used to pretend that I was sick. When doctors didn't believe I was unwell, she'd *make* me sick. I spent time in hospital getting tests, having procedures, to find out what was wrong with me. There was nothing. For a while she convinced me that I wasn't well, and that if I didn't get treatment, I might die like my father had. Munchausen by Proxy, some people called it. Others called it Factitious Disorder Imposed on Another, which I always thought was a mouthful.'

Matteo reached out, took her hand in his. Squeezed her fingers.

Take my hand, Louisa.

Somehow, his touch made her feel braver.

'My God, I had no idea.'

'Nobody did.'

He shook his head. His thumb gently rubbing back and forth across her skin. Somehow settling her racing heartbeat, grounding her as memories of that time came flooding back.

'When did it start?'

'After my father died.'

'That's when you were only six. Just after…'

After she'd left Mae's for that last time. Her mother wouldn't let her go back, no matter how many times she'd asked to or Mae had invited her. Her mother probably knew Mae would see through the lies.

'Yes, just after that summer.'

'How did the doctors not see?'

That was a question she'd asked herself numerous times over the years since. Or the other, which he was kind enough not to voice.

Why didn't you say anything?

'My mother was clever. Doctors knew she was grieving. I believe they simply couldn't comprehend her being the one to make me ill, given my father had died. She told me that she was trying to make me better so that I didn't die like he did. That was an easy way to control a child because I was terrified. It was easy to make me look sick too. She started cutting back my food. Said I had intolerances. Fed me Dad's medications. I was always so thin and tired. Cutting my hair…'

Matteo made a wounded kind of noise, like coming deep from his soul. Clenched her hand a little tight. Released it.

'*Louisa...*'

'It's okay. Really. I've moved on.'

But had she? Regular people didn't panic when someone suggested a haircut. They just got a trim. They didn't
get overwhelmed buying clothes, or in a bustling city. Did
they?

'It's not okay. It will never be okay. For all my parents'
faults, they were *desperate* for Felicity to be well. To imagine them actually making her sick... Why did she do it?'

That was the question that would never be answered. The
answers died with her mother. All she could do was guess.

'I think it's because she was seen as a martyr, caring for
my dad. When he died, she had nothing left.'

'She had *you*.'

The expression on his face was pained. Louisa gave a
weak kind of smile.

'I wasn't enough. My mum and dad were everything
to each other. Sometimes, for her at least, I think I got in
the way.'

'I understand that sentiment.'

She looked at their hands, joined on the table. Giving
each other support. They both had their crosses to bear.

'How was your mother found out?'

She withdrew her hand from his. Wrapped her arms
round herself. Shrugged. 'I only know what I was told.
One time when I was really sick, a nurse became suspi-
cious. Blood tests were off. My mum had contaminated
my IV. People began watching then, put up CCTV in the
room. It all unravelled.'

'There was no press. There was nothing.'

Louisa gave a short, sharp laugh. 'My mother was a
Bainbridge. Of *course* there wasn't any press. The family tried to convince me not to say anything to the police.

Said she wouldn't hurt me any more because she'd learned her lesson.'

Matteo sat across from her, his eyes darkening. A heavy frown on his brow. 'Is that when Mae took you?'

'Yes. And she promised me that everything would be okay. Nothing would ever hurt me again. That I'd always have food on the table, that I'd be safe. And she kept that promise, till the day she died.'

Matteo clenched his jaw so hard it was as if his teeth might crack. What that family had done. They would have returned her to a perpetrator so long as it didn't hurt the damned Bainbridge name.

Instead of her living the kind of life any child should have, there'd been attempts to silence her. Then she'd been taken in by Mae, who'd wrapped Louisa in a fantasy world. Didn't challenge her, didn't encourage her to live the life a young woman should. Instead, kept her in a kind of prison, one of safety and no risk.

Louisa needed more. She needed everything. A chance to explore the world and not be trapped by her own fears of it.

He was even more determined now to make the family suffer for what they'd done. To him, and to her.

'No one paid for what happened to you.'

'I'm free of it. That's enough.'

'Don't you want to be avenged?'

'I want to forget.'

Yet would she ever really be able to? That kind of thing left scars. She was still trapped by what had happened to her. He saw Easton Hall for what it was: a prison. He could show her a life that was something else. Something new to see every day. One on the move. He was an expert. In the meantime, if she wanted some forgetting, he could help with that too. He tamped his anger. Tried to remember that this night was all about her.

'We *were* here to celebrate you and your achievements.'

It was hard to tell under the magical string lights and in the candlelight, but he thought she might have blushed. She seemed to glow more rosily in the soft light.

'I guess we were, small though they are.'

'Don't undersell yourself. Your illustrations are magnificent.'

Now he was *sure* she blushed, her cheeks flushing a beautiful dusky shade. He didn't think it had anything to do with the cute pictures of frogs he'd seen. He bet it had everything to do with the other pictures. The erotic ones. Darker. No whimsy about them. All passion.

Then something changed in the mood of the evening. A switch, as if their sharing had opened a door of secrets, letting out deeper desires. He took another sip of champagne. Tried to shut the sensation down yet what he'd seen seemed to breach his barriers. She'd said she didn't want to get married. Her pictures were ones of passion. What if intimacy was what she wanted, without messy and inconvenient emotion?

'Thank you. It's something I love, imagining that my drawings are bringing joy to children.'

She was lying to herself if that was what she thought they were talking about here. But he could see it. Children would adore her with her beautiful flowing dresses, her fiery copper hair. Looking like one of the magical creatures she'd drawn. They'd flock to her. He didn't know why that left a pang in his chest. A sense of...nostalgia almost. It made no sense, so he didn't dwell.

'Do you have any other projects?'

'Nothing immediate. I have some time to myself now.'

That was perfect. They were here, now, yet there was a whole world waiting out there for her. Properties everywhere. All the time he needed to show her what she was missing.

Course after course materialised. Magnificent dishes local to the area. More champagne, which she'd begun to savour. The little bubbles tingling her tongue, the sensation like happiness sparkling through her. Something between them had changed over the meal. They'd each given of themselves. Shared their pain.

'A burden shared is a burden halved.' That was what Mae used to say. Louisa had never believed it before. She'd carried her burdens close because the telling had been too painful, but now?

It was as if a veil had lifted. The night appeared somehow brighter, everything around her seemed to gleam.

She ate the last mouthful of a magnificent dessert. Pannacotta. It melted on her tongue and she moaned.

'I'm guessing you enjoyed that?' Matteo said, his voice a little deeper, in a way, somehow raw.

'The whole meal, everything. Tonight. Thank you.'

'It's what you deserve. Never doubt that.'

If only she could believe it. Sometimes, the demons still dwelled close. That was what her dreams were about, which was why she drew them. When viewed in the daytime they seemed to have less impact.

'I don't think I'd be able to fit in a dinner like that too often. I feel like I could almost roll all the way home.'

Home...it was the first time she'd really thought about any place other that Easton Hall in that way. But Matteo's Lake Como mansion wasn't hers. It was just a place to lay her head. Wasn't it?

'If you're done, we can go. Walk. As you said, it's not far.'

'I—I'd like that.'

She relished the idea, because she didn't really want the night to end. She had a fear that if it did, she'd lose something that she'd never get back.

Matteo stood and moved to her chair, helping her pull it out. A prickle of awareness shivered down her spine, pleasure at his closeness. She shut her eyes for a moment, simply absorbing the sensation.

'It's a date.'

It wasn't. She needed to remind herself, once again, that it was something people just said. A turn of phrase.

But a date was exactly what she wanted this to be. She wanted it all, whatever 'all' was. A yearning simply overtook her, for the things that a young woman who'd had a normal kind of life with a loving family might experience. She'd never grieved it before, but she did now. Because her life had been about survival, getting through each day without fear. It had never been about her other needs being met.

It was as if those locked-in emotions began spilling out around her. That was the problem with sharing them. It was hard to stuff those errant feelings back in when the sharing ended.

They left the restaurant after saying their goodbyes and she felt almost giddy. The sensation unfamiliar, till she realised that it was something like happiness. Or perhaps it was just the champagne. Whereas once, all she'd wanted to do was melt into the shadows like a little mouse, now she craved to skip down the streets in a way that would draw attention to herself. To laugh out loud and not care who was watching.

She didn't feel like a mouse now.

Night had settled solidly over the town. The streets still awash with people. Some local. Some tourists. Eating at cafés. Talking. There was music, a jaunty kind of folk tune. Singing in the distance. People coming alive as she felt. She and Matteo ambled in silence as she took in the wonder of it all. The cobbled streets, the stone buildings. Geraniums and petunias blooming in pots.

'This is a gorgeous place.'

'I'm glad you like it.'

'With your Italian heritage, will you keep looking for your birth parents?'

He shrugged. 'I'm unsure. I was trying to find out about myself, my history. The Bainbridges love their family stories. Mine. My *real* story, became…important somehow.'

The Bainbridge family had never been titled. Their money derived from trade, a brickworks in the distant past, which meant, no matter how much money they held, they had always been seen as something less. Yet their once vast riches meant power, and that power opened doors. Tarnished now by poor management and a belief that things would always remain the same. Riches squandered.

But the power, it notionally remained.

It had never been used for anything good. And it hadn't saved her. The family name and preserving it was everything to the Bainbridges. Anything that might risk it was discarded, even people. Children, like her and Matty.

'Sometimes I think you can know too much.'

'I knew so little,' Matteo said. 'Apart from being dropped off at a hospital with a slip of paper pinned to my clothes, naming me Matteo. I suppose it was a kindness my adoptive parents kept my name. Or perhaps it meant they never really saw me as their family in the first place.'

'I'm sorry,' she said. They'd left the town centre now,

moving towards the lake. 'But I think family's more than what you were born into. Anyhow, you can make your own.'

'I don't want a family. From past experience, they're vastly overrated. I prefer being on my own.'

She laughed, acknowledging the truth of that statement. 'Yeah. They are, aren't they?'

They began laughing together.

'We shouldn't, you know,' she said, through giggles. Wiping tears from her cheeks. 'It's not really something to laugh about.'

'Better that than cry, Lulu.'

He'd used her nickname. A warmth settled over her as she wiped the tears of mirth away, bittersweet though they were because they were born of a shared pain. An *understanding* settling between them.

'What if I'm crying from laughing?' she asked, and they both laughed some more.

When had life ever been so much fun? She'd enjoyed the days tourists came to Easton Hall. Dressing up like one of the past women of the house. Showing people round. Answering questions. But she could never remember a time where her life seemed suffused with simple happiness like this.

They began to walk down a slope. Her shoes slipped a little. Matteo steadied her. 'Take my hand. I don't want you to fall.'

She slid hers into his and Matteo simply *engulfed* her. His strength, his solidity. A breeze caught them as they strolled hand in hand along the roadway back to his villa. The air sweet with the drifting scent of citrus blossom. She looked up as they left the lights of the town, a few stars winking in the sky. The moon, bright and bold. Lighting their way.

It was perfect.

It's not a date.

Though what did it matter if she pretended, just for a little while? She'd never go on a real date, and imagining didn't hurt anybody. As always, her imagination had been the safest place for her to reside.

'On a moonlit night you get a beautiful view of the lake from a balcony upstairs. When we get back home, would you like to see it?'

He'd used the word home again. It struck her that it was the first time he'd said it in a way that didn't seem pejorative.

'I'd love to.'

The large iron gates of the villa loomed in the distance. They made their way to the house then he led her upstairs to a private balcony she'd not visited before. The lake lay ahead of them, an inky mark on the landscape. Along its edge, towns and little villages glittered. Lights weaving up the hillsides like threads of silver and gold stitched into the landscape. The moon rose high in the sky, painting a silver stripe on the rippling surface of the water.

She stood there, her hands on the balustrade. Giddy with it all.

'This is so beautiful.'

A breeze picked up; swirling round them. She clutched at her wrap and shivered. Not from the cold as such, but from…she didn't know. It overwhelmed her. The dinner, this. So perfect. So romantic.

The emotion of it all. The need pulsing through her with every heartbeat.

When had someone cared for her like this? As if she was a woman, and not something fragile and breakable. Broken.

'You cold?' Matteo asked, shrugging off his jacket. Draping it gently round her shoulders. 'Here.'

The residual warmth in the clothing left from his body

seeped into her. The scent of him, rich spice, enveloping her. Going to her head. Matteo drew her close, then. Gently, almost reverently. Wrapped his arms loosely round her. She didn't know what to do with any of it, but the way he felt... Strong, solid. Louisa relaxed into his arms. Placed her head on his chest. Closed her eyes. Allowed herself to imagine that this meant more. That it could go further.

Allowed herself to simply *want*.

Heaven and hell were this, standing here in the silvery moonlight with Louisa, soft and pliant. Relaxing into his body. As she nestled into him, he was struck by a startling sensation. In his arms was where she was meant to be. He didn't want to let her go.

His body reacted in a way that he might have said was an inevitability, holding a beautiful woman. All the while a voice inside tried to tell him this was not right. He had a job to do here. She was work, another responsibility.

None of it mattered.

Everything about this was as right as a moment could be. Yet something niggled in the recesses of his brain. A warning that things were about to change.

What was life without change? As far as he was concerned, it remained the only constant. Anyhow, Louisa needed some care. Some kindness. He could never have imagined the deprivations she'd suffered. A little girl, losing her father. Hurt by her mother. Yet the family had tried to convince her to stay silent to preserve the Bainbridge name?

They were rotten to the core whilst pretending to be good. How many of them saw what was happening to her and simply ignored it? The volcanic sensation bubbled inside. Rage at the injustice of it all. The need to avenge what had happened to her rising up like magma inside of him. His arms tightened around her, drawing her even closer and then the heat turned into something else. A flame that simply flicked to life inside him like a pilot light. Desire for something else.

For *her*.

He couldn't unsee her fantasies inked into the pages of a book. Running like a film reel through his head. She was an adult with wants too and it seemed she'd been denying them for years. Living a solitary life in the country, hidden away. Jewels like her shouldn't be hidden. They should be brought out to sparkle. He could show her *everything*. Her hand lay on his chest, thumb gently stroking him. Did she even realise it? The way she was pressed into him, as if wanting to meld into his body? She might be an innocent, but she had desires. He wanted her. What did it matter if she wanted him too?

She shifted in his arms. He loosened his hold as she lifted her head from his chest. Louisa looked pale and ethereal in the moonlight. Wearing his jacket. Something primal and possessive gripped him.

'I can't thank you enough for tonight,' she murmured. Her voice somehow lower, huskier. The sound arrowing right through him. His arousal sharp, all-encompassing.

She shouldn't give him thanks. He was a bastard, both literally and figuratively. A cold, hard businessman who knew what he wanted and took it. People respected him and sometimes cursed him, but never gave him thanks. He found he wanted it, wanted hers, all for himself.

They were so close. The moment perfect and fragile, bathed by the magical moonlight, where it seemed anything could happen. Her hands smoothed over his chest. Almost as if she was trying him out. The slow slide over his pectorals and up to his shoulders where they rested.

He was hard. Aching. Matteo had sampled the earthly delights of any number of women and he knew the signs that someone wanted him. Yet part of him was all uncertainty, when uncertainty was something he didn't do. For some reason he knew that she had to take what she wanted from him. Make the first move. His instincts had served him too well to ignore that if he tried to push too hard the night would end.

He wanted this to be only the beginning.

Not of a relationship, but of an awakening for Louisa. If she could just open herself. To life…to him, she'd see what more she could have, and it would change her whole world.

'You deserve all things good, Lulu. Never doubt that. You've denied yourself enough.'

'You think?'

'I know.'

He gently circled his thumb on her lower spine, and she trembled in his arms, pressed herself against him once more. She'd feel what she did to him. There was no hiding it. She flexed her hips against him and if he hadn't already been standing in the moonlight under the night sky, he might have seen stars. Her little gasp, the soft intake of breath, was better than the music of an angelic chorus. He'd never experienced desire like it. Something lit inside him with a rush, like fuel to a bonfire.

'It's time to ask for what you want, then take it,' he said, his voice rough with need. Yet he knew the value of waiting. The benefit of gentle to break down walls rather than hitting everything head-on, with a sledgehammer. He was a patient man, and he could wait for her.

'Be brave, Lulu.'

Be brave…

She was in the arms of a man that she could no longer deny she was attracted to with a relentless craving. She'd pretended her interest was somehow detached, that he was a magnificent man but that it didn't really affect her, that what she saw in him was somehow removed from who she was. Somehow...academic.

All lies.

Louisa wanted him with a ferocity that should make her afraid. He wanted her too. There was no mistaking how she affected him and that gave her a surge of something that felt a lot like power, when her whole life she'd been powerless.

Not any more. This man did things to her. Lit a fuse that made her come alive in his arms. She wanted more of it, needed it like her next breath of air, like the food on her plate.

Ask for what you want, then take it.

Him.

How did she ask for that? This was all new to her. Old fears began to chatter away in her head. That she didn't know what she was doing. That she'd make a fool of herself. Louisa refused to listen to them, listening to her instinct instead.

She wanted to thank him, so she'd give him a kiss.

He towered above her and she felt so protected in his arms. Holding her as though he cradled something precious. Moving slightly, she stood up on her toes. Pressed her lips to his. Unlike the last time their lips touched he didn't move. His mouth soft against hers. She wasn't sure what else to do now, so she lingered for a few moments, hoping, before breaking away.

He'd done nothing, so that was that. Her great experiment. She could tick that off the list. Kissing Matteo twice. Brilliant.

Then he smiled. It was a slow metamorphosis into wickedness, the way his lips curled in that knowing way of his. He lowered his head to her as she tilted her head up. Hoping and praying that he was going to kiss her back. Instead, he moved his lips to her ear. Said nothing for a moment, seemed to simply breathe her in as if he wanted to absorb her. His breath caressing the side of her neck, making her tremble with desire.

'Do you want me to kiss you back?' he murmured.

She hadn't asked for what she wanted. Now he was forcing her to tell him. The whole of her was a pinpoint of yearning. Her breasts ached, nipples hard points in her bra. Needing his touch to soothe them. She'd thought she'd known emptiness, but she'd had no idea. This. Imagining him filling her. It was like an obsession, a drumbeat pounding inside.

She knew what would happen if she said yes, and she didn't care. It was time to be brave.

'Yes.'

He moved then. His nose gently drifting over the soft skin behind her ear. The sensation overwhelming her. She relaxed into his arms as he slid one hand onto her backside, drawing her close and flush against the hardness of him. Then his lips began to move, skimming over her neck. The tip of something slick and smooth drifting over her skin, then cool air. His tongue. As if he was tasting her.

Matteo gave...not a moan as such, but a pained exhale. It mirrored her own.

He lifted his lips from her body and looked down at her. His gaze almost assessing. She knew what this was, a pause to allow her to say stop. No. She didn't want him to stop. She wanted this moment to never end.

After a few heartbeats his assessment, or whatever it was, ended. He dropped his head and simply *claimed* her.

She'd marvelled at how soft his lips were on such an un-compromising man, but there was nothing soft about the kiss as his mouth took hers. Her own began to move, like instinct. Wanting more, wanting everything. His tongue teased her lips and she opened to him, letting him in. An entrée to the main meal. Somehow, he managed to make the kiss so many things. Coaxing, encouraging, demanding. She simply fell into it. Let it overtake her. Rejoicing at his hardness against her softness.

Then the kiss slowed, but she chased more. What if that was all she got tonight? Her body was ready to fuse with him. To become part of him. It was as if she'd die if she didn't. Needing him to fill her.

He gave a wicked, low chuckle that rippled right through Louisa's body. It could have sounded mocking except for his arousal pressing, insistent, against her. She'd done that to him. Made this uncompromising man want *her*. Matteo traced a finger down the side of her face, her neck, the top of her chest, a light, feather-like stroke. Barely there yet it set her on fire. Her nipples burned as that finger made its way lower, towards the top of her breast and then…

It stopped. She whimpered. Wanton and needy.

'Am I neglecting you? Do you need something more?' He leaned in, his lips close to her ear. 'Do you want me to stroke your nipples, ease their ache? Make you come?'

His breath feathered over her throat as he kissed there. A hand sliding up her waist to rest just under her left breast, waiting for permission.

'Yes. Please.'

His lips found hers again as his left arm drew her close once more and his right…it slid up, the lightest of brushes over her nipple, which beaded and tightened under his ministrations, heat spearing between her legs. Setting her on fire.

Could she come like this? In the dark of night when she allowed the fantasies from her drawings to overtake her, her own orgasms seemed to be hard-fought yet in some way feeble and lacking.

Now, she was overwhelmed by the sensation. The conflicting feeling of being so full yet so empty, all at the same time. He kept stroking her nipple, and she began to move against him, wanting and wanting…just *more*. It was like the most exquisite torture. She didn't know how she'd survive it. Didn't know if she even wanted to. Any desire for self-preservation simply fled under his talented hands and mouth. In this moment she would have done anything for him.

There was no slowing, he simply tore his lips from hers, breaths coming in heavy gusts. Her own lips well used, plump and tingling.

'I want you. I want everything.' He growled as if the words were wrenched from him, almost sounding inhuman with the need he clearly felt himself.

The power of that tore through her. That she could do this to a man who no doubt had vast experience. Who could likely have the pick of any woman he wanted, and still he wanted *her*. She stood at a crossroads. All her life had been about safety. Being a passenger. Now, she wanted to take control. To take something for herself.

Matteo. She wanted him. She'd had so little voice of her own, as a child. Trying to find it as a broken teenager. Yet even into adulthood she'd held something back. No longer.

'I want everything, too.'

'And what do you think "everything" is?'

He was making her say it, be explicit. So there'd be no

misunderstanding. If she made this choice, it was because she'd voiced her desire openly, with clarity of mind.

She'd never wanted anything more.

'Sex. You.'

His exhale sounded part pained, part relieved. 'Take my hand.'

He held his out. Another choice between yes and no. There was only one answer tonight. Yes, always yes. She slipped her own hand into his without hesitation. Greedy for his touch. His grip as he curled his fingers round hers firm but gentle.

Matteo led her back the way they'd come. Through the doors from the balcony overlooking the lake, inside. Her legs barely carried her, weak with need. Time slowed, as if she moved through syrup. Such sweet anticipation with the spicy thrill of something else.

Desire.

Then Matteo stopped. Was he having second thoughts? Instead, he turned to her. 'This isn't fast enough.'

He swung her into his arms as if she weighed nothing. The sensation of being cradled, held in his strong arms, an overwhelming one. Like the night he carried her out of Easton Hall. Saving her. Yet this night, there was none of the fear. Only anticipation. In that moment as he strode through the villa, it was as if she was the most precious, cherished being on earth.

They crossed the threshold to a room she presumed was his bedroom, light to semi-darkness. Only illuminated by the moonlight through the windows and a glow from his en suite bathroom. He set her feet on the floor but he didn't let her go, as if knowing that she needed to be held, or she might sink into the carpet in a puddle of desire.

Whilst she could combust from the *wanting*, Louisa had

to tell him. That no matter what those drawings might have implied, she was a virgin. Yet what if he hadn't realised, didn't want her?

Be brave.

'I've never done this before,' she whispered.

His arms tightened around her for a moment, as if to comfort.

'I know. Don't worry, I'll be careful.'

His words made her feel somehow…lacking. She wasn't some porcelain doll that could be broken easily. 'I—I don't want careful.'

She wanted…wild. Unfettered. Untamed. Something that took her out and away from herself. Made her feel like a woman.

'Then I'll take care. Do you want more lights on?'

She hadn't thought of that. She wanted to see him with his shirt off. His muscles, his own desire as he looked at her. But something else made her hesitate. Would he judge her, her body? No doubt he was experienced. Would he find her in some way lacking?

Her mind raced.

'I can hear you thinking, Lulu. So I'll take it the answer is negative. How about you relax and I make the decisions for a while? If there's anything you don't like, you can say no, and we stop.'

She nodded, her heart a pounding ache in her chest. Not of fear, but of anticipation. He took his jacket from her shoulders and tossed it onto a chair. Unhitched the chain belt from round her waist and dropped it to the floor. Grabbed the sides of her dress and pulled it, ever so slowly, over her head where it followed her belt. Then he unclipped her bra, eased the straps over her shoulders and cast it aside. She hesitated, wanting to raise her arms. Cover herself.

'No. Never hide your beauty. Stand proud. Let me look at you.'

She did. Arms by her side as he stood back and simply stared.

'You're magnificent,' he said, his voice rough with promise and desire. 'Lie on the bed.'

She did as he asked. Stepping out of her shoes and pulling back the soft covers. Climbing onto a bed that felt like lying on a cloud. But she didn't know how to lie there, in a way that seemed bold. On her back? On her side? Then Matteo pulled off his shirt and any logical thought fled.

The moonlight streaming through the windows illuminated his magnificent torso that looked as if it had been cut out of marble in the cool light. Almost like the statue of David, she'd drawn in her sketch book. Broad shoulders, generous muscles. So magnificent that if he had been a sculpture, the artist would have wept upon its completion. He was every midnight fantasy as he strode to his side of the bed and came to her.

'Your trousers?'

'They'll come off soon enough. For now, it's about you.'

He crawled over the bed like some stalking animal. Kneeled between her thighs. Dropped his head and feathered kisses over her stomach.

'Tonight, I'll kiss every freckle I can see.'

She trembled with need as his kisses drifted lower, till his lips were on her underwear. His breath hot. Breathing her in. He hooked his fingers into her panties. Drew them down her body as goosebumps peppered her skin. Every part of her over-sensitised, as if all of her shimmered with delight at his reverent touch.

'Open your legs.'

His voice was a command she obeyed immediately. Never a question she was going to do what he asked of her.

'I'm going to touch you.'

'Please.'

She'd die if he didn't. Her world became a pinpoint of desire. The agony at the juncture of her thighs she knew only he could ease. He stroked his fingers along her upper thighs, feather-light, and she arched her back. Trying to get closer to him.

'I won't leave you wanting any longer,' he said. Slipping two fingers to her clitoris where she craved him most. Stroking. Circling in a slow, steady rhythm.

'I wish you could see what I'm doing to you. How hot you are. How wet. How desperately your body wants mine inside you.'

She moaned. This was beyond her experience. Alone, in her bedroom, imaging, drawing, had been nothing but two dimensions. This was *all* real. Her breaths coming sharp and fast as the exquisite pleasure of his fingers wound her tighter and higher. He was right. She wanted him inside her, desperate for him to fill the craving deep in her core.

'That's right, Lulu. Open your legs wider, sweetheart. Let me slide one finger inside. See how good it feels. Do you want that?'

Right now, she feared she'd give him everything if he asked it of her.

'Yes, yes. Please.' Her voice breathless, barely able to make the words.

His clever fingers left her clitoris and she moaned again.

'So needy for me,' he said, almost sounding reverent.

She arched her back again as one of his fingers toyed with her entrance. 'This is going to feel so good. I promise.'

He slid a finger deep inside her and moaned himself. 'So hot. My God. Lulu. Feel what you do to me.'

He took her free hand in his, pressed it to the crotch of his trousers. The thick, hard length there. She whimpered. The size of him. Her body flushed as if fevered. He flexed his hips into her hand.

'Soon. But I need to make sure you're ready.'

'I am. Please. Right now,' she chanted. The ecstasy held just out of reach, driving her on. It didn't matter how big he felt, all fear fled in the face of this need.

'You won't be ready till you're only capable of sobbing my name.'

It sounded like a promise wound in an erotic threat. Another flush of goosebumps shivered over her.

'Now, let's get started on that. Feel this?' He did something inside her, found a spot with one finger that tore through her like an electric shock. Unbidden, a wail of pleasure ripped from her.

He chuckled, low and dark like some evil genius. Which she was coming to believe him to be, the way he manipulated her body.

'Two fingers now. Would you like that, Lulu? More?'

'Yes,' she said on a sigh. Barely able to voice words now, meaning he was on his way to make good his promise that she'd only be able to say his name. He slid one finger out and then there was a little more pressure as he inserted another, in and out, in and out as if testing her body.

'I want you to be ready. I want this to be good for you.'

Every part of her trembled, balancing on a terrifying precipice. Her breaths coming in sharp gasps.

'You're so beautiful. So perfect like this. So soft. Almost there, almost ready. So close.'

Then he did something inside again. Curled his fingers.

Found the spot. 'I'll keep giving you what you need. We have all night. I won't stop. I promise. Don't fight this. You're on the edge. I'll look after you. Just let yourself fall.'

Her body shook as she fought to do exactly what he asked of her. That edge was so close, yet just out of reach. The torture inside her relentless, his fingers not letting up on their sensual assault.

'Come for me, Lulu.'

Matteo dropped his head, his mouth to her clitoris, licking, sucking, and she was torn in two, sobbing. Tears streaming down her cheeks as she cried out his name over and over.

Matteo drew Louisa close, holding her in his arms as she wept, gasping his name. The desire, craving her, needing her, warring with his need to give her this time to absorb the pleasure that had overwhelmed her. A voice in the back of his head whispered that he should feel guilty for what he'd done. But how could he feel guilt when it was all about pleasure? Showing Lulu the things she'd missed in her life. Sharing this with her.

He stroked his hand over her, murmuring that she was beautiful and perfect, till her sobs stopped and she drew back, kissing him. Her mouth fervent on his own. Demanding, desperate. He returned the kiss, her lips luscious and soft. Her hands tugging at his trousers, sliding over his skin as she tried to get closer.

He pulled back. 'Do you want more?'

'I want it all.'

Her voice was still tremulous, breathy. Breaking with emotion. It should have screamed a warning but the only chant in his head was yes. *Yes.*

He stood, undid his trousers, slower than he wanted but

this was for her, a show. Time for her to back away. Louisa watched him, her eyes widened, but now gleaming with desire in the soft light, as her gaze tracked over him. He felt it, her appreciation. Firm as the stroke of her fingers against his flesh. When had it ever meant so much?

Matteo dropped his trousers, his underwear. Kicked them aside and stood, naked. She gasped and he wasn't sure what her sharp intake of breath meant. Desire? Fear? He clenched his fists, flexed his fingers. Waiting a few seconds for her to say something again. Then she licked her lips and the simple move almost unstitched his tight control right in front of her. He wanted to pounce on her, devour her, rather than taking the tender care that she deserved. He moved to the bedside table, grabbed a condom. Tore the wrapper with haste but sheathed himself slowly as she watched him roll it down his length, her lips parted. Lying there on the covers, her skin pale. Her freckles in beautiful relief like a thousand stars sprinkled over her.

He crawled back onto the bed, stalking towards her. She gripped the covers as if they were the only thing stopping her from grabbing him. He hungered for her touch. Matteo lay beside her, stroked his hand between her breasts. 'I need to be inside you.'

'I need that too.'

Matteo kissed her, his lips gentle caresses over hers, till she deepened it. He let her lead for a while, before taking over. Wanting to show her more pleasure than she'd ever dreamed. To be the only man...

No. He was the *first* man.

This was her start, not her ending. He was only showing her what was there for her, how life could be for a woman like her out in the world. Yet why did something dark and possessive overtake him in that moment? A craving to lock her away, keep her to himself. Keep her safe.

He ignored it. This was all about her freedom, not an imprisonment. He eased a hand between her legs and they opened for him once more. Checking to see she still remained wet, ready for him. Then he moved over her, notched himself at her entrance, looking into the green pools of her eyes.

'You're so beautiful. I want to make this good for you.'

He began to ease inside, watching her for any hint of pain. Her eyelids fluttered shut as he moved, rocking into her. Deeper and deeper with each gentle thrust into the tight, hot depths of her till he could go no further. He groaned on her corresponding sob. The glory of it, unlike anything he'd experienced, like his first time it seemed so new.

Then he began to move and for a moment she lay there, hands flexing over his back. Till she began to move with him, as if driven by instinct.

'Good?' he asked, the word grinding out of him.

'So good.'

They were the words he wanted to hear and he lost himself in the rhythm of their bodies. His mind blank to anything bar the biting pleasure. Her smooth skin. Her breathy sighs. His body wound itself tighter and higher as he thrust harder. Her movements becoming faster, un-coordinated. Her breathing more desperate as he drove her towards the edge again.

'Take your pleasure, Lulu. Take what's yours.'

She stiffened. Her fingers digging into his back as she pulsed round him on a wail. His mind blanked in a burst of white light and blistering pleasure as his orgasm burned through him like an electric shock. Wiping him clean.

CHAPTER TEN

LOUISA HELD ON TO Matteo's hand as he helped her from the boat on his private dock. They'd spent the morning motoring about the lake. He'd taken her to see the village of Nesso, with its waterfall and Roman bridge. She'd watched as some tourists leaped into the lake for a perfect social-media moment, swimming and laughing. They'd explored Bellagio and strolled along the waterfront under sweetly flowering nerium, eating gelati in the sunshine.

How her life had changed since spending the night with Matteo. This need for him all-consuming. In the next few days after that first explosive evening, rather than exploring round the lake they'd spent their time exploring each other. Their bodies like undiscovered countries they needed to map with lips and hands.

She could never have imagined this life for herself, when the thought of even walking to the village round Easton Hall had filled her with a kind of foreboding. Something about telling Matteo about what had happened to her, that sharing, had released something inside her. How he'd pushed her just a little, had changed everything.

He'd talked about taking her to Paris, where something was happening with one of his hotels that might need his personal attention. Each day she found another place in the world he had a hotel or retreat, another place he'd explored.

He hadn't mentioned his quest to turn Easton Hall into another of his hotels. Perhaps he no longer saw the need? Life seemed so full and bursting with happiness.

'I have a challenge for you,' he said, pulling her from her thoughts.

'What sort of challenge?'

After settling her on the dock he smiled, and it made her warmer than the sunshine in which they stood. That smile of his could chase away all darkness.

'You'll see. I think you might like it.'

He took her hand again, so strong and secure. It was hard to know when she began to think of him like that. A place of safety rather than the man who wanted to take everything away from her. A pang almost like pain struck her belly. She wouldn't think about it. He hadn't mentioned anything. After what they'd spoken of, he must now under-stand why Easton Hall was so important to her. Anyhow, she'd overheard him talking on the phone to someone about repairs. Surely that meant they could return home soon?

As much as she loved the small slice she'd seen of Italy, Matteo's villa in Como, Louisa still yearned for that place to go back to. Cool and green. The place where her forma-tive happy memories had been made.

'I can hear you thinking again,' Matteo said. 'Remem-ber, you can always say no.'

That shook her from her introspection. The thing was, she didn't want to say no. Her life had been cloistered. Louisa realised how stuck she'd been and now she wanted to catch up. Experience what other girls at her school had talked about, before her imaginary illness had taken over her life. Travels with their families, dreams of kissing boys, adventures…she was making up for years of lost time. She said no so often, to invitations from people in the village, to the young man at the grocer's who'd asked her for a coffee once. She wanted her life to be full of yes.

'I trust you,' she said and squeezed his hand. He squeezed back. Instead of going to the house he led her through the gardens to an open-sided pavilion, surrounded by marble columns. Inside lay a gleaming blue swimming pool the colour of the sky, the water sparkling in the sunlight.

'I thought you might like to learn how to swim, or, at least, to get in the water and see what it's like.'

He'd kept his promise. When they'd first arrived here, she hadn't believed he would. But now...tears stung her eyes. He remembered. He hadn't forgotten.

Matteo let go of her hand and pulled his polo shirt over his head, tossing it onto a recliner that sat on the tiled surface surrounding the pool.

'Do you want to try?'

Her mouth dried. Would she ever get over the look of him? That caramel-brown skin, so different against her own. The hair smattering his chest, arrowing down to beneath the waistband of his shorts. Those muscles, ridged and rippling across his torso. She wanted to keep looking. She wanted to touch. Except...

'I don't have a swimming costume.'

'What a shame.' His grin in response was pure wickedness. 'Do you need one?'

She stilled, flooding with heat. The thought of him and her, bodies slick against one another. Then reality bit.

'People might see.'

'There's no one around. My staff have the afternoon off. If you don't want to, I'll just take a quick swim and we can do something else.'

He unbuckled his belt, undid his shorts and pushed them

down. She'd almost hoped he'd be naked but he wore black swimming trunks underneath.

She nodded to him. 'That seems hardly fair.'

He laughed. 'Life's not fair, Lulu.'

He strolled to a panel on the wall and pushed a button. Louvres of the pavilion ceiling closed halfway. 'The sun's bright. I don't want you to burn.'

His thoughtfulness, it almost undid her. She could dissolve on the spot, right here. Matteo didn't seem to be aware of how he affected her. He turned and dived into the gleaming water. Swimming a lap of the pool under the surface before coming up at the other end then swimming back to her in freestyle, powerful strokes slicing through the water. When he reached the end he stood, water to his waist. Dripping from him like diamonds. Shook his head then ran his hands through his hair.

'Coming in?'

She looked out into the secluded garden. She caught a glimpse of the lake from here, but it was mainly hidden by shrubs. Nobody would see her other than him. Her heart thumped a skittish rhythm, something like nerves. He'd seen her naked before, and after the things they'd done she wasn't sure why nerves should hit her as if she were an innocent all over again. But she'd promised herself that she'd be open to these new experiences. Her hair was in a long plait today, so she didn't have to worry about it getting knotted. There were really no excuses other than her own fears, so she took a deep breath, kicked off her shoes, grabbed her dress and pulled it over her head.

His wicked smile fell away. His mouth, partly open. A look crossed his face then, something far more intense and focussed. Desire written all over him. Her nipples beaded. All of her flushing under his admiring gaze.

'The stairs are right there.'

His voice ran rough across his skin as he pointed to the side of the pool. She unclipped her pretty lace bra. Wriggled out of her matching panties. Walked to the water's edge and put her toes in, the water cool against her over-heated skin. Then she stepped ankle deep, down further to knee deep, then to mid-thigh.

Matteo held out both of his hands as she hesitated, trying to recall the few times she'd ever been in a pool before, experiencing the mix of joy at the feel of the water against her skin with the terror of what would happen if she went under.

'I won't let you go.'

'I know.'

She took both his hands as he walked backwards, and she stepped off. It wasn't deep here, yet her mother's voice kept whispering in her ear. *'What if you drown?'*

She tried to shut out the words. Matteo wouldn't let anything happen to her.

'What are you thinking?'

'How do you know I'm thinking anything at all?'

'You get a tiny frown, here.' He stroked a finger in the middle of her forehead. A tiny drop of water fell on her face from his fingers. He gently swiped it away.

'My mother told me not to swim. She always asked what would happen if she wasn't there and I drowned.'

Matteo grunted. 'That woman shouldn't invade any of your thinking time. She never cared about what was best for you. I'm prepared to work diligently to make sure you forget what she's said to you.'

He drew her towards him, arms around her. His mouth descending on hers in a slow luxurious kiss she fell into, pressed against his body. The heat of him, the cool of the water. Delicious, conflicting sensations. Pressed together, she sensed him harden against her.

He pulled away, his breath coming hard and fast matching her own.

'I said I'd teach you to swim.'

'You did.'

'Let me take you deeper.'

She was already in way over her head. She tried not to think about what all of this meant. It probably meant nothing at all. She hadn't ever expected to have any kind of relationship. Love equalled loss, a dark and tangled web where those two things were inextricably entwined.

Though why she should be thinking about love right in this very moment, she wasn't sure. Love had no place here. He'd been clear he didn't want it, and neither did she. This, sex, it was enough.

He walked back and back, cradling her in his arms.

'Okay?'

She nodded.

'I did some research,' he said.

The idea that he'd investigated teaching her how to swim, spending time she'd not known about, planning this for her, struck her as more than considerate. It showed that he cared. That he was beginning to understand what she needed.

'What did you find out?'

'That you need to learn how to float first. How about you lie on your back, and I'll support you?'

He helped her ease back in the water, his hands gentle against her body. Even though she knew he'd keep her safe, her breaths came a little too fast.

'I'll keep hold of you. Put your arms out. Try to relax,' he said and she did, looking up into slivers of blue sky through the louvres in the pavilion roof as she floated. The water caressing her naked skin as Matteo moved slowly about the shallow end. She shut her eyes for a moment, sound muffled by the water. Simply drifting on trust as he supported her.

'I'm going to let you go for a moment,' he said. 'I'll always be here, but you can do this on your own.'

His hands left her body for a few seconds, and she lay still in the water. No panic. No fear. Only trust that nothing would happen to her if Matteo was by her side. She didn't know how long she lay there, till his hands returned under her shoulders. Louisa opened her eyes, meeting with Matteo's own. He bent down, brushing his lips against hers.

'There was a terrible flaw in my plan,' he said. Shifting to lift her from the water up against him.

'What's that?'

'You're naked, and I want you.'

His arms snaked around her, pulling her flush against him. She wrapped her arms round his neck, her legs round his waist. He supported her as his lips met hers and they kissed. Deep and lush. She notched against his body, hard and ready. The friction delicious.

'I should be a better man,' he said as she tried to catch her breath.

'You are that man. I don't know why you don't realise it.'

He dropped his head to hers. 'There are things you shouldn't forget, Lulu. I didn't get to where I am without getting everything I wanted. Every time. Nothing stood in my way.'

But she was sure he hadn't found everything he wanted. He was looking for his birth family and hadn't found them. Had accepted he never would. She suspected he wanted a real family despite his denials. He didn't have that either. Matteo struck her as a man who was searching, and she wondered if he even realised what he was looking for.

'You can have what you want from me. I'm not standing in your way.'

His nostrils flared. Of course, she was talking about sex, but it was fun for a moment to be held here and believe that the possibilities were endless.

'Be careful what you offer me. You might find I take it, and I don't have much to offer you in return.'

She wished he could see just how much he had. How kind he'd been to her. And yet she didn't think he'd want to hear it, when it was clear there were things he couldn't accept about himself.

She flexed against him, and his eyes darkened to the richest of warm chocolates.

'You have exactly what I need right here, right now.'

He groaned and crashed his lips onto hers once more as she lost herself in the rhythm of his kiss.

CHAPTER ELEVEN

LOUISA SAT IN the warm morning sunshine on a sheltered patio overlooking the lake. She closed her eyes, relishing Matteo's gentle touch. The way his fingers threaded through her damp hair, separating the strands so they could dry.

'We should go inside soon; I don't want you to burn.'

'Just a little while longer,' she said, breathing in the scent of lavender that drifted on the breeze, which she'd always now remember as the smell of summer. Relaxing further as he stroked down her back. If she were a cat, she might start purring.

'It's like silk on fire,' he murmured as if to himself. 'Magnificent.'

'My family were hoping for the Bainbridge blonde.'

Matteo grunted. 'What have I told you about anything they had to say?'

Louisa opened her eyes. Stared out across the lake, like a well of blue ink on the landscape.

'To forget them. I do, mostly...'

Some days, the voice in her head could be persistent. Though around Matteo, the negative chatter had less power. His praise and his words tended to drown them out till they held no more irritation than a gnat she could swat away.

'*Mostly* should become *always*. They didn't deserve you.'

His grip on her hair gently tightened. Drawing her head back as she smiled. Goosebumps shimmered over her as his mouth descended on hers.

She opened for him. Their tongues touching, the kiss deepening. Each day seemed like a kind of miracle. A dream she didn't want to wake from. *This* was far better than any reality she'd ever lived in. And Louisa knew reality would have to intrude eventually, but she had time. There were no pressing deadlines. She could continue to drift in this warm, sunshine-filled fantasy for a while longer.

Matteo's phone vibrated on the table close by, drawing her from the moment. An interruption from the world that wasn't polite enough to stop for them. She drew away.

'Take it. I know you have a business to run. I'll be here when you get back.'

He smiled and it was warmer than any sunshine she might be sitting in. 'I'll hold you to that,' he said as he grabbed the phone and wandered into the house.

She stood and strolled to the railings of the patio overlooking Lake Como. Little boats skipping across its surface. Louisa had never thought she could love anywhere as much as Easton Hall and its surrounds, but this came close. In the UK, everything was about the safe and familiar. Here? She wondered whether she'd love it without Matteo. Because everything about the villa was bound up in him. This patio, where they had a breakfast under the dappled shade of enormous potted olive trees. Their days filled with exploration of the lake and its surrounds. Nights filled with exploration of each other. A sense of no end date. Just a future with a person not a place…

No, that couldn't be right. No futures had been discussed. Except he had offered to show her the world, his hotels, his retreats. His other houses. *That* was a future of sorts. And their nights, his whispered words in the darkness, of being unable to get enough. Of more, more, *more*. What was that, if not a future? Her heart fluttered against her ribs. Not a sensation of dread but one of excitement, of possibility.

The sun brightened, warmer as the morning aged. Matteo would worry if she burned, so she moved to a large cantilever umbrella he'd had set up here, so she could sit under cover whilst looking out over the lake. That care, that kindness. It meant something, didn't it?

Movement at the door drew her from her introspection. A liquid heat flooded her veins as Matteo stalked through. She couldn't get enough of him. His power. Strength. It all made her feel safe, protected. *Wanted*. She might *never* get enough of him. Except…

The look on his face. Jaw hard. Eyes narrow. His body not lax and loose but strung tense like a bow. Obviously, business was not going well.

'Problem?' she asked.

'The family seek to challenge the will.'

It was as if her heart forgot to beat. Like everything, the breeze, the birds, all…stopped.

'Can they do that?' She could barely get out the words. That they would try to take it all away…

'They've been rattling their sabres. Seems they're finally ready for war.' His fists clenched. Released. Looking as if he was priming for battle. He gave a short, sharp laugh. 'I expected it. They can try. But there's no doubt they'll fail.'

He strode to the balcony, planted his hands on the carved marble balustrade. Looking out over the lake, he reminded Louisa of a king, surveying his domain.

She stood, walked over to him. Her legs almost unable to support her weight. Her insides twisting in painful knots. What if they *were* successful? She'd lose her home. She'd lose everything.

This, here, Matteo's house on Como. She loved it, but it wasn't *home*. She'd be happy to travel, but there was a place of her own she always wanted to know she could come back to. Easton Hall. In that moment, she wanted to return. Ground her feet on the cool green grass, walk through the gardens, by the chalk stream with him. Make a home there, with Matteo. They could still travel together but they'd always have a place. It was then it hit her with a blinding strike of realisation, the endless possibility. How she...

How she *loved* him.

She could be his family. *They* could be a family.

'What if—?'

'No. This is the chance to truly destroy them.' He turned his head towards her, his eyes bright. Almost fevered with a zeal she'd never seen before. 'I own Easton Hall and they'll *never* get it. It *will* become part of my company's property portfolio. Generations will be able to enjoy it but none of them will be a Bainbridge ever again. It will be lost to the family for ever.'

Did he forget? He was a Bainbridge. Her mother had been one too. And there was the not so small matter of her inheritance.

'But...what about me?'

'What about you?'

The words hit her like a slap. She almost reared back. He wasn't thinking of her at all. Hadn't she figured as part of his plan for a future, for anything?

'Easton Hall is my home.'

He snorted. 'You can live anywhere in the world. Pick a place. My hotels, my retreats, they're all available to you, free. Easton Hall is nothing but a crumbling symbol of a family that needs to be shown for what it is. Not paragons of virtue, but fake to the core. A façade for liars and cheats. You should have no interest in it, at all.'

'And yet, Easton Hall is *all* you can think about. You're obsessed with it.'

He wheeled round to stare down at her, nothing on his face other than the hard clutch of fury. 'Obsessed? I want to destroy what it represents. You should too after what was done to you.'

He still couldn't see. This between them was worth fighting for, revenge wasn't. It could only destroy, yet she finally saw a future and understood that love, the right *kind* of love, could build.

'Don't you see, Matteo? You say you don't care about place, don't care about a home, but you do.'

'You think you know me so well. You know nothing.'

She shook her head. He truly couldn't see, so blinded by hatred of a family that wasn't worthy of his time, it obliterated everything else.

'You said my mother shouldn't invade any of my thinking time, yet you're not taking your own advice. Forget the family.'

'*Forget* them?' His eyes were wide, incredulous. A sneer of disbelief on his face. Yet he couldn't see what she could. Louisa needed to make him listen.

'Everything about you yearns to find *your* place. You've been searching for your birth parents. Discovered Italian heritage so bought a house here. What is all of that if not a need to find where you belong in the world?'

She hated the way her voice was so small, lost. Almost

pleading. As though she had no agency here, when she did. She had the right to stay in the home till she decided to leave it permanently, or marry...

Marriage. She realised that with Matteo she wanted *everything*. Louisa reached out, settled her hand on his arm, the whole of him tense, as if one wrong move and he'd shatter. It was a surprise that he didn't pull away from her, but she had to make him see.

'You don't just want it. You *crave* it. Your safe place. Somewhere to call your own...'

Louisa took a deep breath to conquer her fear. To be brave and make her greatest pitch. To the man before her, to the boy he'd once been. To *Matty*. To the universe. To crack open her chest and hand him her heart. Hoping with every beat that he'd take what she was offering him.

Matteo pulled back, began to pace. How couldn't she see? This was his chance. The final hammer blow, and she thought he wouldn't take it? That some nebulous idea like 'home' could stop him? He'd never stop. Not until he got what he had planned for.

'I've told you. I don't *need* any of that.'

Louisa held out her hands, as if imploring him.

'You're lying to yourself. You own retreats. Boutique hotels. Escapes, sure. But they're still places where people live, for a while at least. Ask yourself why that's the business you chose. Why you're so successful. Your company is called Arcadia. I looked up what that means. A place of rustic idyll. Of innocence and pleasure. What does that tell you?'

He shook his head. She was looking for signs that didn't exist.

'It tells me nothing other than it's a lucrative business

and I excel at it. My company's motto isn't "Beyond home, your ultimate haven" for nothing.'

She looked to the heavens, almost like asking for divine guidance. 'For a reason. Matty, can't you see? That just proves my point. You're searching and searching for your *place*, because you're lost. And now you're trying to take away the only home I want. Where I've always been safe. The home I believed I'd live in for the rest of my life.'

She didn't feel safe with him? Her words were like a knife to the gut. Louisa couldn't see. She was still trapped by her past.

'You're a young woman. You need—'

'I need to be where I'm happy. We both do, and I realise where that is. You don't have to search any more. I love you Matty. Make your home with *me*.'

Her words brought him to a halt. His heart pounding a sickening rhythm. No.

'You don't love me.' That was impossible. Matteo knew he should care but couldn't. Not with this sensation of heaviness in his chest. His heart pounding as if it would burst from his ribcage. She'd offered him something he didn't want. That he'd never asked for.

'You don't get to tell me how I feel,' she said. Something about Louisa seemed to crumple, fold in on itself. As if part of her had broken. She turned her back to him, voice cracking. 'And you don't get to tell me what I want out of my life...'

Matteo raked his hands through his hair as that heaviness increased. Squeezing the life out of him. There wasn't enough air to take a breath. 'I thought you'd be the one person who could understand. That family wanted to silence you. Send you back to the woman who hurt you to preserve their pristine name. The family who cast me aside because I wasn't a true Bainbridge, no matter what my adoption made me at law. They're craven and soulless, and they *will* pay.'

Victory was so close he could almost taste it.

She shook her head. 'How do you expect to make them?'

'They want a fight, they'll get it. There are reasons why Mae left the home to me. A right to reside to you. I believe those reasons have everything to do with the way that family treated us. It'll all come out in court, if not before…'

All the colour bled from her face, as if she'd seen a ghost. Her eyes widened.

'How could…how can…? You know what will happen. It'll be splashed all over the press.'

He laughed. That negative press would destroy the family and the image they'd built. The damage would be irreparable.

'It's perfect. They sow the seeds of their own demise. They won't even see it coming till I have them.'

'No!' She slashed her hand through the air, stalking towards him, fists clenched. 'I don't want that story to become who *I* am because that's all anyone will ever remember about me when they hear it. You want to use my pain, what I went through, as fodder to get back at the family I've left in the past. You care about revenge more than you care about me.'

He gritted his teeth. She thought to take it all away from him? What he'd worked at for so many years? For what, some meaningless declaration like *love*? His parents had told him they loved him, and they'd abandoned him when someone better came along. And where had love got her?

'If you cared about *me* at all, loved me as you claim, then you'd understand. But you *don't* love me. That's an illusion.'

Louisa's shoulders slumped. Her chin trembled as she took a shuddering breath. 'I—I thought...but I was wrong. I've told you before I'm not leaving Easton Hall. I thought you'd understood. I won't be a party to this, I can't stay and watch this happen... Because it will destroy everything.'

Louisa turned and began to walk into the house.

'Where do you think you're going?'

She didn't break her stride, kept moving as he followed. 'Away. Anywhere but near you.'

It was as if a weight pressed on him. Relentless. Crushing. Right now, he felt like Atlas, trying to hold up the sky. She wouldn't leave. She *couldn't*.

'You'll *never* survive on your own.'

Louisa stopped then. Turned, slow and deliberate. Head held high. Jaw clenched hard. Eyes narrow, spitting fire.

'Just you watch me.'

Matteo paced through his Como villa, to a window overlooking the lake. The day outside gleaming beautiful and bright. Blue skies and sunshine. A perfect day for exploring the small inlets, villages and surrounding countryside. Yet nothing about this was perfect. In a place he'd always felt settled, nothing seemed to fit any more. *He* didn't fit. It had been a week since Louisa had turned her back and walked away. In his arrogance, he'd been sure she'd return within an hour after she'd left. Then time had ticked by and night had fallen. There'd been no tearful return. Only silence.

A sensation had clawed at him. Fear. That she was alone and he wasn't protecting her as he'd promised. *Damned promises.* He'd gone to the village and searched. Silently stalking the streets and laneways. Visiting the *trattoria* they'd dined in, but she'd melted away. He might have called the police, had he not received a message via his assistant saying Louisa had been in touch to ask that he pack up her things and she'd provide a forwarding address.

That address hadn't yet come. Now thoughts of her plagued him. Was she safe? Did she have enough to eat? How would she cope without her familiar things? His gut wrenched at the worry that she was alone, together with a terrible sense that he'd forgotten something or, even worse, lost something irreplaceable. Because she hadn't walked away and left everything behind. She'd walked away and left *him*.

That distinction was vital.

He'd reflected on their final, terrible conversation. At first not understanding why she couldn't see that every living Bainbridge should be punished for what they'd done. To her, to him. That he had the means to lash out and destroy, as if that would somehow blunt the pain. However, he'd come to realise that the pain had turned inwards and now flayed him alive.

She'd offered him her love, and he'd thrown it back in her face. All because of fear.

Matteo turned away from the view that had once given him peace, and now reminded him of what he'd lost. He'd convinced himself that he didn't want relationships. Had spent most of his adult life alone, travelling, making his fortune. He still had everything he'd started this journey with, and had a fight ahead over Mae's will. As Louisa had requested, he'd asked staff to pack up her things, ready to send them to her whenever she gave word. They'd almost finished the job. There was one room left, which he'd told them to leave till the end. The room containing her drawing table and her art supplies...

He wasn't sure why he'd asked for that space to be

packed up last. Hoping that she'd return, perhaps? But she wouldn't. Like his birth mother, like his adoptive parents. It was a familiar pattern. Everyone left him behind. That was why he kept moving. If you didn't stop, you couldn't be left. People had trouble *catching* you. Matteo started walking then. Not really knowing where he'd end up, yet at the same time finding himself unsurprised that he'd made his way to where Louisa had done her illustrations. After it had been so important to her, he'd found it hard to fathom her abandoning everything here. It told him how much she'd wanted to get away.

Her sketchbooks were stacked in a neat pile. He ran his fingers over the spiral bindings. The need to open them, to look, as if that would somehow connect him to her, became overwhelming. To immerse himself in the joy and innocence of her illustrations. Except he'd stolen that innocence from her. Tried to corrupt her. Taken a woman who deserved so much more than the cracked and broken man he was. Tried using her to satisfy his own needs.

He'd dismissed her as if she'd meant nothing to him at all. It was no wonder that she'd walked away without looking back.

He rubbed at the ache in his chest as he slid a random sketchbook from the pile. Flicked through book after book of whimsical drawings, sketches that he didn't understand. All the while the pictures connected him to her inner beauty. He marvelled at how untainted she'd been by what life had thrown at her. How she'd retained any sense of wonder at all was a miracle.

She was a miracle.

He took out the final book, one that looked a little different from the others. Opened the first page. Stilled.

An illustration of a little girl with flaming-red hair and a little boy, in a forest. A title page...

Matty and Lulu's Stupendous Adventures by Louisa Cameron.

It was as if his heart forgot to beat. Time simply stopped. He flicked through page after page. Stories of a sun-drenched summer where two sad and lost children found each other and made their own magic.

The memories of that time blazed on the pages. Funny, glorious. He'd forgotten how they'd found a nest of hedge-hogs. Tried to catch fish with their hands in the stream. Sneaked through the secret passageways of Easton Hall, pretending to be chased by ghosts.

The only ghosts now were the ones he'd created for himself and they haunted him with a vengeance.

Back then he'd been a scared boy, full of bravado. He questioned how much had actually changed. The fear gripped him now, of what else he might find as he turned those pages. What other stories it would show. And yet there on the pages were tales of a holiday when two children were simply allowed to be themselves. A little boy, a little girl. Both of them perfect and innocent.

Somehow in the intervening years he'd lost that innocence, whilst Louisa had retained it. He'd spent his life building a business, accumulating money and for what? Because he realised it now. That childhood summer was one of the best times of his entire life.

No. There was something that eclipsed it. This present summer, before Lulu had gone.

How had he not recognised it? How everything had seemed softer focus, in so many ways, gentle. A glowing warmth that had nothing to do with the weather outside but was carried around inside him. An emotion so foreign he hadn't understood it.

Happiness, and something more.

Something expansive, that hinted at a future. Something vast, unfamiliar. Never-ending.

A choking sensation throttled him, an inability to breathe. Lulu brought out something in him, a side that was patient, thoughtful. That could care and take care. Matteo gripped her art desk, riding the wave of panic and realisation. This emotion was all-encompassing. Something like he'd never experienced before, and that could only mean one thing.

He'd loved her yet had refused to believe it because everyone he'd loved had walked away. Like Louisa, except in truth that was a lie he'd told himself. He'd pushed her away. Ended it when she'd refused to be trapped in the same hatred and anger that had consumed so much of his life.

Hadn't he done the same to his sister as well?

He sat down with the book and finished reading the stories. Some he remembered. Like eating berries till their fingers were stained and bellies were full. Others he'd forgotten, like trying to talk to the bees after Mae told them she'd knocked on the hives in the days after Great-Uncle Gerald had died, letting them know that he'd gone but she would look after them. Whilst reading, he searched for a skerrick of that innocence inside himself. He wanted that again, the optimism. He craved it.

Almost as much as he craved a woman with flaming-red hair and a beautiful heart.

He slid his phone from his pocket. Thinking of the people he'd pushed away in the fear they would somehow leave him anyway. Losing them all the same because he hadn't had the courage or faith that he was enough to keep them close. That stopped now.

He looked at his sister's messages. Texts. The attempts to reach out that he'd tried to ignore. Took a deep breath. Called her number. She picked up immediately.

'Matty?'

'Flick. I'm sorry I haven't been in touch. It's been… busy. How are you?'

He tensed, waiting for the response. Was she well? Was she sick?

'I'm really well. Busy too! Hey…'

The conversation washed over him, about a trip she was taking to Australia nannying for her employer, as did the relief. One bridge being rebuilt. And he needed to learn how to do that properly before he attempted to mend what would be the most important, if that was possible. His biggest failing and greatest loss.

Lulu.

She'd offered herself. Opened her heart and made a place for him in it. For the first time in his life, he'd felt settled. Now it dawned on him that she was right. He'd been searching for a home. His surprise was finally acknowledging that he'd found it. Not in a place, but a person.

He needed her innocence. He needed her love.

He needed *her*.

And he would fight to get her back.

CHAPTER TWELVE

LOUISA SAT AT a small table on an ancient stone terrace overlooking Lake Como. The universe had put on another perfect sunny day for her, as it had every day for the two months since she'd walked out of Matteo's door. It hardly seemed fair when all she'd done for the first week was cry. Why couldn't there be rain, as if the world were crying with her? But she'd been delivered sunshine and, in the end, guessed it was said universe sending her a message. That no matter walking away from Matteo had felt like an evisceration, she'd survive it.

The world kept turning. Life went on.

After leaving Matteo she'd holed up in a *pensione* for a day, trying not to crack and break into a billion pieces. Not to drown in the tears that had fallen when he'd rejected everything she'd offered him. Her heart. Herself. Her love. Then she'd taken a deep breath and tried to make a decision. Her first instinct was to run back to the UK, back to Easton Hall. She'd called Mrs Fancutt, who'd told her the home itself was still under repair, but the gatehouse was empty. She'd considered it, but something about going back there felt like immersing herself in the past when, for now, she needed to start dreaming of a fresh future. Because who knew what would happen with the Bainbridge challenge to the will? She wasn't sure she could go back to Easton Hall only to have it taken away from her again.

Instead, here she sat, torturing herself in a tiny one-bedroom house she'd found on the lake for a good deal, when a long-term holiday letting had fallen through. She had money, she had time, and refused to allow memories of what had happened with Matteo taint this beautiful place. Of course, the universe had another trick up its sleeve. She looked across the wide blue expanse of water. A little boat zipping across the surface towards the small town in which she was staying. In the distance was a pale blotch on the landscape. In the days after she'd come to stay here, she'd discovered that what she could see across the lake was Villa Arcadia. Matteo's home.

'You'll never survive on your own.'

She rubbed at the ache in her chest. Those words cut deep. Of all the pain she'd suffered in her life, none had hurt as much as that. She'd thought Matteo had *seen* her. Come to know her. What a fool she'd been about it all, about him.

Louisa stood and left the terrace to stop herself gazing at a speck on the other side of the lake, obsessing over a man who didn't want her. She walked inside to where some sketchbooks and pencils she'd ordered online, sat on a rustic kitchen table. Here she was, surviving despite him.

She'd learned to cook with the help of the Internet and the generosity of the kind woman who owned the home. Who'd taken one look at a heartbroken English girl and had seemed to feel sorry for her, teaching Louisa how to make pasta. She'd found more work, another commission. Otherwise, Louisa tried to make sense of her life, to reorganise it, without relying on anyone.

The one good thing about what had happened was that

she'd finally grown up. Her life wasn't in stasis as it had been when Matteo had first arrived on her doorstep, when she'd been frozen in time. Now she was growing into herself as a woman. If nothing else, she had that to thank him for.

Louisa slipped on her glasses, picked up a pen, and began doodling on the page. Scribbling little curlicues and circles, allowing her mind to wander. She'd been contracted to do some illustrations for a nature-themed diary. It was easy work. She didn't really have to imagine much. Only the changing seasons. Drawing animals, fruits and flowers. Yet her heart didn't seem quite in it. Part of that heart, she'd left behind in a villa next to a sun-drenched lake. Not her home, but the place she'd truly found herself.

She looked at the page and found herself drawing a little frog prince. Louisa dropped the pen, the ache in her chest intensifying. A sting in her eyes and burn in her nose. Despite saying it was something she'd never wanted because she didn't think she'd survive the inevitable loss and betrayal, she'd fallen in love all the same.

Yet here she was, alive and breathing. And even acknowledging the pain, she had to admit one blinding truth. Had she been given the chance to do it all over again she would, with no hesitation. Because those moments with Matteo were pure, unadulterated magic.

It had sneaked up and caught her by surprise under that warm Italian sunshine. All the laughter, and happiness and *wanting*. The sense that what was happening seemed timeless and endless. It was only at the very end that she'd realised what she'd been looking at was a future.

Then he'd taken it away from her, because he didn't want the same.

She wondered how he was. Whether he was fighting for

Easton Hall and revenge against a family who had never truly accepted him. Whether he had found the peace and belonging that she knew he so desperately needed. But she couldn't worry about him. Revenge had no part in her life, letting the anger destroy her. Louisa knew there had been choices to make and, in the end, she'd chosen to save herself.

Which was what she was doing right now. She picked up her pen again. Turned to a fresh page, ignoring fallen frog princes. Was sketching out a few more ideas when a knock sounded at the door. Today was Wednesday. Working Wednesdays, she used to call them. Her life less rigid now, fewer fears about everything. She wondered who it could be. Perhaps the owner of the house. She'd promised to teach Louisa how to make gnocchi next, since Louisa had admitted she loved it so much. She left her chair and trundled down the stairs, opening the front door.

Against a backdrop of the glorious sunshine stood Matteo. In a polo shirt, wearing sunglasses. Hair, windswept. She gripped the door frame as her knees weakened. He was the last person she'd expected to see, and yet she drank him in like a woman dying of thirst. It didn't seem to matter what he'd said, the emotions came flooding back. The exhilaration, the despair. Jumbled together in such a potent mix and she didn't know whether to shout at him to leave, or fall to her knees and beg him to stay.

But his path didn't intersect with hers, so staying wasn't an option.

'Lulu.'

'Matteo.'

He winced, but he'd ceased to be Matty the day she'd walked out of the villa. When he showed her what he was prepared to do to exact revenge against a family who was not worth either of their time. Showed her exactly what he thought of her too. Rejecting her offer of love, of home.

'May I come in?'

She held out her hands. 'Can I stop you?'

He stood there looking as magnificent as ever. Tall, imposing. His skin a warm, tanned brown from days in the sun. Though now she noticed other things. He strangely held his shoes in his hands. His tan chinos rolled up to mid-calf, darkened with water at the bottom. They hung a little loosely against his lean hips. The stubble shading his jaw seeming to be more of a rough beard. How under his eyes had taken on as bruised an appearance as her own.

He looked like hell. It should have made her feel good, feel satisfied.

It didn't.

He gave a pained exhale. 'Lul—'

'No, just no. I'm not Lulu. You're not Matty. They were two children who should have grown up a long time ago. They don't exist any more.'

Why, after all he'd said, did she still want to reach out and comfort him? It made no sense, but she guessed love was like that. He was the man who'd shown her herself. Held up a mirror and forced her to look. In the process she'd liked who she saw, just as she believed he'd liked her too.

'I'll leave if you want me to.'

The thing was, she didn't. It made her angry. She was trying to get over him and he turned up here? How long would it take now to forget him after seeing him in the flesh? It was like some cruel game.

Still, she stood back, inviting him inside.

'Come on through,' she said. The space seeming to shrink with his imposing presence. He dropped his shoes

inside the door then followed Louisa up the stairs to a
tiny kitchen, where she put the kettle on. When the water
boiled, she made a cup of tea for herself. He shook his
head when she offered one to him, gripping the back of a
kitchen chair till his fingertips blanched white.

'I thought you'd be living at Easton Hall.'

'It doesn't feel like mine now,' she said, leaning against
the kitchen bench.

'You have a right to be there.'

'Do I? Really?' Louisa took a sip of the hot tea. 'I
thought you'd be happy to find me here and not staking
my claim.'

He rubbed his hand over his face. 'There are things I
need to say.'

'I won't stop you. But I guess you should sit down rather
than looming.'

She didn't want to be so sharp with him, but all those
old hurts came flooding back. How she'd trusted him.
How she'd believed in him. How she'd thought he believed
in her too. And she realised in many ways that was her
flaw. She'd been desperate to find things in others, things
that she really hadn't developed herself. She'd expected
so much of him when, in reality, he was only human. Just
as she was.

He pulled out the chair. Sat. Seemed to try to make himself…smaller in some way. Perhaps he'd taken the looming comment to heart. She pulled out a chair and sat too.

'The family's claim on the estate…' he said.

She waited to hear whether they'd issued proceedings
yet. Had resigned herself to the years of litigation. The
crippling fear he'd reveal to the world what had happened
to her, despite her wishes. No certainty over the outcome.
No certainty about where she'd live. Because Matteo would

tangle them up in litigation for as long as would cause the Bainbridge family the greatest pain. It was all so exhausting. So pointless.

'It's over, Lulu.'

Her heart rate spiked. She put her cup down on the table with a thud, although still holding on to it as if it were her only tether to reality. 'What do you mean, *over*?'

His golden gaze held hers. She was afraid of what he might see if he looked too hard. 'I needed you to know there's no risk to Easton Hall.'

Louisa tore off her reading glasses and tossed them on top of her sketchpad. 'What did you do?'

Matteo's gaze left hers for a moment, settling on the little frog prince she'd drawn. His focus seemed to be distant. The corners of his mouth kicking up before he came back to himself and turned to her once more, clasping his hands in front of him.

'Your home's safe. They won't be coming after it any more.'

Louisa sat there, mouth slightly open, hand clasping her cup of tea. She looked beautiful. With her hair wild and loose. Her verdant green eyes that had haunted so many of his thoughts, glimmering. It was clear she'd made changes in her life, moved on. Those changes appeared to have been good to her. When he'd spoken to Mrs Fancutt to check how the staff were faring back in the UK, she'd commented about it. Telling him he'd done well. That Mae would be happy.

Louisa's grown into herself.

Yet he'd done nothing except cause her pain. He wasn't responsible for her growth. It was all down to her. He realised she'd been underestimated. She'd kept her past with her mother so well hidden that no one recognised the depths of strength this woman held within herself, to merely survive.

Now, she was so cool and sharp. He deserved every part of her disdain. The hardness that seemed to coat her in a thin veneer. He hated that he might have done that to her. Might have made her somehow disappointed in life, because he was sure she was disappointed in him. That disappointment was the most painful wound she could have inflicted, because he'd realised in the days after she'd left that he'd basked in her approval like an elixir.

Craved it, because what he truly wanted was her love. A love she'd freely offered and that he'd unthinkingly rejected.

'How did you do it?'

'The why is probably more important.'

She narrowed her eyes. 'Yet that's not the question I asked.'

The burn was well deserved. She wanted answers, and he was here to give them to her. To apologise, to beg for forgiveness. To ask her to allow him to come back into her life. To say that he would take her love if she still offered it, and cherish her, rather than flinging her emotions back in her face.

'How did I get them to call off their legal action?' He shrugged. That had been the easy part in the end. 'I offered them money.'

A great deal of money, but he'd come to realise it didn't matter. Why should it, when his quest for revenge had lost him someone whose importance had become vital to him?

'That must have hurt,' she said.

The pain was nothing compared to the agony of watching her walk out of the door. Waiting for her to return in the assuredness she would, then realising she had no intention of coming back. Though he didn't think she'd want to hear that, not right now.

He shrugged. 'Money's nothing when compared to certainty. They did a lot of posturing, so I did a little of my own. I've been investigating their charities but haven't been able to pin anything on them. Just rumours, suspicions, reports that didn't add up. I warned them they'd attracted my attention and that they could use the funds to rectify what I suspected were anomalies in their accounts. It seemed they took my advice.'

Whilst he didn't have solid evidence, he'd seen the fear in their eyes. They wouldn't learn. One day they'd slip, and there would be no more of his money to bail them out. The regulators would catch them. He'd wasted too much of his life on them already, the hatred, the revenge. What he wanted to focus on now was love.

'Is that all you came to tell me?'

He had so much more to say. That life without her had become a cold, dark place. How, when she'd walked away, the meaning for everything he'd done in the past and what he'd worked towards in the future had simply evaporated. How he'd thought she was trapped in the past when the person who'd been trapped all along was him.

But even more, he wanted to reassure her that Easton Hall was safe. That she could live in it, and that he'd never try to take it away from her.

'I came to tell you that I'll continue with whatever repairs Easton Hall needs. Anything you want will be done. The house is your home to live in for as long as you want. For ever, if that's what you choose. Because all I want, Lulu, is for you to be happy.'

* * *

Louisa stood up, her chair scraping on the rustic tiles of the kitchen floor. She couldn't sit still. She wanted to pace. Only a few months ago this would have been everything she'd dreamed of. Yet she realised all of her dreams since leaving Matteo were still bound up in him. The passion, the pleasure.

That didn't make dreams reality.

'What if I don't want to live there?'

'Then you don't have to. After what you've inherited already from Mae's estate, you're a wealthy woman but, as you've reminded me, Easton Hall has been *your* home and you still deserve part of it. If you want to move away for ever, we can calculate the value of your right to reside, and I'll pay you for it. Then you can go anywhere you want in the world.'

What did she really want? She wrapped her arms around herself, turned away and looked out of a small kitchen window to Lake Como and the tiny dot on the other side that was Villa Arcadia.

There was so much she had to say, she hardly knew where to start. Though, where better than one of the things that had hurt her the most?

'You said I wouldn't survive on my own.'

She heard Matteo's chair move out from the table. A prickle at the back of her neck. A slide of warmth telling her he was close.

'I was wrong. You didn't just survive, you thrived.'

Thriving might have been a bit of an overstatement.

'How do you even know?' she asked.

He gave a short, sharp laugh. 'Don't you think in the days after you left, that I didn't look for you? I needed to make sure you were okay. I knew you'd left a *pensione* in the next village. Then I spoke to Mrs Fancutt and she told me you were still in Italy. In the end, I found you here.'

Her heart began to beat a quick and thready rhythm. She'd thought that he didn't care at all, that he'd completely washed his hands of her, and yet here he was admitting that he'd known what she was doing all along. That she was just across the lake from him. Then why did it still seem like an unbreachable gulf?

Louisa wheeled round, the burn of tears threatening. Her voice catching in her throat. 'You hurt me, Matteo. You made me feel special and then you took that all away because revenge against the family was more important than anything. It would *never* be me.'

He took a step forward. Stopped. A moment of hesitation as if he was unsure of himself.

'I've never dwelled on my mistakes. I've lived a life with no regrets, believing that I was relentlessly moving forward. But, Lulu, I have regretted every moment of that last conversation with you. Analysed every word that would have caused you pain. I've obsessed. Immersed in a past I can't take back but wish I could change. I came to realise that anything I wanted, revenge, business, success, money, it was all hollow without you in my life.'

Everything stilled. It was as if she forgot to breathe, as if her heart had missed a beat. 'What are you saying?'

'I can't change the past, that's what shaped me. It's the future I have some control over, and I've come to realise that my past has held me hostage for long enough. I said I'd accepted that I'd never find my birth family, but I lied. To myself more than anyone else. You were right. I was searching and searching for something that never really existed. Now I've stopped.'

'I don't understand.'

'My whole life has been about temporary. I didn't believe another person could give me love. I figured deep down that you'd walk away and leave me, so I pushed you away as if that would protect me. Instead, I came to realise whether I pushed you away or whether you walked away on your own, that knife plunging into my heart hurt just the same. My search was for family when what I'd been looking for was standing right in front of me, imploring me to choose her. When I realised that, everything became easy. I want you. I choose you. I love you.'

Her back pressed into the kitchen benchtop, hands gripping the edges to hold her up, because she could hardly believe what he was telling her. 'You love me?'

'How could I not?' He began to move forwards again. 'You said I was looking for a home. When you walked away, I realised what I hadn't before. That home isn't a place.'

He was talking about a *home* now? What about the man who travelled the world, who never stood still…?

'You want to make Easton Hall your home, with me?'

He was so close. She tilted her head back to look up at him and the hard man of that last, awful day had simply disappeared. Melted away. All she saw was softness, for her.

She saw *Matty* again.

'Did you miss the part about me saying I love you?'

She gave a tremulous laugh. Was this a dream? Could this be real? 'No, I kind of got that bit.'

'*You're* my home, Lulu. Wherever you want to be, I'll be too. My place is with you. What I'd really like is for you to say you still love me too. But if you don't, if you don't trust me yet, then I'm prepared to work at it. Diligently.'

Everything seemed so shaky in this moment and yet heat began to flood over her. 'I really like it when you're diligent.'

The corner of his mouth kicked up in a wry grin. 'I hoped you might.'

'What if I said that I've never really loved anybody before? It feels thrilling, it feels terrifying, and I really don't have a single clue what I'm doing.'

He laughed. Rubbed a hand over his face. 'Don't worry, neither do I. We can practise together, till we make it perfect. But right now, I'd really like to hold you.'

Matty opened his arms and she walked right into them. He wrapped her tight. That comforting sense of belonging returned. As she relaxed into his embrace, his damp chinos brushed against her legs. She pulled back to look at him.

'Why are your trousers wet?'

The corner of his mouth kicked up. 'I motored across the lake to see you. There was no mooring, so I had to wade to shore.'

The little boat she'd seen, that was him. If she could have fallen even more in love with him in this moment, she would have. But that was impossible. Her heart was too full already. All the times she'd gazed out at his villa, just a speck in the distance. Wondering whether he was still there. What he was doing... 'Did you look across the lake to me?'

'Every day and every night from the time I discovered where you were.'

They'd been watching each other. Tears pricked her eyes and one escaped, tracking down her cheek. Matty gently brushed it away with his thumb.

'Marry me, Lulu? I can't bear the idea of another day away from you. I want to prove that we should never be apart again. We can forget everyone else and make our own family together.'

'You don't need to prove anything to me, Matty. I'll marry you because I love you. I can't think of a better reason.'

He threaded his fingers through her hair, brushed his lips gently across her mouth.

'There's no better reason in the world.'

EPILOGUE

MATTY TOOK LULU'S hand as they walked through the cool, soft sand on his Whitsunday Island resort, which he'd closed to other guests for the duration of their stay. A warm breeze blew, sunset painting the sky in pink and gold. It had been two years since their wedding, and for their second anniversary he'd decided to celebrate by revisiting their honeymoon destination, where he'd shown her the beach for the first time.

'Where are we going?' she asked. Lulu looked beautiful tonight in a sheer and shimmery kaftan that moulded to every curve, the same colours as the sunset. Her copper hair loose, streaming down her back. Lit up like fire in the golden light.

He smiled. 'I have a surprise for you.'

She smiled back. He'd never thought Lulu could look more beautiful than she had on their wedding day, in a magnificent vintage wedding gown under a bower of roses at their Lake Como villa, but he'd been wrong. Each day surpassed the rest, as if she were created anew each morning, just for him.

'I don't need surprises. You're enough.'

She gazed up at him, her tropical green eyes filled with warmth and love. He understood, she was enough for him as well. He wanted for nothing with Lulu in his life. Each day, now complete.

Since their wedding, they'd spent time travelling the world, chasing summer. Visiting his houses, his hotels, and resorts. Even though they had plenty of places to stay they kept two homes. Easton Hall, now renovated to its former glory, and Villa Arcadia. Both, places of rustic idyll. Innocence and pleasure.

He looked down at Lulu, her gaze heated. Lips parted; pupils blown wide. A delicate flush on her cheeks. Okay. He grinned. Perhaps more pleasure than innocence... But he wasn't complaining. Life was an adventure in hedonism with his incredible wife.

An adventure in other ways too. After some thought and a little encouragement from him, she'd submitted her stories and illustrations about their stupendous childhood adventures to a publisher. Soon, Lulu would have a series of children's books in her name and could add author to illustrator on her résumé. Warmth like the sun kindled in his chest, his pride at her achievements. She amazed him every day, the way she overcame and grew. He gently squeezed her hand, she squeezed back.

'What are you thinking?' she asked.

That he couldn't wait to get to where they were going. Even though she said she didn't need it, Matty loved to surprise her as a way of thanks. For freeing him from the exhausting quest for belonging he hadn't even realised he'd been on.

'That every day with you is the happiest day of my life.'

She sighed. 'When I thought you couldn't make me swoon even harder... Oh... Matty... This is *beautiful*.'

They'd arrived at what he'd organised, a tent of jewel-coloured silk high on the beach. Surrounded by flaming torches, waiting for night to fall. The floor was covered with soft blankets, strewn with plush pillows. With cham-

pagne on ice and a basket full of delicacies, he had everything he needed to celebrate how much he loved her.

'You did this for me?' Her voice trembled, cracked.

'A romantic picnic for two,' he said. 'I've given the staff
the night off.'

They wouldn't be disturbed unless he called for something. They were as alone as they could possibly be. Ship-
wrecked together. He led her inside, and they sank into
the cushions. The waves a gentle hiss on the sand in front
of them. He grabbed the champagne from the ice bucket,
poured two glasses.

'A toast.' He held up his glass to her. 'Happy anniversary, Mrs Bainbridge.'

'Happy anniversary to you, Mr Bainbridge,' Lulu replied.

That once disparaged family name held no power over
him any more. Not now that he and Lulu shared it with
each other. It was only a name, not something that defined
him. Anyhow, it was the name his sister carried too, and
he loved her. With so much love in his life, there was simply no room for negativity.

Lulu looked out over the ocean. Blue turning to purple
as the colours in the sky deepened. She took a sip of her
champagne, put down her glass. 'It's going to be hard to
leave here.'

'Where would you like to go next?'

She looked up at him and smiled. 'So long as I'm with
you, the "where" doesn't matter.'

His heart felt as if it would burst. Matty put down his
glass to join Lulu's as he leaned into her, cupping her
cheek. Stroking his thumb over her soft skin. Their lips
touching, their breaths mingling as the kiss deepened. Lulu
slid her hand under his shirt, stroking his back as he became fire, each nerve setting alight as he eased her onto
cushions behind them.

'Are you thinking of skipping dinner and going straight for dessert?' he asked.

Her breaths came in heavy gusts. 'I thought that was your idea.'

'Then dinner can wait a little while.'

'I was thinking…' Lulu's copper hair fanned out behind her. She took her lower lip in her teeth, worrying it. When she released it, he kissed the reddened flesh better.

'Yes?' he murmured against her mouth, contemplating where to kiss next.

'Maybe we could try for a baby.'

Matty stilled, sat up. They'd talked of family. Wanted children. But they'd never talked about a timeframe.

'Now?' he asked.

A baby. A family.

'It's what I was hoping, if you want.'

'I want *everything*,' he said, his voice rough with emotion. He stroked his hands over the silk of her dress, her nipples tight under the fine fabric.

'Are you…wearing anything under that?'

Lulu's lips curved into a seductive smile and his desire speared low and hard.

'No.'

He eased the filmy fabric over her head. Tossed it aside. She lay on the pillows and blankets beautifully naked, arms above her head. The sunset painting her skin rose gold.

His mouth watered. He was starving, but not for food.

'I see you came prepared.'

She laughed, the sound lighting him up like the flaming torches surrounding them. His breath caught as she tugged the hem of his shirt, pulling it over his head. She cast it aside as he worked his way out of his shorts and underwear till he lay gloriously naked as well, the sea breeze cool on his overheated skin.

It was as if they were the only two people left on earth.

'I need you,' he murmured.

'I need you too.' Her voice was a fervent whisper in the approaching twilight. 'Now. Don't wait.'

She didn't need to ask. He kissed her again. Moved over her body, skin to skin. Into her as she opened for him. Sliding deep, welcomed by the hot velvet depths of her as she arched into him with a moan. Losing himself utterly as they moved together in perfect synchronicity. Breathing each other's breaths, their hearts beating like one.

He'd never felt so unprotected as he lost himself to the ecstasy that was his wife. With thrusts and gasps and scorching pleasure they came as one. Shuddering. Replete. Matty was overcome by the same sensation as he'd experienced on his wedding day.

That this was the first day of the rest of their lives.

As they drifted back into reality, still joined, he looked down at her, Lulu's eyes dreamy and half focussed. A flush across her chest and throat. Lips plush, pink and well kissed.

'Every day, Lulu, you honour me,' he said. 'You are my beating heart.'

'I love you, Matty. You always hold mine.'

Whatever adventures were yet to come, they were in it together. For ever. Lulu lifted her hand, threaded her fingers into his hair. Pulled his head down.

'You showed me the world,' she whispered against his lips.

'You led me home,' he said before deepening their kiss.

And there was nowhere else in the world he'd rather be, than home with her.

* * * * *

HIS CHOSEN
QUEEN

BELLA MASON

MILLS & BOON

For Brad, without whom none of my books
would ever have been written.

In you, I have found my king.

CHAPTER ONE

IT WAS REMARKABLE how some days could seem completely
ordinary. How the sun would beat down as it always did, how
the sounds in the air didn't change, how people could go about
their lives as normal and yet everything could be different.
Changed.

Prince Vasili Leos, 'spare' to the throne of the small Medi-
terranean island kingdom of Thalonia, located in the Ionian
Sea, sat in the darkened office of the private secretary to the
King. He'd never liked this office, and would try to avoid it at
all costs. The wood-panelled walls and polished wood floors
were suffocating. It wasn't a room to make anyone feel at ease,
and ease was the last thing on his mind now.

Only the barest hints of sunlight passed through the slats of
the dark wooden blinds, landing in penumbral stripes on the
highly polished desk that was devoid of all clutter. And in the
centre of all that light and dark, as if a divine spotlight was cast
upon it, sat a letter with his name on it. A letter that currently
consumed his existence. A letter that he wouldn't have had if
it hadn't been for the news that had broken his world apart.

The King of Thalonia was dead.

Vasili was now King.

His brother Leander had been flying over the mainland
when his plane had crashed. There were no survivors.

The King's private secretary, Andreas Kyriakou, was speaking, but Vasili barely heard a word.

He was numb. Mere hours ago he had been sharing a drink with his brother, the rightful King, and now he was gone. An entire life wiped out. His only real family. And now he sat in this uncomfortable chair, hardly feeling the carved wood his arms rested on, to be told they had to move on swiftly.

Vasili had never wanted to be King. He was the spare. The insurance policy. The 'Playboy Prince', as he had been dubbed. He had never been intended for the throne and he didn't want it.

'Your Majesty, are you listening?' Andreas asked, halting his pacing.

No, Vasili wasn't listening. He didn't want to. Everything was happening so fast it was a blur. The sun was still low in the sky. The morning had barely begun. And in that time he had been summoned to Andreas's office and, without any pre-amble at all, had been told his brother was dead. Now, without waiting or caring about how that news had landed, they had already read Leander's will. The letter had been left in his brother's care to be given to Vasili in the event of his death.

Vasili glared at the white envelope. He shouldn't have received it. Not yet, at least.

'We need you to take the throne immediately. You need to speak to the people. Make sure they know the monarchy stands strong.'

Vasili curled his fingers into fists. He was still trying to process the fact that his brother was gone and all Andreas could do was talk of his ascension. Still, he remained silent. In this void he had landed in the thrum of his steady heart could be felt throughout his body. All he could see was that letter. A physical representation of the fact that Leander was gone and that Thalonia was now looking at a twenty-nine-year-old king in the seat of power. It was ridiculous. Just as ridiculous as the fact that yet another letter had been left to him by his father. A man who had shown him nothing but disapproval. The rebellious son...

The first had been after his death, barely a year ago, but Vasili had had no interest in what his father had had to say. In anger, he had immediately tossed that letter into the fireplace, and he had no inclination to open this letter either. He didn't know if he ever wanted to read it. The contents could stay buried for all he cared. Just like the man himself.

His illness had come on swiftly, and before they'd known it the Kingdom had been plunged into mourning and Leander had ascended the throne. A role he had trained for his whole life. A role never meant for Vasili. One that the more superstitious of his people had come to believe was cursed.

And now allaying their fears would have to fall to him. It had to be some sort of cosmic joke! His people would once again sink into a pit of mourning and he couldn't blame them. Leander had been a popular king and, given the fact that only Andreas was in this office with him, Vasili surmised that Carissa, their communications secretary, was making the announcement to the people as they spoke.

'Thalonia requires stability, Your Maj—'

Vasili cut Andreas a glare that had him falling silent. He rounded the desk, sitting in the overlarge chair behind it.

'Your Majesty, I understand that you do not wish to hear this, but I will say it again. Thalonia requires stability and it is your responsibility. This is your duty.'

Vasili wanted to laugh, but there wasn't an ounce of humour within him. All there were were jumbled thoughts, and at the forefront of all of that was this blasted letter.

He could not fathom why his father would have left it to him for this moment. Throughout his entire life neither his father nor his mother had had any time for him at all. He was the spare. His existence merely a tick-box exercise. Why would they care about him when Leander has been the son who would one day lead the nation. They were King and Queen after all. Their time had been much too precious to be spent frivolously.

So what could the great Athanasios Leos have to say to him now? If he couldn't even invest the barest hint of time in his youngest son when he'd needed him, what could he say now when he didn't? Had he not been the one who had warned Vasili not to waste Leander's time as a child? And yet here he was being asked to rescue the very institution for which he had never been good enough.

In fact, the only person who had been there for him as he'd grown up had been his nanny. The palace had employed several royal nannies, but only one had ever tended to him. She had raised him. Had given him the support and love he had missed so badly from his parents. She had been the only person he'd known he could count on, but when he had turned fifteen she had been let go, and that was when he'd known without a shadow of a doubt that whatever he wanted or cared for meant little to the crown.

So he had swallowed down his grief and decided that the crown meant nothing to him either. Resentment and rebellion had been born bright in him. He didn't care about the throne. He didn't care about being a prince. If he was of so little value, then all his family stood for held little value for him. And so he'd become the 'Playboy Prince', with no interest in ruling. It had seemed to be what aggravated his parents the most, so Vasili had freely indulged himself in his hedonistic lifestyle.

Rebellion had suited him well. Especially when all his parents had focused on was the monarchy and Leander.

Vasili had understood that. He'd understood the dedication that ruling a kingdom required. He'd even understood the attention Leander received. He was meant to be King. What he hadn't understood was why those things had made his life void.

At least none of it had affected his relationship with his brother. Vasili had often been ordered to refrain from distracting his brother, and he'd obeyed, but that hadn't stopped Leander from sneaking into Vasili's room at night. From the time he was little they would share pilfered treats from the kitchens, until they'd grown older, when they had shared a drink.

While they hadn't been able to be as close as siblings ought to be, or even really friends, Vasili had still looked up to his brother. Admired him even in adulthood. And now he was gone. Without a warning or a goodbye. He would never see Leander again. His brother was dead and what was he left with? An advisor he could barely tolerate and a kingdom that would be disappointed.

Vasili closed his eyes for a breath, the reality of the situation crashing upon him. With his mother having long since passed, and having buried his father only a year ago, now losing Leander meant he was alone. Completely alone.

This palace, grand and ostentatious, with its Rococo architecture, was the jewel of Seidon—Thalonia's popular capital—and had been home to generations of his family and a battalion of staff, and never once had it felt quite so empty.

Of course Vasili had friends. An entire network of them. People who loved to party as much as him. Who were after a good time. And not a single one of them could he call now. Not one could he lean on or go to for support. He couldn't think of what he would say in any case. Love and support were alien concepts to him, having never had the privilege of experiencing it for himself. So he would have to deal with this, with his immense grief, as he dealt with everything else in his life. Alone.

'Your Majesty,' Andreas said more forcefully. If he was at all aware of Vasili's spiralling thoughts he didn't show it. 'You are now King. This is something you must accept. We have to move immediately. Thalonia cannot be without its king.'

Vasili was aware of that, and yet Andreas's constant badgering had lit the wick of his anger. He needed a moment—one moment to himself. Alone. A moment to say goodbye to his brother and steel himself for whatever was to come.

'And, furthermore, we need to move quickly to secure the future of the crown. You need to settle on an adequate bride and you need to marry and produce heirs as soon as possible. It is imperative—'

'Enough!' Vasili spat angrily, pushing to his feet and silencing Andreas.

He had heard just about as much as he could take from the older man. Swiping the letter off the table, Vasili strode out of the gloomy office, slamming the door shut behind him.

His angry footsteps echoed through the marble hallways of the palace, and a swirling cloud of fury and grief consumed Vasili as he tried to put as much space between him and Andreas as possible. Because right now it would take nothing for the tether on his temper to snap entirely.

Sensing his dark mood, the palace staff kept their eyes low and gave him a wide berth as they continued with their day. Vasili wondered if they already knew Leander was dead. They had to have been informed, and yet none offered him even hollow words of sympathy.

Seeking solitude, Vasili was grateful, but wouldn't show it.

There was only one place he could go where he would find the peace he was after. The library. The silence there would be welcome.

He pushed open the gilded door and stepped into the grandest library in all the Kingdom. It was a cavernous two-storey space, with rows upon rows of shelves, every single one packed with books of every colour and topic. Branching off the main space, with its gleaming marble floors, were passages to rooms and alcoves looking out over the palace gardens, where there were even more books. Frescoes in shades of pastel blue and pink covered the ceiling, drawing the eye up the gold-accented white walls.

There weren't too many things Vasili was grateful to his forebears for, but this place was one. Even though he had rarely stepped into the library in the last few years, the colours in here always reminded him of the island itself. Of early mornings when the sky was painted in pink and blue with streaks of gold. When the turquoise waters were a siren's call to all who looked upon them. White clouds in the sky and sand on the beach.

Except today he didn't revel in all the ways he enjoyed this place. Today he just found a seat in a comfortable chair in a quiet corner and closed his eyes.

He prayed for just a little peace. His brother had died. He hadn't been told if there was a body to recover. He hadn't even gone back to his brother's room to whisper a quiet goodbye. He was already being forced to move on. This entire institution was heartless. He had learned that at fifteen, but it seemed he was having to learn the lesson all over again.

Vasili was thankful that it was quiet. It was still early enough that the library was completely empty. He had no idea where the librarian was—was just happy that whoever it was had left him be.

But this was a day that was meant to test him, and what little peace he had hoped to get was shattered when the library doors were thrown open and in walked Andreas, followed by the communications secretary, Carissa.

Vasili groaned. His temper frayed further.

'Your Majesty,' Andreas said, dripping disapproval.

The man had served his father and brother, and was clearly unhappy that the crown would now fall to him. Vasili could see it.

'You cannot simply walk away from this.'

'Please, Your Majesty...' Carissa tried a different tack.

A tall woman with straw-light hair, cut sharply along her jaw, impeccably clad in a dark tailored suit, she took the chair angled towards his and spoke to him in a tone he assumed must work wonders in getting anyone to do as she bid. But no amount of charm or authority would work on him. Not now.

'Just listen,' she said. 'And then we can decide on a way forward that works for everyone.'

Vasili huffed. 'For everyone?'

'Of course, sir. We're in a tough situation and we all want to do what's best,' Carissa said.

'She's right,' a still-scowling Andreas agreed. 'It's imperative that you listen to us. You have to marry and produce heirs. King Leander didn't do so quickly enough, and now the crown sits in a precarious position.'

Vasili tilted his head, studying the private secretary. 'Let me guess…it's my duty to save the monarchy?'

'Of course it is. Thalonia needs its king,' Andreas replied.

Vasili shook his head. Saving the system he had rebelled against his whole life—the very thing responsible for him being cast aside—was the last thing he wanted to do.

He was sorely tempted to let it all fall to ruin. One family didn't make an entire kingdom. Besides, he hadn't been enough at any point in his life before, so why should he be now? Vasili believed he was the very last person who should ever marry. He didn't want marriage. Commitment wasn't something he had ever considered. He much preferred losing himself in a beautiful woman who understood his needs. Knew that it was only for a night. That there would never be a future with him.

He was trying to escape the cage, not invite others to join him in it.

His mother had once called him a Lothario and Vasili would much rather wear that title than the title of King.

'Clearly not just a king,' Vasili all but growled.

Carissa cut Andreas off before he could utter whatever was brewing on his tongue. 'We understand your trepidation, sir—'

'I doubt that.'

She continued as if the new King had not interrupted her. 'But we are here to help you take on this task. You can lean on us, and we can guide you through these changes.'

How weak did these people think he was? With their pretty words that blatantly told him they would try to control him.

'And one such change is your lifestyle,' Andreas chipped in. 'Not just because it is unbecoming behaviour for the King, but because it would also be highly inappropriate when you wed.'

When? It had gone from something Vasili *should* do to an inevitability. As if his choices, his life, didn't matter.

'We can help you find an appropriate bride.'

'What?'

Fire exploded in his veins. Andreas's eyes widened at his low, icy tone. Anger burned through his grief, igniting every rebellious urge he had ever had. He wouldn't be controlled. Wouldn't be dictated to. If the old King and Queen hadn't been able to control him, what made these people think that they could?

Marriage and children had never been on his radar, but if they wanted him to get married so badly it wouldn't be to someone they deemed 'appropriate'. Some generic royal who would be as selfish and self-obsessed as all the rest. No. He would do things on his own terms, exactly as he lived his life. Vasili couldn't care less what Andreas and Carissa wanted. To him they represented all that was wrong with the entire institution of royalty.

Feeling every bit the recalcitrant prince he was known to be, Vasili once again rebelled against the system that he could never escape. He looked over their heads, defiance etched in every line on his face, and with teeth bared he ground out, 'Fine. I'll marry *her.*'

Both royal secretaries turned around in unison, to glance in the direction of the new King's gaze, and found the librarian staring wide-eyed at the three of them, clearly having overheard the entire conversation.

'Your Majesty…' Andreas whipped back around, his face a mix of horror and frustration. 'You can't be serious.'

'Andreas is right. You can't marry the librarian. She isn't an appropriate queen for the Kingdom,' Carissa tried to reason with him.

Vasili stared hard at the communications secretary. 'And just who would be an appropriate queen, exactly?'

'You need to marry a noble. It's tradition. Every consort in our history has been a royal in their own right. It projects the right image. Of strength and endurance. Please, you have to think of the throne.'

Carissa's words were like kindling to flame. And the realisation that she had said the wrong thing was soon reflected in her eyes.

'Are you questioning your king?' Vasili challenged.

He didn't have to raise his voice or stand over these two people he had quite honestly had enough of for one day. If he was now King, then they would see the kind of king he would be. Not one easily controlled or cowed.

Andreas looked horror-struck, as if the insinuation was the greatest insult. 'Of course not. We would never second-guess the King. But it is my job to act as his closest advisor. I have done so for your father and your brother, and as such I have to say that this is not the best course of action. King Leander was to have married a princess in two weeks.'

'Well, it seems that I need to remind you that I am not Leander. Nor will I ever be. It's best that you heed that very important fact, Andreas,' Vasili said smoothly.

'Be that as it may, sir, she is a librarian.' A puce tinge coloured his neck. 'She may work at the palace, but she is a commoner, and never in the rich history of this kingdom has a commoner ever sat on the throne. Need I remind you of our heritage? Thalonia was named after Thalia, Queen Consort of the first King. A princess before that.'

'Firstly, Andreas, I would mind my tone if I were you.' Vasili rose gracefully from his chair to stand towering above

Andreas and Carissa, who hastily got to her feet to show respect. 'And secondly, there is a first time for everything. Your
king has spoken.'

Vasili turned towards the librarian, still frozen at the counter. His eyes locked with hers. An arresting shade of turquoise,
they widened in shock. Her heart must be beating a frantic
tattoo—he could see the flutter of the pulse in her neck—but
in that moment the world stood still. All that existed was him
and her and nothing else.

A beat passed.

Maybe two.

Maybe an entire eon.

Then Vasili ripped his gaze away from hers and with his
jaw clenched tightly, strode out of the library.

Helia tracked his movement, still rooted to the spot.

Her eyes were still locked on the door through which the
new King had vanished.

'What…?' She whispered to herself in utter shock, her heart
pounding furiously.

He couldn't be serious! He had no idea who she was. Marry
her? The utter insanity!

Yet her heart still beat frantically, its rhythm changing,
thudding, as she remembered his eyes on her. He had never
looked her way before, but in that moment Helia had felt as
though he was looking into her soul. As if he could see the
very essence of her. Those golden-brown eyes had been a trap.
Ensnaring her. And for a heartbeat she would have given up
her every secret to that look. It had excited her.

Which was an immensely ludicrous thought, even though
it was one she wished were true. No one went from seeing a
person for the first time—a person they had never noticed before—to choosing to marry them.

Prince Vasili was grieving. He had only just found out his

brother was dead—from what she had overheard—so no one could possibly take him seriously. Could they? Of course, not. His advisors would probably rush after him and that would be that.

Helia thought back to when her father had died. Grief had clouded her every thought and she had only been a teenager back then. Surely Andreas would see that the King was not thinking straight. The King would need a moment to collect his thoughts and then he would speak to his advisors calmly and this whole crazy interaction would be forgotten.

She would be forgotten.

Whatever hope she'd had of him having seen her flared and died with that one logical thought—but at least she would have the memory of the one time King Vasili had seen her and how good it had felt.

CHAPTER TWO

Unfortunately, given the looks on the advisors' faces, that seemed unlikely.

Andreas and Carissa approached Helia with grave expressions.

'Come with us,' Andreas instructed. 'Quietly. We need to discuss this in private.'

Helia still couldn't believe the words that had left the new King's mouth. She couldn't think that anyone would.

'Is this really necessary?' she asked.

'Yes.'

Something like hope fluttered in her belly, because that would mean Vasili really had taken notice of her. So she followed Andreas and Carissa through the palace to the private secretary's office. Not once did her heart steady its rhythm. Helia couldn't wrap her head around how her ordinary day had turned into this circus, all because the King had looked her way in a moment of madness.

'Take a seat,' Andreas instructed. 'Wait here, we'll be back shortly.' He left the room, with Carissa at his side, and closed the door.

Helia was left alone in the unwelcoming office. She could hear agitated voices beyond the door, but couldn't make out what was being said. She tried to block them out, attempting, instead, to make sense of what had happened. To unravel her feelings. But that thread seemed to be well and truly tangled.

So she waited. A glance at the polished antique clock on the desk revealed that she had been waiting ten minutes. Which turned into an hour. Which turned into two. Every so often she would hear hurried steps and hushed, frantic voices. Whatever was going on out there it was certainly chaotic.

Helia's patience was growing thin. She knew she couldn't defy an order from Andreas, but waiting alone had her shoulders growing stiffer by the moment. Surely if they were going to tell her that it had all been mistake they would not have been gone this long—which made excitement once again flare in her belly. She tamped down hard on it.

Just when she had decided that it wouldn't matter if she waited here or in the library, where she could be alone, and where she would have a distraction, the door opened and in walked an irate Andreas. Carissa followed closely with a scowl, closing the door. He rounded the table to his throne-like seat, while she elegantly perched on the chair beside Helia's.

Andreas was a starchy character, but it had never concerned Helia before. Yet now she was filled with a sense of foreboding that warred with her earlier excitement and state of shock.

'I'm sure you have gathered as much, but I should officially tell you that King Leander is dead.'

That was obvious, but Helia would not interrupt until she could fully understand the situation she found herself in.

'Which means that Prince Vasili is now His Majesty, the King of Thalonia. As such, he is required by law to marry and bear heirs.'

Heirs!

Silence pierced the air.

The hope, confusion, excitement all died. Helia could no longer feel that frantic heartbeat. Her jaw dropped as she pieced together what he meant. 'You're not serious!'

'I'm afraid I am.'

'Andreas, you cannot expect me to marry someone I don't even know.'

Marry and have children with them? That was completely unreasonable! She hadn't even thought about having family yet.

'This makes no sense. His Majesty cannot possibly want to marry someone he has never seen before,' she said, attempting to reason with them.

Yes, Helia had admired Prince Vasili for years. She had allowed herself fantasies of what it might be like if he one day took notice of her and it had felt good. Incredible. But never had those fantasies been like this.

'You can't take my choice away from me!'

'Look,' Andreas said in a severe tone, his fingers steepled under his chin, 'we are even less happy about this than you are, but whether we like it or not, Prince Vasili is now King and he has spoken. We have no choice but to obey.'

Irritation flashed through Helia. But Carissa nodded along with Andreas, as if agreeing to this absurdity.

'Whether you like it or not?' Helia asked. 'Is that because you disapprove of me, a commoner?' She directed this at Andreas—the person she had to report to in her responsibility over the palace archives, who didn't even have the good grace to look embarrassed. 'Or is it that you have a problem with King Vasili himself?'

'How long before we can get her and the country ready for the wedding?' Andreas asked Carissa, completely ignoring Helia's questions.

She felt a sharp pang of sympathy for Vasili. It was no secret what nobles thought of people like her, but to hold Vasili in such disregard was disrespectful, and she could only imagine hurtful to him. She remembered his reaction in the library, thinking that she would have been far less pleasant if the roles had been reversed. But his words had been reckless, and had very real consequences for her now.

She couldn't help the ember of anger burning in her from that. However, it was the two people with her in this room now who truly irked her. Their blatant disrespect for her and the King was entirely unacceptable. The way they looked at her, as if she was some kind of irritation they had to deal with, had her grinding her teeth. She wasn't the one who had put them in this situation. Vasili was. He was the one who had said the words, but even he wasn't entirely to blame.

'Don't ignore me,' she said.

Andreas cut a glare her way which she chose to disregard.

'No one has agreed to a wedding. What would this mean for me? My career?'

It was all too much. She needed them to spell out exactly what would happen to her—because right now she was completely overwhelmed.

'You would be Queen, of course,' Carissa said impatiently.

'And you would not return to your job,' Andreas added.

Helia's fingers curled in her skirt. Their tight grip was the only thing stopping her from hyperventilating. Her career was everything to her. She was a librarian, not a queen! What did she know about ruling?

Her stomach roiled at the thought.

She had spent two years among the palace's books and archives. Had scraped and clawed her way from nothing to end up here in the palace library.

Following her father's sudden passing when she was just a teenager, she had moved in with her uncle, her father's brother and business partner. He was meant to be her guardian, to take care of her, but he had only done so when it served him. Helia's father had left her a substantial inheritance—a nest egg meant to provide security for her when he could not—but she had never seen a penny of it as her uncle had cunningly taken it from her. And once he'd been in possession of it he had promptly dropped her off at the local orphanage. At a time when she had needed her family the most, she had been abandoned. Left to fend for herself. To deal with her grief and her anger alone.

She had found solace in books. Not that the orphanage had had very many. But they had filled her with a quiet happiness.

It had been no surprise to anyone, least of all herself, that she had become quiet and withdrawn. She hadn't been able to find it in herself to be the happy, effervescent person she had been with her father. She had been lost to her misery.

Only a single solitary spark had brightened those long, dark days.

While at school she had spent every free moment in the library. Until the librarian had taken pity on her and had allowed her to assist during breaks and after school. Bit by bit, in those dusty stacks, she had slowly come back to life. It was then that she had decided what she wanted to do with her life. She wanted to spend it among the books that had become her family and her escape. And she didn't want to be just a librarian at an underfunded, somewhat forgotten school. Oh, no, she wanted much more than that.

So she had earned herself a scholarship, and studied at one of the best universities in Thalonia, and immediately after that had gone to work at the city library in Seidon. Every day she would glimpse the palace on her commute to work and think to herself that one day she would work there. When the job she had dreamed of had finally become available, Helia had pounced on the opportunity. Now, at only twenty-eight, she was head librarian at the grandest library in the Kingdom, home to Thalonia's archives. It was a job she was immensely proud of.

They had another think coming if they thought she would take any of this lying down.

'What if I don't agree to this marriage?' she asked, interrupting their conversation.

Andreas dropped his hands to the carved armrests of his chair, staring Helia down. 'I don't want you to, Ms Demetriou. You are not the right queen for this kingdom. It goes against our traditions, not to mention brings us the nightmare challenge of getting you anywhere near ready to be a royal. But unfortunately for all of us King Vasili has decided, and none of us has the power to overturn his decision.'

His words were like a red rag to Helia, but she knew he was right. She wasn't ready to be Queen, and that would be a challenge, and Vasili had in fact picked her. His gaze had been intense. Filled with intent, but also grief and anger.

'I still haven't agreed.'

'Why wouldn't you agree?' Carissa very nearly sneered. 'Women don't often get the chance to become Queen.'

She's right, Helia thought to herself.

Most women never became Queen or gained any kind of power or influence, but the position had been presented to her now. It might not have occurred in a way she would have chosen, but surely there was an opportunity for her to make a difference.

Helia thought of those years at the orphanage, when funds had been low but there had been mouths to feed and growing bodies to clothe. When the temperature had dropped but they'd only been able to make do with what they had. When the children would talk about their dreams knowing they probably would never achieve them—because who would pay for their tuition?

She had come from among the forgotten citizens of not just Seidon, but Thalonia at large. Those without a voice who often just fell through the cracks. She remembered wishing she had the power to change things. Hoping that one day she would find a way to help. She had been volunteering at the orphanage whenever she could for years. A lot of those kids felt like her own. They were the closest thing she had to family.

Now there was a chance for one of the forgotten to sit on the throne, so maybe fighting this would be a mistake. It would be foolish of her to squander this opportunity—even if saying yes did mean that she would have to deal with attitudes like those of Andreas and Carissa every day.

Helia was conflicted. She didn't want to lose her career. It was all she had. All she loved. But she cared about the kind of children she'd grown up around...and beyond that there was Vasili.

She still remembered the day she had arrived at the palace. He had been the first royal she had seen. His beauty had rendered her speechless. With his short dark brown hair in soft, wavy curls and his golden-brown eyes, he had been a sight to behold. Let alone the fact that he had been climbing onto a black motorcycle at the time, clad in leathers.

He was the most unusual royal, and over the years she had noticed him more and more. Each time she did, a small attraction for the Prince grew. While she had almost never had any reason to directly interact with the royals, she'd noted how different he was compared to them. He always had a bit of time to chat to staff who were mostly treated as if they were invisible. He had a smile for everyone except when no one was watching him. But she did.

Helia was not delusional. She was entirely ordinary, and he had never once noticed her. Why would he? She spent all her time in the library that he never visited.

Now she felt foolish for feeling hopeful about being tied to him.

Her heart had skipped a beat when he had walked into the library today, in suit trousers and a button-down shirt that was open at the neck, but her appreciation had been halted by the expression on his face. He'd seemed to be caught somewhere between weariness and anguish...

Still, appreciating the Prince—or rather the King—didn't mean she could be a queen.

The mere thought had her hands trembling, and instilled a very real fear in her. She was confident around books, but had no idea how to navigate a royal court. She came from nothing. But didn't that make her perfect in a way? Vasili had been born to this life. He knew precisely what he was supposed to do. Could she show him what he *should* care about?

They were opposite forces, but together they could be something special. The thought filled her with equal parts trepidation and excitement.

'I'll do it.'

The moment the words left her lips, Helia's heart began to race.

'Of course you will.'

There was a look of smug satisfaction on Carissa's face that had annoyance bursting through Helia, eclipsing her nervousness.

'Think what you will, Carissa, but unless either of you can get His Majesty to change his mind I'm all you have—and I have my reasons for agreeing.'

Like the fact that *all* of Thalonia's people would be able to count on her, not just the rich and aristocratic, whether they realised it or not. Her every decision would have serious repercussions.

Her pulse hammered and her palms sweated. She tried to focus on her breathing. Panicking wouldn't help her.

She was still torn. Her whole life had been changed in a matter of minutes. The career she had fought for would be taken from her and replaced with something far more influential and terrifying. She hadn't really been given much choice, but her traitorous heart still beat just a little faster at the thought of being with Vasili.

* * *

Vasili sat in a plush white chair in Leander's office. *His* office. He had hardly ever come in here…the seat of power for Thalonia. He had hated this room with a passion growing up, and had been pleased when Leander had made changes to it. The walls still had frescoes from centuries long past. The blue of the sea was evident on nearly every wall, and the gold accents still glowed as if the metal had been poured straight onto the plaster, but everything else had changed.

Light poured in through the large arched windows, illuminating the white couches and the armchair where he sat. Towards the far end was a meeting table with six chairs, and directly in front of the window, as if all of Thalonia and the sea stood behind the man who sat there, was a behemoth of a desk.

An empty desk.

This office reflected Leander perfectly. How he'd tried to marry his modern views with a traditional past. It wasn't Vasili.

He leaned his head against a backrest carved in the Rococo style and closed his eyes, uttering a soft curse. He should never have lost his temper. It never helped any situation. But when he thought about Andreas and Carissa trying to foist a bride on him his blood started to boil all over again.

They were loyal to the crown, to Leander. The latter he could forgive, even respect, but the former…? That angered him immensely. Because wasn't that exactly like his parents? Loyal to the crown to the detriment of him?

Vasili understood that they were unhappy he would have to take over. But he didn't *have* to do anything. Not only had he never been meant to be King, but he also never wanted it— and he could only imagine who his 'trusted' advisors would pick for him to marry. Another thing he was simply expected to accept without consideration for how he felt. And for what? To save the crown? Why would he care? He hated it.

That was certainly no secret. All his life he'd wanted out, yet he knew he was stuck in his gilded cage—which was why he'd rebelled just now. As he always did. Except this rebellion made him feel guilty, because he had left no room for argument. He could only imagine how pushy that would have made Andreas and Carissa. The chaos his staff would now be consumed by as they navigated his decision.

A groan sounded through the silent office as he replayed the moment he had chosen the librarian to be his wife. He didn't even know her name, for pity's sake! But even in that moment of madness he hadn't been able to help but notice how stunningly beautiful she was. Entirely arresting. Her eyes had brought to mind the untameable seas around the Kingdom.

He'd made a reckless decision, thinking Andreas would see it for what it was. See that he needed to grieve. He had just lost his brother. That still didn't feel entirely real. He needed time to come to terms with that...with these massive changes. But they hadn't seen that, or had simply ignored it, and Vasili knew time was something he was never going to get.

He had awoken that morning with two women in his bed and the thought that today would be like any other day. He had decided to ride down the coast, where a lavish party was planned for the evening.

A part of him still wanted to do that. To turn his back on the palace and forget all of it for a few hours.

He heaved a sigh and walked to the large window, staring out at Seidon. Earlier he had had the thought that he would like to let the crown fall into ruin. He really liked that idea. More than ever the temptation to abdicate seduced him. He wanted to reach out and grab on to that notion with both hands. Leave it all and walk away. He liked his life as it was.

Vasili had just decided a ride on his motorcycle was precisely what he needed when he heard the door open. He knew who it was before he even spoke.

'Here you are, Your Majesty,' said Andreas, as he entered and quietly shut the door behind him.

Vasili was struck with a vivid fantasy of throwing the man out. He had seen far too much of him for one day. He wanted to ask if Andreas was done with terrorising the librarian, but he said nothing. While he might not have received quite the same training as Leander, Vasili knew how to use silence as a show of power, and something told him he would always have to wield that power with Andreas.

Turning around with his hands clasped behind his back, he pinned Andreas with a stare that had the older man stopping before he could cross the room all the way.

Andreas cleared his throat. 'We have spoken to Helia Demetriou, sir, but we need to discuss this decision. She isn't what this kingdom needs.'

'I suppose you know exactly what that is?' Vasili challenged.

'In this instance, yes. We need a queen who can take the throne immediately. She cannot do that. We have no time. King Leander's wedding has been planned. Every vendor is confirmed. Every part of his wedding was meant to showcase Thalonia to the world, and people are still relying on us to move forward with the event. As much as it might hurt us, we need you and a queen on the throne. We need the coronation to happen as soon as possible, or we risk damaging our people financially. That takes priority. God forbid, but should something happen to you, Thalonia will be in serious trouble. We need to have faith that the Queen could rule in that situation.'

A spare ruler. Not just that, now he was to be a filler-in at someone else's wedding. His life truly meant nothing. Vasili was a spare in every way.

All he could do was shake his head.

'Allow me to speak freely,' Andreas went on.

'Nothing has stopped you before.'

'The wedding has to go ahead. But Carissa and I feel that while Miss Demetriou has agreed, we believe we could come up with a better solution. I'm sure she has her appeal...she just isn't the best choice given our time constraints. We will have the entire staff running around trying to arrange a wedding, a coronation and training—which ordinarily would be far simpler than what we have to do now. Which is to teach someone how to be royal. I have got people trying to figure out how to impart an entire lifetime's worth of training and knowledge in a few short weeks. But this isn't going to work. It's an impossible task.'

Vasili still said nothing. He simply cocked a brow, indicating for him to continue.

'Please, Your Majesty, just listen.'

Vasili didn't want to. He knew he was being ridiculous—but so was this entire situation.

'So what would you propose? Hmm? A marriage to someone I would have nothing to do with?'

'It doesn't have to be that way. Princess Allegra is still an option—'

'You have to be out of your mind! I am not marrying Leander's fiancée.'

The idea was abhorrent.

'She understands how to rule. She is ready to be Queen and you have tolerated her in the past.'

'Tolerated? Is that how low the bar is for a royal consort?'

The bite in Vasili's words had Andreas flinching.

'She is one option, and there are other options that you need to look at for the good of the Kingdom. We would have to alter our traditions, our processes, to accommodate Helia. How long would that take? You know Princess Allegra—you know nothing about the librarian.'

That was true. He knew nothing about her. But he would take her over any of the royals he knew. Any of the nobility.

And if it took time to ready her to be queen then that was all the better for him. At least he would get the time he needed then.

'Your parents knew each other as children. They were both of noble blood and were probably the most loved royals we have ever had on the throne.'

Except they hadn't loved each other. They hadn't loved him.

'I have said it before and I will say it again, Andreas. I am neither my parents nor Leander. You'd best stop expecting to see them in me. I don't care what you have to do—that isn't my problem. No matter how many times you come to me with this, my decision will not change.'

'Vasili!' Andreas snapped. His frustration was pouring off him in waves.

'Excuse me?' Vasili all but growled.

Andreas took a very deep breath. 'Apologies, Your Majesty, but you don't seem to be listening. We *cannot* make this happen. Not in the time we have.'

'Andreas,' Vasili said, with a calm he did not feel, especially when the fuse of his temper had once again been lit. 'I've had just about as much disrespect as I am going to take from you, and this will be the last time. I understand your panic, but my word is final. Now, bring Miss Demetriou to me. I wish to speak to her in private.'

There was no emotion in Vasili's voice. Every swirling thought and feeling was locked away securely deep within him.

'Of course.'

He watched Andreas leave and turned back to the window. He needed to find out why Helia had agreed and then give her an opportunity to back out. After all, this wasn't a decision he had made for her—it was a decision he had made against being the King they wanted.

It wasn't long before Vasili heard footsteps on the other side of the door. Silently it swung open and in she walked. She took the breath from him. He couldn't speak. All he could do was stare. How had he never noticed her before? She had to be the most exquisite creature ever to have graced the palace.

It took a gargantuan effort to wrestle his thoughts back into something that made sense. He had called her here for a reason.

Clearing his throat, Vasili instructed her to close the door and take a seat.

Of all the things she could have done, she curtseyed.

'Your Majesty,' she said politely, and did as she was told.

The action was so at odds with how his day had gone, Vasili did well to hide his laughter.

He followed her with his eyes as she sat down. 'Given our current situation, I think we are past formalities, wouldn't you say? Call me Vasili.'

'My name is Helia,' she replied in a soft voice.

For the first time since he'd been told his brother had died, Vasili wanted to genuinely smile. She was a little gauche, and he couldn't help but find it endearing. She was a lamb in a den of wolves. A woman like her should never be shackled to a debaucher. Especially not one who held the throne in such contempt.

'I would ask you how you are, but I imagine you have no good answer right now, and for that I must apologise.'

'I appreciate that, Your— Vasili.'

Her skin was tinged red and Vasili had the mad impulse to run his fingers over it. Would she feel hot to the touch?

He took a steadying breath. Seeing Helia in front of him had brought home just what he had set in motion. 'I realise I have placed us in a difficult situation, but I want you to know that you can be honest with me. In fact, I insist on it. And I will do the same. Understood?'

Helia nodded.

'I need you to say the words, Helia.'

He saw the flash of her pupils dilating and he imagined a different circumstance when he might say those same words. Her name felt like a caress on his tongue.

'I understand.'

'Why are you agreeing to this madness? Surely you were given the choice to refuse me?'

Helia looked away. Wavy caramel curls fell over curved shoulders, and she avoided his gaze before she straightened, and looked him in the eye. At first Vasili had thought her meek. Timid. Now he could see there was fire in her. It shouldn't tempt him as much as it did.

'If I can make a difference to people as Queen, in any way, I would be a fool to say no. I may be a commoner, but I think that gives me a voice few ever get to use. I know better than most what it's like to be forgotten.'

Vasili walked to the front of the large desk and perched on the edge, getting as close to Helia as he dared without touching her. 'What do you mean?'

But she didn't respond. He couldn't blame her. He had asked for honesty, but not for her to bare her secrets. Even if she seemed attracted to him, she didn't know him, and she had no reason to answer. So he respected her silent request for him not to push.

'Helia, you are not being forced to accept this situation. If you feel there are needs not being met in our kingdom…if you feel that you need to be the voice of those without one…that's fine. You can talk to me and I will listen. You don't have to sacrifice your life for it. Regardless of what anyone says, you have a choice. You always have a choice.'

He hadn't anticipated that things would reach this point, but he now realised that he had doubled down on his decision only because Andreas had caused him to snap. He'd reacted in the way he always did. By resisting.

Helia was trying desperately to banish the flight of butterflies in her stomach. Her heart was racing, as it had been since she'd walked into the office. Having worked at the palace for two

years, she knew exactly how to behave in the presence of royalty, and she was certain she had always come across as polite
and self-contained. Yet from the moment she'd walked into this
room she had been overwhelmed by the new King's presence.

It took a mammoth effort for her to focus on the words he
had been saying. It seemed surreal that he was saying them,
and speaking had become difficult.

'I respect that,' Helia said, trying to keep the wobble of
nerves from her voice.

He had told her to be honest, but she didn't know if her
thoughts were too bold to say out loud.

'Whatever is on your mind, you can say it, Helia.'

She wasn't so sure about that...

'You have agreed to be Queen,' Vasili said with a small
smirk. 'How are you going to do that if you can't talk to me?'

She had agreed, and now she wondered if that had been a
terrible mistake. What was she thinking? She couldn't be the
King's equal. But she couldn't waste a chance to help the orphanage.

'I will offer you a thought if you offer me one. Does that
sound fair?' he asked.

She nodded, still unsure and feeling completely out of her
depth.

'I'm wondering how you could agree to this. If you're actually okay with the thought of being Queen...of being married to me. I see how tense you are and I think that you aren't
okay, and that this world I live in might be more cut-throat
than you are prepared to handle.'

Helia hadn't realised how perceptive he was. Of course she
hadn't. She had never been in his company long enough to
notice anything. She hated it that he was probably right. She
didn't know how to deal with royal business, and that in particular scared her. As honourable as her intentions were, the

worry that she might fail spectacularly as Queen still sat at the back of her mind.

Helia swallowed thickly. Vasili had spoken his thoughts—his doubts—and in doing so had shown her it was safe for her to express hers, even if it made her uncomfortable.

'It seems to me that you do not wish to marry.' Whether it was to marry her or marry in general, she didn't know. She couldn't blame him for not wanting her, she was entirely ordinary compared to him—the antithesis to the women he was normally seen with. 'Surely you could choose not to. You are King and you are entitled to grieve.'

Vasili shook his head, a sombre look passing over his features. 'If only that were true. It's best you find out now that being a royal doesn't leave you with much room for choice. This...' he waved his hand between them '...will be the last big decision you get to make on your own. Everything you do from now on, everything you say, will be watched and dissected. Andreas and Carissa are only the start of it. I made a reckless pronouncement that affects you...how much time did you get before you were forced to make a decision? How much choice were you given?'

He was right. She hadn't been given much choice or any time to digest what had happened. And once she'd agreed she had been almost immediately brought to the King. She was in a tailspin, fighting to gain control. But she had had no choices most of her life. She'd had to survive. And even though she was finally comfortable and thriving, she knew she could survive again.

'Even as a commoner you don't get many choices. You have to make do with what you're dealt.' She hoped she'd hidden the deep sorrow that lanced through her.

'Don't call yourself that. Andreas may have certain ideas about tradition and propriety, but I do not share them. There is nothing common about you.'

The vehemence in his words had Helia's heart skipping a beat. He made her feel off balance, and she desperately wanted to believe that he thought her something special. It was beginning to dawn on her just how out of her depth she truly was. Wishing to share a moment with Vasili should have been the last thing on her mind—she should be singularly focussed on what it meant to be Queen. Who she was doing this for.

All that thought did was make her panic.

'If you agree to this, Helia, it will not be an easy life.'

'Life isn't easy anyway.'

She bit her lip to stop herself saying more and his gaze flashed to her mouth, darkening. The atmosphere between them seemed to change. Become charged with something intoxicating. Her eyes darted to his lips, but quickly flicked up, meeting his. Heat flared within her.

'No, it isn't.' Vasili's voice came low and raspy. 'I didn't intend for you to get caught up in this battle. The decision I made was meant to do nothing more than—'

'Shock?' she offered, forgetting herself, lost in his golden-brown gaze.

Vasili's lips twitched with a suppressed smile. 'Yes. And just meant to earn me a reprieve.'

'The next few weeks are going to be difficult,' he warned, curling his fingers around the edge of the table to stop himself from reaching out to Helia.

'I expect so. But I'm not backing out of this.'

It was barely above a whisper.

'Why?'

She looked away, her fingers fidgeting, and for a moment he thought she wouldn't answer.

'A lot of people helped me. As Queen, I can be there for them and so many more. No one else cares about them, but I do.'

'You will lose any semblance of a life. Your career. Is that what you want?'

She continued to stare down at her hands. He wanted to force her to look at him.

When she answered, her voice was strong. 'No, it's not. But we can only work with the cards we are dealt. May I ask you a question?'

'Of course.'

'You don't want to get married...'

'No, I don't. I probably never will want that.'

'Then what *do* you want?'

It was the question Vasili had wanted to hear all his life. It was sad that the only person to ask was someone with no power to change anything. Still, he'd promised her honesty, so he would answer.

'To leave. The throne...this kingdom. All of it.'

'Then why don't you?'

'Because, as much as I would love to abdicate, the well-being of the people rests on my shoulders. I would love nothing more than to cast it all away, but unfortunately I was born to a duty that I can't escape.'

Vasili hated the defeat in his voice. Earlier he had wanted to climb on his bike and leave, but no matter where he went he knew the truth of the matter wouldn't change. He had to be King.

'So where does that leave us?' Helia asked softly.

It left him with little choice. It left him with a kingdom to run and a marriage he didn't want. His sole choice was either to marry the beautiful woman before him, or a royal that his staff approved of.

He realised he had taken too long to answer when Helia stood and with a glance back at him walked to the door.

Except he couldn't let her walk out yet.

His steps ate up the distance between them, and just as she

placed her hand on the door he flattened his palm against the wood, preventing her from opening it. Standing behind her, he could finally truly see what a delicate thing she was. Her head would comfortably tuck under his chin. But he left the smallest of spaces between their bodies.

He bent down slightly, his lips close to her ear. 'Be sure you want to go through with this, Helia. The crown…this world… It is not made up of good people. It's full of people like me.'

She turned around then, leaning back against the door. Her tempting body was almost underneath him. That fire was back in her eyes. Raging in full force and calling to him.

'You are King now. The crown can be whatever you want it to be.'

Who *was* this bewitching creature?

Vasili ached to know more about her. He was filled with a curiosity he had never experienced before. He wanted to touch her. To run the backs of his fingers down her cheek. To brush his lips against hers. They were nothing to each other, but she had woven some sort of spell around him, because for the first time that day he could breathe. Helia had pushed away the forces suffocating him.

And so he had his answer. He would marry Helia over anyone Andreas chose. At least she would be his choice. But, given that he didn't wish to marry at all, he still didn't feel like it— which made him want to lash out. Except he couldn't. So he simply withdrew into himself and stepped away from Helia, feeling the fight in him go out.

'To answer your question, it leaves neither of us much of a choice.'

'So we'll marry,' Helia said.

It wasn't a question. Merely an agreement.

'Yes. Your life as you knew it is over. I'm sorry.'

CHAPTER THREE

HELIA STOOD IN the antechamber of her suite, which func-
tioned as a receiving room. The luxury she found herself in
was not something she could get used to. She had been given
these splendid rooms the day she'd agreed to be Queen, and
she had been in shock then. She wasn't entirely sure that it
had worn off yet.

There were paintings on her ceiling! And Helia was certain her whole apartment would have fit numerous times into
this suite.

She hadn't been allowed to return home. Her belongings
has been sent for. As Vasili had warned her, once she'd agreed,
she'd had little choice.

Two weeks. That was how long it had been since Helia had
given the King her word that she would marry him. And that
time had been filled with what she called her 'Queen Lessons'.

Being a librarian had given her vast knowledge on many
different topics. She was proud of how well read she was. But
no level of intelligence or knowledge could have prepared her
for this.

Every single day was filled with lessons on politics, deco-
rum, history… She'd had every part of her scrutinised. From
her posture to her table manners to her appearance. It made her
feel lacking in a way she had never considered before. She'd
been given a list of literature that it would be appropriate for
a queen to have read. She didn't mind that so much—at least

she had the books for company—but she loathed being told what she was 'permitted' to read. She'd let it go for now, keeping her eyes on the reason she was doing any of this. Besides, when she was Queen her requests would not be ignored. Or so she hoped.

She had even been made to undergo a physical examination with the private royal physician, and it seemed so had Vasili—as evidenced by the copy of his all-clear results that was given to her. It made sense, considering they expected her to bear his children at some point. But she still didn't know how she felt about that.

She required a great deal of patience, as every 'lesson' was filled with jabs at her background. Comments on how the lessons would not be necessary if she were a royal. Whispers that she should not be going on the throne. That her very presence had thrown their plans into disarray. Helia was set to be their queen, and yet none of them saw fit to hide their disdain.

All it did was make her square her shoulders and lift her chin. She would show them that she would not let them drag her down, even if their words pierced her armour and broke down what little confidence she had.

Those two frantic weeks had gone by in the blink of an eye. And now here she was. Standing alone in her suite in the most spectacular wedding dress she had ever seen. A sheath of fine, hand-made lace, it caressed her chest and fell to the floor. She touched the band of lace around her upper arms, exposing her golden shoulders. The full-length mirror that had been placed in the room reflected a woman who looked like her, but couldn't possibly be.

She turned slightly, admiring the way the dress hugged every part of her. From below her shoulder blades all the way down, ending in a long, dramatic train. It reminded her of the bubbly wash along the shore as the waves broke.

Perhaps it had reminded others of it too. Which would explain the sapphire and diamond tiara in her hair, which had been styled into an elegant chignon. It sparkled like a sprinkling of the sea. There were sapphires in her ears too. Dainty little drops that would take no attention away from the masterpiece that was the dress.

My wedding dress, she thought, her hands growing clammy.

She tried taking deep calming breaths as the full extent of what she was about to embark upon crashed over her. Was she doing the right thing? What if all the whispers were true? She was an orphan who had come from nothing. Would she be an adequate queen? Did she have any right to believe she could be?

Helia turned to fully face her reflection in the mirror, wondering if she had been naïve about the reality of her future. But these doubts were her own to bear. She couldn't back out now. This was her only way to help all the forgotten people, like herself when she was in the care system. Most kids from the orphanage didn't grow into powerful adults. They became people just doing what they could to get by. She was one of the lucky ones, and fortune had truly smiled down on her. It would be foolish to think there wouldn't be a price to pay for it. So she would use whatever royal power she could to help those who meant the most to her.

She was under no illusions. Helia knew this would be one of the hardest challenges she would ever have to navigate. But she stood on the precipice of fulfilling a wish she had held so dear for all these years. A wish that she could make a difference.

And there was another reason why she couldn't back out. One that felt as vital as breathing. She'd given Vasili her word. He'd given her a chance to back out and she had said she wouldn't. That promise might mean little to him, but it meant something important to her—because she had made it to *him*.

She was well aware that he didn't want this marriage, but duty had given him no choice. She had to find a way to get him on her side and keep him there, so that she could realise her plans. She would have to learn to be the Queen he needed. Yet another thing to make her feel uneasy...

Helia hadn't seen Vasili at all in the two weeks that had passed. The lessons had taken up all of her time, and she assumed he had been coming to terms with being king. So there had been silence. She supposed she could have reached out in some way—but so could he. At the end of each day she'd been so tired she'd often fallen asleep as soon as she'd collapsed on her bed. She hadn't even been allowed back to the library, which had made her miserable. But at least she had the comfort of some books in her room.

She didn't know what to expect when she walked down the aisle. There had been no dress rehearsals. Andreas and Carissa had simply explained the order of events to her.

Would Vasili be there at the end of the aisle? Or would he choose to go against the wishes of his advisors? What would she do if he wasn't there? He had admitted that he wanted to leave. She remembered with great clarity the remoteness in him when they had agreed to marry. His reluctance.

It had stung, but she couldn't hold it against him.

She took a deep breath. Then another. Falling down this spiral would help nothing. She had a duty. If Vasili wasn't at the altar, she would deal with it then.

A firm knock sounded on the door and she whirled around just as Andreas walked into the room, dressed in a tailcoat.

'Good, you're ready.'

Helia was used to his lack of greeting by now, as if he was far too busy to waste even precious seconds.

'I think you could pass for a queen already.'

'I think that could almost pass for a compliment,' she retorted.

Her relationship with Andreas was now in a rather odd place. He was no longer her boss. In fact, once she was Queen she would be much higher up the hierarchy than him. But he still had far more knowledge of this royal world than she did. His disdain for her was certainly still on display, but it couldn't last for ever. She would learn what she had to in order to deal with all the palace staff—including him.

'Perhaps.' He stepped fully into the room and closed the door behind him. 'How are you feeling?'

'A little ill,' she said truthfully.

'To be expected. Just remember what you're supposed to do and say, and it will be fine.'

Helia nodded. As pre-wedding pep talks went, Andreas's attempt was abominable, but she hadn't really expected comfort from him.

'The carriage is outside,' he informed her, before taking a step closer. 'And my offer to walk you down the aisle still stands.'

'I appreciate that, but my answer is still no, thank you.'

'That isn't our tradition.'

Helia wanted to say that neither was the King marrying someone who wasn't of noble birth, but she held her tongue. Andreas had made the offer several times. She knew it wasn't out of kindness but rather wanting the right image. But she had always known that she would have no one to walk her down the aisle if she ever married. Her father had died, and no one else deserved the honour.

Helia had had to rely on herself for a long time, and she wasn't the only one who did so. The world she came from was filled with people just like her, so she would walk herself. It would be a show of strength and solidarity for them, even though it was another break in tradition.

'Shall we?' She gestured to the door.

Andreas held it open and several women stepped into the room, each of them holding up part of the long, lacy train of her dress as they set off through the palace and then helped her into a waiting carriage, pulled by four magnificent white horses. The carriage itself was white, with gilding and hints of lapis lazuli. Pure opulence.

As soon as the door was closed, they set off for the cathedral.

Vasili stood at the altar of the largest cathedral in Seidon. Alone. There were cameras all over the place. As discreet as they tried to be, he still saw them. Media trucks crowded much of the square outside. The royal wedding was being televised throughout the nation. Vasili pretended they didn't exist. This wedding was a show. He found nothing sacred in it.

He cast his gaze down the long aisle, where a thick red carpet had been laid over the stone floors. Pillars topped with elaborate white flower arrangements stood proud on either side. Light filtering in from the high windows illuminated them. Slight shadows played on the sculptures attached to the columns that towered all the way up to the vaulted ceiling. Row upon row of people dripping in wealth sat in their finery, waiting for the arrival of the would-be queen.

Vasili ignored all of them. He kept his eyes firmly fixed on the closed doors, standing almost preternaturally still with his hands clasped at his back. His only movement was running his thumb back and forth along the gold accents on the cuff of his jacket. He was decked in full royal regalia. A gold sash sat over his jacket and there was a ceremonial sword at his waist. He felt ridiculous in the uniform. He would never have worn it given the choice, but nothing about what was happening was about choice. He knew he projected the kind of image a king should. Strong and regal. Inside, he wanted that door to open so they could get this wedding over with.

Standing alone meant he had every eye on him. Having someone beside him would have diluted the attention, but he hadn't wanted anyone to stand with him. The only person who should have had the privilege was dead. And, while he was getting married and ensuring Thalonia's future, he wanted no one to forget that Leander was gone. One king was dead and he had already been replaced by another. There was a celebration planned, and a coronation would follow the wedding. He found it all repugnant.

This should have been Leander's wedding, not his. Vasili would have happily stood beside his brother. He was the one groomed for the life of a king. He could almost hear fate's shrill laugh as he waited for his bride to arrive so he could become the King no one had asked for. But, no matter how much he hated the situation he was in, this was the very reason for which he had been born. A fact he'd had to come to terms with over the last few weeks. He hadn't seen Helia at all during that time, but she hadn't been far from his mind.

The image of her pinned beneath him against the door assaulted him frequently. Particularly in his dreams, when he would wake up hard and panting. It was perhaps a mistake to have kept his distance. Andreas had informed him of her progress during her lessons. The older man's disapproval had leaked into every report, but it had made him smile. Vasili cursed himself now, because he could have used that time to get to know her. See if they had anything in common. Find out what she loved other than books—because he was yet to meet a librarian who didn't. Truly get to the bottom of why she was martyring herself like this.

Perhaps rebellion was so rooted in him that he had hated what was occurring so much that avoiding Helia had been just another way to rebel against the crown. It was a belated realisation, he knew, because now they were on the verge of getting married and he still wished to bolt from the church.

The doors slowly swung open, and it was officially too late.

How did she feel about him staying away? he wondered. The palace was already full of pretentious snobs—he could only imagine how lonely the past two weeks must have been for her. He regretted his actions now. He should have given her a way to contact him. After all, it was his fault that she was being taken from her comfortable life.

Was she reluctant to go through with this wedding? Was she nervous? Would she walk through those doors at all? Given how he felt towards the throne, he wouldn't hold it against her if she decided not to show up. He had certainly given her a reason not to say yes. No doubt Andreas would quickly take the opportunity to find him a different bride. One who fitted in with his idea of the perfect queen.

He half expected to see the man walk in now, to tell him his bride had left. And for some reason the idea of not seeing those caramel curls or those blue eyes felt like a loss he didn't want to endure. But then the hum of numerous people getting to their feet sounded through the cathedral and a lone violin played chords that were both beautiful and sorrowful, making the hairs on Vasili's arms rise.

But it wasn't the music that stole his breath. It wasn't the magnificent building with all its rich history. The sole reason he felt as if he was in the crushing depths of the sea, with no air in his lungs, was the woman standing in the doorway. Her curled hair was pulled back, with a few loose tendrils framing her face, catching the filtered light like a corona around her…a divine crown. He didn't blame anyone for the gasps he heard echo around the chamber. If he'd had any air he might have gasped too.

She stood alone, just like him. A pillar of regal strength. And he felt it then: her eyes latching on to his as she glided down the aisle. Her dress trailed long after her in an ocean of lace, as if she carried the sea wherever she went. A more perfect queen he could not imagine. Vasili hadn't even known of Helia until just two weeks ago, and now he wondered how a secret like her could ever have been kept in this place.

She was utterly, heartbreakingly beautiful.

He didn't expect the swift punch of guilt that came next. This stunning woman was an innocent. He knew nothing about her. Perhaps she had a life she loved. Maybe she loved being in that library. And just because she'd happened to be in the wrong place at the wrong time, he had dragged her into this madness with him. Vasili had thought of her as a secret, and maybe she'd been safer that way. Because the moment he had seen her, he had turned her world upside down. For that there should be no forgiveness. He deserved his punishment of life as the King he didn't want to be, locked in a loveless marriage he didn't want, but there was no way Helia deserved that fate. She deserved a life of pure happiness. Especially since back in his office he'd sensed a hardship she didn't want to talk about.

But he couldn't stop the wedding. Not now. It would cause unspeakable embarrassment to her, and he just didn't have it in him to be that cruel.

As Helia drew close, the corner of her mouth kicked up just the tiniest fraction, and he returned her small smile with one of his own. He held out his hand once she was close enough, feeling a current tingle across his palms as her skin made contact with his. He helped her up the small step.

'Hello, Vasili,' she whispered as she came to stand in front of him.

He swore he could see relief on her face. Had she been worried that he wouldn't be here? He supposed he'd given her no reason to trust that he would.

'Helia.'

He smiled down at her, taking her in. From the tiara on her head to the lace band around her bare arms, to the dress that kissed the ground with her every movement.

Vasili lost the battle of trying not to touch her, grazing his finger along what was hardly a sleeve. He pulled his hand back as the bishop let out an amused chuckle. He barely heard the man speak. All he could concentrate on was Helia. So he took her hands in his, and immediately the calm he had felt in her presence before descended upon him.

It was more than calm. It was as if every ounce of his attention was being drawn to one place. Helia. To that hum between their bodies. To the current travelling along their skin. There was temptation here.

'Vasili…' Helia whispered with a tiny smile, urging him to pay attention.

He heard the bishop gently clear his throat.

He was so focused on Helia that he hadn't even noticed it that the moment in which he would have to promise himself to her was upon them. The moment when he would have to say words he didn't believe in. He still did not want to be married, but there was no way around this, so with great effort he held his frustration at bay and made his vows.

He slid a large blue gem onto her finger. The French cut blue diamond reflected the light infinitely, like crushed ice, as the two smaller white diamonds on either side twinkled prettily in their platinum setting. The jewel had been in his family for generations, but none of the previous Queens had worn it. All had opted for something far more garish, but he couldn't think of a better suited choice. Helia was different from all those who had come before her, and that was something worth celebrating.

'Vasili…' Helia's voice rang out sweet and clear. 'I take you to be my husband, for better, for worse, to love and to cherish. And to stand by you alone, for all of our days.'

He didn't understand the feeling that overcame him at hearing those added words.

Helia had fire in her and would not bend to the will of others. Not easily at least. Understanding her message, he couldn't help but smile. She would stand by him alone. Not by Andreas or Carissa or the demands of the crown. She had just announced to all of Thalonia that she intended to be his partner.

You are King now. The crown can be whatever you want it to be.

He would have her support to do just that.

'You may now kiss the bride.'

Vasili heard the words. The moment he had craved and dreaded was upon him. For two weeks he had wanted to kiss her. Images of her against the door of his office flashed in his mind once again. He had wanted a taste of her then, and after replaying that moment so frequently he wasn't sure that he would be able to stop once his lips met hers.

So, with her hands still in his, Vasili mustered every bit of control he had and leaned in, placing a chaste kiss upon her lips. But as if it were a trap, designed just for him, that one simple touch caused the very air to snap around them.

He couldn't stop kissing her if he tried.

A buzzing warmth trailed over him from the contact of their lips, winding through his body, until his arms went around her and her hands found their way to his chest.

He couldn't think. Couldn't breathe. This innocent kiss was more overwhelming than any he had had before. Every other kiss he'd experienced in his life had been a means to an end. Merely a seduction to make the pay-off greater. Every one of those fell into the shadow of this one.

Without even realising it, he brought up a hand to cup her face, angling his head to kiss her more deeply. And, as if they had danced this particular dance before, she moved with him, opening to him as his tongue caressed hers. Igniting his blood.

He swallowed the sigh she breathed into him.

He'd thought there was nothing sacred about this wedding, but he found the divine in Helia's pillowy lips. She was soft and sweet and tentative. Everything he realised he had been imagining she would be, but more. Calm and crazed. Trapped and free. This embrace devoured him. Her eager responses spurred him on to kiss her harder, deeper.

He was utterly lost to the current that swept them both away, and it was only the sound of polite clapping and an amused chuckle close by that broke through the haze, wrenching him back.

With careful tenderness he pulled away, noticing the look in Helia's eyes, like a raging sea. And he knew she was just as affected as he was.

Maybe there was an up-side to this marriage after all.

CHAPTER FOUR

THE CORONATION FOLLOWED immediately after the wedding ceremony.

Vasili knelt on the step in the cathedral with Helia by his side and Helia glanced sidelong at him. She could see how hard he was gritting his teeth. She herself trembled on the inside. This feeling was far beyond nervousness. This was fear. Anxiety that she couldn't control but couldn't show either. She just had to dig down deeper, to find a way to fake the calm serenity the world expected from her.

But the fear refused to abate. She was terrified she would fail. She knew she already had with her little act of defiance. Adding to her vows made her a failure as Queen because she hadn't done what was expected of her. But she and Vasili had agreed on honesty. Besides that, he was King. She needed to show she was on his side, and maybe then he would be on hers.

Once their coronation oaths were said and the ceremony was over, Vasili offered Helia his arm, which she took with a small smile, letting him lead them out of the cathedral and into the square where their carriage awaited.

Helia waved to the people, ensuring her smile never faltered. A mask that would hide her nerves and help her do exactly as she was told.

Helia couldn't forsake her defiant heart. After all, it was what had helped her survive her years in the orphanage and beyond. Adding to her marriage vows was proof of that, but she would still take instruction on how to provide the right image for Thalonia's queen. She had to appease Andreas to a certain degree—and more than that she had no idea how to be Queen. It was a tightrope to walk, but she had to do it for the orphanage.

For herself.

For Vasili.

She could feel his burning gaze on her skin, but she refused to look at him. She was afraid of what she would see. Afraid that she would expose her attraction to him. Afraid that her mind would morph whatever that look was on his face into some sort of lie, telling her he wanted her too.

She couldn't lose her head.

The palace drew closer, and when the gilded carriage finally stopped Vasili stepped out and then placed his hands on Helia's waist. Her eyes locked with his as he lifted her out. His hands tightened around her, the touch rendering her breathless. His hold had safe. Steady. As if he wouldn't let her falter.

Helia knew that was just the hope in her heart talking and she had to control it.

'One more show, Helia,' he said to her softly, setting her on her feet.

'I know. Are you ready?'

'No, but let's do it anyway.'

'I feel like that might be a theme for our reign,' she said.

She laughed, covering up the way her heart pounded from the thought of what they were about to do. From his proximity.

Vasili chuckled. A look of surprise flashed across his face. 'Come, Your Majesty, your adoring public awaits.'

She saw straight through Vasili's attempt at levity. There was an intensity about him that was entirely at odds with his words. He hated this, but he needed to play his part just as she was.

They walked through the palace in silence, making their

way to the second floor, where they stopped before a set of closed double doors. He unlinked their arms as he turned to face her, placing his hands on her shoulders. It was as if he was bidding her to look only at him.

As if she could look anywhere else.

'Once we go out there, every person in the world will know who you are. Your privacy will be non-existent. Do you need a minute?'

She had been more apprehensive about this part than any of the others, because now she would be on show as Queen of the land. Every other part of the ceremony had been behind closed doors. It had felt controlled. But now she had to face the people and put on an act that Andreas would approve of. One that would reflect well on Vasili. All the while feeling like a fraud.

'I'm fine,' she said with a smile.

'And I'm going to remind you to be honest,' he said.

She glanced out through the doors, made up of numerous panes of glass, at the crowd beyond. 'I'm nervous—of course I am—but delaying helps no one.'

'If you're sure?'

'Do *you* need a minute?'

'More like several years. Let's get this over with.'

She nodded as he laced their fingers together, her heart jolting at the touch, and then, as one, they opened the doors and stepped out onto the balcony to face the crowd gathered just beyond the gates.

They might have clapped or cheered or waved flags. Vasili couldn't tell. All he felt was the weight of his new role. The consequences if he should fail. It wouldn't be he who suffered, but the ocean of people he now looked upon. Helia was waving. With the ever-present Andreas and Carissa at their backs, she didn't put a foot wrong—but he would not perform.

They were meant to share a kiss on this balcony. It was what every media outlet was waiting for. The perfect picture to splash on every news site and newspaper in Thalonia and beyond.

Vasili clamped his jaw shut. There was no way he would be kissing Helia in front of all these people. Not when the risk was getting sucked into that space where it was just him and her and this maddening attraction that he didn't want.

As soon as they were back inside and the doors had closed, Vasili handed his mantle to Andreas before helping Helia out of hers. Without another word to his private secretary, he escorted her to the King's quarters.

It was an enormous suite, with a luxurious sitting room. Beyond that was a pair of double doors, and the largest and grandest sleeping quarters in the palace. A second door off the sitting room led to the adjoining Queen's rooms, but Vasili wouldn't take Helia there.

'Make yourself comfortable. This is where you will sleep.'

'Where are you going?'

As much as he felt like a cad for doing so, Vasili didn't answer her. Her presence was a constant current, zapping over his skin. He could still feel her lips on his. And, heaven help him, he wanted to kiss her again. But there were too many warring emotions in him. Too many thoughts. He needed some space to re-centre.

'You can call for anything you need.'

He took her in one more time, standing there in her wedding dress with a look of confusion that quickly morphed into a blank slate.

'Vasili, we have a role to play here.'

He knew that.

'We have both made sacrifices today.'

Something else he was well aware of. But he couldn't be in this room with Helia a second longer without her affecting his judgement.

'You're right—we have. And it will make no difference to what happens tomorrow or the day after once I'm out through that door.'

'I can understand you needing to escape. I sympathise. But I have given up a great deal, and with Andreas watching my every step I can't afford to put a foot wrong. I've done everything expected of me today. I can support you, but I need you to do the same.'

Helia calling him out shouldn't have any effect on him, but damn him if her defiance didn't appeal to him. Still, he bowed to no one, and even though she had just become his queen and his wife, she would not be the exception.

'You *have* done well. But no one—not even you, Helia— gets to dictate to me.'

She nodded once and he left, making a bee line for his old bedroom.

The second the door snicked shut he ripped off his ceremonial baldric. It and his sword were tossed aside, before he dropped into the dark leather chair in the corner of the room.

As soon as he was old enough Vasili had removed every hint of the palace from this space. His sanctuary. Now it was modern, with dark wooden floors and walls so blue it felt like being in the crushing depths of the sea. The artwork above his headboard certainly reminded him of water, and this was where he needed to be to centre himself.

Staring out of the window, he ran his finger along his lip and cursed. He was still thinking of that kiss. Of how much he'd wanted to kiss her in the carriage and again in the King's suite. But he knew it wouldn't have stopped there, so he'd had to escape.

Because that kiss had been different. It had made him feel instead of just being a physical indulgence. That kiss had made him need Helia, even though he never needed anyone. It had made him want to do anything, be anything, so he could keep kissing her. He had been so ready to give in to their chemistry after their kiss. Had thought that maybe they could have a little fun in this marriage... But it felt like a risk.

She already had a power over him he couldn't explain. What would happen if he was to have sex with her? Open himself up to her like that? A kiss was a means to an end, but that wasn't the case with Helia. Did he really want to risk flaying himself like that? Because he knew sex with her would be different. If a kiss could feel divine, sleeping with her would not be just a physical act. He couldn't allow it.

But the chemistry they had couldn't be ignored. It buzzed under his skin even now. They needed an outlet for it somehow. A way they could indulge without getting too close.

What about the fact that he wanted the monarchy to end with him, yet he was required to produce heirs with Helia? An heir and a spare—just like him. Perpetuating the same toxicity he had experienced with his own flesh and blood. Children. Innocents who would never have asked for this world.

He didn't really know what Helia wanted either—only what she'd agreed to. He didn't know whether she wanted children or not, and this life was certainly not going to give her a choice in the matter.

Concern for his people might have taken the choice of abdication away from him, but that didn't mean he had to ensure that the throne endured. It would end with him. Yes, he had married, as was required of him, and since this role of second-best ruler was what he'd been born for, he was now King. However, he could choose not to have children. It would be easy enough to control that.

Vasili crossed the room to a table that held a crystal decanter filled with amber liquid. He poured a measure into a glass and took a sip, relishing the burn in his throat.

He was resolute that he would not have any children just to have them forced into the life he lived. No one should have to suffer his fate…the fate of the King who shouldn't have been. And now he was expected to move into the King's quarters. He detested the idea but, thanks to tradition, he didn't have a choice. He would have to deal with the ghosts of that room. A room meant for his father and his brother but never him. Just the same as the role of King.

He would have to share these walls with people who had never seen the value in him. Who had always found him lacking. Bitter, awful people, who hadn't ever been happy, hadn't known love—who had held him in such disregard even though all he had ever wanted was to live his own life. Not to be placed aside just in case he was needed.

So he had lived in spite of them. The sex and the parties… they were all part of a life lived as hard as possible. But now that had to be put behind him. Now he had to look out for the people of this kingdom. People who probably wished that it had been him and not Leander on that plane.

He could feel it even within the palace walls. In the words Andreas said and in the silences he held. Perhaps it would have been simpler if it *had* been him. Nothing would have changed then. It would have meant little for Thalonia.

Vasili drained his glass and placed it on the towering stack of books on his bedside table.

Running his fingers through his hair, he realised these thoughts would get him nowhere. What he needed to do was decide how he would take on this new life. He had made a commitment to Helia.

Simply thinking her name had him wondering what she would be doing now, in that large room by herself. Wondering if she was upset or hurt. God, she was beautiful. She was his queen, and he would have to help her navigate this life, but she would in turn have to understand what their marriage would and wouldn't be.

Perhaps he should have discussed it with her before their

marriage, but he hadn't known then just how much she could affect him.

That damn kiss!

He needed to talk to her, but he couldn't do it now. A night away from her was a good idea, but tomorrow they would forge a new path. One that he carved out.

Helia watched the door close in disbelief. She hadn't really known what to expect after the ceremonies. Of course she had been told what *should* happen. That she and Vasili should retire to their rooms with the unspoken expectation that they would consummate their marriage.

While Thalonian royals of eras long past had had separate quarters, that wasn't a practice followed by modern-day rulers, and certainly wasn't an option for them. Because they had to sell the image of a strong union which meant sharing a room.

She hadn't considered that Vasili would leave her standing there in her wedding dress immediately afterwards, as if he couldn't stand to be in her presence any longer. And it made her feel alone. A feeling she'd thought she was used to.

Helia tried to squash the hurt that needled at her.

What did you expect? Helia quietly chastised herself. Vasili had been honest about not wanting to be married. Just because they were in this together, it did not mean that would change.

Heaving a deep sigh, she bundled the long train of her wedding dress in her arms and walked into the bedroom, hoping to find something there to change into. A stunning white chemise was laid out on the bed. She ran her fingers over the delicate fabric but then snatched them back. She had no reason to wear such a garment.

She turned her back on it and marched into the large bathroom, where she found a thick robe.

With some difficulty Helia managed to get out of her wedding dress. She reached for the dressing gown, but stopped short of taking it off the hook. It was her wedding day and, while it might not have been the day she had dreamed of, why shouldn't she enjoy what came with it? She might have a reluctant groom, but he wasn't here now, and all indications were that she wouldn't see him again that day. She would never have been able to afford such a fine item before becoming Queen, so she marched back into the bedroom and slipped the chemise over her head, luxuriating in the way the fabric kissed her skin as it slid down her body.

She sat on the edge of the bed, taking the fabric between her fingers. There would be a lot to get used to now. Not least of all a husband who had little interest in her despite her attraction to him. That kiss during the ceremony had taken her by surprise. She had anticipated that Vasili might try to avoid it, or perhaps give her a peck on the cheek. But that kiss... It had robbed her of breath and clouded her mind. She had been intoxicated by his presence. His scent. The feel and taste of him. She had forgotten where they stood, giving in to the liquid heat consuming her.

If she closed her eyes, she could feel the phantom warmth from his fingers still ghosting across her cheek. She could have sworn that his eyes had darkened. That he'd been as breathless as her. But then she remembered it was she who was attracted to him. Any feelings from that kiss had been one-sided. After all, she had been the one to notice a handsome prince...he had never noticed an invisible librarian...

Until he did.

Vasili was simply playing a part. As much as she thought she might possibly grow to love him, there was no good outcome to losing her heart to Vasili. She could allow herself to enjoy his touches, but she had to remember it was all a show. Because he would not be married to her if he had been given a choice.

Would he ever have noticed her if she hadn't been in the library that day? What if one of the library assistants had been there instead of her? Would they be sitting in this room now? She suspected she knew the answer to that. After all, she was not good enough for the Prince who was now King. No one in the palace seemed to think she would be an adequate queen.

Helia ripped the tiara from her hair and tossed it upon the dresser. Had she made a mistake? Or was she just letting the fact that Vasili had walked out unsettle her?

He's not the reason you're doing this, she reminded herself.

But she had to acknowledge that that was only half true. Her attraction to him was part of the reason, but the biggest part was that she would finally achieve her goal. Helping people like her was something she had always wanted to do, and she had vowed to find a way one day. Well, one day was here. She had chosen this union with her eyes open in order to serve her wants. So she would not second-guess herself simply because her husband needed space.

And it was obvious that he did.

From the moment the coronation ceremony had commenced Vasili had become withdrawn. There had been a haunted look in his eyes when he'd helped her out of the carriage that he hadn't been able to cover up in time. What if it wasn't just her but also this place that he'd needed to leave so urgently?

Helia had seen that he understood her addition to the vows, but maybe he needed to know that she would be on his side. This marriage needn't be a trap to make him miserable.

She would give him tonight, but tomorrow they would find a way to turn the crown into something they could both live with.

CHAPTER FIVE

THE SUN HAD barely risen. There would be little sign of life in the palace. But Vasili was already fixing the cufflinks on his shirt and pulling on his coat. He had contemplated his next move for most of the night. There were things that had to be done that neither he nor Helia could change, but he had to think bigger than just the next steps. Ground rules had to be outlined for their marriage. Boundaries neither of them would break. It was the best course of action for both of them.

First, he would have to apologise for his abrupt departure after the wedding. It had not been his finest moment, but Vasili was glad he had taken the time to sort through his thoughts.

Picking up his phone, Vasili called down to the kitchen. The one place that would already be hard at work.

'We will not be eating in the dining hall. Have breakfast sent to the room,' he instructed, not having to clarify which room he meant. He was supposed to have spent the night with his new wife. No one knew that he had instead spent the time in this room.

Hiding out.

He banished the thought. He wasn't hiding. He was strategising.

He had no idea how Helia would react, and hoped a calm chat over breakfast in private would lead to her easy acquiescence.

With that thought Vasili left his room and made his way through the quiet halls to the King's room. *His* room.

He knocked twice and turned the knob, expecting that Helia would likely still be in bed given the hour. But when he entered he found her hurriedly shrugging on a satin peignoir.

As quickly as she tried to cinch the belt around her waist, Vasili still caught sight of the gossamer fabric of her chemise beneath. Arousal flared bright in his gut. All thought had been wiped from his mind save one: to kiss her. The blush creeping up her neck did nothing to quash his reaction. He wanted to peel that peignoir away. To see how far that blush travelled. Kiss her again like he'd done at the altar, but this time find out where that road would lead.

Vasili had slept badly, and when he had, he had dreamt of her. In his arms. In his room. For just a second his willpower to keep her at a distance wavered. He could show her such pleasure. He wanted to know more about her. Was desperate to. That desperation broke through the haze of want. Getting to know her, being intimate with her, exposing himself to her, was forbidden.

No one wants you like that. She *wouldn't want you like that.*

Of course she wouldn't. That was why he couldn't give her any reason to think they could be a normal married couple. They weren't. Not by any stretch of the imagination. More than that, he couldn't let her think that they could fall in love. Because he didn't love, had never been loved. It wasn't in his genetic make-up.

That didn't mean they needed to live a life without passion.

Vasili cleared his throat. 'I'm glad you're awake. We have a lot to talk about.'

'Good morning to you too, Your Majesty,' Helia sniped.

He had to bite his cheek to stop himself smiling. Either Helia was still upset by his hasty exit the day before or she was not a morning person. Perhaps both. It was an idea he found oddly endearing and he filed the information away.

'Good morning, Helia. Did you sleep well?' Try as he might, he couldn't hide his amusement.

'Marvellously, thank you.'

'I've taken the liberty of sending for breakfast.'

As if it had been planned, a knock sounded at the door.

'That will be it right now.'

He opened the door and stood aside as a servant wheeled in a trolley with several cloches sitting on top.

He greeted Helia and Vasili with a bow, and was about to serve the new King and Queen when Vasili stopped him with a smile.

'That's all right, we can handle it from here.'

He closed the door, then pushed the trolley towards the small table in the room and went about lifting the lids before taking his seat and pouring two cups of coffee.

'Join me?'

Vasili might not have had the same level of rigorous training to be King as his brother, but he did know that he needed different approaches to win different people over. Sometimes a blatant show of power was needed, but at other times a softer touch was more effective. Given Helia's irascible mood, and the subject at hand, he knew he would need to be amiable. Charm her. And that was something he could do effortlessly.

He handed one of the cups to her, noting that she added neither cream nor sugar before taking a sip of the steaming hot drink.

'Pancakes?' he asked.

He watched Helia study him closely before she answered.

'Yes, please.'

He loaded her plate with pancakes, cream and fresh berries, before serving himself the same. If what he wanted to speak to her about hadn't been so important, he would have laughed at her confusion.

He watched her drain her cup before starting on the pancakes. If he was going to have a civilised conversation about their way forward, now was the time.

'Helia, I would like to apologise for my behaviour yesterday. Both at the wedding and after. I shouldn't have kissed you and I most certainly should not have left the way I did.'

'Why did you leave?'

She seemed focused on cutting up her food. Her calm indifference had to be an act. Still, he was glad they had a distraction of sorts for this conversation.

He picked up his utensils. 'I needed to think. The situation we find ourselves in is not an easy one to navigate, so we need to set some ground rules. Discuss our expectations.'

'Go on.'

'I know you have been told that in agreeing to be Queen you will be expected to bear heirs to the throne.'

Helia's cautious gaze landed on him. 'I have.'

'I don't want you to be concerned about that. I do not expect a physical relationship. You will not bear us any heirs. We will not have sex.'

After that kiss, he couldn't take the risk. He needed this boundary for himself.

Vasili waited for his words to land. Watched her stiffen as she speared a strawberry.

'Would it not have been prudent to mention this to me before we were married, Your Majesty?' she snapped.

'Your Majesty?' Vasili repeated, taken aback by the sharpness of her tone.

'Seems appropriate, given how you are dictating to me. And what about the crown?'

Her fork clattered on the plate as she placed her hands on the table. Vasili noticed how she forced herself to flatten her palms on the tablecloth as they tried to curl into fists.

'It will end with me.'

Regardless of whatever Helia said next, he would not budge on this. He had decided he would not have children, and nothing would change his mind.

'Do you want children?' he asked. He had to know, because if she did, all of this would have to end right now.

'I don't know. I hadn't had the luxury of thinking about the possibility all that much until two weeks ago, when I was *told* I would be expected to, and now again I am being *told* that I won't. It's my body, and possibly my family, but clearly I don't get a say in this decision?'

She was right, so he couldn't blame her for being angry.

'Are we still being honest?' she asked, after taking a breath, but he could still hear her temper in her voice.

'Always.'

'Then why? Help me understand.'

'I will not have an heir and a spare. It is my mission to move this kingdom to a system of governance that will never again require a royal.'

'You really hate it.'

'I do.'

'And yet you're willing to do the duty you hate for the people you are now responsible for.'

The fire had gone out of her tone.

'What's your point?'

There was a shimmer of emotion in her eyes that she blinked away. He could see there were more questions she wanted to ask.

Helia shook her head. 'It doesn't matter. Not at this moment at least. But I need to understand a few things.'

'Of course.'

'You are aware of your reputation. I have seen all the women you entertain, Vasili. If I am not the one in your bed, and if you are choosing not to have heirs—children—what does that mean?'

That tension she had managed to let go of earlier was back in her shoulders. He supposed he had earned his playboy reputation and could understand her concern over the potential embarrassment she would suffer.

'Are you asking me if I will stray?'

His voice had dropped an octave. He didn't like her calling his integrity into question. He knew his reaction was unfounded, because he had chosen the path his life had taken, but he would never deliberately hurt anyone. Especially not Helia.

'I am. If I am to be Queen—'

'You *are* Queen.'

She stared him down and continued, despite his interruption. 'I will not be embarrassed by a scandal. My goals are too important to endanger them like that.'

Vasili placed his knife and fork on his plate and pushed it aside, clasping his hands on the table as he leaned towards her. 'I will not be unfaithful to you, Helia.' She looked down at her plate, but he needed her to understand. 'Look at me,' he demanded. 'I may not have wanted to marry, but I did make a promise to you. Despite what might be said about me, I am a man of my word.'

'But—'

'But nothing. I am well aware of my reputation, but what you need to understand is that I have never wanted to be a royal.'

It looked as if Helia wanted to interrupt, but he wouldn't let her.

'We agreed on honesty from the start, so that is what you're going to get. I am sure you have noticed that I tend to rebel against this institution…' He waved his hands through the air, to indicate the palace and everything in it. Helia smiled, as if to say obviously she'd noticed. 'My philandering was nothing more than rebellion against how I was supposed to act as Prince. And it was effective. But I don't need it. It was simply an act meant to serve me.'

'That may be…but never is a very long time, Vasili. To say that you won't miss the company of women or won't want children…'

'I can say that I won't want children, and I am not saying I will have no company. There is chemistry between us Helia, I'm certain you feel it.'

He could tell by the way she swallowed that she did. It was impossible not to.

'What I am proposing is a marriage with no sex, but one in which we explore this thing between us. One with passion and pleasure. Helia, I will never love you—I am not capable of it—but I will remain faithful to you and expect the same from you. This marriage isn't about love. It's about duty. But why should we deprive ourselves because of it? However, you have to make the choice.'

Helia was dumbstruck. It irked her that he was dictating to her, but the truth of the matter was that she was married to Vasili. She doubted anyone else would turn her head ever again. Besides him, no one had since her first and only relationship.

She didn't understand why he would want passion without sex. It had been a big part of his life before. Was it her? Was this some sort of unfortunate attraction for him and he didn't truly want her?

Helia didn't want to admit how much that stung, but she was a realist, and just because she was extremely attracted to him it didn't mean he had to reciprocate. But to go through a whole life without love would be lonely. Especially without children. Without family.

Except she hadn't had love since she was orphaned, and she had survived. Why did she think her life now would be any different? Besides, it wasn't as if she would be without distraction. The prospect of experiencing pleasure at the hands of Vasili was exciting. So exciting, in fact, that her thighs squeezed together under the table.

So maybe she would be lonely, but she would also have passion unlike anything she had ever experienced.

And maybe it was a blessing that he was so set against having heirs. It was by far a better choice than having children he didn't want and would regret having. Children who might possibly be abandoned or bear the emotional scars of not being wanted—or, worse, children who would be left alone if something were to happen to her and Vasili.

But could he really manage a lifetime without sex?

'Tell me what you're thinking,' he said.

Helia wasn't sure she wanted to. It was evident that Vasili had had to deal with a lot of doubt when it came to who he was and what he could do, so she didn't want to speak hers aloud and add to the voices.

'Tell me,' Vasili insisted.

'I don't know if you would be able to turn off such a big part of yourself. You admitted that was who you had to be for a long time, and it doesn't seem possible to me for you to just switch off those urges.'

'If it was that important to me we wouldn't be having this discussion now. I would do as I pleased. As I have always done. I don't need it, Helia.'

Helia thought about it. His words didn't feel much like reassurance at all. And there was still the issue of children. She hadn't thought about having her own. Not when all her life she had been focused on surviving. When she had been alone. She hadn't even thought about children when she was in a relationship, and that had been doomed to fail.

'I need time to think about it,' she said.

'About what?'

'All of it.'

'Fine. I will give it to you.' Vasili sat back in his chair and took a sip of his now cooled coffee. 'We will have to make a public appearance—our first official appearance—when we return from our honeymoon.'

'Honeymoon?'

That caught Helia off guard. She hadn't known there would be one, but she realised she had been ridiculous not to think of it. Naturally there would have to be, for appearances' sake.

'Yes, Helia, a honeymoon. You can take all the time you need to consider what we have discussed here while we are away. I know what it is I have just proposed, and we will not be physical in any way until you come to a decision.' He placed his cup down and in a gentler voice said, 'I think we both need to come to terms with all that has changed.'

He was right. She definitely did.

'When do we leave?' she asked.

'Today.'

She nodded, not bothering to ask where they were going. It didn't really matter.

'Now, about our first appearance... I want you to pick what we do. I realise it will take you some time to get used to your new life, so choose something that will make you comfortable and Andreas will arrange it.'

'Andreas will arrange something *I* choose?' Helia challenged with a cocked brow. She stopped short of scoffing.

'Yes, he will. Need I remind you there was a coronation yesterday? You are Queen. You have power. Use it. And should you need it, I will support you.'

There was a look she couldn't decipher that passed over his face, but she appreciated the words, nonetheless. 'Thank you.'

'That's what a husband is for.'

Despite all that they'd spoken of, Helia laughed. 'Is it?'

'So I hear. Other things include reminding their wives about unpleasant events—like the coronation banquet that will be held a few weeks after we return.'

She could tell he was trying to keep the atmosphere light, but the tic in his jaw and the fact that his smile hadn't reached his eyes betrayed his true feelings.

'Why does that bother you so much?'

Vasili studied her intently before heaving a deep sigh, as if the weight of the world sat upon his shoulders. She supposed it did.

'It sickens me that Leander died only two weeks ago and yet now a banquet is being planned. We've had a celebration in the city. It just…' He took in a deep breath and glanced out of the window, grasping the armrests of his chair.

Helia understood. Vasili was grieving more than anyone realised or cared to acknowledge. Yes, the Kingdom had lost its king, but now it had a new one. Vasili had lost his brother. His flesh and blood. Not a title or someone who could be replaced.

'Vasili,' she said gently. She wanted to take his hand in hers but refrained from doing so. He was looking at her, and that would have to be enough. 'I know this marriage isn't what you chose, but I meant my vows. I will support you. This union between us can be what we make it, and if you want to postpone the banquet then that is what we'll do. If you want to have a ceremony to honour Leander instead, we'll do that. You have lost your brother, and you should do what you need to be free of all the chains your advisors have wrapped around you. So, tell me what you need and I will help you make it happen.'

'Helia…'

Her name was a breath on his lips. He said nothing else as he stared at her. Whatever emotion was contained in that one word was not reflected on his blank face.

It was clear Vasili had loved his brother deeply. And he cared about so much that he wouldn't reveal. He was willing to do something he truly hated because he cared about his people. If there was anyone who would support her goal it was him. And she felt her silly heart give up a piece of itself to the King.

'Get dressed, Helia. We will leave shortly.'

His voice had grown low.

Helia nodded and closed the door to the bedroom behind her, feeling utterly devastated for him.

CHAPTER SIX

HELIA FOUND HERSELF in the King's office. Vasili's office.

After their chat over breakfast, she'd readied herself as quickly as possible in clothes she didn't recognise and made her way with Vasili to this room. It didn't suit him at all. Everything seemed to have been carefully chosen to project an image of modernity, but without pushing the boundaries of tradition. That wasn't Vasili. Since she had first seen him, everything he had done had smashed down tradition's stifling walls. He didn't toe any line. He challenged it. It felt as if everything here had been designed for someone else and Vasili was the understudy that didn't fit.

The notion angered her.

'I thought we were meeting with Andreas,' she said, turning away from the fresco she had been examining.

'We are, but we're making him come to us. In fact... Would you come over here, Helia?'

Without thinking, she obeyed, walking over to Vasili, who had pulled his chair out.

'Have a seat.'

Helia stopped short. It might not be the throne, but that was most certainly the King's seat. Arguably the most important seat in the Kingdom. And he was offering it to her.

'I couldn't possibly.'

'Of course you could.'

He waited. Clearly he wouldn't back down.

Helia's heart thumped in her chest. She didn't know what to make of this. She sat down and he pushed the chair in, then rounded the table to face her.

'You look good there, Your Majesty.'

'Vasili, don't tease.' Obviously it was all in her head, but the chair, the table, this whole office, suddenly felt far too big for her.

'I'm not. Here are a few things to remember, Helia. Firstly, always make them come to you. Especially Andreas. Use my office or your own—it doesn't matter. Never go to them. Secondly, you're the Queen of Thalonia. The title might chafe, but it brings power. Wield it.'

'It's not that easy,' she admitted.

'No, it isn't. I understand this is all overwhelming, and that everyone here might seem as if they know more than you do, and that's fine. Learn from them, but don't ever let them forget who they're talking to.'

She understood what he was doing. In giving her his chair, Vasili was establishing the power balance between her and his closest advisor. Gratitude clogged her throat. But there was no time to express it because there was a knock at the door. Vasili held her gaze a moment longer, then turned around and perched on the edge of the table.

Andreas's attitude generally frustrated her, so she watched with some satisfaction as he entered the room and stopped in his tracks when he caught sight of them. The older man's brows knitted together, and for the first time she was glad for the change in her wardrobe. She doubted this would be nearly as effective if she had still been dressed like a librarian.

'Your Majesties.' Andreas inclined his head as he sketched a small bow.

'Andreas,' Vasili said. The authority in his voice was impressive. 'Have a seat.'

Helia watched him sit down in the chair opposite, casting a cursory glance her way before fixing his attention on the King.

'We wish to speak to you about the public appearance to be held once we return from our honeymoon.' He didn't take his eyes off Andreas. 'Helia, why don't you tell him what we have decided?'

She knew she needed to pass this initial test by wielding her power with a man who still attempted to intimidate her. She hoped her nervousness wouldn't show in her voice.

'Our first outing will be to the Seidon orphanage. We will meet with the caregivers there and the children. In that meeting we are going to find out exactly how the home is run, what help they need, and then work on measures to help.'

With every word she could see Andreas growing more and more unimpressed, until he could no longer keep his opinions leashed.

'Absolutely not.'

'I'm sorry?' replied Helia, afraid that her idea was going to die in this room.

Andreas took his time answering. No doubt choosing his words as diplomatically as possible. 'As admirable as your intentions may be, that is not an appropriate choice for your first sighting as King and Queen. The point is to introduce you both to the Kingdom and the world—because make no mistake the world will be watching—and show you in the best possible light. Not doing something that will take the focus away from you. We don't want the first thing we put on show to be—'

'Our country's failures? Should we hide everything that's wrong so that it will make everyone look good?' Helia challenged.

She knew she needed to be calm—she felt anything but. Her voice had risen as anger had coursed through her. Men like Andreas were the reason she and the other children had been cold in winter. Why they'd had to make do with what little they'd had.

Andreas didn't even look slightly uncomfortable. 'Every kingdom has its issues. It's an unfortunate reality.'

'Issues?' Helia exclaimed in disbelief. She was certain that this was not how a queen should behave, but she couldn't stop herself now. 'We need to do something about it.'

She could see the battle she would be facing to have her goals met. With Vasili having accepted his duty purely for the concern of his people, she reasoned that he would be on her side in her quest, but getting everyone else to play their part would be a fight.

'Eventually we may be able to look into it.'

A non-committal answer if ever there was one.

'We need to look at more appropriate public appearances and I am happy to help you with that.'

'What is more appropriate than showing an interest in help-ing the children of Thalonia? Where will this kingdom be without them? You are determined to secure the future of our nation, so surely this fits in with that objective?'

Gone was the quiet librarian. Right now, in this office, she would fight with all she had for her people.

Andreas had gone tense with frustration. 'I didn't say we wouldn't do anything about it, only that we need to choose wisely for your first public appearance. We have numerous options available to us. There is a charity concert being held by the symphonic orchestra. That would resonate well, as pre-vious kings and queens have often chosen the same event. It will show the people that you are willing to uphold our tradi-tions despite your history.'

Helia didn't miss the jab, but Andreas ploughed on.

'There is the annual polo match—or even a charity ball. Any of those would work well. Which should I arrange?'

Rage. That was what burned through Helia now. Andreas assumed that she would back down and listen. She wouldn't.

Just as she was about to argue, Vasili spoke. His voice was calm, but no one would dare oppose his tone. It would be enough to silence Andreas.

'That's enough. We brought you here to inform you of our decision. Your queen has given her orders. We are going to the orphanage.'

'My apologies, Your Majesty,' he said rigidly. 'It shall be arranged.'

'Good.'

Andreas swiftly exited the office, leaving Helia alone with Vasili. He had been so opposed it concerned her that he wouldn't plan the appearance.

'Do you think he will follow through?' Helia asked, feeling ashamed that she had reacted so strongly. She had let Andreas control her emotions instead of being the one in control. She had failed her very first test.

'Yes. Andreas may not be happy with the situation, but serving the royal family is something for which he holds a great deal of pride. Regardless of his opinions, he will do as he is ordered.'

Helia hoped so, but she wasn't given much time to brood over the matter when Vasili appeared at her side, offering her his hand.

'Come, we have to leave.'

She placed her hand in his, ignoring the flutter in her belly, and allowed him to lead her through the palace and out to the expansive gardens at the rear, where a gleaming red helicopter waited. She was debating whether or not she should apologise.

The rotors swished as they approached, quickly gathering speed and creating an almighty wind. Goosebumps erupted on her skin when Vasili's hand came up to her nape, forcing her thoughts away and making her bend slightly to see a man in a black suit with an earpiece standing at the door.

'Why are we travelling by helicopter?' she asked loudly, so he could hear her over the din.

She waited for an answer that only came after he had helped her inside, ushering her into one of four cream leather seats.

'Because, Helia, only two of our security detail can travel with us,' he said as he buckled her into the harness.

The touches made it hard for her to pay any attention to his words.

'I figured you would be far more comfortable alone with me than an entire entourage.' His eyes flicked to hers.

She was at a loss for words. Vasili hadn't wanted to be married, or to be King, yet he continued to show her more consideration than anyone else. If she wasn't meant to love him, his actions would make that very difficult. How was she supposed to keep her emotions out of a physical relationship if he was to treat her with such kindness?

She couldn't trust herself to keep to that promise if she had to make it. Did it mean she would have to keep her distance? She couldn't see another way to ensure that she would never fall in love with him. To mitigate the risk of that ever happening.

After all, her plans depended on her remaining as Queen, so she would have to agree to Vasili's emotionless marriage.

Some honeymoon this would be.

'You're right. Thank you,' she said now.

'Are you nervous?' Vasili asked as he strapped himself in.

'A little. I've never flown before,' she admitted.

More and more she was coming to realise how out of her depth she was in this life.

The flight took barely over an hour, and in that time she couldn't tear her gaze away from the scenery around them.

It was Thalonia as she had never seen it before.

The turquoise waters of the Ionian Sea glittered as if it was covered in jewels. The city gave way to beaches and cliffs and dense green forests.

The only thing that challenged the view was Vasili's presence. She kept stealing glances at the King, who had a faraway look in his eyes.

He caught her staring, and she knew she should look away, but she couldn't. There was something unreadable in that intense gaze. It almost seemed as if he couldn't look away either. A muscle in his jaw flexed. They were stuck in this world where beauty existed all around them but had faded to nothing.

It was the slight bump of the helicopter touching down that wrenched them away.

Vasili exited first, silently helping Helia out afterwards, and, with a hand on her back and her heart thumping furiously at his touch he guided her away from the aircraft.

She paid no attention to where she was being led because, to her, they had arrived in Paradise.

Protected by steep cliffs on all sides, the resort was a hidden gem, with only a few white chalets. She heard Vasili say something, but couldn't make out the words as they stepped onto a wooden pathway that was flanked by all sorts of plants, winding between each chalet. They were spaced so far apart they would have complete privacy. And as they walked forward she saw a private beach emerge, with pristine shore and clear waters. She noticed each pathway emerged onto the sand, like a delta meeting the sea.

'Leave us,' she heard Vasili say, and turned around to find their security detail disappearing off onto another path.

She looked to Vasili, who answered her question before she could ask it.

'They will be staying on site in the furthest chalet from

ours. No one is here, Helia. Apart from the resort staff, we're alone.'

For days on end she would have only Vasili for company.

A thrill of excitement shot through her at the prospect. But so did trepidation, and a little loneliness, at knowing she had to keep away from him.

She stepped inside the chalet and had to pinch herself to remind her that now she spent her time in places like this.

The chalet was by far the most luxurious place she had ever seen. Her old apartment could have fitted in it many times over with space to spare. It was large and airy, with fluttering gauzy curtains hanging at windows and archways. She flitted from room to room. There was so much light, so many openings to the outside, that it barely seemed they were indoors at all.

And then she spotted a set of doors that undoubtedly led to the bedroom. Helia rushed through, but was drawn short. Not by the spectacular views, of which this particular chalet must have the best one, nor by the plunge pool that could be stepped into right from the bedroom itself, despite there being an enormous swimming pool out on the deck, but by the bed.

The very large, very singular bed.

Helia's excitement morphed into anxiety as she remembered their talk. She hadn't yet agreed to his terms and he had promised they would not be physical in any way until she did. But how would she be able to think, to keep her distance, if she was in the same bed as him?

She knew she had to while they were on this honeymoon, but she couldn't help wonder what it would be like to share a bed with him. Did Vasili even want to?

She searched around the room, hoping for some sort of solution to magically make itself known. There was a chaise in the room, and several couches in the living area, one of which would be large enough to sleep on should things become awkward. But she couldn't tell the King not to sleep on the bed. Especially not when they should be on their honeymoon.

Helia supposed she was small enough that she could comfortably sleep there. If there were staff in the grounds, their sleeping in different chalets was not an option—just as it wasn't an option at the palace. They were the newly married King and Queen and they had to keep up appearances.

'You look uncomfortable.'

Helia jumped at the deep, raspy voice behind her. She hadn't heard Vasili enter.

'Did I startle you?'

'No.'

She didn't need to see his face to know that he didn't believe her lie. His sharply exhaled breath did that more than adequately.

'I can sleep elsewhere, Helia. Relax.'

His voice had come from above her head, but it was his heat at her back that she felt most intensely. She would have loved nothing more than to lean into that. See if his embrace would ignite her like his kiss had, or if his immoveable hardness would comfort her.

But that was not the marriage they had, and she had to remember that fact.

'I can't let you do that.'

She took a few steps away from him. Distance was what she needed, or she knew she would want to savour his very presence.

'You'll find there's very little that anyone can forbid me from doing.'

'I get that you're the King, Vasili. But I also very much doubt you would fit on that couch.'

His lips twitched as if he was battling a smile. She didn't see what was so funny. This was an impossible situation. There was no way she would let him be uncomfortable for the entirety of their stay. And what if the staff entered to find one of them sleeping on the couch? They were definitely on hand. As discreet as she was sure they were, gossip would get out, and all the hard work they were doing—had already done to ensure everyone believed the monarchy stood strong—would be undone.

There was just no way around this.

'I appreciate you thinking of my comfort,' he said. 'But I didn't say I would sleep on the couch.'

It took her a moment to understand his words. 'But you can't sleep elsewhere. What happens if the staff notice? Or a picture gets out? We can't afford the gossip. *I* can't afford the gossip.'

'We'll handle it,' he said gruffly.

'I refuse to give anyone ammunition to use against me. Most of your advisors are already against my being Queen. My goals are too important to jeopardise. Look, I know what we agreed to, but we're going to be sharing a bed in the palace anyway.'

She could see him thinking it through. He looked as if he wanted to say no. Did he think sharing with her would be so bad? she wondered.

'Are you certain you are prepared for that?'

'Yes,' she lied.

He didn't look as if he believed her.

'Very well,' he said stiffly.

Helia couldn't get a read on him. Only knew that he was far more tense than he had been at any point during the day so far—including when he had strapped her into the helicopter seat. Perhaps an escape would do them both good.

'I'm going for a walk.'

She hoped the sea air would settle all her conflicting feelings.

Helia returned to the chalet after dark, having had time to process what the week might possibly be like. Vasili was nowhere to be found, so she ordered room service, which she enjoyed on her own, and then readied herself for bed.

She wheeled her suitcase into the bathroom, cursing as she pawed through it. Her earlier gratitude for having her wardrobe changed had vanished, and was now replaced with mortification. She had already come to terms with the fact that her own wardrobe was not fit for royalty, but surely her nightwear didn't have to be collateral damage in this war on her identity. No one would ever see her in it.

Unfortunately, as she picked through everything that had been packed for her, she found nothing that she would have chosen for herself. No comfy yoga pants or soft shirts.

Every negligee was more flimsy or weblike than the last. She could appreciate the beauty of them, the luxurious feel of the fabric, but how could she wear something like these without Vasili thinking that she was accepting his terms when she hadn't yet come to a decision?

Helia put on what she thought to be the most modest of the lot. The deep red satin was vivid against her olive skin, but at least it covered her up.

She shut off the light and stepped back into the bedroom to find Vasili already in bed. He was sitting against the headboard, shirtless, paying no mind to her as he read something on his phone.

She had felt the hardness of his body, had seen the way he moved with a powerful grace, but she was still not prepared for the vision of his naked chest, which looked as if it had been carved from stone. The sculpted, shadowed dips and peaks of his stomach were highlighted by the lamplight. The bedcovers were tossed carelessly around his hips, and she could just make out the band of his underwear.

She couldn't take her eyes off him. Vasili was glorious.

Her heart gave a sharp throb, and she realised that she had been staring.

She forced herself to move and, as carefully as she could, slunk towards the bed, slowly climbing beneath the covers to avoid catching his attention. She settled as close to the edge as possible, trying exceptionally hard to ignore the fact that she was now sharing a bed with the man she was impossibly attracted to but from whom she was determined to keep her distance.

'You're going to fall out of the bed. Come closer.'

When she didn't listen, Vasili dropped his phone onto the duvet and reached around her, pulling her away from the edge. The touch scalded him to his core. His body rejoiced at her nearness.

He hadn't been able to concentrate on a single word in the email he had been reading. How could he have been expected to concentrate when he had felt Helia's gaze dragging across his body like a touch? How could his every nerve not have been attuned to her when she'd walked out of that bathroom looking like an enticing dream? If the people of Thalonia had still believed in mythological deities, she would undoubtedly have been one.

He tried not looking at her, hoping that would be enough to wrangle the arousal coursing through him into submission. He had to control himself. He would not make this any more uncomfortable for her than it already was. Helia had agreed to this marriage without being given much of a choice, and to him that was no consent at all.

Which was why he had said there would be no physical relationship. No matter how much he wanted to slip his hand under all that satin, explore her body... It was the very reason he wanted to sleep away from her—he couldn't allow it.

He took a breath to master himself. Not that it helped much when he could smell her floral fragrance and wondered if she would smell that sweet everywhere.

Helia was embedded in his mind, and she wasn't going anywhere soon. He had wanted to bow down to her in his office. She had been regal in that chair, and more than that he had been proud of the way she had handled Andreas. He had wanted to kiss her afterwards, and even though he'd managed to hold back, there had been no reprieve.

Buckling her into her seat in the helicopter had been another test he hadn't felt prepared for. To be so close to her. To touch her and feel every contact like a white-hot shock. That flight had seemed like the longest he had ever taken. Every minute had been spent figuring out a way that he could either avoid Helia on their honeymoon or how he could get a taste of her without getting close. And then she had looked at him. Trapped him in a bubble that silenced the world. Quieted his anxiety.

And now, as if all of that had not been enough for one day, there was the bed.

When she had suggested that they share, Vasili had wondered if there would ever be a point in his life when the universe wouldn't answer him with cruelty. He didn't want to sleep with Helia. He didn't want to let his guard down around her. To be vulnerable. There was no control in sleep. Nothing to stop warm embraces. No shields to stop them gravitating towards each other.

It had been test upon test, and he felt as if he was failing miserably because he simply could not contain this chemistry between them.

He had kissed her once and it had given her some sort of power over him. He couldn't allow it—which was why he wanted to enforce the boundaries in their marriage. That was the end of it. No matter how badly he wanted a taste, Vasili refused to give in.

'Go to sleep, Helia.' He reached over and flicked the light switch.

'Goodnight, Vasili,' she replied in a barely-there whisper as the room was plunged into darkness.

If he'd thought the black night would allow them to relax, he couldn't have been more wrong. With nothing to focus on apart from the weight of each other in the bed, and their audible breaths, he felt the tension between them magnified by the dark until they could focus on nothing but each other.

Vasili's entire body was alert to the proximity of Helia. He wanted so badly to reach out to her. She was so close. He felt her hand twitch against the sheets, but refused to allow himself to think of what it would be like if she crossed that small expanse between them.

He lay awake for hours, and knew Helia did too. They were keenly aware of each other, and of the mounting current in the air. Desire was like a fog, suspended around them, but neither would reach out. Vasili would not break his word to her or to himself.

There was a scraping against the sheets…a tug he felt.

Clearly Helia felt the same.

CHAPTER SEVEN

THE SOUND OF crashing water was the first thing Helia heard. Then she felt a warm weight around her body. Slowly, other sounds met the first. Chirping birds. Soft breaths. As Helia was roused, she took in more of her surroundings. She was in bed, with light pouring in from all the open doors and windows. She was lying on her back, and when she looked over she saw Vasili sound asleep. Lying on his side. One arm was under her, the other was over her stomach, holding her close. His leg was wrapped around hers.

She had no idea when they had ended up in this position. She had tried to keep a physical space between them, and had been so tense she hadn't thought she would fall asleep at all.

But she obviously had.

She turned slightly so she could get a good look at Vasili.

The King.

Her husband.

He was so beautiful. Dark, thick lashes fanned over his cheeks. His slightly curly hair fell in mussed waves. Fleshy pink lips were slightly parted. And then there was his body, which she could feel but couldn't see, because he held her so close.

She was warm in his embrace. Content. Helia savoured this moment. A memory she would keep tucked away safely.

She had always wondered what it would be like to be held by him. Wondered what his lips might feel like. Even in those days spent in the library, when she had admired him from afar, she would let herself dream that one day he would see her. Would want to caress and kiss her. Now she'd had a taste of him. Knew what kissing him really felt like. And no imagination, no matter how creative, could have compared. Now she had an idea of what it would be like to wake up in his arms every morning, and a very significant part of her wished she could have more.

But she couldn't.

He would never be doing this if he was awake.

He wouldn't give that to her.

It was dangerous to think these thoughts. Dangerous for the goals that rested on her being the Queen Vasili needed, and especially dangerous for her heart. Only heartache awaited down that path. Because even though she was happy to be in his arms, it would feel even lonelier soon. When he woke and pulled away she would have to deal with that warmth abandoning her.

All these feelings told her that she was already struggling to separate the emotional from the physical. They had simply needed to sleep, but she was wishing for more.

Being in this bed wasn't doing her any favours. So, as carefully as she could, she slipped from his embrace and quietly went to the bathroom, where she changed as quickly as she could into a jade bikini, and threw a long beach kimono over it. The pattern reminded her of an antique vase.

She left the chalet and walked barefoot along the slatted wooden path until she stepped onto the beach. The sand was still cool beneath her feet, but she knew that wouldn't last long. Not with the summer sun that would beat down soon enough.

Helia walked all the way to the water's edge, where the warm water fizzed over her toes, catching the very edges of the kimono that fluttered around her ankles. She was utterly alone on the beach, and she felt a part of her settle in the peace.

For two weeks, every day had been a rush—a constant hum of voices and activity. She had missed the tranquillity of the library but now, on this beach, where there wasn't another soul for miles, Helia found what she had been craving.

It had been quiet the night before, too, when Vasili had turned out the lights. Except that silence had been deafening. As loud as a scream. All she'd been able to feel in the dark was his presence. The want that coursed through her. The need to reach out and touch him.

When he had turned out the lights it had felt as if they had entered a void where there was no escape from her attraction to him. Where it had become a physical entity. There had been no distraction in the darkness. Nowhere to focus other than on herself and him.

Her nails had scraped against the sheets as she had fisted the linen, trying to stop herself doing something terrible like reaching for him. She had almost considered erecting a physical barrier between them. There were enough pillows in the room. But she'd known she couldn't do that and show Vasili how much he affected her.

Then she remembered how she'd woken up, and that felt like a dream itself.

She walked the length of the beach before turning around and walking back towards the resort. But she couldn't go back there yet and risk facing him. She dropped down onto the sand, hugging her knees as she gazed out at the water, pondering how much her life had changed.

It hadn't been that long ago when she'd wished she could see more of Thalonia. She'd earned a comfortable wage working at the palace. More than comfortable. But, as much as she'd wanted adventure, staying close to her books was safe. Books kept the loneliness at bay. Books couldn't be taken from her, wouldn't desert her.

The life Vasili was proposing would be a lonely one. She

wanted to experience passion with him—of course she did—but how could she agree to never falling in love or never having children when she had no idea what the future might hold?

And now she was in a paradise she would never in her wildest dreams have been able to visit before, on a honeymoon that was simply a pause. Because once they returned to Seidon, Helia would have to fight to achieve her dream. Then it would no longer be a dream...would no longer be a niggle at the back of her mind, something she wished she could make happen. It would be reality.

Helia was lost to her thoughts as she stared out at the turquoise waters. Paying no attention to her surroundings, she heard nothing when someone stepped onto the sand, surprising her as she felt him sit beside her.

'Good morning, Helia,' Vasili said. His gaze was cast out over the sea as well. 'Did you sleep well?'

Not at all. But she couldn't admit to the reason.

'I did, thank you.'

'I always forget how beautiful it is out here.'

'Have you been here often?'

'Not as much recently.' He glanced over his shoulder at the resort. 'But a few times in the past.'

Of course he had. Helia's stomach sank as she imagined the kind of company he had come here with.

'It's a beautiful morning for a swim.'

'I don't think that's a very good idea.'

Not for her, at least. While it wasn't an invitation on his part, she needed to ensure that they spent as little time together as possible. And besides, swimming was never an option for her.

'Why not?'

She could feel him looking at her, so she turned towards him to give him an answer. It was another way in which she was lacking. Another simple skill that the Queen of Thalonia didn't have. And what an embarrassment that would be. Yet another way she was inadequate.

'I can't swim,' she said softly.

Shock crossed his face. 'How is that possible? We live on an island. The sea is in our blood.'

'I love the sea. There is a quiet little spot near the lighthouse where I go to be alone. It's my favourite place.' Helia could see the curiosity on his face. Turning back to the water, so he couldn't see the pain on hers, she continued. 'But I've never been in the water.'

'Ever?'

'Ever.'

The grief that often reared its head when she thought of her father smashed into her, but she had learnt how to keep it from showing to the people around her.

'My father owned a business and was always too busy to teach me how to swim. It wasn't something taught at our little school, and after he passed away I never had an opportunity to learn.'

It was as if a tidal wave of sorrow poured from Helia, even though Vasili could see that she was trying to hide her feelings. It made him want to pull her into his arms and protect her from this heartache that she carried around.

Vasili was fighting his curiosity about her. He shouldn't want to know more. What he learnt would make no difference to their strange relationship, no matter how much he lusted for her.

'What about your mother?' he asked.

She shook her head. 'I never knew her. She died when I was an infant.'

'So it was just you and your father?'

'Yes.'

Vasili had always felt alone, despite having a family, but

Helia…she truly was alone. Well, not any more. Because his ring did sit on her finger, even if it was impossible for him to be the kind of husband she would want.

The way she looked at the water, with such longing, broke his heart. It was true that Vasili had to protect himself from Helia. To prevent her from getting too close. But he wouldn't let the situation they were in change the man he was—and that man would never be cruel enough to leave someone drowning in their grief. In their loneliness.

Like you are?

Standing up, he ignored that voice, holding out a hand to her instead. 'Come with me.'

She hesitated before placing her hand in his. 'Where are we going?'

'You'll see.'

He released her hand as soon as he'd pulled her up, leading her to the massive sparkling blue pool on the deck. He descended the steps one at a time, feeling the water rising with each step, until he was waist-deep, his feet planted firmly on the floor of the pool.

He turned back to Helia then, holding out his hand with an inviting smile. 'Join me.'

Vasili watched her closely as he waited at the wide steps.

Her eyes darted the length of the pool. Fixating on the deep end.

'Don't think about that yet. Just join me over here.'

Satisfaction and heat battled for dominance within him as he noticed the way her gaze travelled from his upturned palm to his body. She was drinking in every inch of his bare skin.

'Trust me.'

The two words had her gaze meeting his, and then, with a deep breath, she screwed up her courage, peeled off her kimono and slowly stepped into the water.

Pure pride washed through him, but he pushed that aside.

Pride wasn't something he would allow himself to feel for this person he was trying to keep at arm's length.

Vasili moved towards her, and she latched on to his hand the moment he offered it.

'That's it,' he encouraged, leading her to the next step, and the next, until she was standing with him.

'How do you feel?' Vasili asked. He could see how tense she was.

'Okay for now.'

'Just breathe, Helia. The water is shallow. Relax.'

She nodded, but his heart twisted at seeing all her confidence vanish.

'I won't let anything happen to you.'

'I believe you,' she said, in a slightly tremulous voice.

Her beauty paralysed him. Vasili stood in the water with her, taking in the way her swimsuit covered her up but left little to the imagination. As bikinis went, it was modest. Vasili had been on boats with women who wore far less. Yet this green garment had him in a chokehold. It revealed just enough of her breasts for him to picture kissing them. Leaving his mark on them. Her bare stomach was flat, with little droplets of water...

He spun Helia around in order to regain control over himself.

Swallowing thickly, he lowered his voice just a little as he placed his hands on her arms. 'We're just going to get you used to a simple movement.'

He felt her shudder but pushed on, moving her arms in slow circles.

'I'm no expert, but shouldn't I be doing this *in* the water,' she teased.

'You could try, but I don't think you would enjoy being underwater all that much. I hear breathing is difficult.'

'Fair enough.'

How was it that she made him smile, laugh so easily, when

that was the last thing he wanted to do. Why did she make him feel lighter?

Vasili made her practise the strokes until he was certain that she was doing them perfectly.

'Now come to the side,' he instructed. 'You're going to hold on to the wall and kick your legs. Don't worry, I will be holding you,' he added, when he could see she was about to protest.

He helped her into position, placing his hands on her stomach under the water, holding her up while she learnt how to kick the right way. He could hear himself giving her directions, but all he could think about was that she was exactly as soft as he'd thought. That he wanted to say screw the swimming lesson so he could hold her against his body and show her what that damn bikini was doing to him.

Slowly he moved her away from the wall so she could get used to the feel of the water.

'Don't panic. I've got you. I'm not letting go.'

He never wanted to, and now he was cursing himself for offering to teach her—because he might not be able to see her beautiful face or her tempting breasts, but he had a constant eyeful of her perfect derriere. Everything about her was perfect. It was driving him mad.

Every time he had her doing a different movement she would clutch onto him as if he was her lifeline, her body rubbing against his. His hands were all over her, and he was going crazy with want. He couldn't think straight any longer. All he wanted to do was press her against the wall and kiss her. Kiss her until she knew nothing but his name. Hear her scream out for him as he pleasured her in every way he knew for as long as possible.

He drew her back to the shallow end, putting a little distance between them. He had to, or he would have no willpower left.

'I think that's enough for one day.'

'Oh. Um…okay.' She frowned.

'It's been hours. I don't think you want to exhaust yourself on the first day.'

Excuses. And flimsy ones at that. He was trying to run from her because she made him let down his guard. She made him feel less alone. And he couldn't give that power to her.

'Vasili…?' he heard Helia say.

Maybe it had been a mistake, marrying her. If he had listened to Andreas and married some princess he didn't care about he wouldn't be tempted like this. Wouldn't be so attracted to her that he was in physical pain. He would have loathed her too much ever to get close.

'Are you okay?'

Helia had started moving closer to him, and all he could do was make his way to the steps.

'Yes, I've just remembered I have some things to take care of. Will you be okay to entertain yourself?'

'Yes, of course.'

He nodded once and then, without another look at his wife, Vasili grabbed his towel and disappeared into the chalet.

CHAPTER EIGHT

HELIA STOOD BEFORE the large mirror in the bedroom, painting a deep red colour on her lips. She had been told that as Queen she would need to be ready to be photographed at any time. Day or night. If she was in public, she was fair game. And, while she hoped they would have privacy in this secluded, empty resort, there were still boats out on the water. Who knew which of those were equipped with telephoto lenses? Helia couldn't take any chances.

The sun had gone down, but the air was still warm. Which was a good thing, because the white toga-like dress she wore offered little protection from the elements.

Vasili had left a note saying they would be dining together. She supposed that to the world they were on honeymoon, and it would be highly unusual if they weren't seen together.

As Helia walked along the path, she couldn't stop thinking about their time in the pool earlier.

She had been apprehensive about accepting his offer, but the idea that she could learn to do something she had always wanted to had been too tempting.

Vasili had been kind and patient. He'd made her feel at ease despite her anxiety in the water. It had been hours of him holding her and touching her. Hours of her heart skipping a beat with every one of those touches. And his voice... It had poured over her like silk.

She had revelled in his attention, despite the fact that she knew she should have kept her distance, and had fought hard to listen to his instructions—before he had pulled back so hard all she could compare it to was a rubber band snapping back after being stretched to its limit.

Spending time with her couldn't have been so abhorrent to him, could it?

Except it could. Her mere existence had been enough for her uncle to toss her away.

Vasili had fled. And she hadn't seen or heard from him since. Well, apart from the invitation to dinner...

Helia followed the long path until she came to a large deck that extended out onto the sand. Upon it was a single, square table with two chairs, laid with a setting for two. A candle sat in the middle with a dancing flame. And there sat Vasili in a white linen shirt, sleeves rolled up, exposing his forearms. His eyes, his hair, seemed so much darker in the muted light.

A dark prince.

No.

A dark king.

She noticed his eyes widen briefly as she stepped into view, but he quickly recovered, moving to pull out her chair, which he helped her onto before joining her at the table.

'Is something wrong?' Helia racked her brain, still trying to figure out her mistake in the pool.

Vasili simply shook his head. 'Nothing.'

She knew that was a lie.

'You look beautiful.'

'Th-thank you,' she stuttered, feeling off balance.

She looked over his shoulder, just able to make out the water. The sounds of lapping waves formed the soundtrack to their dinner.

'Wine?' he offered.

'Yes, please.'

Helia could see he was stiff, despite trying to put on an air of ease, and there was something off about the way he spoke to her.

'I don't believe you,' she said, taking a sip of the fruity wine.

'About what?' Vasili was busy pouring himself a glass.

'When you say nothing is wrong. We've only been married two days and already I know something is off. Tell me what I've done.'

'Don't worry about it, Helia.'

'How can I not? We're supposed to be honest with each other, remember?'

Helia thought back to the pool. Everything had been fine and then he'd withdrawn. As if a switch had been flipped. She couldn't recall doing anything to upset him, which left only her actual presence. She should have refused him in the first place.

'I remember. And if something was wrong, I would talk to you about it.' He glanced away from her as something caught his attention. 'The food is arriving.'

'Please don't insult my intelligence.'

She leaned back in her chair and plastered a pleasant smile on her face, thanking the servers as they laid a starter between the two of them. It was a honeymoon dinner meant to be shared between a happy newlywed couple. Not two people awkwardly navigating a marriage of convenience.

Marinated olives, dips and sliced wedges of pitta sat between them. Helia could picture other honeymooning couples feeding each other. A meal to bring couples even closer together. A seduction before returning to their room.

As soon as the servers walked away from the table she leaned forward and spoke softly enough that they wouldn't be overheard. 'If you would like, I can go. I can feign some illness...perhaps say I've spent too long in the sun...so no one would be any the wiser.'

His molars locked. 'I don't want that.'

Helia sighed. 'Fine. Then how about this? A thought for

a thought. I'm currently thinking that I did something to offend you earlier, and that if we remain together like this people are going to know something is wrong between their king and queen. So I'm going to offer you a solution. I don't want you to feel forced to spend time with me. For image or for any reason whatsoever. I am well aware of what this marriage is supposed to be, given all I have to think about. We have complete privacy here—you've made sure of that. So you should use this time to mourn your brother in peace and I will respect your privacy.'

Vasili hated himself. Had he thought the way he'd left earlier wouldn't be noticed? That Helia wouldn't take his leaving as a reflection on herself? She had done nothing wrong and yet here she still sat with him, so poised, any emotion on lockdown, offering him a kindness.

He had wounded her. For that he should be the one punished. And yet Helia was the one hurting. It was obvious in her words. She told him he wouldn't have to spend time with her as if that was something to suffer through. Despite whatever negative feelings he had her experiencing, she still considered *his* feelings. His grief. When had anyone ever done that?

She had known him only a few days, but had already shown him a support he hadn't experienced. He hadn't known it could feel like this. As if there was an immovable wall at his back. Someone to say, *I've got you.*

But he couldn't accept the offer. Tempting as it was. He wouldn't mourn when it was convenient. He wouldn't ask for help. The void that had been torn into him when he'd been told his brother was dead only yawned wider, but he would deal with his grief just as he had dealt with everything else in his life. Alone.

And just like that the safety of that wall disintegrated and he was alone, fighting through the world on his own again.

'That won't be necessary, Helia.'

He reached over, picking up a piece of pitta to give his hands something to do, somewhere safe to focus, and spread dip along the bread. He noticed that apart from her sip of wine Helia reached for nothing else. Once the bread was loaded to his satisfaction he placed it on her plate, wishing he could pull her onto his lap and feed her instead.

'Vasili...'

Was that exasperation in her tone?

'Helia...?' he mimicked, and chuckled at the unimpressed look on her face. 'I am sorry for the way I left earlier, but I don't need time to mourn.'

'Of course you do. Everyone does.'

'"Everyone" doesn't have the same responsibilities I do,' he replied as he took a bite of his own bread, happy to see Helia had done the same.

'No, they don't, but that doesn't mean you have to ignore your needs. You don't have to deal with everything alone, you know.'

If she only knew. 'I'm not alone. I'm with a beautiful woman.'

'You're changing the subject.'

She plucked an olive from the bowl, and his body stirred to life as he watched her bring it to her lips and close her eyes as she savoured the taste. But then she blinked, tilting her head to the side. Something he'd noticed she did whenever she was trying to understand him.

'Why is that?' she asked.

'I'm *not* changing the subject.'

'And now you're lying. You have a tell. Did you know that?'

'What?'

'You blink and look away,' Helia said matter-of-factly.

'It seems to me you have far too much time on your hands if you've been studying me so closely.'

'And now you're deflecting.' She smirked.

This woman. She was driving him crazy.

'Fine, we'll talk about something else,' she said. 'You've been here before?'

The change of topic seemed safe, but Vasili had the distinct impression that he was not the one on higher ground in this conversation.

'I have.'

'I imagine the parties here would be rather spectacular.'

She was fishing, and the realisation had a smile curving his lips. 'I wouldn't know.'

'You wouldn't?' She frowned.

'I wouldn't, because I have only ever come here alone.'

She constantly made him feel as if he was standing on quicksand—well, now he saw an opportunity to flip the tables on her.

'This is where I come when I need some privacy. A bit of peace and quiet away from everyone.'

She was about to take a bite, but placed her food back down. 'But you've brought me here. Why would you do that?'

Vasili reached over and picked an olive off her plate, popping it into his mouth. 'Why, indeed.'

'I don't always understand you,' she confessed softly.

'Well, then, maybe you need to study harder.'

The idea that someone would know him was enticing—because no one had ever bothered to. The only person who had was taken from him when he was a teenager and all those who were left would never see the value in his existence. Vasili had never invested his time in relationships because they were fleeting anyway, but he knew that he risked becoming a cold ruler who thought only of the Kingdom and not of his wife.

Wouldn't he then become the very thing he didn't want to be? Just like his parents? Of course he would. But want wasn't need, and he needed to ensure that he never let Helia behind his walls. If only she'd agreed to his terms they would have something else to focus on, and he could distract her in ways that kept him safe.

That night, when they climbed into bed and Vasili turned down the lights, he was prepared for his body's response to his wife.

Preparation didn't make it any easier to bear.

'Vasili?' Her voice cut through the darkness.

'Hmm?'

'Can I ask you something?'

'Anything.'

'Why do you hate it so much?'

'Hate what?'

'The throne. The title. Everything.'

He trained his eyes on a spot in the distance. With all the doors and windows open, he could see a sliver of moonlight cast across the craggy cliffs. He didn't know how much to reveal, so he opted for the shortest, safest answer.

'It's a cage.'

It caged one's heart, so one could never show real love to those who deserved to receive it. Caged one's spirit, so one would always be what the institution expected. Caged one's soul, so one would never have true freedom.

He knew Helia would be reading something into the silence that followed. She was perceptive. Intelligent. She would know there was so much he wasn't saying.

'I know I haven't agreed to your terms yet, and that we may never have a traditional marriage and I won't expect one. But maybe we could be friends.'

He could tell she was waiting for him to respond, and when he didn't, she went on.

'I just think we could both use a friend on this journey, or it could be a very long, very unhappy life. And I don't think either of us deserves that.'

Still, he couldn't respond.

She let out a sigh and turned over so her back was to him. 'Just think about it. Goodnight, Vasili.'

He lay there in the dark night, listening to the ocean and replaying her words in his head. Finally, he heard her breath even out, and once she was soundly asleep he said, 'I don't know how to be a friend, Helia. All I know is how to be alone.'

CHAPTER NINE

THAT NIGHT VASILI lay awake for hours, and when he did fall asleep it wasn't very long before he woke. He found Helia in his arms, but instead of extricating himself from the tangle of their sleepy embrace he pulled her more tightly to him. Breathing in her scent. Pondering the fact that even in sleep their attraction had them gravitating towards each other.

It was exactly what he had been afraid of. And even more worrying was how much he wanted to keep holding on to her. He couldn't need her like this. He wouldn't allow himself to.

She was right, he had to concede. It would be an unbearably long life spent in misery if they continued as they were now. He was only twenty-nine, she barely a year younger. They had their whole lives ahead of them. The issue was that Vasili had spent most of his life alone. There were always people around him, and yet there was never a person *with* him.

If he didn't have friends, how could he be one?

He wouldn't consider himself an adequate one for Helia, that was for certain. She was a good person. Didn't she deserve a better friend than he could be?

Even as he thought that he knew he couldn't stay away entirely. He wanted to explore her body. To know her. So, while he might not have the ability to be a friend, or a husband, or even a good king, he could make an effort for Helia while maintaining his boundaries. He would endure this attraction until she gave him her promise that she would accept a life on his terms.

Which meant he would have to start spending time with her and not fleeing as he had done the day before.

Vasili eased away from Helia and slipped a shirt over his head. He called room service for coffee while thinking about how he could spend the day with Helia while remaining cordial and pleasant, and then he made another call.

He settled on the edge of the bed. 'Helia,' he said gently. She scrunched up her nose, letting out an irritated grunt that made his heart twinge. 'I have a surprise waiting. I think you'd be most displeased if you missed out on it because you'd slept all day.'

'It's not all day,' she mumbled.

She tried to turn away from him, and Vasili could see the exact moment that her brain caught up with the rest of her. Eyes widening, she moved to sit up.

'Vasili, I'm—'

'Come on, there's coffee waiting and you need to get ready.'

'Why are we awake so early?'

Helia ran her fingers through her hair, bunching it over her shoulder. Vasili followed the movement, picturing his fingers tangled in her locks.

'You are a prickly one in the morning—do you know that?'

She only looked at him, with no expression on her face.

He felt his lips twitch into a smile. 'The surprise is out on the water.'

'Great. So it's not for me.'

'Oh, no, you don't.' He grabbed the covers as she tried sinking further down into the bed. 'I expect you outside in fifteen minutes.'

With a glare and a few mumbled words she tossed the covers off. 'I'm up.'

It didn't take her long to get dressed, and when she emerged in yet another mind-boggling bikini, with a sheer dress over it, Vasili knew it would be a very long day.

'I didn't think kings were meant to wear shorts,' she teased, taking in his outfit.

'They do when they're on honeymoon at the beach.'

'So where are we going?' Helia asked as she fell into step beside him.

'You'll see.'

He led her along various paths, all of which he had explored on his own over the years, until they came to a pier with a single boat docked. Polished wood and shiny fibreglass gleamed in the morning sun.

'Vasili, I can't…'

'I won't let anything happen to you, Helia.'

He'd anticipated that she would be nervous, and waited for her to give him a sign that she was ready to go aboard. Eventually she gave him a small nod, and he climbed aboard the luxury runabout then helped her in.

He felt a tremor running through her as the vessel bucked and swayed. Her eyes darted to each end of the boat and out to sea. She was nervous. That much was obvious. And with her not being able to swim he wasn't surprised. But he'd meant what he said. He would never let any harm befall her.

Vasili picked up a bright red lifejacket and brought it around her, guiding her arms through the sleeves, his eyes locked on hers as he did up the clasps on the front, his breathing turning heavy as goosebumps erupted on her skin. Gently pushing her arms out, Vasili found himself once again tightly strapping Helia up. Her body obeyed his silent commands so easily. She was so soft…so delicate. He had to concentrate to ignore the desire coursing through him from having Helia beneath his hands.

'Sit here.' He helped her into one of the four seats in the open boat. 'Nothing bad is going to happen, but you can hold on to this handle if you need to,' he said, his voice growing gruff as he placed her hand on one of the grip handles. 'Even if you end up in the water, don't panic. Your jacket will keep you buoyant and I will get you. Do you understand?'

'Yes.'

'Good.'

He wanted to lean down and kiss her, but he would not touch her yet, and wrenched himself away to the steering wheel. He refused to look at Helia. Instead, he eased the boat away from the pier and out to open waters.

'Where are we going?' she asked.

'Somewhere special,' he answered.

They were already somewhere special. Choosing to honeymoon at this resort had been for his own benefit as well as hers. Everything they would do after they went back to Seidon would be for public consumption, so a little break with some privacy was a small comfort he could offer Helia. Why he was taking her to another special place was beyond him. And he wasn't going to examine it.

They left the resort far behind as they approached a small island in the archipelago. Slowing the boat down, he brought it to a halt at a tiny uninhabited island. He grabbed a basket from the rear seat—judging from her confused frown, Helia hadn't noticed it. He wasn't surprised. She'd been nervous on the entire boat ride, holding on to the handle in a white-knuckled grip.

They made their way onto the beach—Vasili's favourite place in the whole of Thalonia. People didn't usually come out to this island, so apart from the sound of the water and the gulls flying above there was utter stillness. Even the sounds of the water seemed far away.

'It's beautiful here.'

He glanced over at Helia, who had her arms wrapped around

herself, staring out over the calm water. The breeze was blowing her hair out to the side.

'It is,' he said, putting the basket down and moving behind her. He lowered his head so his lips were at her ear and pointed over the water. 'See those cliffs on either side?' He felt Helia nod. 'They keep the waves out, so the water here is always calm.'

It was true. There was just a gentle lapping on the shore. All the beautiful violence of the waves was contained in the distance.

'It's safe for you to get into the water here. With me, of course,' he added.

'This is a wonderful surprise. Thank you for bringing me here. Even if you drove the boat too fast.' She stared accusingly at him as he stepped away.

'You'll get used to it.'

Would she? Did he plan on bringing her back here? Vasili hadn't consciously thought about it, but he felt centred here. As if he could be anyone. With a million choices before him. It was likely that Helia would need a break too, over the years to come, so why wouldn't they return?

That answer was a cloud hanging over them... What if her answer to his rules was no?

'What's that?'

She broke through his musings, tipping her chin towards the basket.

'I'd hope a librarian would know.'

Helia rewarded him with an eye-roll.

'I've had a picnic prepared for us. The question is, do you want to swim before or after?'

'Before. I'm already nervous as it is. I don't need to eat before getting in the water.'

'You'll be fine, Helia. Swim it is.'

Vasili pulled his shirt over his head, depositing it on the

sand, and watched Helia shedding her dress to reveal a bright blue swimsuit. His hands curled into fists as he attempted to smother the urges running rampant through him.

With her hand in his, they waded out into the water, and when they were chest-deep he stopped and allowed her to get used to the push and pull of the current.

'Please don't let go,' she begged.

'I won't. You can trust me.'

'I do.'

Vasili wanted to warn her that she shouldn't, but he couldn't deny that it satisfied some deep need in him to hear someone say it.

'I used to watch the crowds back home playing in the water and wish I could join them. It's funny…something as simple as frolicking at the beach can mean so much.'

Helia looked around the cove, seeing nothing but nature. Vasili had not only given her a taste of something she had always wanted, but he'd made sure to do it somewhere she would be safe and away from prying eyes.

'Why are you being so kind to me?'

His grip on her loosened. 'Would you rather I did not care about your well-being? I thought you wanted a friend in this marriage?'

'I do, but after you've been forced to be King and to marry me, I don't understand why you would do something like this for me.'

Helia knew he was kind. She had seen it in his interactions around the palace. But now that his kindness was directed at her, it was hard not to feel something for Vasili—and this was exactly why she hadn't yet agreed to his terms.

'I was forced to marry, Helia. I wasn't forced to marry you. I made that choice.'

She noticed a frown flash across his face. There and gone.

'You weren't given much choice either, and that is my fault. This is the least I can do. I wish I knew your reasons for agreeing…maybe one day you will be comfortable enough to tell me.'

'Maybe.'

'I know so little of you.'

'What do you want to know?'

'Anything. Tell me about a good memory.'

That wasn't what she had expected. She'd thought he would ask all the standard questions people asked when they attempted to get to know someone. Not Vasili. He wanted to know her heart. And maybe she could understand that, since he would have had to question the motives of every person in his life.

Helia wasn't accustomed to sharing parts of herself with others, but for some reason she knew her most treasured memory would be safe with him.

'My father was a florist, and every evening he would return home with a flower for me from the shop. Just one. I had a vase in my room, and by the end of every week it would hold a bouquet of beautiful mismatched flowers. I loved it.'

'Which were your favourite?' Vasili asked.

He seemed genuinely interested in her answer, and it allowed her to lose herself in the memory. It was as if she didn't have to have her guard up, protecting her precious memories.

'The irises. There were so many colours.' Helia looked away, a small huff of laughter passing through her lips.

'What?'

'It's just that I've never told anyone about that before.'

Maybe that was because she was too afraid to form friendships, lest those friends abandoned her too.

Hope had lived in the halls of the orphanage. A blessing and a curse. There had always been the hope that someone would be chosen by a family and would leave. It had rarely happened. And even if it had the rest of them would soon be alone again. If you were old enough to hope, you were usually too old to be adopted.

Vasili's hand went around her waist, while the other cupped her cheek. There was nothing but utter sincerity in his eyes. 'I'm honoured that you would tell me.'

It scared Helia that when it came to Vasili she was hopeful again. That was why she'd told him such a personal memory. She knew he couldn't leave, given the reason they had married, but was it smart to open herself up to him when he wouldn't ever be there for her emotionally?

It was then she noticed that while she had been distracted he had taken her further out, and she had been treading water just as he had been. As if her body naturally followed his lead.

What would it be like to dance with him?

She wondered where that thought had come from. She had never danced in her life.

'I can't believe I'm doing this,' she said, incredulous.

A pulsing rhythm beat between them. The air was growing taut. Could Vasili feel it too?

'You're a fast learner, but I'd rather not push you. Shall we go back to shore and see what's in the picnic basket?'

He was forcing her away, but she knew then that he was just as affected. 'I'd like that.'

After drying themselves off, and keeping a respectable distance from each other, Vasili pulled two flute glasses and a bottle of champagne from the basket, followed by strawberries, dips, and an assortment of finger foods. The resort kitchen had gone all out.

Helia picked up a particularly deep red strawberry. Vasili's eyes darkened and she saw him track the path of the fruit to her lips and the bite she took. Sweet flavour exploded on her tongue. Juice dripped down her hand, and she quickly licked it away.

It looked as if he was grinding his teeth.

'So, I told you a memory—now it's your turn.'

He cleared his throat, and his voice seemed a touch lower. 'What do you want to know?'

'The same. A good memory.'

She could see him thinking. Taking a long time to do so.

'Is it really that hard to think of one?'

'Yes.' But before she could comment further, he was talking. 'When Leander and I were children he would sneak into my room at night. At first he used to steal treats from the kitchens and bring them up, but I got better at it than him. I would smuggle our contraband into my room and every night we would spend a few hours gorging on snacks.'

'You were close?'

'Not especially. He had a destiny he had to be prepared for. It didn't leave us a lot of time for bonding.'

Helia didn't want to point out that from where she sat it seemed they'd been incredibly close. What she wouldn't have given to have had a sibling all those years in the orphanage. She also got the distinct impression that Vasili wasn't telling her the full truth. That was okay. She would just listen to what he felt safe revealing. Maybe one day he would share more.

'You miss him a lot, don't you?' she said.

'I do. Champagne?'

'Yes, please.'

She allowed him to change the topic.

'You said you hadn't flown before, but have you travelled anywhere?'

'A few times we went on holiday to a cabin in the forest a few hours outside of Seidon. It was beautiful there. Peaceful. Just my father and I.'

'May I ask how he passed away?'

She was aware of how closely Vasili watched her. 'An aneurysm.'

Like a switch, her whole life had changed after that.

'I'm sorry.'

He reached over and took her hand in his. Over the years, Helia had grown numb to the sympathy she would receive when anyone found out she was an orphan, but with Vasili she wanted to lean into him. It felt as if he was offering comfort and warmth. It was that dangerous hope again—but this man had shown her there was a depth to him that not many chose to see, so Helia believed his kindness.

'Thank you. Can I make a confession?' she asked.

'Should I be concerned?'

'No.' She laughed. 'I saw you the first day I started working at the palace.'

'You did?' He sat up straighter, enticed by this titbit of information.

'You were wearing black leathers and climbing on to your motorcycle. I thought you were rather sexy. Unusual, but sexy.' She could feel herself blush.

'You did, did you?' He smirked.

'I also thought your ego probably didn't need inflating.'

'Lie.'

'What?'

'That was a lie, Helia. I'll let it go this time. If you like, I could take you on a ride.'

'A king out on a motorbike?' she scoffed.

'Why not? Who's going to stop me?'

Helia held her glass between both hands as she leaned towards the King. 'You know, you say you don't want to be King, but you seem to have taken to it just fine.'

Vasili shrugged.

'Also, there is no way I'm getting on that death machine.'

'Scared?' he taunted.

'Yes! I can't even drive a car, and that has four wheels. You're out of your mind if you think I'm getting on two.'

'You can't drive?'

Helia shook her head. Another thing she'd never had the opportunity to learn. A fairly basic skill at that.

'Well, then, we'll just have to teach you how.'

Helia laughed, even though the idea appealed to her more than it should. 'I'm not sure we'll have the time.'

'I'll make the time.'

'I know I've said it before, but thank you for bringing me here, Vasili. It's the most relaxed I've been in a long time. You know, I never dreamed of anything like this. A life like the one I'm living now. It feels like I've stepped through a portal into an alternative reality and I'm struggling to wrap my head around it.'

'You can ask for help, Helia.'

Just like her, he kept his gaze over the sea, and she was grateful for that because it made it easier to be honest with him.

'From whom? Andreas? Carissa?'

'Me?' he replied.

Helia shook her head. Of course he would offer. He was ensuring his queen would be competent, and the woman in the palace office before they'd left was not.

'I'm sorry for failing with Andreas. I don't know how to wield this power I have just yet. I'm so afraid of doing or saying the wrong thing.'

'You'll learn, Helia. I don't expect you to handle this world with the level of mastery that only comes with years of experience. And there was no harm done. I was there to support you as I said I would be.'

'But what if you weren't?' Helia challenged.

'That won't happen. I got you into this—I'm not going to abandon you to the sharks now.' Vasili abruptly stood and turned to her. 'I'm going back in the water.'

Helia moved through the shallows to perch on a rock. She watched him keenly as he waded out into the sea. The muscles on his back rippled as he dived in. She bit down on her lip, appreciating the way the water glided over his body as he surged through it in powerful strokes. That was her husband. A man she had admired. And as she peeled back the layers of him, she found there was so much more to him.

Helia was coming to realise that she was growing fond of him—which meant that she couldn't accept his terms. They hadn't shared in any pleasure yet, and she was already developing some sort of feeling for him. Not to mention the fact that she still didn't know where she stood when it came to children, which meant that wasn't a firm no, as Vasili wanted.

That didn't stop her watching him swim until he was a speck in the distance, and she didn't take her eyes off him until he was walking towards her. Beads of water raced down his sculpted body, raining down from his hair. He was a masterpiece, and maybe her lust for him was evident on her face because his gaze was fixed on her too. Devouring her.

They might have been outdoors, but the air had become thick. Charged like it had been at the church when they'd kissed.

The force of his presence tugged her off the rock and, paying little attention to her movements, she slipped. But there was no splash of her falling into the water as she'd expected to. Instead, strong hands caught her, and when she looked up golden-brown eyes were all she saw.

She couldn't stop herself then, but neither could Vasili, and their lips crashed together, stealing the breath from her. Making her heart pound and liquid heat pool in her core. Then his tongue caressed hers and she shivered against him. His arms tightened around her, making her forget where she stood or why she was there. Forget all that she had decided moments before.

His lips slid against hers, tasting of the salty sea. Her skin heated. His touches were making her light-headed. She was reminded how explosive they were together. This could be hers to experience for all her life...

Helia really didn't want to step out of Vasili's embrace.

So what if they wouldn't have children? She didn't have them now, didn't have any family, so it wouldn't change anything. And even if he couldn't be there for her emotionally, she hadn't ever needed anyone to be. She had survived and made it this far on her own. But their chemistry...? This was new. This was exciting. And she wanted much more of it, so maybe it would be enough.

'Vasili...' His name caught in a breath. He hummed low in his throat, igniting a spark in her belly. 'I agree to your terms.'

CHAPTER TEN

'SAY THAT AGAIN,' he'd breathed against her lips.

'I agree to your terms, Vasili, all of them.'

It had been as if her words had unleashed the tidal wave of want he had been trying to control, and he'd kissed her. He'd kissed her as he'd carried her out of the water, and he'd kept on kissing her until the sun had travelled across the sky and they'd had to return to the resort.

Now they sat on the deck once more beneath the night sky— still in their beachwear, having not bothered to return to the chalet—after enjoying yet another dinner. This one had been far more pleasant than the previous one.

'Take a walk with me.'

He had meant it to be a question, but it hadn't come out that way. Not when he wanted so much to extend their day.

'Of course.'

It should have worried him that Helia was so ready to spend more time with him, but he couldn't care now. He took her hand in his, leading her away from the deck and onto the sand, where they kept walking until they reached a dark beach the lights of the resort could not reach. The moon was reflected on the water, giving only just enough silvery light to see where they were going.

'What are we doing here?' Helia asked.

'You'll see. This should be fine.' He sat on the sand, pulling her down with him. 'Lie back.'

He let go of her hand and folded his arms behind his head, pleased when she followed suit.

The black sky was covered in silvery twinkling stars. The Milky Way was like an airbrushed stripe across the sky in blues, purples and blacks.

'It's breathtaking!' Helia exclaimed.

'It is. The lights in Seidon are too bright to see the stars, so whenever I come out here I take a moment to appreciate them. The quiet…'

'It's so peaceful. Thank you for sharing this with me.'

He wanted to thank her for being there with him. Even if she hadn't agreed to his rules it would have been a good day. Probably the best Vasili had experienced in a very long time. Maybe ever. He didn't want it to end—which was probably rather selfish of him. Helia was likely tired. He knew he should let her retire for the night. But he couldn't let her go. And yet he couldn't ask her to stay. He had never asked for anything in life. He moved through it alone. Did things for himself. He didn't need people, so the words would not form.

The sand beside him shifted. Helia had moved closer. As if she could sense the need in him. He couldn't stop himself. He unfurled one arm, placing it under her, scooping her closer to his body.

'You know, according to myth, Hera created the Milky Way.'

Helia placed her palm on his chest. The warmth seared him to his core.

'Heracles needed that strength for his labours.' He took great pride in the look of surprise on Helia's face. 'What? Do you think princes don't read?'

'It's not that. I just wouldn't have expected you to be allowed to read about mythology when you must have had a prescribed book list.'

'I could read whatever I wanted to. Why would you think otherwise?'

'I've been given a list of what *I* should read.'

'You can read whatever you want, Helia. You're the Queen. As someone once said, "Make it so."'

'Just like that?'

'Just like that.'

Vasili brushed his fingers through her hair. Now that Helia had agreed, and he had permitted himself to touch her, he couldn't stop. He hated it. And he loved it.

'There may be things you need to read to prepare you for ruling, but you're not limited to what Andreas thinks is appropriate. He's pining for the kind of rulers he's never going to get.'

'What about you?'

That was a loaded question. What did Vasili want? Initially he had been opposed to being King, but now he had accepted the title. He was King; and when he thought about who should rule beside him he could think of no better option than her. Which had him answering honestly.

'I'm happy with the Queen I have.'

He didn't wait for her to respond. Couldn't bear to see what reaction she might have. So he pulled away and stood up, ripping his shirt over his head and offering her his hand.

'Take a swim with me.'

'Now?'

'Yes.'

'But...'

'Don't be afraid, Helia. Trust me.'

He wanted her to, and when Helia put her hand in his it was easy to ignore that voice at the back of his mind screaming at him to get away from her. Warning him that he was getting too close. He wanted to listen to it, but at the same time he craved that closeness with equal measure.

Vasili took her into the water. His hands tight around hers. 'Please don't let go of me.'

'I won't.'

When they were waist-deep, he turned to look at her. He had thought at the cove that she looked like some sort of sea nymph, with those eyes the colour of the water, her golden body and the blue bikini, but now... Now she looked ethereal. Utterly ravishing in the pale moonlight. Who cared about Hera or the Milky Way when he had a goddess in his arms? Except she wasn't...not yet.

He let go of her hand to wrap his arms around her waist, holding her close. Her sharp intake of breath raised the hairs on his body. He wanted to make her gasp. He wanted to make her as crazy as she made him.

Eyes locked on hers, he leaned in...waiting. Praying that she would close the distance between them. Making sure that she was certain it was her choice. He would let her go if she didn't. Let her go back to the bedroom and give her enough time to fall asleep before he went anywhere near the place and faced another night of little to no sleep. Of craving Helia like air and avoiding even the barest hint of intimacy.

But he wouldn't have to. While he knew he would still have to face his battles, Vasili rejoiced as she closed the gap between their lips. Pressing hers against his in a desperate bid to get closer. He angled his head and she parted her lips for him. His fingers were digging into the soft skin at her waist as their tongues met in a sweet dance. She clutched at his back, wanting more. And he would give it.

He deepened the kiss, growing hard at the sound of her moan. She would feel his length pressed up against her, he knew it, but he couldn't step away. He wanted her so badly it was a buzzing throughout his body.

'Helia...' he breathed against her lips.

Was he asking her permission to go further? Was he trying to stop? He didn't know.

He pulled away slightly and her soft fingers came up to his lips. Tracing the outline of them. Need was singing through his blood.

'Is this real?' she whispered.

'Yes.'

It was all he could manage before his hand was at the back of her head and he was kissing her again. Harder. Deeper. Nipping at her lip as desire flooded his body. Her hands were sliding down his chest, making his breath catch, but they stopped on his stomach and he almost begged her to keep going. He trailed his lips along her jaw, to her ear. He understood her question...it seemed like a dream to him too.

'I need to touch you. Please,' he begged.

'Yes.'

One little word that nearly undid him.

With one arm firmly around her, he slid his other hand down her neck, over her chest, cupping her breast. She mewled against him as he rubbed his thumb over her nipple, so he did it again.

'I need more,' she begged him.

'Tell me what you want,' he said against her neck.

'Vasili, please...'

'Tell me how to serve you, Helia.'

'Touch me...there.'

He trailed his lips over her neck and cheek and just as slowly trailed his fingers down her stomach, dipping below the water and under the waistband of her panties. She shuddered against him. Moaned as his lips closed over hers at the same time as his fingers slipped into her core, finding her slick for him.

He stroked her until she was panting. Every sound she made was driving him into a frenzy of lust. He was painfully hard now, but all he cared about was Helia's pleasure. He needed

her release as if it was his own. It was a new feeling to him.
Pleasure was always mutual, and then it was over, but here in
the water with Helia he never wanted it to end.

Helia could barely think. His kisses were stoking the flame
of her desire while his fingers pushed her further and further
to the edge. But she was afraid of the fall. It felt so good here.
She didn't want to think of what came after. So she tried with
all her might to hold on to this feeling. This blazing heat consuming her. The water was doing nothing to extinguish the
flames. If anything, the constant gentle waves were adding
to her pleasure.

Her fingers slid down Vasili's body, gripping the waistband
of his shorts. She felt him tense. Felt the twitch of his hardness
against her body. She wanted to touch him.

Helia had fantasised about this. Being in his arms. To give
and receive pleasure. Her fantasies had been positively dull
compared to what she felt now. Her rough breaths grew ever
more rapid. There was a coiling in her belly. She wanted him
to feel it too.

'You feel like heaven, Helia,' Vasili said, kissing his way
down her throat.

'I want to touch you too.'

'Not yet.'

'Why not?'

'Because right now I need you to come apart for me. And
when you do touch me I want to be able to see you...and for
you to see a king fall apart at your touch.'

Helia was barely hanging on, his words sending a shock of
arousal through her. And as if Vasili could tell just how close
she was, he slipped a finger into her, then another. He was
curling them and making them hit a spot that had her seeing
stars far brighter than the ones overhead.

'Vasili!' she cried out as she shattered around his fingers.

He pulled her against him even tighter, kissing her hungrily, stroking her and drawing out her pleasure until she felt weak-kneed.

And then she was in his arms and they were moving out of the water, Vasili carrying her to their chalet.

He took them straight into the large shower, where they washed off the sea and sand. Vasili made her come apart on his fingers again, and all the while he wouldn't let her return the favour, making her grow tense. Self-conscious. Maybe he'd had a taste of their passion and found her lacking. Her experience was limited, after all.

She climbed into the bed and he slid in after her, propping his head up on his hand. Lying on her back, she looked into his eyes, and could see swirling thoughts behind them. In the light of the room she could see the haze of lust dissipate, gone from his features to be replaced by something else.

She prayed it wasn't regret.

'Just say it, Vasili.'

He put an arm over her, holding her tightly against him. 'I don't yet fully understand your reasons for choosing to marry me, Helia, but I can only imagine a marriage like this isn't something you envisaged for yourself.'

Marriage was something Helia had only thought of as a concept—not as something she would ever truly experience. Not when she was so afraid of being abandoned. Trust didn't come easily, and it was far safer to be on her own because she knew she could rely on herself. It was a huge part of why her only relationship had failed.

She tried to respond to Vasili, but he silenced her.

'Let me finish. I want you. Probably more than you can comprehend...'

Helia had an idea, but she wouldn't tell him how she felt about him and for quite how long she had felt that way.

'Tonight...what transpired between us...it's only the tip of the iceberg. And I was honest with you. I do want you to touch me. I do want you to give me pleasure in the way I have given it to you. But I need to be sure you understand and have fully considered our terms. I can't love you, Helia. I'm not capable of that. We won't ever be husband and wife in the traditional sense. And I am sorry about that, but it's just the way it is.'

All Helia had done since their talk was consider his terms, but her heart still broke at hearing the words. She'd always known she wouldn't be enough for him. Being just an ordinary woman from Seidon. They were worlds apart, and his words struck right at those insecurities. But she was also hurt at him saying he wasn't capable of love, because the very fact that he was grieving for Leander meant that he was.

Maybe his problem wasn't that he wasn't capable of love but rather that he loved too much—not that it would mean much for her. He had just admitted that he couldn't ever love her.

'I have already agreed, Vasili.' She hoped her voice would not betray the hurt she was trying to hide from him. 'I remember we are united in our duty as King and Queen to the world's eyes, and that in our home we explore this attraction between us. But no sex. No love. No children.'

She waved between their bodies.

'This is the only way I can give myself to you, Helia,' he said. 'And if you have any apprehension at all, then I think it's best if we don't cross that boundary.'

'I thought you weren't interested in me? You said you shouldn't have kissed me.'

'Nothing could be further from the truth. I have made my attraction to you plain. I meant that I shouldn't have kissed you like I did at the wedding, but I had wanted to since you walked into my office.'

Helia hadn't realised that she could feel two such conflicting emotions at the same time. It hurt to know that no matter how long they would spend together she would never have his love, but she did want to be with him. And to find out that he was so attracted to her had made the unbroken parts of her heart soar.

However, a lifetime was a very long passage. To travel the entirety of it without love would be difficult. Would their chemistry last? Was it a good enough substitute? Could a physical relationship ever be enough?

If she didn't accept these terms then she would have no relationship with him at all. Perhaps a cordial friendship, with time. And that seemed like a path filled with misery. Not to mention the fact that her goals depended on her remaining as Queen. So she really only had one choice. Because she did want to be with him, and having some of him was a much better prospect than having none of him.

'I can do this.'

She placed her hand on his cheek and he leaned into her palm. Right then, despite the fractures forming through her, she knew she made the correct choice.

'I want this.'

He kissed her palm and then her lips in a slow, lingering caress. 'That makes me happy.'

She ran her fingers through his soft hair, saw his golden-brown eyes alight with heat. 'Me too.'

But she was feeling nowhere near as euphoric as she'd thought she would.

'I'm going to show you so much pleasure,' he whispered in her ear.

And she let the intoxication of his embrace carry her away from the heaviness in her heart.

CHAPTER ELEVEN

VASILI OPENED HIS EYES. It took him a few moments to remember he was back in the palace, sleeping in the King's bed. Gone were all his books and his tranquil walls. Instead, his senses were assaulted by a gaudy room and an ornate four-poster bed.

Also behind him was his honeymoon.

The remaining days had passed far too quickly, with Vasili exploring Helia's body for as long and as frequently as he'd been able to. He had taken great pride in making her scream out his name or having her forget what she was saying with a single look from him.

He was happy that Helia had fully accepted the terms of their relationship, and having an outlet for their attraction made it easier to be in her company—especially since he could barely keep his hands off her. It was a shield between him and Helia while they safely explored their physical connection without any risk of growing attached. But still, every kiss, every taste of her drew him in. So he knew sex was still too big a risk. That kind of intimacy with Helia would be different from anything he had before, and he had to protect himself.

He heaved a sigh. This would take a great deal of getting used to.

What made it all the more unbearable was the fact that his wife was asleep in his arms. A more perfect sight he couldn't imagine, and it was the reason he had struggled through yet another night without much sleep.

The nights, he found, were the hardest.

In his previous life Vasili hadn't minded sleeping next to his conquests, because he'd known they would be gone as soon as the sun was up and he would have little or nothing to do with them again. With Helia it was much, much different. She was meant to be his partner, and he was growing fond of her, but sleeping in the same bed as her for the sake of appearances without the excuse of sex still felt far too intimate. As if he was inviting her into his heart for her company. For her heart. To create a bond.

He couldn't have that.

Not when all he'd experienced was being cast aside when he'd craved a bond with his family. When he'd been young and naïve and had trusted that they would be there for him and love him even if they were busy. It had never happened, and it had taught him a lesson to keep his heart walled off. To forsake the bonds that people usually sought.

So he couldn't lower his guard, which meant he never relaxed enough to rest, and therefore was continuously tormented by her presence in the dark.

'Helia,' he called gently as he pulled away from her. 'We have an appearance to make.'

As he had been instructed, Andreas had ensured that the orphanage was ready for their visit.

She groaned, burrowing deeper into her pillow. Vasili curled his hands into fists, fighting the urge to brush her hair away from her face.

'You don't want to keep the children waiting.'

'No.' She yawned, stretching her body, and Vasili couldn't help himself. He pulled her under him, kissing the strip of her exposed stomach. Kissing a path up her torso until his lips locked with hers.

'A girl could get used to this sort of wake-up.'

'A queen,' he said, low-voiced in her ear. 'And you'd better get out of this bed before I keep us both here indefinitely.'

It was so much easier to fall into passion. To ease the ache of want with physicality that still allowed him his barriers.

'Don't threaten me with a good time, Vasili.' She grinned. 'Are you ready for today?'

It was one thing for her to be a queen within the palace walls, quite another to be one in public.

'I think I am. Andreas went over the itinerary and what is expected of me. I think I'm prepared.'

'There will be media.'

He could see her tense. The apprehension in her face.

'I'm sure I'll manage.'

'You don't have to manage, Helia. If it becomes too much, lean on me. Understood?'

He was far more experienced at dealing with all the attention, and truthfully still felt a twinge of guilt for having brought Helia into this mess. The least he could do was make it easier on her. Vasili was aware that there was still a chance that this life could turn him into someone like his parents, so he would choose to be different—and being considerate of his wife was one of those choices.

'Yes,' she said.

She placed her hand on his cheek, and he felt his body responding to the warm touch. If he didn't leave the bed now, he wasn't going to.

Vasili waited in the palace hall dressed in a blue suit. Everything had been picked out for him. Every piece considered for the image the palace wanted to present. He could only imagine what Helia would be put through this morning. He hoped Andreas and Carissa were going easy on her. It ground on his nerves, the way they treated her, and he would very soon be having a conversation with both of them.

Thankfully, he wasn't allowed to stew for very long as Helia descended the grand staircase, looking an absolute vision. Her hair had been left curly and loose, pulled back, away from her face. Her make-up had been done softly enough that the woman he'd been on honeymoon with was still clearly on display. And that dress... White satin flowed over her body to her narrow waist, where it flared out in pale blue and green flowers to her calves. He wanted to run his hands all over her. Place them on that narrow waist and whisk her away somewhere they could be alone.

'Beautiful,' he said.

'You don't look too bad yourself, Your Majesty.'

He could see the way she looked at him. As if she would like nothing more than to rip away his suit. In just a few days, Helia had gone from being shy and inhibited, unsure if she should touch him, to demanding. Almost confident in her want for pleasure. It satisfied him greatly that she would share that side of herself with him.

Vasili took her hand in his. They would no doubt be photographed from the moment they stepped out of the palace. Together they climbed into the waiting Rolls-Royce bearing the flags of Thalonia.

The ride to the orphanage was longer than he'd thought it would be. Upmarket buildings faded into modest storefronts, which morphed into more battered structures. Seidon had always been the pride of the Kingdom. Its streets were supposed to be rich. His parents would have had everyone believe that the people were happy, but here they looked forgotten. There was none of the vibrancy, none of the life he would have associated with his home. These streets were nothing like the ones he had partied in or ridden his motorcycle along. There wasn't any freedom here.

'Even as a commoner, you don't get choices. You have to make do with what you get dealt.'

Helia's voice came back to him...her words from their first meeting.

Without realising it, he curled his hand tighter around hers and she squeezed back.

They arrived at a nondescript white building. Cameras were already flashing. A line of people waited at the entrance, and once the car door was opened Vasili stepped out, then helped Helia, who emerged with a smile and a wave. It wasn't a bright smile. There was a tightness around her eyes.

'Your Majesties...' The first person in line—a world-weary-looking woman—greeted them with a curtsey. Vasili extended his hand. The woman shook it with ill-concealed hope.

'It is good to see you, Maria.' Helia smiled, holding both the woman's hands.

Vasili was taken aback by the familiarity between them. He wondered if Helia had volunteered here, and that was why she'd chosen this place for them to make their first appearance. She'd had a life before he'd plucked her from it, and she had shown so much kindness and consideration. It was a theory that made sense.

As they greeted the line of people, he noticed the warmth with which they all received her. He placed a hand on the small of her back and hazarded a glance behind him. Andreas and Carissa stood further away, allowing all the attention to fall on the new King and Queen, but his private secretary had an inscrutable look on his face, and Vasili didn't understand how he couldn't show at least a little emotion, standing where they were.

'Shall we show you around?' Maria asked.

'Please...after you.' Vasili gestured ahead of him.

The outside had barely prepared him for the inside. It was clear they were doing the best they could, with the funds they had, but calling the place shabby was as generous as he could be. There was a large, outdated kitchen, a common area, and numerous bedrooms with two to three children sharing each. He was relieved to see a recreation room of sorts, but it was severely lacking. The offices weren't that much better.

Helia had told him that she wanted to help the forgotten people of Thalonia, and he hadn't really known who that could be. Now, he hated it that he had been blind to this side of his kingdom. All those years he'd spent rebelling against the crown in a way that served *him* he could have spent rebelling in a way that served others. It had always been obvious that the politicians favoured the wealthy, as had his parents. But he could have used his rebellion for good, and it angered him that he had been so ignorant. Angered him that he had been lectured on propriety in his behaviour as a royal, when a royal was meant to serve everyone. His family didn't do that.

'Is there somewhere we can discuss matters?' he asked Maria.

'Yes, of course.'

'We would like to speak with all of you as well,' Helia said to the other staff.

They were taken into a room with a large table and some boxes stacked against the wall.

'I apologise. We can't offer you a better meeting room. Unfortunately, we don't have much space.'

'No apologies are necessary,' he said. 'We're here to listen. It's obvious that you're struggling—where are the issues?'

Maria needed no further encouragement than Helia nodding at her to speak. It was amazing to watch her interact with these people. *His* people. He had been worried about how she would fare today, but he hadn't needed to be. She was warm and listened carefully to their grievances, interjecting only to clarify their points. She showed a patience that he was struggling with—because it seemed Maria had to manage too much. There wasn't a proper organisational structure that would benefit the orphanage or the children. Hardly any of them would achieve any kind of greatness simply because there were no avenues for their betterment. Most of the staff were volunteers. How did this help anyone?

Things had to change.

He was grateful to Helia for showing him what he had been blind to. She was promising Maria things would improve. A move that had Andreas scowling.

Upon re-entering the main building, they finally got to meet some of the children that this place helped. From babies who grasped his heart in their tiny little fists to teenagers who were far too jaded for their young years. He could tell that Carissa was pleased they would get pictures that she could spin into something wildly positive, but if it hadn't been for Helia's presence beside him he would have been completely untethered. Sucked into his disappointment and anger.

He pulled her closer. Wrapping an arm around her waist as they further spoke to the volunteers. He needed her near.

But just as he had the thought, she was whisked away—and it couldn't have made him happier to see her go.

A little hand clasped onto Helia's, and out the corner of her eye she saw several of the royal entourage step forward. With a single look she ordered them away—not even stopping to reflect on the fact that she had controlled everyone wordlessly—and allowed the little girl to pull her out of Vasili's embrace.

This excursion had clearly been a shock to him. She could feel his emotions radiate through him. Frustration, anger, disappointment… Despite what he believed, he was a good man, and she could only imagine what seeing this side of his kingdom was doing to him—which was why she'd remained so close.

For her, this visit was monumental. Helia was more at home here than she'd ever felt at the palace. This was where she'd grown up. Where she'd spent her free time. When Helia had turned eighteen and left, it had been to start a hopeful new life. But now, returning as Queen, it was to bring a hopeful future for them all. This place—these people—had given her a home when she had none. A place that was now giving others a home. Like the little girl now tugging her away, so she didn't feel bad for leaving her husband.

'Where are you taking me, Anastasia?'

'Come and see what we made.'

The little girl she was well acquainted with from her volunteering led her over to a group of children sitting on the floor, playing with building blocks.

'We built a palace.'

Anastasia tugged at Helia to join them on the floor, and she kneeled on the threadbare carpet. Andreas—barely hiding his displeasure—and several others looked as if they wanted to intervene.

'Stop,' Vasili commanded them.

She locked eyes with her husband, thinking the admonishment was for her, but there was something shifting in his gaze she couldn't decipher. There was a thread between them, and it went taut as he approached her. She watched him sit on a nearby couch, her heart full to bursting, as he examined the plastic brick construction.

'It's where you live,' one of Anastasia's little friends piped up.

'I think this is far more impressive than where I live,' she replied making the child's face light up.

'If this is Queen Helia's palace,' Vasili said, picking up a few stray bricks, 'then it needs a very big library.'

His eyes flashed to hers and her heart skipped a beat. She could feel heat creep up her neck. A heavy ache in her core that she had to hide. But he saw it. She knew by the small smirk on his face which he disguised with a broad smile for the others in their presence.

The feeling didn't go away in the time she and Vasili spent with the children. It meant more than she could say when he spoke to the older kids, who had tried to stay away, and within these walls where hope so often burned and died, Helia found herself hoping. Wishing she could have more with Vasili. With her husband who clearly cared for these people. *Her* people. And a deep sense of affection for him overcame her, flaring bright, but was quickly doused with an acute loneliness as she remembered all they were and all they could never be.

'We will be in touch. In the meantime, if you require anything contact our staff and it will be yours,' Vasili said, shaking Maria's hand.

'I promise things will get better.' Helia hugged the woman that she had known for most of her life and left with Vasili holding her close.

He remained silent on the drive back to the palace. Physically, he kept close to her. And a jolt of electricity passed through her at their every touch. But it seemed he was withdrawing into his thoughts, and she didn't like that. He had taken the title despite wanting to abdicate—a choice made for his people. Helia hadn't known how much of Thalonia's suffering he'd been aware of before, but seeing the look on his face when they'd toured the orphanage had answered that. He was her ally in this quest, so she needed to know what he was thinking.

'Are you okay?'

'You're asking me if *I'm* okay?'

She could see something flicker in his eyes before he sighed.

'No, Helia, I'm not. I didn't know it was this bad.' He rubbed his eyes with his thumb and finger. 'I should have. I was always aware of how much my family favoured those with power. Wealth. But I never stopped to consider what that would mean for others.'

'Maybe that's true—but, Vasili, we are doing something

about it *now*. Those people back there were happy to see you for a reason.'

He huffed a humourless laugh. 'Don't try to placate me, Helia.'

'I'm not. I'm just telling you what I saw.'

She couldn't understand why he wouldn't acknowledge how much his words and actions meant to the people at the orphanage, but there wasn't much more time to dwell on it before they had arrived back at the palace.

They made their way to Vasili's office for the debrief that would follow. She'd expected both Andreas and Carissa to appear. However, it was only Andreas who did, wearing a deep scowl.

'I'm sure you have an opinion about today, Andreas, but let's recognise that it was a success,' Vasili said.

'I won't deny that Carissa will have what she needs to introduce you both to the world, sir,' Andreas said stiffly.

He was not happy, but Helia couldn't possibly imagine what could have set him off. She had remembered everything she needed to. Plus, Vasili had pledged his assistance, and it was the start of what she wanted to achieve.

Andreas turned to her. 'But *you*, Your Majesty, did not act in a way befitting of a queen.'

Helia could feel her buoyant mood dissipating. The high was gone and instead she was plunging back to earth. She thought she had done well. How could she have read the situation so wrong?

'I did everything expected of me,' Helia defended, recognising that she shouldn't have to, but also that Andreas knew so much more than she did. He had so much power over the staff and the politicians.

She'd fought to keep the steel in her voice, and felt Vasili move to stand at her back. She so badly wanted to lean on him now, but that would show weakness. Something she was not.

She had given up her career, sacrificed everything for this mission. She would lean on no one.

'Meeting in a storeroom. Making promises that we don't know if we can keep. *Sitting on the floor.*'

Andreas's cheeks flared pink. Oh, he was angry.

'Never in all my years has any royal done that. We are meant to show strength. That we bow to no one. And yet you behaved like one of those ordinary volunteers. You acted without thought.'

He was right. She had acted without thought. She'd seen those children and seen herself in them. She hadn't felt like a queen when she'd played with them—she'd been just Helia. A woman who cared so much that she would say goodbye to the one thing she loved for them. Queens didn't do that. Queens found solutions that didn't affect them personally. But how could she do that when that very place was her past?

'You are not one of them any longer. You are Queen Helia Leos and you need to start behaving as such.'

'Enough.'

The gruff voice had come from beside her. There was a warm hand on her back, grounding her. Andreas fell silent.

'That's quite enough, Andreas. Leave us—and for your own sake, I suggest you do so quietly.'

Helia watched him march angrily through the door and once he was gone she turned to Vasili.

'You behaved like those ordinary volunteers.'

What if she had embarrassed Vasili? She relied on him to help her with this cause. What was more, things had been going well. She was growing to care for him more and more with each day. She couldn't bear the thought of hurting him in any way. She had to apologise.

'Vasili, I'm so—'

He cradled her face, seizing her lips, cutting off her apology with a hard kiss that had her letting out an unexpected moan.

His tongue plunged into her mouth, setting off an avalanche of arousal through her body. She gasped as Vasili hooked his hands under her thighs and lifted her, setting her on the edge of his desk, making her just a little taller. Flame licked at the base of her spine as he stepped between her legs, deepening the kiss. He tasted of mint. The scent of his aftershave—cool and fresh, with something spicier that she could only describe as *his* scent—wrapped around her, chasing the apology from her mind. But she had to make it.

She pushed at his chest and he stopped immediately, his lips reluctantly leaving hers.

'Vasili, I have to say this—'

'No, you don't.' His voice was low. Rough. 'Don't you dare apologise.'

'But Andreas—'

'I don't care what Andreas said. All I saw today was a woman who cares.' He pressed a soft kiss to her lips. 'And I've wanted to kiss you all day.'

'Then do it.'

Vasili leaned in. Taking her lip between his teeth. Watching the way her eyes fluttered closed. He brushed his lips against hers, licking the seam of them, taking his time. Stoking the fire between them.

Seeing Helia interact with everyone at the orphanage had done something to his heart. He didn't care what his advisors said. The woman before him was the Queen this kingdom needed. He had wanted to kiss her then, a million times over, but he hadn't been able to. Their passion was behind closed doors. That was the agreement. But the need in him had built and built. Now, the noises she made as he tasted her had him growing hard. But he couldn't stop kissing her. He trailed kisses and bites down her neck, marking her. Everyone would see it. He would see it. It was a primitive thing to want to mark one's territory, but he couldn't care less. Especially when she called his name in that breathy way that satisfied something deep within.

Vasili recognised that he needed to step away from her for a moment or he would have his queen laid out on his desk.

He picked her up and carried her over to the couch, where he settled her on his lap, tucking her head against his shoulder. While he knew he needed to clear his head of the lusty haze, he didn't want to let her go. Not yet. He still had questions, and while they had privacy he was going to ask them.

'I need to thank you, Helia.'

'For what?'

'Showing me how we've failed.'

'Vasili...'

He looked down into her bright turquoise eyes. Her hand came up to his cheek and he laid his over hers. At first he thought he was going to remove it, but that wasn't possible. He craved her touch too much.

'*You* haven't failed at anything,' she said. 'Not yet, at least. You didn't run this kingdom before.'

'I could have done something sooner. I rebelled selfishly. Don't excuse my actions.'

He was angry at himself. So angry for not having bothered to look further than his own suffering.

'I'm not. But you saw something that was wrong today, and instead of making excuses you listened to them. You offered them help.'

But he needed to do more. And he still needed to know why it meant so much to Helia.

'As did you.'

'It's different for me,' she admitted.

'Why? Why is the orphanage so important to you? Why choose that for our first outing today? Andreas was right in that you could have picked something easier—not better, but certainly easier. I need to understand. Is this why you agreed to marry me?'

Helia pulled her hand from his face and glanced away, making Vasili worry that he had pushed too soon. But he needed to know. He felt Helia's chest expand as she took a deep breath, and without looking at him she started speaking in a low voice that failed to hide her pain.

'I grew up there.'

Which explained why she'd been received so warmly. She was one of them.

'I was barely a teenager when my father died, and with my mother having passed away long before, my Uncle Giannis became my guardian. They were close, Giannis and my father. They were business partners. My father was the creative one. He was warm and kind and people loved his flower arrangements. Giannis was the opposite. Coldly logical. He was great at business and finance, so their partnership worked well. My father had made him executor of his estate.'

Vasili had a bad feeling he knew where this was going.

'My father had left the business to Giannis. It employed enough florists that it would still make money without him, but he'd also left a monetary inheritance for me. A substantial amount. It would have taken care of me. Helped me study. Get a start in life.'

The light flowing through the large windows sparkled on a tear as it fell, kissing her cheek before disappearing. Vasili brushed the wetness away and wrapped his arms around her.

'I went to stay with Giannis. He had always been nice to me when my father was alive, but he changed. He became cruel. He would tell me that I was a burden. That he hadn't wanted a family and what made me enough reason to change that about his life? I tried so hard to be good. To make sure he didn't notice me more than he needed to. I would do chores, and try to cook, but nothing I did was good enough. I missed my father and my uncle was awful. Maybe he had always been that way and everything else was an act. I don't know. Anyway, he dealt with the lawyers and the banks and everything else. I was at the will-reading, so I knew I was getting an inheritance. What I didn't know was that Giannis had opened a bank account for me and he had full signing rights on it because I was a minor. My inheritance was paid into it, and once the estate was settled he moved every penny into his own account. He said it was what he was owed and then he packed me a suitcase— just one—and dropped me off at the orphanage.'

Vasili tightened his arms around her, trying very hard to rein in his temper. He wanted to find Giannis Demetriou and make him pay for his sins. For making Helia question her worth.

'Maria was the director back then too. She tried to get me to make friends with the others, but I couldn't. I withdrew from everyone.'

Vasili didn't blame her. She had been abandoned—why would she want to trust anyone? He could understand that.

It dawned on him that she was trusting him enough to tell him her story. Vasili had never been protective of anything, but now, as he listened to Helia's story, the need to protect flared blindingly bright in him. He wanted to shield her. Keep her safe from everyone and everything. Nothing would touch her again. He vowed it in that moment.

'I had to change schools. A forgotten little school with a terribly small library. But it was something. The librarian there let me help out, and slowly things got better. I knew then that a librarian was what I wanted to be—but you saw what it's like at the orphanage. It's only the fortunate ones who go on to achieve their dreams. I swore that one day I would find a way to help them…which is why I volunteer there when I can. But have always wanted to do more.'

Vasili hadn't thought he could get any angrier, but here he was, trying to hide his trembling from Helia. The crown hadn't done enough. Not for people like Helia. Not for those having to live away from the bright lights of Seidon. His family had failed for generations.

He kissed her temple, cradling her to his body. He could have told her that he was sorry she'd had to go through that—because he was. He could have told her he wanted vengeance in her name—because he did. But he didn't say any of that because he couldn't change the past.

Instead, he said, 'Helia, I am King of Thalonia and you are my queen and together we will fix this. We will fix what's broken in this kingdom so that no one else will have to endure what you did. No one will be forgotten while we rule.'

'Vasili...' she breathed, in a way that stopped his heart.

With eyes full of tears she kissed him. Tugging on his hair as she pulled him closer. He lifted her and placed her over him to straddle his lap, letting her control this frantic kiss until he wanted more.

He threaded his fingers in her hair, angling his head so he could kiss her more deeply, and then he pulled away for just a breath. 'I escaped into books too.'

Helia laughed against his lips. The single most joyous sound after her tears had cut through him. His lips were back on hers instantly. Something molten was stirring within him. Scorching him with every pass of their lips. And then his hands trailed down her body, digging into her soft flesh as the overwhelming need to be buried inside her gripped him in an iron hold. He dragged Helia's hips forward. Her core brushed against his hardness, making him moan. Low. Deep. He flexed against her, driving them both mad.

Crazed. That was how he felt. All he could think of was more.

'Helia...' he groaned, biting her chin, her throat.

He slipped his hands under her dress and knew she would be slick for him. How easy it would be to shed these clothes, these flimsy fabric barriers, and push into her.

Her sighs and mewls had every link on the chains he had around himself breaking apart. He wanted her. Now.

His fingers tightened around the band of her panties. He could tear them right off her. Feel her warmth against his skin. Feel her clench around him.

No! a voice at the back of his mind shouted.

What was he doing? He couldn't have sex with her. Especially not now, when they were both raw. He couldn't let them seek comfort in each other like that. Not to mention he had no protection.

Vasili tore his lips away from Helia's and pressed his forehead against hers. Their breaths were ragged. He had been so close to forsaking his mission. The thought of what might have happened if he'd entered her bare was sobering. He couldn't risk having a child. The throne wasn't meant to endure. But he had found Helia so tempting he had forgotten what he was working towards.

'I'm sorry…' he panted.

'For what?'

Her pupils were blown wide. Skin flushed. How wonderful it would be to see her writhing under him.

'This isn't what you need right now. Not after what you told me.'

It was an excuse, and he knew it, but he couldn't tell her that he didn't want to have sex with her, because that would be a lie, and he couldn't tell her that they shouldn't, because he could barely remember why. But he could tell her he would take care of her—because he would.

'I'm not going to have sex with you, but I am going to take care of you. Allow me that?'

Helia studied his face. Searching, he presumed, for an answer he couldn't give her. And maybe she understood, because she nodded and shifted off him.

He stood and adjusted the evidence of his arousal, then took her hand, leading her out of the office. Their union wasn't meant to include sex, but he couldn't ignore their physical reaction to each other. And now he thought maybe there was more to it than that. Because every thought he had in this moment centred around his wife.

Vasili told himself that he had to do better...to remember why he held himself back. He couldn't lose control again.

CHAPTER TWELVE

VASILI HADN'T SLEPT a wink. All he'd been able to think about was what Helia had been through. He had known loneliness, but even though his family had never been there for him, he'd still had a brother who had cared to a degree. He hadn't been entirely abandoned—not like Helia. To trust someone, to think they had your best interests in mind, and then to be so betrayed at such a young age would have broken anyone. Especially at such a vulnerable time.

Vasili still didn't know how to react to the trust she had shown in telling him. He'd never had anyone wanting to be that close to him. Now the first person to do so was the one person he was trying to keep at arm's length, and it was proving harder and harder every day.

Having her confide in him had made him feel fulfilled in a way that was alien, even if it also angered him that she'd had to deal with so much strife.

At least now he understood why she'd married him. Why this mission of hers was so important. Seeing the people at the orphanage had affected him, but to know that Helia had been one of them both crushed him and ignited a determination to help her. Which was why he had finally given up on sleep and worked on the solution that he would propose to her. He would include her in every step.

As soon as the rest of the palace had awakened, he had sent for her.

For now he sat with Andreas, a folder open before him. He studied his advisor and personal secretary, who seemed hell-bent on pushing for a bill that went against everything Vasili was hoping to achieve. He kept one eye on the door. Helia would be arriving shortly. He could already picture her expression when she learnt about this.

'This does nothing to better Thalonia,' Vasili said, tossing a page back into the folder.

'Of course it does, Your Majesty. This would benefit everyone.'

'Everyone whom you deem important,' Vasili corrected. 'This is trickle-down economics.'

'Nothing is more effective.'

'Don't try to sell that to me, Andreas. We both know it doesn't work that way.'

'It's my advice to you to sign off on this bill.'

Vasili stared Andreas down. There was absolutely no way that he would. Bills like this were the reason why places like the orphanage existed in the state they did. Why the poor of Thalonia suffered in silence. His father would have signed off on it, but Vasili was determined on being a different kind of king.

Through the tension, a knock sounded on the door and in walked Helia. She was frowning as she looked between him and Andreas.

'What's going on here?'

It wasn't a tentative question; it was a demand to know.

Vasili could see how she was blossoming into her role even if she still doubted herself at times.

'It's nothing for you to be concerned about, Your Majesty,' Andreas said.

Vasili knew that tone. But disregarding Helia would never be something he accepted. His father had ruled absolutely. His mother, though she'd been Queen, had only ever been allowed power over things he'd deemed acceptable for her. Vasili had hated it then and he hated it now. Perhaps it was the rebellion in him which he probably would never be rid of. The need to do things his way.

Helia was his partner. They had agreed to show a united front to the world. That included his advisors, so as far as Vasili was concerned, and she would always have a voice.

Holding Andreas's stare, he slid the folder over to Helia, who had come to stand beside him. 'This is a proposed tax bill that I will not be passing.'

Helia read through the pages in the folder, grateful for her background as a librarian. All the knowledge she had absorbed over the years helped her understand the document in her hand now. One that made her heart sink. This was proof of the barriers she needed to overcome to ensure the people who needed help the most received it.

The one shining light was Vasili. He was already opposed. A fact that made her breathe a sigh of relief. The problem was Andreas was obviously pushing for it.

'I'm no expert, but to me this would only benefit those already wealthy. There is no benefit for the poor. They're likely to be forgotten. Seems like you're pushing for something only the upper echelons want,' she said evenly as she set the folder down.

'That is exactly it,' Vasili agreed.

Vasili had told her to wield her power. Had said to her numerous times that she was Queen. Reminded her when he kissed and touched her. And after their talk the day before it was finally starting to settle—because the only person whose opinion she should value was her husband's.

When they had returned from the orphanage Andreas's words had had her doubting herself. She could see that he didn't care for everyone. But she did. And Vasili did. So she would no longer allow him to make her feel as if her title was an ill fit.

'Vasili is right. We can't pass this. As Queen, I am opposed.'

Just as she had expected, Andreas did not take well to her statement.

'This is irregular. It is the King who has a say in the policy of our country. That was how King Athanasios did things, and that was how King Leander did as well.'

'It would appear that once again you need reminding, Andreas, that I am not my father, nor my brother. I will accept the counsel of my queen because she is the only one amongst us who is intimately aware of how our policies affect and fail the ordinary citizens of Thalonia. Helia has as much of a say in the wellbeing of our people as I do, and we are both opposed. If you want this bill passed in Parliament, I suggest it be reworked.'

While Vasili did not raise his voice, Helia was taken by the power in it. He might be a reluctant king, but to her he was already a good one.

She turned to Vasili as soon as Andreas had left and said, 'Thank you.'

'We agreed to fix things together, did we not?'

They had, and he was already following through on that promise. He treated her with consideration, valued her opinions, and it was making it so much harder for her to keep her feelings under lock and key. She was forbidden from falling in love. He didn't want them to fall in love. But he made it so hard. She already trusted him. He had asked for her trust in small ways, but had earned it in the biggest, which was why she had felt comfortable telling him of her past. Helia hadn't told anyone the whole truth, but she'd told Vasili, and it hadn't scared her to say it.

It was clear that she was well on her way to breaking her promise and losing her heart to him, but he would never do the same. How could he treat her so well, help her and listen to her, and then refuse to love her?

'We did.'

'But that isn't why I asked you here.' He stood and offered her his chair, pushing it in when she sat, then lifting the lid of his laptop. 'This is what I want to discuss with you.'

Helia skimmed through the document, her breath catching. 'When did you do this?'

'I couldn't sleep,' Vasili admitted, perching on the corner of the table, looking down at her. 'What do you think?'

'You want to make orphanages a palace concern.'

'Yes. That way we can secure funding that I get to dictate without having to go through the politicians. That's not all. I plan on creating an educational fund that the orphans will have access to for further study.'

'How would we make that work?'

'Possibly some sort of bursary fund.'

That would be perfect. She knew first-hand that not everyone shared in academic dreams, it would be a standout achievement for them to say that the palace had taken notice of them. It would give them the leg up in the world that they desperately needed.

'And for the orphanages?'

'Those funds would be dealt with separately, and with your help I think I can come up with a framework to allocate resources fairly.'

With her help.

Not only was Vasili helping Helia achieve her mission far sooner than she had dared to hope, but he also wasn't taking it away from her. He wanted her to be a part of it. And that meant more than he would ever know.

'This is going to be a big project, Helia. Of course you would be part of it. After all, this is your mission.'

Helia felt a burning in her eyes, but she wouldn't allow herself to cry. It didn't matter that she was happy. She needed to keep her emotions at bay long enough to make it through the rest of the discussion. But she knew he was coming to understand her. Read her like no one else ever could.

'What's this about schools?' With all the emotion clogging up her throat, her voice came out strangled.

'That is my decree increasing the national spend on education.'

'Thank you, Vasili.'

'No, don't thank me. This change is long overdue. You and I…we're changing this kingdom, Helia. I will not be toeing any lines to keep people who have watched Thalonia suffer comfortable. We need new traditions.'

Helia didn't have words for how much this meant to her. Once she had taken him to the orphanage—only once. And this was what he had done. She couldn't contain herself any more…couldn't deny what she felt for him. Vasili was kind and considerate and caring, and she knew without a shadow of doubt right then that she was hopelessly in love with him.

Helia couldn't find the moment when it had happened, and realised she had fallen for him in little bits from the first time she'd met him. That was why she trusted him. Why she'd told him about her past. It was because she loved him.

Without thinking, she flung herself at Vasili and kissed him. He didn't hesitate, not even for second, and he kissed her back.

Hands on her waist, he held her firm as she wrapped her arms around his neck. Lightning crackled through her veins as his tongue delved into her mouth, stroking her. Making her come alive. Then he spun them around, placing her on the large desk, and moved to stand between her legs. She cursed the tailored trousers she wore, because she wanted to feel the warm hand that was travelling up the outside of her thigh.

She wanted him to lay her down on the desk and feast on

her. She wanted to show him with her body what he meant to her because she couldn't say the words.

Helia wrapped her legs around him, sinking her hands under his jacket. Scratching down his sides over his perfectly starched white shirt. She felt the muscles beneath her fingers tense.

'Helia…'

He moaned out her name and angled his head, kissing her deeper. Wilder. And she wanted this. She wanted him to break free with her. He was only barely managing to restrain himself. She felt it in the tremor of his arms and the scrape of his teeth. It awakened such a wild desire, which was only further fuelled by the torrent of love within her.

'Vasili…' she breathed into his ear.

He cursed, pulling her hips to the edge of the table, grinding his hardness against her core.

Her whimper sent shockwaves of lust racing through him.

He couldn't stop this time.

Vasili realised that when it came to Helia, he wasn't the one in control. And he was tired. So tired of wanting and not having. So tired of the rebellion that had given him choice but taken just as much away.

Choosing Helia had been a rebellion, but denying himself his need to take her to bed was a rebellion too. A rebellion against his need for her. He hadn't forgotten why he didn't want to have sex with her, but he was losing his grasp on his willpower and the want coursing through him strangled him.

For once he wanted to ignore everything else and take what would make him happy.

'Let go with me,' she told him.

He wanted to. He was barely hanging on by a thread. The hold on his barriers was beyond tenuous now. All he wanted was to be deep inside her.

'Is this what you want?'

He gritted out the question, hoping she would say no. He needed her to, because she was the only thing that could stop them now. And yet he was praying she would say yes, because he wanted her so badly he couldn't think straight.

'Yes.'

It was the key that unlocked every shackle on him. He had nothing left in him to resist her any more. He only prayed that this would not be his ruination.

She tugged him even closer to her, but he shook his head. He wouldn't allow their first time like this to be a rushed, torrid affair on his office desk.

He placed a gentle kiss on her lips, then took her hand and led her from the office.

Vasili walked right past their shared bedroom. He didn't want her there. He was taking her to what was his room. His quiet sanctum.

He shut the door, not giving her a chance to look at their surroundings before his lips were on hers again, and without breaking their kiss he picked Helia up. Her legs wrapped around him without him having to tell her.

Vasili didn't want to think of what this would mean for them. He didn't want to think of why it seemed that they danced perfectly in sync with each other. All he wanted was to lose himself in her.

He pressed her back against the closed door. His breath hissed from his lips as he pushed his hardness against her. Her gasp was music to him. The sweetest sound.

'Please, Vasili, I need you.'

He needed her too, with an urgency that defied all thought or logic. But there was no room for thought. Not now.

With sure steps he crossed the room and laid her gently upon the bed. Seeing her lying on his dark sheets, staring back at him with hooded eyes, he felt a savage sort of possessiveness overcome him.

This woman—his queen, a goddess—was his.

But she had been so timid when they had first become intimate... He needed to know just how inexperienced she was.

'Have you done this before, Helia?' He kneeled over her, supporting himself on a muscular arm beside her head.

Her skin burned red. 'Yes, but—'

'But?'

'It doesn't matter.' She looked away.

Holding her chin in his fingers, he forced her to meet his gaze. 'It does to me. Honesty. Remember?'

'I had sex with someone I had dated, but it wasn't enjoyable. It was always uncomfortable. And after him I avoided it even if I wanted it. I couldn't let go. I couldn't allow myself to trust.'

Anger burned alongside Vasili's lust. He couldn't do anything to change her past experience, but he would make sure she knew only pleasure now.

'I won't hurt you.'

'I know.'

He ran his hand along the side of her body. 'Let me show you how a king worships you.'

'A king doesn't worship a queen.'

She ran her fingers through his hair. He caught her wrist and kissed her palm. 'A king worships a goddess.'

And that was what he wanted to do. For weeks she had haunted his thoughts and dreams.

'I have wanted you for so long, Helia. I've dreamt of this moment. Of what you will feel like when I sink into you.'

'What did you do in your dreams?'

'I peeled every maddening layer of cloth from your body. Slowly. Until you wanted to tear them off yourself.'

With his teeth, Vasili pulled down the zipper on her trousers, never taking his eyes off her. He kissed the lace peeking between the parted fabric and peeled it off her legs. Her breath was coming in heavy pants.

He kissed his way up her body, running his lips over her neck, making her shiver as he undid the buttons on her blouse. She clutched at the sheets. At her hair.

'Just like this,' he whispered in her ear, only to draw away and remove the rest of her clothing with the same teasing slowness until her pupils had swallowed up most of the turquoise in her eyes. 'And then I kissed you.'

He brushed his lips over hers, then took her mouth hungrily. Teasing Helia like this had unleashed a firestorm of want within him, but he didn't care about his need for release because he craved seeing Helia come apart for him. The sight was addictive.

He broke the kiss, pulling away, and he chuckled when Helia tried to follow. He kept her down on the bed, saying, 'But not here.'

'Where?'

He grinned as he settled between her legs, seeing her slickness on her golden skin, and lowered his mouth to her mound. His tongue slid through her folds as he kissed her deeply. He became lost in her taste and her scent and the symphony of her moans as he made her soar further, higher, until she reached her release with a keening cry, sobbing his name.

He kissed every inch of her body, sucking her nipples into his mouth, marking her perfect skin with his teeth, drawing out her pleasure until she calmed, and then he kept going until she was panting once more.

Vasili shucked off his clothes and reached into a drawer, retrieving a foil square. He saw Helia's eyes follow him.

'Vasili, I'm on birth control.'

'I'm glad to hear it,' he said, brushing his fingers through her caramel curls.

He truthfully was glad, but accidents did happen, and even

though he wanted nothing more than to feel Helia around him, he was determined that they would never have heirs. He couldn't. So he ripped open the packet and rolled the protection along his length.

And then he had Helia's hips in his hands, spreading her thighs apart so he could see himself sinking into her. A hurricane of pleasure consumed him. Stealing his breath. Grabbing his heart in a fist.

She felt like heaven. Like everything he had known she would and so much more.

He cursed on a breath. 'Helia...'

This was so much more overwhelming than Vasili had anticipated. It felt too good—and not just in the way the pleasure rolled over him in unending waves. It felt too much like home. As if being with Helia like this was fated.

Vasili had crossed a boundary he knew he shouldn't have. Because he would never want to stop doing this with her. It was exactly as he had feared.

CHAPTER THIRTEEN

VASILI HAD MADE her wait for this and it was worth every minute. With him sliding in and out of her, Helia's voice flowed from her in unintelligible moans. None of her fantasies compared. She hadn't ever felt current like this in her body, this heat in her veins and a coiling deep in her core. And then there was Vasili. The sheen of sweat on his sculpted torso. The look of ecstasy on his face. There was also vulnerability there. Something he would normally cover up. But he couldn't now.

'More...' she begged, and he obliged.

Wrapping his arms tightly around her body, he fused them together. His thrusts were growing harder. Faster. His breaths were coming in a constant rapid rush. She had thought it couldn't possibly feel better than it had when he'd had his mouth on her, but *this* was all-consuming.

She lost her whole heart to him. Feeling utter pleasure. Treasured. Protected.

His rhythm was growing erratic as he drew close to release and Helia was right there with him. Stretching. Coiling. Reaching for her peak. And as he slammed his hips into her, tensing as he spilled, she shattered around him. Calling his name as he dropped his head into the crook of her neck and they rode out their pleasure together.

'Helia...'

Everything had changed. She felt it. Heard it in his voice. They had crossed over to somewhere new. Except she didn't know where that was. What it would mean for them. For her and this new, pulsing love that thrummed faster than her heart.

'Don't move.'

Vasili kissed her forehead, then disappeared into the bathroom to dispose of the condom. She heard running water and he returned with a warm towel that he used to clean her up. Then he tossed it aside and drew her into his arms.

By now Helia had lain in his arms numerous times, but this time it was so different. She turned towards him and Vasili held her against his hard body. She kissed the base of his throat, knowing that her heart was his. She loved him, but she couldn't say it.

Helia looked into his face and saw that every one of the barriers he had erected around him had come crashing down. She didn't know how long it would last, but for the moment at least he was hers.

So she settled into his embrace and looked at their surroundings. At the modern room and the books and the art.

'I've finally found a place in this palace that looks like you belong in it,' she said.

'Is that so?'

Helia was coming to understand Vasili. She could tell when he was trying to cover up his feelings.

'Yes. The title suits you. You are the King, Vasili. But that office doesn't suit you.' She kissed him lightly on the lips. 'You should make it yours. Like it is here.'

His arms tightened around her. She felt his lips on the top of her head.

'I was barely out of my teens when I ordered the change. I needed somewhere to belong.'

Soft words that had the power to break a heart. Helia wanted to ease the hurt in him, but to do that she needed him to open up to her.

'What was it like growing up here? Being a prince?'

BELLA MASON 155

'Lonely. The only reason my parents had me was because they had to have a spare. Nannies raised me from as far back as I can remember. Well, one did.'

'What was she like?'

Vasili smiled. Sad, yet fond. His eyes were focused on some faraway place. 'Sophia was…warm. She was funny and playful. Kind. Smarter than anyone gave her credit for. And she took care solely of me.'

'You two must have been close.'

'We were.'

There was a gruffness in his voice that had Helia trying to move even closer to him. Trying to soothe an old hurt.

'Until my parents ordered that she be fired when I turned fifteen. She said nothing to them. Refused to report to Andreas or thank anyone for having worked here. She broke all the rules of propriety by addressing only me before she left. She told me never to bow.'

Helia could see the connection between Vasili and Sophia. Kind, rebellious souls. 'Do you know where she went?'

'No, I wasn't allowed to look for her. Not until recently, when I found that she had passed away a few years ago.'

'That's awful. I'm sorry.'

Helia could only imagine how hard it would have been for him to lose the person closest to him because she had been taken away. Forced to abandon him.

'There's a lot of that in these walls, Helia,' he said, matter-of-factly.

'You couldn't lean on Leander either,' she said, speaking her thoughts out loud.

Vasili sighed. 'I was ordered by my parents not to waste Leander's time. He was being raised to be King, so I kept my distance as much as I could.'

'Except at night.'

She remembered his story from the beach, and thinking then that he had in fact been close with his brother, but maybe Vasili had never got to have the relationship with him he wanted.

'Yes.' He chuckled. A low rumble in his chest. 'We once stole an entire tart. Sophia found it the next day.'

Helia laughed. 'Did you get in trouble?'

'No,' Vasili said, as if the idea was preposterous. 'We ate a little more of it before she got rid of the evidence. I couldn't get in trouble.'

'Because you were the Prince?'

'Because someone has to care, and as long as I stayed out of the way no one did.'

'But your parents—'

'Were the King and Queen of Thalonia and had no time for me. I was an insurance policy, Helia. Nothing more than that. Being their son or behaving perfectly—none of it was worth anything. I wasn't worth their affection.'

Helia had never felt such anger towards people she'd been supposed to admire. Andreas had told her how Vasili's parents had been loved throughout the Kingdom. The perfect monarchs. She wanted to laugh. How could they have been perfect monarchs, people meant to care for an entire kingdom, when they hadn't even cared for their own child.

Her heart ached for the young boy alone in this big palace.

Alone.

Lonely.

Just like her.

'How did you cope?'

It was hard to comprehend that someone who had every right to be angry and cold was anything but.

'I told you—I rebelled. At first I would escape into the library and books...'

Helia had spied the stack on the bedside table. She couldn't help but think it was a sign of a deeper connection between them.

'Afterwards I acted out. Rebelled against the idea of being the perfect son. The perfect prince. I didn't want to be a prince at all. The partying, sex, women—all seemed to get a bigger reaction. And since all I wanted was to live my life, I figured living hard was a win all round.'

'But it didn't make you happy.'

'No, it didn't. And I regret my choice of rebellion now.'

Helia looked into his face then, attempting to read his thoughts. 'Why?'

'Because seeing the other side of Seidon…the orphanage… I knew I could have done something real.'

'This world is not made up of good people. It's full of people like me.'

But he was good. Vasili was better than he realised. He had been hurt over and over by the people who should have loved him most. He hadn't seen love from his family, and the one person who had loved him was taken away. So Helia understood why he'd told her he didn't love, but knew he was blind to all the ways in which he showed that he did.

'It's why I don't blame the people for wishing Leander was still on the throne. I'm sure they would rather our places had been switched.'

Helia looked up at him, horrified. 'Surely you don't believe that!'

He said nothing.

'Is that what you think? That it would have been better if you were on that plane?'

More silence.

A knot formed in Helia's throat. He really was an island. Alone at sea with all his hurt. So much so that she was certain he didn't even love himself.

'Vasili, look at me.'

He looked down at her, his normally bright, intelligent eyes showing nothing at all. They were perfectly expressionless and she hated it.

'You didn't know. And now that you do, you have a plan to fix things. You are helping me with the thing that means the most to me. You are good and kind and your people love you. I hate what your parents did to you, but it's their loss. Do you hear me? You were and are entitled to the way you feel. You are entitled to affection.'

'Helia…' he said in a low voice.

'Do you hear me?'

He huffed a laugh and kissed her lightly. 'I hear you.'

'Good.'

She was quiet for a moment, thinking through everything he'd revealed to her. She completely understood why he didn't want to be King, but she had no doubt he was the King Thalonia needed. She also finally understood why he was so set against having children. In his place, she would feel the same.

'You not wanting heirs…is that the reason you held back?'

'It's not that I don't want children, Helia, it's that I know what kind of life awaits them if I do. I won't do that.'

'No, you won't. Because it's not in you to be cruel.'

She remembered how good he'd been with the children at the orphanage. Every one of them. Yet he thought he wasn't good. Helia wouldn't allow it. She'd noticed that he avoided her question, which meant not having children wasn't the reason he tried to keep his distance. She considered that maybe this lonely, unloved boy still couldn't trust anyone to be in his corner. She certainly hadn't until Vasili came along.

Whatever he thought, Vasili needed love. And lying on his bed, in his arms, Helia vowed that she would be strong enough to love him. Even if it meant he could never return it. Even if she craved hearing the words he might never be able to say, she would love him still.

She was risking her heart, but that already belonged to him.

It did scare her that Vasili was the first person she'd admitted to loving since losing her father. If he ever found out how she felt he might decide to abandon her too. But there was absolutely no way she would allow Vasili to feel that he didn't deserve love or had to earn it.

He was enough, and she would show him. Even though her heart was further fracturing at the thought of how lonely it would be to spend a lifetime in this vortex of unrequited love.

CHAPTER FOURTEEN

HELIA WALKED DOWN a golden lit passage. Her dress swished along the marble floors. She barely felt her arm in her husband's as she reflected on the days and weeks that had followed their first time together. They'd been some of the best and the worst. But each day had started with them wrapped around one another and ended the same way. Each day she'd felt stronger. Settling in her role as Queen.

After the clash with Andreas over the tax bill, things had improved with him as well. Perhaps he was coming to accept how different the new King and Queen were, but Helia didn't know for sure. What she did know was that since then she had dealt with him with an authority that sometimes felt uncomfortable, but was always fuelled by her pursuit of her goals.

She and Vasili went about their duties, made their appearances together and apart, and worked on their project. They were achieving many of their objectives quickly.

She read a different story about her and Vasili every other day in the media, and they were all greatly positive. The people liked it that she was one of the masses, now a queen.

Yet every day felt harder.

Every day she would love her husband. Show him that she did but never utter the words. Every day that one-sided affection had her growing lonelier. And when she looked to the future all she saw was this path stretching on. Just her and Vasili, stuck in this magical, desolate connection.

Vasili didn't want children, and she had knowingly agreed to his terms, so that meant she would have no family—ever. No outlet for all the love inside her. No one to want and need her as much as she wanted and needed them.

Helia only realised they had arrived at their destination when she was jerked to a stop.

'You seem distracted,' Vasili said.

Helia looked at the shut double doors and shook her head, keeping her every thought well hidden. 'Just a lot on my mind.'

Of course she would be nervous about the coronation banquet. Vasili thought to himself.

It would be her first interaction with foreign dignitaries. He didn't want to be here either. His reasons for hating the event hadn't changed, but he had resigned himself to doing his duty.

Even as he'd walked down the passage with Helia on his arm he'd still been wishing he didn't have to step through these gilded doors, but this tradition served a purpose.

'If it helps, think of it less as a celebration and more as an opportunity to meet everyone as King,' Helia offered.

There would be politics to navigate. Every word more than it seemed. Alliances and threats made with smiles on faces and warm hands to shake.

Vasili hooked a hand around Helia's nape, pulling her in for a kiss that heated his blood as it always did.

'I wasn't prepared to wait.'

Especially when she looked so beautiful. Soft and feminine in a pale blue dress falling in layers of chiffon and tulle that reminded him of flowing water. Her hair was pinned up at the centre of her crown, an heirloom of diamonds and sapphires donned by every queen at the coronation banquet. And on her finger sat his ring.

She placed her hand over his heart, on the gold sash that sat on his black uniform. He thought she looked like the very heart of the Kingdom, and if she was its heart he had to be its immovable pillar of strength.

Helia laughed. 'You never are.'

'Ready?'

When she nodded, the doors to the ballroom swung open and in they walked to a room full of splendour. Gold and frescoed walls. Elaborate floral arrangements atop tall pillars. Gentle music flowing from the string quintet.

It was also a room filled with people. Royalty, dignitaries, politicians, billionaires...so much power, so much influence in one place.

They were announced, and then it began. Introductions and handshakes. Pleasantries and carefully worded welcomes that didn't sound welcoming at all.

Once they'd made their way around the room, Vasili excused them and spun Helia onto the floor. It was an invitation for everyone to join them in dance. But Vasili didn't care about that. He just wanted his wife in his arms.

'Everyone is looking at us...it takes a little getting used to,' Helia said as she placed her free hand on his shoulder.

With his palm on the small of her back, he tugged her a little closer, leading her through the ebb and flow of the swirling melody. Perfectly in sync.

'I'm not surprised that they're looking.' He bent low, pressing a kiss to her cheek. 'I have the most beautiful woman in my arms.'

He smiled at her blush. Helia had shown such strength and intelligence in the weeks since they had married. She was a force in her own right, but he still loved being able to make her blush and then watch her go from blushing to being demanding and enthusiastic in bed. He got to see all the many facets of Helia, and he wasn't sure he deserved the privilege.

But now he knew what everyone else would be seeing. He could feel it between them. An energy that caught everything around them. The current in their touch and the electricity in the air.

'I want to take you to bed and have my way with you.'

Helia wrapped her arms around his neck, pulling herself closer until her lips were at his ear. She said, 'Well, you're just going to have to be patient, Your Majesty.'

'Not a virtue of mine. In fact, I'm not very virtuous at all—you should know that by now.'

'What I know,' she said slowly, 'is that the longer I keep you waiting, the happier I'll be later.'

'Tease…'

'You wouldn't have it any other way.'

She pulled away from his embrace and with a sly smile over her shoulder made her way back through the crowd. She was right—he wouldn't have it any other way. She was perfect, and somehow she managed to make him feel lighter than he ever had before. Somehow she managed to help him not just to accept being King, but to like it. She had opened his eyes, and now he had the power to effect change.

Vasili kept an eye on Helia even as he was drawn into group after group of guests. After what seemed like the thousandth conversation along similar lines, he lost sight of her.

She was still within the palace walls. Safe. But he couldn't ignore the way her absence grated on him. It was ridiculous when he had known her for such a short time.

'She's doing well tonight,' he heard Andreas say beside him.

Vasili wondered what it had cost Andreas to admit that. 'Yes, she is. She has been all along.'

He glanced at his private secretary knowing he wouldn't get any response. It was then that the crowd parted, and he caught sight of her with the Queen of a neighbouring island kingdom. As if she had a sixth sense for where he was, she turned and smiled at him from across the room, never once halting in her conversation.

He wanted her back by his side, so with sure steps Vasili crossed the room.

'I'm sorry to interrupt, but I need to steal my wife away.'

Vasili slipped his arm around Helia's waist, pulling her closer in a move that was unapologetically possessive. It was not missed by the woman in their company.

'My apologies, Queen Arianna,' said Helia. 'It was lovely to meet you.'

The visiting Queen smiled in a knowing way, waving off Helia's apology. 'I too was once young and in love. I hope to see you soon.'

Vasili heard Helia promise that she would, but his mind was firmly fixed on that one word. *Love*. It wasn't love that he felt. He didn't love. It wasn't possible to feel something one knew nothing about. What he and Helia had was pure passion.

He led Helia out onto the cool, brightly lit balcony. Soon he was kissing her with an urgency that she returned. Proof that he was right.

Helia frowned at him when they broke apart, a question in her eyes, but before he could address it, they were being approached by a group of men he hadn't thought of in weeks. Hadn't heard from or contacted.

'Vasili,' his friend Stavros greeted him.

'*King* Vasili,' another corrected.

'We haven't seen you in a while.' His friend snapped his gaze to Helia. 'But I guess you have been busy. Your Majesty.'

Stavros inclined his head, a familiar smirk painted on his lips. It had never bothered Vasili before, but now he wanted to shove Helia behind him. Be her shield until the lot of them left.

'It's a pleasure to meet you,' Helia said pleasantly.

No, it was not. Not to him. These were the people he'd partied with. Nobility. Members of the highest echelons of society. But he couldn't deny he hated seeing Helia interact with them.

'Why so tense, Your Majesty?' Stavros asked.

Normally the man's inability to take anything seriously entertained him. Not today.

Vasili pressed Helia further into his side. 'Maybe I don't like you talking to my wife.'

'Territorial?' Stavros laughed.

Anger bloomed in his chest. Not at Stavros, but at himself. Because the man was right. Vasili didn't like seeing Helia with these people because they reflected the ugliest parts of himself. He was selfish. Not worthy of anything meaningful. The women of before had known not to expect a relationship with him. He hadn't cared about their feelings. He'd been out for a good time. Which made him no better than Stavros or any of the men now talking to his wife. They weren't his friends. He didn't have any of those. None of these people had contacted him after Leander's death. None of them had reached out when he had married or taken the throne.

And he hadn't missed any of them.

Realisation dawned that he wasn't even worthy of the most superficial, disposable affection. Of affection of any sort. He had learned that over and over with his parents and now he learned it again.

'You're damn right, I am.'

'Never thought I'd see the day...'

Helia was no longer paying attention to the group of men they were talking to. Her heart had hammered in her chest as Stavros's words had landed. Vasili had lived a very different life from her own. He had been with women so unlike her. None of whom he felt anything for. And even though she was his wife, she wasn't any different—because now she was in his bed. She got to enjoy his touches and his attention, and to a certain degree, his support. But nothing more.

'I too was once young and in love.'

Except Queen Arianna was wrong. Vasili didn't love her.

She had been the one to break the rules. *She* had been the one to fall in love. And all she'd got in return was an increasingly lonely existence. Because she realised now that she had always craved having someone to love and to love her back. She wanted Vasili to love her back...but he had said so many times that he couldn't do that.

She didn't want to spend her life pining for the man in her bed, wanting him in a way that she couldn't have. She wanted more.

And in that moment her crown fell away. All the people disappeared. She was alone in a dark, quiet palace, seeing for the first time what she would really have in the long life ahead of her.

No one.

And she couldn't keep pretending that everything was fine as she had been doing all night.

Helia knew then what she had to do. It would take strength, but she had already proved to everyone—including herself—just how strong she was. She'd wanted to be there for Vasili, and she had been, but now it was time to choose herself.

Helia pulled herself back to the present. To the music and lights and people and took control.

'All good kings are territorial, are they not?' Helia said pleasantly. 'They have entire kingdoms to protect.'

Vasili's hand squeezed hers at her side.

'End of an era, then, I guess,' Stavros said, making a show of sliding his hands into his pockets. 'I would say you will be missed, but I'm greedy, so there's just more for us.'

'Have at it. I've grown tired of the scene anyway. I have more important things to concern myself with.'

'Enjoy the banquet,' Helia said, before any of them could say any more. 'If you'll excuse us?'

She walked hand in hand with Vasili through the room until she found Andreas.

'We will be leaving now,' she told him. 'Do what you need to.'

He looked between her and Vasili, nodded once, and set off.

It wasn't long after that when she was thanking everyone for attending and inviting them all to stay for as long as they liked. Vasili didn't challenge her as she took centre stage, all the while looking like a king who didn't bother himself with the opinions of anyone.

A lion in his den.

When they finally left, she kept silent until the door to their bedroom had clicked shut.

'Vasili, we need to talk.'

She watched him take a deep breath, then remove his sash and walk up to her. Gently, he removed the heavy crown from her head and took her hands in his.

'Helia, I want you to know how well you did tonight.'

'Thank you,' she said, and felt a crack forming within her as she steeled herself to say what she needed to.

She stepped away from his reach, knowing how weak she was for his touch. But not even that could stop her now.

'Thank you for allowing me to share in this life, Vasili, but it's time we faced reality.'

'What do you mean?'

He tried reaching for her again, but Helia shook her head and watched his hand drop.

'This life that we agreed to…it isn't going to work. For the kind of life you want to live, you don't need a queen.'

The words shattered the heart that she had exposed to him as if it was made of nothing but glass. Her vision was blurry, but she refused to cry.

'Helia—'

There was a flash of panic on his face that made it hard for her to speak, but she powered through it.

'I agreed to marry you for two reasons: the first being my need to help the orphanage, to help those who never get a chance to live the life Thalonia offers to its wealthy, the for-gotten. And the second reason, Vasili, was you. I had admired you for so long, but those feelings paled in comparison to the way I felt seeing you with my people…how I feel about you now. But I realise that isn't enough.'

'Helia, you knew what this was,' Vasili said, his face a care-fully blank mask.

'I did. But I also know that I deserve more than a lonely existence and a loveless marriage.' She stepped forward, plac-ing her palm on his cheek. A single tear rolled down her own. 'You're a good man. A great king. And I know you'll see our project through.'

'Of course, I will. But Helia—'

'But nothing, Vasili. We both deserve more from this life, and I hope one day you will find it in you to let someone past your walls.'

Helia had known loving him would be a risk. She'd taken it anyway. And now, even though she tried to hold herself to-gether, and even though she knew she was doing the right thing, her heart felt as if it was being ripped out of her chest.

'My advisors were right. You aren't an appropriate queen, because an appropriate queen wouldn't be good…like you. I wanted this to work.'

'So did I. Goodbye, Vasili.'

He held her gaze. Gritting his teeth.

Without a word, he turned around and left.

Helia waited until she heard the outer door close before she set herself into motion. Her heart in pieces, she could barely breathe through the agonising fracture carving through her.

She had to get out.

As quickly as she could, she gathered only the belongings that she would need and then left the King's quarters, slip-ping through the interconnecting door into a room she hadn't set foot in.

The unfamiliar surroundings were a small comfort. There
were no memories here. No hope. No laughter or stories shared.
And that helped her keep control over her shattering emotions.
Without much thought, she stepped under the shower, needing
to wash Vasili's scent away. The memories would be punishment enough. She didn't need to smell him on herself as if he
was beside her. He wouldn't be again.

With ruthless efficiency she scrubbed at her skin and her
hair. Once she was done, she went in search of a bag, but she
found only one. It would do. Helia stuffed her clothes in it,
paying attention only to the next task and the next. It was the
only way she could think around the pain in her chest.

She tied up her damp hair while instructing her chauffeur
to meet her in the underground garage in the least conspicuous
vehicle. She could hear the man's confusion, but he obeyed.

And then she was on the road. The black SUV with highly
tinted windows was rolling through the gates and away from
the palace.

Every atom in her wanted to look back. Wanted to look at
the home she'd had with Vasili. Wanted to look for him.

Distance grew and it felt wrong. It was all wrong. They
shouldn't be apart. But she needed to do this for herself. To
give herself a chance at a happy life. She felt as though a
thread was rapidly unspooling between them, going taut as
they reached the end of the road and then snapping free completely when they turned the corner.

Helia covered her mouth to stifle the sob that bubbled up.
She could no longer see the palace. She wouldn't see her husband again.

CHAPTER FIFTEEN

VASILI SQUINTED AWAKE. Bright sunlight fell across his bed through the open curtains, nearly blinding him. He rolled over, his hands on the cool sheets beside him. He had slept in his old room to give Helia space. Space that he'd hoped she would use to rethink her decision. She wanted to leave, and yet the days leading up to the coronation banquet had been perfect.

They'd kept to the agreement.

But now that very agreement might have cost him his queen.

She wouldn't have left in the night, he reasoned. Not with so many people in the palace. Perhaps he would be able to speak to Helia. Find a workable solution.

Throwing the covers off, he got out of bed and went about readying himself for this conversation. He didn't feel prepared for it, but it had to be done.

The palace was quiet when he stepped out of the room. So vastly different from the night before, with all the people, the music, the bright lights. It was as if a sombre hush had descended—but maybe that was a reflection of his own mood.

'Helia?' he called, knocking on the door to the room he had left her in the night before, but no answer came.

So he stepped inside and found everything exactly in its place.

Unease crept down his spine.

He opened the bedroom door and found the same. A bed that hadn't been slept in. There was no sign of her in the bathroom either. He rushed out of the room, moving towards the interconnecting door. Maybe she had needed to sleep elsewhere, just as he had. But again he found nothing in the sitting area. The only evidence of her was her discarded dress and the jewels on the bed.

Vasili rushed to the room she had used before she became Queen, feeling more desperate, more frantic with every passing second. And when he found no sign of life at all in that room, he pulled out his phone and called her.

'Damn it, Helia, pick up!'

But it went straight to voicemail.

It was obvious what had happened. He could feel it in his bones. In the silence.

Helia had left. She had said goodbye, and now she was gone.

He dropped onto the edge of the bed, his elbows on his knees, head hanging. If she didn't want to be reached he had to respect that, but it didn't stop the worry that was breaking him.

Was she okay? What if something happened to her?

She was the Queen. If anything had happened he would know. He told himself to hang on to that thought.

When she was ready, they would talk. When she was ready, he would lay out the terms of a new agreement.

Except he couldn't. He refused to be dictated to, but this time Helia had seized control. This time Helia had decided the terms, just as he had been doing before.

He curled his hands into fists. Of course she was unhappy. He had made her that way.

Vasili felt numb. Dead inside. As if a black hole had opened inside him, sucking away all the joy, all the happiness, leaving him empty. With a pounding headache.

'What have I done?' he whispered to the empty room.

Helia looked out of the window of the small mountain cabin. Filtered green-hued light poured into the modest lounge. Tall, lush trees stood on all sides of the little dwelling. There wasn't another person in sight. She was alone. As she had been for days.

The book she had been attempting to read for distraction lay discarded on the coffee table. Instead, she stared out of the window with a cup of coffee warming her hands despite the heat of the day. A tear trickled down her cheek.

Once she'd been alone, she hadn't been able to stop them, and they still wouldn't abate. As if this pain was infinite. It had had a beginning, but there was certainly no end. She mourned the loss of Vasili. She'd loved him fiercely. She still did. She knew it had been a risk to fall in love with him. To show him that love without once telling him. But maybe now he would find the right person to share the burden of rule with. Some-one he could keep at arm's length that his advisors would ap-prove of.

The thought sent a fresh wave of tears down her face. It hurt more than she could bear to picture him with someone else.

But she had seen them. Those women who were his equals.

They'd been at the banquet. Tall and polished in a way she would never manage. Maybe one of them would wear his ring…

She looked down at her finger, at the ring she still wore. At first it had been an oversight. In her hurry to leave, she hadn't even thought of it. But now, alone in this cabin, she couldn't bring herself to take it off. The last link to Vasili. She would have to return it eventually, but for now she curled her hand into her chest, replaying all the memories with him she held so close.

It would take a lifetime to get over Vasili—if she ever did. But she had to try. Because she couldn't be alone for the rest of her life. She had come to realise that she wanted children. She wanted love. And Vasili simply could not give that to her.

Helia spent that first week vacillating between hurt and

anger. Vasili was one of the few people who could understand loneliness, but he was blind to hers. And now she had nothing. Not someone with whom to share a laugh or a knowing smile. She had lost everything. Her love, the career that she had worked so hard for, and her mission—although that had been achieved.

It was only in her second week of being holed up alone in the cabin that she felt she could breathe a little. As if she could pick herself up enough to restart her life. Could think through the pain. She needed to get her career back on track, but it couldn't be in Thalonia. Not when she had briefly been its queen. She would have to find a new home.

Her heart broke for yet another reason. This love had indeed cost her everything—including her home.

Hollow. That was what Vasili was. What his days were. Robotic. Mechanical. Vasili went through the motions every day. Eat. Barely sleep. Work.

It had been two weeks. Two weeks of hell. Two weeks of feeling bereft. Broken. The palace seemed even colder since Helia left. Emptier. Everyone avoided him when they could. He didn't have it in him to make small talk or exchange pleasantries. There was nothing to be pleasant about. So he threw himself into his duties instead. Or tried to.

As Vasili sat behind his desk he heard the door open, followed by the sound of Andreas taking his seat for their meeting. But he couldn't concentrate on the task at hand. There wasn't anything in his life that didn't remind him of Helia. Of her words before she left.

She was right—she deserved more than a life of loneliness. Wasn't that what he wanted? Why he had tried to be in her corner? Because he knew loneliness. Except now it was dawning on him that maybe it was his own fear that had allowed his loneliness to persevere. It was his fear of being hurt that had had him erecting barriers around himself.

For a shining moment on their honeymoon he had known what it felt like to have someone care about him. To have support at his back. And what had he done? He'd pushed Helia away the night she'd offered to give him the space to grieve.

And he'd kept pushing her away.

Every single day he'd enjoyed being around her. Wanted her and cared for her. Every day he'd enjoyed her wit and affection and consideration. And in return he'd given her nothing but empty touches.

Except they hadn't really been empty, had they? He'd had to fight his feelings for her. He'd made that rule not to be intimate to protect himself.

Vasili had had to fight hard to ensure he didn't grow attached to his wife. The last time he'd trusted his heart to someone in any kind of bond he'd been fifteen, and Sophia had been forced to leave. When he and Leander had finally been free to nurture a brotherly bond, he'd been killed.

When he had allowed himself to be with Helia she'd got under his skin, but he had feared that it would only be a matter of time before she too found a reason to leave.

Vasili had been happy to have sex with Helia, for them to appear as a king and queen should, but he had refused to love her—and didn't that make him like his parents?

A throat was cleared. 'Your Majesty…?'

Vasili didn't register the interruption. Not now he'd realised how much fear had ruled his life.

He'd walled off his heart for fear of being hurt like he had been by his parents. He'd kept Helia away when he was grieving his brother because it had hurt to lose Leander. How could he let in another person who would hurt him? That was all he'd known.

But with Helia he had been happy. Relaxed. Less alone. Helia had taken his grief and made it bearable.

He thought back to that morning on the beach, when he'd seen her grief. While he'd taught her to swim, it hadn't been just lust burning through his veins—it had been so much more. It had been finding someone who understood.

'I hope one day you will find it in you to let someone in past your walls.'

He already had. But he hadn't had to let her in—she'd burrowed through with her love and care. She had seen him. Vasili. Not a royal or a son who wasn't worthy.

'Sir...' Andreas said as he quietly closed the binder on Vasili's desk. 'Go to her. Bring her back.'

'I can't do that, Andreas.'

Vasili closed his own folders. He couldn't see anything in them anyway.

'You know, there have been many things I have disagreed with you on,' said Andreas. 'But throughout your rebellions and your disregard of our traditions, none of your sins has been as egregious as this.'

'Watch yourself, Andreas. I'm willing to take your advice, but you are very close to overstepping,' Vasili growled.

'I may have my own thoughts on your queen, but neither of you deserves this—and the Kingdom doesn't deserve a king lost in misery.'

'If I didn't know better, I'd say you miss her,' said Vasili.

'Perhaps I do.' Andreas stopped at the door. 'I am a traditionalist, but my concern had always been for what is best for the throne. And in the end, even if we disagreed, Queen Helia proved those concerns unwarranted. You're not the only one who's had time to think.'

Vasili scrubbed his hands down his face when the door softly clicked shut. Yanking on his desk drawer, to store away the files on his table, he saw an envelope slide forward.

His father's letter.

He picked it up and closed the drawer, turning it over in his hand. He was already in torment—what was a little more? If there was ever a time to read the words of a man who had never cared for much, it was now.

Vasili pulled the letter free and unfolded it, seeing the familiar scrawl. He could almost picture his father with his black fountain pen in hand.

He began to read...

My dearest Vasili,
How I wish you'd never have to read this letter...

Of course he had—because if everything had gone to plan, Leander would have been in this chair.

...I know you will read those words and think I have written this because I never wished for you to be King, and that is my own fault, but the truth is that I wish you still had your brother. That you did not have to be alone.

I mentioned this in my previous letter, but I fear, even as I write that you may not have read the words and that is undoubtedly my fault.

I have many regrets in life, Vasili, but perhaps you are my greatest. I regret that I put the crown before you. I saw every day what my choice did to you. You see, I was deluded into thinking that this throne was the most important thing. That everything else was secondary. Including my family. Including anything as frivolous as happiness. That withholding affection and raising you both to put duty first would create strong leaders. Kings.

I don't want you to make the same mistakes, Vasili. Learn from mine. Do not repeat them and become like me, an old man on his deathbed seeing with clarity for the first time and filled with regret.

You are strong, son. Perhaps the strongest of us all. You stood up for yourself, for what you wanted and believed in. As much as it irritated me, I admired you for it so much more. This is how I know you will be a strong king. A good king.

This throne is a lonely place, son, so find yourself a queen who will not just be what Thalonia needs, but what you need first.

I'm sorry I didn't tell you this enough, and I'm sorry it comes in two letters, but I love you, Vasili. I would stand over your crib every night and marvel at just how much it was possible to love something so little and so precious.

I know it is too late to say all of this, but I am sorry, son.

I love you and believe in you.

With regret for destroying the first letter his father had left him roiling in his belly, Vasili read through this one to his father's signed-off scrawl and then tossed it aside. He propped his elbows on the table, resting his forehead against his laced fingers.

He could have read those words that he'd so wanted to hear a year ago. Could have known he had been loved. And it was his own fault that he hadn't, because he'd been so hurt and angry.

There was so much hurt in his family. That was their true legacy. Vasili couldn't even find it in himself to be angry any more. A letter did not make up for twenty-nine years of rejection, but it did show him a man lost in his misery. In the wrong choices.

Just as he had made the wrong choices.

Vasili had the perfect queen and he realised that he loved

her with a viciousness. She was exactly what he needed. She had been from the start.

So now he sat at a crossroads. He could wallow in all that he had lost and wall his heart off permanently—because no one would touch it as Helia had—and then he would become yet another soulless king. Or he could fight the fear. Find the bravery he had been blessed with to rebel, but use it to go after the woman he loved. The woman who loved him back. Who had changed his life.

And just like at the start of all this madness, there was no real choice. Because the only right answer was to choose Helia.

CHAPTER SIXTEEN

VASILI STOOD AT the door to a modest cabin nestled amongst tall dark trees. Though he could hear the sea, he couldn't see it. He looked over his shoulder at the path he had driven up. The blacked-out SUV looked almost garish in the serene forest.

So much oppressive, insulating greenness.

Helia had retreated and it was his fault, but he would make it right. He had to.

Vasili knocked, and sent up a silent prayer that she would listen.

The door swung open and there she was. In jeans, with her hair piled messily on top of her head, without a scrap of make-up, and she was by far the most beautiful thing he had ever seen.

Vasili finally breathed a breath that didn't feel as though it had been forced through a fissure in his chest.

'Hello, Helia,' he said.

'Vasili...' Shock rippled across her face. 'What are you doing here?'

'May I come in?'

He could see the doubt within her. And, as much as it hurt, he didn't blame her for being uneasy about letting him in.

'Please. I just want to talk.'

He watched her take a breath and stand aside, allowing him to pass through the door. From the entrance hall he could see the sitting area, the kitchen and the dining table. A glaring reminder of Helia's past life and how different it was from his.

And against the wall was a packed bag.

'Join me?' he asked as he took a seat at the table.

It was a reminder of a different time when he had asked the same of her. Except then he had laid down the rules and expected Helia to follow. Now he would give her the choice.

'I don't know if that's a good idea, Vasili. I don't know why you're here, but there isn't much left to say.'

'There's plenty to say. Starting with I'm sorry.'

Helia scrunched up her eyes, wrapping her arms around herself as if she needed protection from him, and it made Vasili furious with himself.

'Please don't. It's not going to change anything.'

'That's where you're wrong. Everything has changed. Let me explain, Helia. I beg you.'

He could hear the rawness in his own voice and wondered if it was his obvious brokenness that convinced Helia to join him at the table. Close enough to touch. But he would not do that until she allowed him to.

His eyes drifted to the bag. 'Are you going somewhere?'

'I'm leaving Thalonia. There's nothing here for me. I need a new start.'

That was the last thing he wanted to hear. Thalonia needed her. *He* needed her. He wouldn't let her leave without a fight.

'How did you find me?' she asked softly. 'I left instructions not to tell you where I was.'

'I know. That's why I paid a visit to Giannis Demetriou.'

Vasili slid an envelope over to Helia and placed a vibrantly purple iris on top of it.

'What is this?'

He heard her voice catch as her eyes filled with tears.

'That, Helia, is every cent of your inheritance. The start in life your father left you. After we're done here today, if you still wish to leave, it will help you. As will I. I'm not going to abandon you.'

'I don't know what to say...'

'Then let me start.'

Vasili could bear it no more and reached for her hand. The spark of her touch restarted his heart, which had grown cold and empty without her. He took a deep breath, trying to find the words. The only thing he could tell her was the truth, but he needed to start somewhere. He needed to lay himself bare to this woman, which was a terrifying thought, but there was no longer room in his life for fear.

'I was scared. I have been afraid for a very long time. Afraid to expose my heart to anyone. I've come to realise it was I who kept Leander away, not the other way round. He tried, but I wouldn't get close. Not when I had been warned away. But I was wrong. I loved my brother a great deal, and I see that now. I also see how grieving him only made me want to wall myself off further.'

Vasili let out a shuddering breath. Felt his throat closing up with the ache of his loss. Helia said nothing, but the squeeze of her hand was support enough.

'I wanted my parents to love me, and when they didn't—or appeared not to—it hurt. But I had Sophia. And then, when she was gone, there was nothing to stop me pushing every-one away. It's why I didn't love anyone. It's why I never had true friends. And it's why I tried to keep you at arm's length. Because you, Helia...you were a danger to me from the start.'

'Me?'

'That day in the library I was lost to my grief. Drowning in it. In my anger at what was being asked of me. My mind was loud, roaring with frustration, with the injustice of it all. But then I looked at you, and for a moment it was peaceful. And when I kissed you, I was lost in it. Moved in a way I had never been. And I knew if you had that power with a simple kiss, you had the power to destroy me. I couldn't let that happen. So I selfishly chose myself over you and I hurt you. I'm so sorry.'

'Why are you telling me this?'

Helia's voice was rough through her tears. Tears he knew weren't just for herself, but because of his own anguish.

'You were so brave to stand up to the King and Queen from such a young age, Vasili, and yet you were a coward when that rebellion led to something real and powerful.'

She was right. He had been a coward. Even though it had been a fight not to fall in love with her, he had done so anyway. And still he'd tried to keep her away from his heart. There was no bravery there.

'I was. And it took you walking out for me to realise what a fearful idiot I have been. You took control. And because of you I can see things so much clearer. Because of you I can finally own up to my feelings. That morning when I woke up and realised you had left...'

Vasili swallowed hard. Swallowed down those feelings that now returned. Anger at himself. Hopelessness. His eyes had been opened that day.

'It broke me. In trying to keep you from destroying me, I'd made it happen.'

'So why are you here now? What do you want?'

'I want you back. I want you in my bed. I want you in my life. I want to change this kingdom with you! I love you, Helia. I love you so goddamn much that I ache with it.'

There they were. The words Helia had longed to hear. And they made her want to run into his arms and stay there for ever.

But his admitting the truth didn't change their situation. Would he still want to end the monarchy, which meant she would never have a family? Was he prepared for the kind of life she wanted?

'I have waited for those words, Vasili. There was something about you even when I didn't know you that drew me in, and when I did get to know you I couldn't help but fall in love with you. But loving each other isn't enough. I need to know what's different now.'

It took a moment for him to respond.

'In my mind, if the people meant to care for me couldn't, how could I be worthy of it from anyone else? From you? But here's the thing... I know I used that as a shield. It came from fear, and I have no room in my life for fear any more. That's what's different. I'm done with shields. With keeping everyone away.'

'But we want different things. I can't return with you now only to have my heart broken later.'

She'd had the strength to leave once, but it had gouged at her soul to do so. She didn't want to do it again. She couldn't. Just thinking about it nearly paralysed her.

'Tell me what you want and it's yours. Anything.'

She could hear the desperation in his voice.

'I want a family. I want children, and a husband who isn't afraid to give me his whole heart. I don't want to be lonely any more.'

Her voice broke on that last word. Her stomach dropped as the chair scraped loudly against the floor as Vasili dragged her to him and cradled her face.

'You have my heart. My soul. And with time we could have a family.'

Helia tried to pull away. 'Don't feed me false hope. We both know how you feel about children.'

'You know, I believe I still owe you a thought,' he said, not letting her go.

Their honeymoon seemed as if it had been eons ago, but she would never forget that night she'd offered to leave. When he'd said he didn't want her to go.

'I dreamt of it once,' he said. 'Our children...with curly

hair and your smile. I craved it but I pushed it aside, thinking that life wasn't for me. I was so convinced I knew what would happen to my children that I wanted no part of it. But then I read a letter my father had left in Leander's care, to be given to me in the event of my brother's death, and I know now that he loved me. He chose not to show it, because that's what he thought he needed to do in order to be a good king. I have said it before. I am not my father and I believe that now. I have made different choices. And that life I dreamt of with you... I want that too.'

Helia could see the sincerity in Vasili's eyes. It made what was left of her resistance crumble, because the picture of life he'd painted was exactly what she was leaving Thalonia to find.

'I hate it that you didn't get the love you needed growing up. I hate it that your parents made such awfully bad choices. And I especially hate it that those choices made you believe that you weren't worthy of love. That they made you stop loving yourself. But you need to know I will always love you. No matter what happens. I will always be yours, and I know that your people love you, Vasili.'

'Helia...' he whispered brokenly.

'Do you know what I saw after our wedding? Happiness. I saw smiles on every face in the crowd. They were happy for you. Happy to have you as their king. The man who treated everyone in his palace with kindness. You think I didn't notice the way you spoke to everyone? You think that was a secret or overlooked? It wasn't. I paid attention. I saw what you didn't.'

He leaned his forehead against hers. 'I wish that I'd met you sooner.'

'Then tell me you want me. Tell me it's not a mistake for me to go back with you. That you won't get scared again and push me away.'

Because Helia wanted to go with him. As much as she was

hoping for the life she deserved, she knew there was only ever one man she would love like this. Only one man who would ever make her heart pound and set her blood ablaze. Her eyes fell on the envelope. Only one man who had ever fought for her. And after these two weeks of constant heart-ache and never-ending tears, in Vasili's embrace she felt hope-ful. Lighter. Happy. As if a light had been turned back on.

'I want you,' he said. 'I want you every day. I want you when you're cranky in the mornings, and I want you in my arms at night. I want you for the rest of our lives and then some. You're it for me, Helia. I promise that I will never push you away and that you will never know another day of loneliness. Neither of us will.'

'Then give me your ring.'

Without hesitation, Vasili handed his gold wedding band to Helia, who gave him hers.

Taking his hand, she said, 'Vasili, I promise to love you every day. I promise to remind you to love yourself when you forget, and to love you harder when you can't. I promise to be the friend you deserve and the partner you can count on. I promise to always be honest with you, and I promise I will never be taken from you.'

She watched his eyes glisten as she slid his ring back onto his finger. These vows were so different from those they'd made last time. There were no secret messages or hidden feel-ings. These words felt sacred. This union was divine.

'Helia, I have a lot to work on, and I promise to work on being better, on being the man you deserve. It might take a while...' he smiled when she laughed '...but we will get there.' He twirled the ring in the sunlight. 'Maybe I always knew it would be you. Maybe I was fighting a truth that already ex-isted. You and I—we're inevitable. And here is your proof.'

Helia looked down at the ring he held, noticing for the first time the Latin phrase engraved on the inside of the thin band.

'It means *My salvation...my eternal.*'

'Vasili...' Helia breathed.

Tears ran down her cheeks and he brushed them away with the backs of his fingers.

'That's what you are, and I promise to show you as much every single day.'

Vasili slid the ring onto her finger and then, in a crash of limbs and bodies and lips, they kissed. They kissed without restraint. They kissed as if they had been reunited after an eternity apart. And they kissed as if this was their start.

'Well, then, Your Majesty,' Helia said as she pushed the envelope back to him. 'I believe this should go to the orphanage. The Queen has little need of it.'

'As you wish.' He smiled. Bright and glorious. 'Let's go home.'

And it felt right. As if a part of her soul had healed. For Helia had found her home. It was here, in the arms of her husband. A man she loved so much. And now that love didn't make her feel alone—instead it made her stronger and more hopeful and blissfully happy.

EPILOGUE

Six years later

VASILI STOOD BETWEEN the two little beds and as quietly and gently as he could tucked the covers around one little girl and then the other.

His daughters. Neither of whom resembled him nor Helia.

Two years after they'd married, Vasili and Helia had made the decision to break with tradition yet again and adopted their first child. A beautiful two-year-old girl. Eighteen months later, they'd adopted their second.

At first, he had been terrified he wouldn't be a good father. That he would repeat the mistakes of his own. But with he and Helia being so closely involved with the orphanage, Vasili knew he loved the children in a way he hadn't been.

He had come to the realisation that it wasn't the throne that he was angry with—it was his parents. The crown had the power to help, to better people's lives, as he and Helia had been doing. All the orphanages were well looked after and well-funded. With the King and Queen involved, they were no longer hopeless places. Children like Helia had been were no longer forgotten. The country's schools were thriving, and all children were able to study without the worry of expense thanks to the Leander Leos Foundation. Even the tax bill had been amended with little fight, and Thalonia was thriving.

The truth he'd had to accept was that the crown wasn't responsible for the lack of affection he'd experienced. Their treatment of 'the spare' had been his parents' choice, and he chose to love *his* children demonstrably. Though one of his children would inevitably become the monarch one day—the first in Thalonia's history not to be royal by blood—none of them would be treated as the heir or spare. Those words were never uttered in the palace.

He'd made peace with the fact that he didn't need to end the monarchy. He just needed to make it better.

He needed to be a better king than the ones before him. A better husband. A better father.

Vasili had kept his father's letter. Had read through it frequently to remind himself of what the wrong choices meant. How love could be hidden and lost because of them. That letter wasn't a punishment he inflicted upon himself. It was, instead, the greatest lesson his father could have imparted, and the reason Vasili had come to forgive the late King.

Together, Vasili and Helia put the girls to bed every night. Though he would always come back in for just a little while longer. It was overwhelming just how much he loved them. His family.

He turned on the night light and made his way to the bedroom, where his wife waited.

Helia...

She was every bit as beautiful to him now as she had been the first day he saw her. She tugged back the covers in silent invitation. One hand rested on her belly, swollen with the son they would soon welcome, the other was holding the duvet.

'I take it they're still asleep?' She smiled knowingly.

He laughed. 'They are.'

'Good. But now, Your Majesty, your wife requires your attention.'

And he was happy to give it.

Vasili had never envisaged a life as perfect as this. Hadn't dared to dream of it. But as he pulled his wife into his arms, and kissed her with a burning passion, he was glad he hadn't. Because no dream could compare with this Elysian reality.

* * * * *

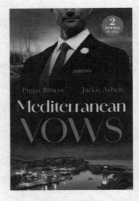

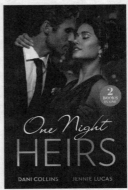

COMING SOON!

We really hope you enjoyed reading this book.
If you're looking for more romance
be sure to head to the shops when
new books are available on

Thursday 20th June

To see which titles are coming soon, please visit
millsandboon.co.uk/nextmonth

MILLS & BOON

MILLS & BOON®

Coming next month

MY ONE-NIGHT HEIR
Natalie Anderson

'You stunned me into silence.' His expression softens. 'I was trying to stay in control. I couldn't do this there.'

'This?'

The brush of his lips is balmy, teasing. His tenderness takes me by surprise as does the moment he takes to lean back and search my eyes. I realize he's seeking my consent.

I can hardly think. 'This is…'

'What I've wanted to do all night.' His gleaming gaze bores into me—intense and unwavering. 'You're why my pulse is racing.'

I just topple right into his arms. He scoops me close and then his mouth is there again—on mine. And I melt.

It turns out that kissing is the best ever way to neutralise panic. The best way to stay in the moment, to not give a damn about anything else in life—not even imminent death. Kissing is the best ever thing full stop.

Continue reading
MY ONE-NIGHT HEIR
Natalie Anderson

Available next month
millsandboon.co.uk

BOOKS

Afterglow Books are trend-led, trope-filled books with diverse, authentic and relatable characters and a wide array of voices and representations.

Experience real world trials and tribulations, all the tropes you could possibly want (think small-town settings, fake relationships, grumpy vs sunshine, enemies to lovers).

All with a generous dose of spice in every story!

OUT NOW

Two stories published every month.

To discover more visit:

Afterglowbooks.co.uk

LET'S TALK
Romance

For exclusive extracts, competitions and special offers, find us online:

- **f** MillsandBoon
- **X** @MillsandBoon
- **◎** @MillsandBoonUK
- **♪** @MillsandBoonUK

Get in touch on 01413 063 232

MILLS & BOON

THE HEART OF ROMANCE

A ROMANCE FOR EVERY READER

MODERN

Prepare to be swept off your feet by sophisticated, sexy and seductive heroes, in some of the world's most glamourous and romantic locations, where power and passion collide.

HISTORICAL

Escape with historical heroes from time gone by. Whether you passion is for wicked Regency Rakes, muscled Vikings or rugge Highlanders, awaken the romance of the past.

MEDICAL

Set your pulse racing with dedicated, delectable doctors in the high-pressure world of medicine, where emotions run high and passion, comfort and love are the best medicine.

True Love

Celebrate true love with tender stories of heartfelt romance, from the rush of falling in love to the joy a new baby can bring, and a focus on the emotional heart of a relationship.

HEROES

The excitement of a gripping thriller, with intense romance at its heart. Resourceful, true-to-life women and strong, fearless men face danger and desire - a killer combination!

 afterglow BOOKS

From showing up to glowing up, these characters are on the path to leading their best lives and finding romance along the way – with plenty of sizzling spice!

To see which titles are coming soon, please visit

millsandboon.co.uk/nextmonth

GET YOUR ROMANCE FIX!

Get the latest romance news, exclusive author interviews, story extracts and much more!

blog.millsandboon.co.uk